The House That Alice Built

The House That Alice Built

Chris Penhall

Portuguese Paradise – Book 1

Winner of

Search for a Star
Finding new talent in fiction
sponsored by
Cat

Stories that inspire emotions!
www.rubyfiction.com

Published 2021 by Ruby Fiction
Penrose House, Crawley Drive, Camberley, Surrey GU15 2AB, UK
www.rubyfiction.com

A CIP catalogue record for this book is available from the British Library

ISBN: 978-1-91255-028-9

Printed and bound in Great Britain by Clays Ltd, Elcograf S.p.A.

*This book is dedicated to Sarah and Hannah and
my incredibly supportive family and friends.*

To Gareth, Ann, Kevin and Barrie

And to Mark, who bought me my first writing desk.

You're all fabulous and I couldn't have done it without you!

Acknowledgements

I would like to thank the Choc Lit and Ruby
team for the opportunity to release this story.

I'm incredibly grateful to everyone that has helped me
along the way, and to Steph Roundsmith for all her
guidance, Tony Fisher and Deborah Stephenson for reading
my early manuscripts, taking the time to give me feedback
and making me feel my story was something to be proud
of, plus Heather, Judith (who helped me research the paddle
boarding!), Sian, Bridget and my other friends who read
the book and took the time to say they liked it! Thanks to
the Choc Lit team for giving my story that extra polish, to
my very wonderful Uni Chicks and their chaps who I've
known forever and who have been there for me through
everything – Jill, Sandra, Sue, Loui, Mark and Mike – my
Essex friends, work buddies, Portugal lovers, Hay Ladies,
salsa pals and all the good people I've met through the
years – here's to more of our dreams coming true!

Thank you to the Tasting Panel readers who passed the
original manuscript of *The House That Alice Built* and
made publication possible: Mel R, Bee M, Sharon D,
Gillian C, Anne E, Alison R, Carol D, Judith C, Maureen W,
Allie L, Stephanie H, Dimi E, Yvonne G, Gill L, Hilary B,
Alma H, Cordy S, Isobel J, Janine N and Leisha Q.

Chapter One

Alice wearily trudged down the street towards home, the rain a constant pitter-patter on her umbrella, her ankles damp from the water kicked up in puddles as she moved. She had opened the curtains that morning to blue skies and fluffy clouds – a perfect day for her friend, Kathy to visit, who had flown over from Portugal for a meet-up for the first time in about five years. She wanted everything to be just right, including the weather. However, it had been a disappointing kind of day, with rumours of job losses murmuring around work, a truculent colleague causing more stress than was absolutely necessary, and the low clouds drawing in. But as she turned the corner towards her little terrace, the early blossom on the trees outside seemed to shine through the rain. It almost felt as if the whole house was basking in a welcoming glow, lifting her mood and making her feel safe, as it always did.

Why, why, why when I have my hands full do my keys decide to jump down to the bottom of my bag and hide? she thought as she got to the door, umbrella handle tucked under her chin whilst she rifled around trying to find them. Kneeling down, she emptied the contents onto the path, accidentally dropping the umbrella at the same time, whilst her laptop case slipped from her arms onto the muddy grass. 'I know you're there,' she whimpered. 'Come out, come out, wherever you are. Please.'

'Lovely weather,' said a voice behind her. 'No wonder I don't come back to London very often.'

She jumped up and turned around, her knees covered in grass and mud, whilst several drops of water slid down her face from her rain-sodden hair. Alice smiled – despite feeling damp – at Kathy standing in front of her, tanned, glowing and laughing. And not wet. In fact, the opposite of Alice in every way.

'You should have taken a taxi from the station,' she said. 'That's how you avoid rain damage. That's why I'm dry and you're … not!'

'Ohhhh, Kathy, Kathy!' Alice stood up, hugging her tight. 'Whoops – you're wet too now. Sorry.'

Kathy laughed again. 'Okay, I deserved that. Is this what you were looking for?' she asked, bending down and picking up a set of keys from the path.

'God, thanks,' sighed Alice, opening the door and picking up her shopping.

'What's that? I hear the sound of clinking bottles.' Kathy grinned.

'A teeny bit of Prosecco and cheesecake for our girl's night in.'

'Night in? We're going out.'

'Are we?'

A slight frown flickered across Kathy's face as she picked up the laptop case from the ground and carried it inside. 'Still bringing work home all the time?' she asked.

'Well, that's my life,' said Alice, bristling a little. 'I've got to keep on top of things otherwise it all gets disorganised and spirals out of control.'

'Even more reason to go out tonight to make sure you don't take a sneaky peek at some training plan when I'm in the loo or something.' Kathy laughed. 'When was the last time we were in London together and went out on the town?'

Alice paused for a second. She couldn't remember. 'A while ago.'

'Come to think of it – when was the last time you went out on the town?'

Alice winced. 'No idea – lost in the mists of time. Come in.'

Kathy put her rucksack down in the hall, gave Alice the laptop back, spread her arms wide and breathed in slowly. 'Oh, Alice – I do love your house. It feels so nice. And it looks so nice. And it smells really, really, really nice.'

'Thank you.' Alice beamed. 'I love it too, as you well know.'

As they walked into the kitchen, she began to move several piles of paperwork that were on the table. 'Don't look at me like that,' she said to Kathy.

'Like what?'

'Like, I do all that work at home. Like I've turned into a workaholic. I am *not* a workaholic.'

'I never said you were.' Kathy calmly pulled out a chair and sat down.

Alice took her coat off and put it in the cupboard under the stairs. 'Work's a bit, well, miserable at the moment, to be honest,' she said.

'Miserable?'

'Lots of rumours of redundancy. It's very unsettling. So, I'm making sure I'm indispensable.'

'Of course you are,' said Kathy. 'You've been working there for years. You're a top training manager now.'

'Several take-overs later, I'm not so sure.'

'Right,' said Kathy, standing up again. 'Time for medicinal action. The fizz is chilled enough for our needs from your walk home. Shall I put the other one in the fridge and pour us a couple of glasses from this one?'

'I was going to put the kettle on.'

'Well, you can have tea with it if you want.'

'Oh, I give in,' said Alice walking into the living room and sinking onto the sofa. 'I'll change later. Bring on the warm wine.'

Kathy brought two glasses over and sat down. 'I just wanted to celebrate seeing you again after all this time,' she said. 'A toast to friendship. Even if it's far apart.'

'Friendship,' echoed Alice, holding her glass aloft.

'Let's down it in one!' Kathy suggested with a laugh. 'Come on.'

They drained their glasses quickly. Alice sneezed and then giggled, enjoying the warm tickle of the bubbles as they fizzed in her mouth.

'Why haven't you come to see me in Cascais?' asked Kathy eventually.

Alice thought for a moment. 'Life, the universe, responsibilities, I don't know … time goes. I visited you when you lived in Lagos though, remember?'

'Indeed,' said Kathy. 'But it was with Adam the controlling arse. It would be more fun in Cascais with me now he's trotting round the world. He wouldn't be allowed to come anyway. Every time I phoned you he'd be the one to pick up the call. He always said, "How are things in Cascayce then?" Always!' She shook her head and smiled. 'And I'd tell him, no, no it's pronounced Cashcishe, Cash … cishe … and he'd ignore me and called it Cascayce again.'

Alice closed her eyes for a moment to try to erode the image of her ex that had just pushed itself into her mind.

'You've still got it,' said Kathy pointing at a colourful ceramic bowl on the coffee table.

'Ah, yes.' Alice smiled sadly.

'I remember the day you completed on the house, the two of you had been out looking for duvets and furniture and everything. And all you managed to buy was the bowl.'

'We were very proud of it, though.'

'Rightly so. It's very pretty.'

'It's the only thing we agreed on about the way the house should look.'

'Typical.'

'Very symbolic.'

'You'd love Cascais. Life is so much more laidback, the weather is better, it's sociable. I'm nowhere near as stressed as when I worked in the city even though I'm working for myself.'

'And how is the beauty business?' asked Alice, noticing how happy and relaxed her friend looked.

'It's going well – I did tell you I moved it to a hotel from the shopping centre, didn't I? Anyway, the whole place is kind of magical.' She poured them both another glass.

Alice shifted uncomfortably. She knew what Kathy was going to say. She had been sending her messages, photos and postcards for some time hinting at the same thing.

'You could have an adventure,' said Kathy. 'He's not here to bother you – you could give up your job, rent out the house and travel the world.'

'I knew you were going to say that,' said Alice, trying to smile, 'I can't give up my job.'

'Why not?'

'I have a mortgage to pay.'

'If you rent it out, you could pay the mortgage – have a bit left over to live on …'

Alice picked up her glass and took a swig from it. 'I can't rent the house out to be honest. Adam is co-owner and needs to sign things and I don't know where he is. He just went one day and left a note. That's it.'

'You can e-mail him – we have the internet and everything these days, Alice.'

'Nope – he blocked me – he told me he was going to. Said we needed a clean break. Said he was going to cleanse himself of social media and the internet. That was in an e-mail he sent me from Alaska. I can't find him anywhere, and I've been looking, believe me. All I get from him are bloody postcards.'

'Bloody postcards?'

Alice stood up, walked to a drawer and pulled it open dramatically. 'Here,' she said, waving some cards at Kathy. 'This one's from Rio, this one's from Guadeloupe, this one's from Costa Rica and this one's from Patagonia. I got rid of all the others.'

'All the others?'

'Yes – he sends them every three to four weeks. So, that's been two years' worth. I tear them into little pieces and throw them in the bin. I sometimes set fire to them.'

'Why does he send them to you? Controlling little—'

'Oh, do you know, I'm past caring,' sighed Alice. 'I've just thrown myself into work, finished off the stuff that needed doing in the house and ... hibernated!'

'You're far too much fun to hibernate, Alice. We used to go off and do all sorts – remember Glastonbury? Remember us trying to learn how to sail!'

'Oh dear, yes. Don't think we'd be welcomed back to that particular sailing school.' Alice took another sip, guffawed suddenly at the memory, and began to splutter.

'When you met Adam, you were both so much fun. What happened to him? He got all ... pompous. Quite early on.'

Alice thought for a moment. 'He did, didn't he? Out of the blue. Never saw it coming. He was pompous for years before he had his mid-life crisis. Now I'm used to him not being here I don't want him back. But I'm a bit stuck. And I wish he'd stop sending those bloody postcards.'

'You need a mid-life crisis yourself, Alice Dorothy Matthews,' announced Kathy. 'A life-changing, mind-bending, irresponsible, irrepressible one. But where I can keep an eye on you. So, you have to come to Portugal.'

'I can't. Like I said, I have to work.'

Kathy laughed. 'Take a break then. You can have one during a two-week holiday, Alice. A short-but-sweet and intense one if you can't manage any longer. Better than nothing.'

Alice swigged her drink again. 'Point taken.'

Kathy looked through the postcards. 'Right,' she said. 'Get your glad rags on – I have an idea.'

'Have you got them?'

'Yes, here,' said Alice, taking the postcards out of her bag, pleased that the rain had finally stopped.

'So – does this seem appropriate?'

'Tower Bridge – couldn't be better. This is where he first kissed me. Bastard.'

'Are you ready to rip and tear?'

'I'm ready.'

'One, two, three … Go!'

The fragments of postcard scattered from the bridge into the River Thames, floating like confetti towards the water.

'How do you feel?' asked Kathy.

Alice watched them sink slowly into the river, and imagined it was Adam disappearing into the cold, grey murkiness. 'I should have done this sooner!' she admitted.

'Right,' said Kathy, pulling her away from the railings. 'This way and don't look back. I've booked us a restaurant in the Shard and we're running late.'

'I feel bad about dropping litter in the river,' said Alice quietly.

'Think of it as bedding for seagulls. They'll swoop down before it lands and use it. Recycling.'

Chapter Two

The girl in the sepia postcard strode along the city street, handbag swinging, purposeful and optimistic, her white sundress almost shining against the damp pavements, her straw-hat protection from the rain, not the sun. Even though she was walking away. Even though you could only see her back, you could tell. She exuded it. Blue skies were coming and that's where she was going. Let it rain.

Alice read the message on the back again.

It was absolutely brilliant to see you the other week. The water's lovely over here. Why don't you just come and dip your toes in it. Portugal awaits. Love, Kathy xxx

She put it on the dresser next to the other one. The black and white one. The one with a solitary cowboy passing through a bleak expanse of sparse, grey fields, framed by a range of hard, desolate charcoal mountains. She didn't have to read the message on the back of that one again. She had read it four times already. The words were seared into her brain without her consent. She didn't want them to be there, but that was Adam all over, she thought, getting under her skin, unwelcome, unwanted and callous.

Hey Alice, just arrived in Buenos Aires for some R and R! Things going well here. Book deal in the offing and a brand-new project in the air. Think it's about time we sold the house. I'll be back in the UK at the end of next month and we can start the process then. Can you be a darling and get a couple of estate agents to value it? Cheers, A.

The cards had arrived at the same time, lying innocuously on the door-mat. How could Alice have known that one was good and one was evil?

Although her mind was fuzzy with stress, she remembered reading Kathy's first because she knew it would make her smile. And then she had read Adam's postcard. It didn't make her smile. It made her panic. It made her sad. And it made her angry. So, she had tried to calm down by putting things in order which is what she always did, instinctively rearranging the postcards and 'The Letter', which had arrived the day before, so they looked neater together on the dresser: the postcards either side, the cream official envelope in the middle. Then she realised what she was doing.

'What the bloody hell am I doing!' she had shouted, walking over to a drawer, opening it and then shutting it again, loudly, just because it made her feel better. 'Three bits of paper that sum up my life. Adam wants the house, Kathy is having a lovely time and wants me to visit. And my redundancy letter. My *redundancy letter.*'

She had run upstairs and thrown herself into cleaning the bathroom, scrubbing and polishing, and putting old bottles in the bin aggressively, trying to escape from the present the only way she knew how, only returning to the kitchen when her heart had stopped racing.

And now here she was – the letter still there, along with the postcards. They weren't going to go away.

She opened and shut the drawer again and paced around the kitchen. Finding herself near the kettle she switched in on. *Hot sweet tea. That'll help. That's what they do in films*, she thought. Sitting at the table waiting for it to boil, she drummed her fingers, staring at the dresser, mind racing wildly. And that's when the girl in the sepia postcard really got her attention.

Why was everyone else having fun except her? Why did Adam think he could just waltz back and make decisions about her life? Hadn't HR at work already made a decision about her life that she hadn't been consulted about? Standing up she poured water over the tea bag, watching it scorch the liquid brown. Shovelling in some sugar and throwing in a splash of milk, she sat down again, sipping it angrily. Picking up Adam's postcard again she scrutinised it just in case he'd hidden his new e-mail address on it by accident.

On the table was the bowl they'd bought when they first moved in. Adam had paid for it, smiling. 'We're going to make this place distinctive and individual,' he had said. 'Our house.'

'Our home,' Alice had said, remembering the first time they'd seen it, how they had planned the way they were going to bring the worn and musty building back to life. But they had bought it in the throes of early, hopeful, passionate love and Adam had slowly abandoned it, both emotionally and materially in the same way he had abandoned Alice.

She took her tea and sat on the stairs for a while, her head against the wall. She was told the news about the job a month ago and had finished two weeks early to use up all the leave she never bothered to take. But she was frozen, unable to look for more work, let alone apply for it, her brain seemingly unable to focus on anything apart from panic. Her shoulders were constantly tense, and her eyes twitched with nerves as soon as she woke up.

But she had always had the house. She felt safe in this house. Her cocoon.

Alice sighed, silently praying for someone with a magic wand to appear, sweeping around, singing and saying wise things, somehow making everything alright, a bit like a fairy godmother. Dragging herself back into the kitchen, she picked up Kathy's postcard and allowed herself to smile. Adventurous, exciting Kathy. Living in Portugal. Making things happen.

I used to be like that, she thought sadly. *Wonder what happened to me.* Her eyes fell on Adam's card again and her teeth involuntarily clenched. She knew she couldn't shred this one. Or set fire to it. Or drop it from a bridge. She had to keep it to keep the anger; she needed to keep the anger so she could decide what to do. Because this time he had gone too far.

This time she had to do something. But she didn't know what that something was.

The fury engulfed her, so she threw on a jacket, left the house and turned her iPod on full blast, hoping some fresh air would give her some clarity. Usually music helped, but for once it was all just white noise accompanying Alice's angry steps, driving her across the road and into the park. With every movement a small voice began to grow louder and louder.

No. it said.

No.

No. It's not your house. It's my house. You cannot sell my house.

No, no, no, no, no.

The path arched through the lawns past a tiny playground next to a café. A little girl in a red coat was soaring high on a swing, chuckling joyfully like a tinkling scale on a piano. Her father was pushing her higher, and with every movement she laughed even more, thrilled with the excitement of flying through the air, as high as the cherry trees bursting with pink blossom next to the stream.

Alice paused to watch, momentarily captivated by the girl's vitality, longing to be like her, just living in the moment, free of all of the worries she'd been carrying around for so many years. She thought of Kathy in Portugal – Kathy in Portugal relaxed and happy and having an adventure – and as she did so it was like she saw a chink of light. An escape from waking up at three o'clock in the morning just to panic about the future and how to pay the bills, from years of working just to stand still.

'A break. A break. I just need a little break from it all,' she whispered to herself.

It seemed so obvious. Adam couldn't do anything if she wasn't there, could he? He couldn't sell the house if she didn't agree with it, not for a while anyway. He couldn't persuade her if he couldn't find her. He couldn't have it. The house they'd bought together. The dishevelled building they'd begun to lovingly bring back to life. The house Adam had stopped paying for ten years ago because the freelance work was a bit up and down. The house Alice had therefore paid the mortgage for because someone had to. The house she had painted and papered and scrubbed and loved. The house he had finally and completely abandoned two years ago.

The house that Alice built.

And for the first time in many, many years, Alice Dorothy Matthews did something spontaneous. She phoned Kathy, her heart beating fast.

'Hi, you've reached the voicemail of Kathy Fonseca. I'm not available to take your call at the moment, so if you leave a message I'll get back to you as soon as I can.'

So much for seizing the moment, thought Alice. She took a deep breath, and after the beep, the words spilled out.

'Hi Kathy. It's me, Alice. Can I come and stay for a few weeks? I mean in a hotel for a holiday. Not in your place, just near it. I've been made redundant and I can't concentrate on looking for another job. Think I need a break to unfuzz my brain. It could be for two weeks, three, or four. Can't make up my mind … and, and—' a stray sob caught in her throat '— and Adam – whatever he wants the money for he can go and whistle for it. Sod him.' She took a breath. 'Bye. Speak soon.'

She walked home, checking her phone every two minutes in case she'd missed a call from her friend. Opening the front door, she kicked her shoes off and paused for a moment, the enormity of what Adam was expecting her do slowly dawning on her. Her breathing quickened as she panicked, then slowed again as she noticed a scuff mark on the wall next to the front door. She rifled through her cleaning shelf in the kitchen and picked out the sugar water and a cloth, then noticed several more marks and lost herself in cleaning until she was interrupted by the phone.

'Alice!' Kathy almost shouted down the phone.

'Kathy,' replied Alice more quietly.

'Right. You said you wanted to come over and visit but weren't sure how long for?' said Kathy.

'Yes,' said Alice. 'I hope that's okay.'

'Of course it's okay. I've been asking you to come over for years. But this open-ended thing, that's not like you. You like everything organised and arranged.'

'No. But it used to be like me. I used to be like that, didn't I?

'You did. Over ten years ago.'

'Well, after a long hiatus, that Alice is back.'

'Is she?'

Alice paused. 'Christ, I hope so.'

'Alice ...?' said Kathy slowly.

'Yes?'

'What else has happened other than losing your job? What did you mean about Adam and the money?'

Alice didn't speak for a moment. She couldn't.

'Alice, what are you doing? Are you still there?'

'Yes, just putting the kettle on to make some more chamomile tea.'

'Right ...'

'It's to calm me down. I bought two boxes with 140 tea bags in. I read about it online.'

'So, what did you mean about Adam?'

Alice paused again. 'I'll tell you when I'm there. I'm fed up of thinking about it to be honest.'

'What's he done?'

'Is there a hotel near you with a lovely view?' asked Alice quickly. 'I honestly would stay with you in your apartment, but I feel I need a bit of independence. Can't really explain it. I'll stay in the hotel for two weeks and if I want to stay any longer I'll find a cheaper one. See you on the 27th. Hope that date's okay. I have to go.' She put the phone down and leaned wearily against the wall. Discussing Adam and the house made her feel physically sick. Every time she had talked to her mother about it a debilitating nausea enveloped her and she just wanted to crawl under a duvet and hide.

Later that day she took the bus to her parents' house and explained her plan.

'What are we going to do when he comes looking for you Alice?' her mother asked.

'Tell him I've gone to Borneo.'

'I'm not sure he'll believe that, darling. But more to the point, what shall we say about the house?'

'Nothing. Say nothing. Feign ignorance about everything.'

Her mother smiled. 'Can't stand the man,' she said. 'I am going to enjoy this.' She put her hand on Alice's wrist. 'Please stop playing with those bracelets, Alice.'

'Sorry, I'm just a bit wound up.'

'Well you'll break them if you're not careful. It's a pity you don't make your own any more. They were a lot nicer.'

'Right, well, will you pretend you haven't got the keys? I changed the locks just after he left without telling him so he can't get in on his own.' Alice placed the new keys on the table.

'Even more fun!' Her mother clapped her hands. 'Let's make the pig pay for breaking your heart and stealing your money.'

'Mum!'

'Sorry, dear. I got a bit overexcited. Do you want that last Hobnob or can I have it?'

'All yours.'

'Anger is a great galvaniser,' shouted her stepfather, Joseph, from the conservatory. 'Nurture it a bit and turn it on him!'

'Good to know I have your support,' she replied.

'Although Alice, you will have to deal with this at some point. He will have rights to the house you know, whether you like it or not,' Joseph said, walking into the room.

'I know, I know. But not yet. In my own time. I just need some time.'

'This is very unlike you, Alice,' he said, sitting down next to her. 'You always like to do the right thing. Do things the right way. Adam will be expecting you to behave rationally.'

'I'm not being irrational, I'm just—'

'That's not an insult,' interrupted Joseph. 'I think it's an excellent strategy.'

Her mother dunked the biscuit thoughtfully in her tea. 'Of course, I'll tell Tara. Your sister needs to know. We have to have a family story for this. I do like a bit of intrigue. A nice plot, you know.'

Alice hugged her. 'I love you, Mum. But remember, this isn't a film. I haven't written a script. There is no plot.'

'Really, Alice Dorothy Matthews, I'm not stupid.'

'No, I know,' she said.

And why are you called Alice Dorothy Matthews? muttered the voice in her head. *Alice is in Wonderland. Dorothy is in The Wizard of Oz.*

'My mother's film fixation, not mine,' said Alice out loud, closing the front door behind her and stepping onto the street.

Chapter Three

Alice moved slowly through each room taking photographs of her home, brushing her hands against the fabrics, unable to smile at the memories of the years she had spent there because of the rage she felt at the prospect of having to fight for it. 'I'll be back in a few weeks,' she said to the kitchen. And there was that ceramic bowl again – the one they had bought before any thought of tables or chairs or beds. She picked it up and pushed it into the rucksack she'd left by the stairs. 'The neighbours will keep an eye on you while I'm gone, house. Adios.'

Then she strode out of the door and clambered into the taxi without looking back. By the time she was ready to get on the plane the anger she had been nurturing for the past few weeks was so strong she was almost high on it. But, it began to dissipate somewhere over France, and was slowly replaced by a much more disturbing mantra. *What are you doing? What ARE you doing? Oh no! WHAT ARE YOU DOING? You should be at home looking for work to earn money. You can't afford a holiday. You bloody stupid woman.* By the time she stepped off the plane and walked along the concourse to passport control the words had developed into a throbbing headache. As she queued to get through Alice began to glance at the people standing around her, wondering why they were there. *Anyone else dodging responsibility and failing to face up to things like a grown-up?* she wondered.

Standing next to the luggage belt to collect her case, she had to stop herself impatiently hopping from foot to foot. The departure lounge could be seen through a glass wall, and for a second, Alice imagined herself somehow climbing over it and getting the next flight back home. No harm done. Then sanity took over. 'It's only a holiday,' she muttered. 'Calm down. Just an open-ended one. But it's a holiday.' Her case appeared, and she grabbed it, almost running towards the exit, repeating in her head over and over again: *It's a holiday, just enjoy it.*

Pausing briefly before the automatic doors towards the arrivals hall, she bowed her head and took several deep breaths. Alice Dorothy Matthews had never run away before. 'Here we go,' she muttered as the door opened and she walked into the bright, white light as crowds of people slowly came into focus. Kathy wasn't there, just a sign with Alice Matthews scrawled across it held by a tall, smiling man with striking blue eyes and hair like a hedgehog's prickles. She waved at him, relieved. 'That's me,' she said.

'Ah, welcome, Alice.' His smile got even wider. 'Welcome to Portugal.' Taking her suitcase, he guided her towards the exit. 'Kathy had to deal with an emergency at the spa at the hotel, so she has asked me to collect you. It was one of her regular customers being a total cow. I think that's what Kathy said.'

'Oh dear,' said Alice, scurrying to keep up with his long, swift strides as he guided her through the arrivals lounge towards the car park.

'That meant that she couldn't leave on time to meet you,' he continued. 'Kathy is a very loyal customer and this is on the house.'

'That's very kind of you,' said Alice, following him outside. The bright blue sky and the midday heat wrapped themselves around her like a warm blanket, with the familiar flutter of excitement she had always felt on family holidays in faraway countries as she had stepped off the planes into enticing other worlds. It was the first time she had felt anything other than panic for the past few weeks.

'Kathy suggested I drive you along the sea road to Cascais – The Marginal – rather than the motorway. It's much prettier,' he said as they weaved around cars and taxis and hordes of people dragging their suitcases towards the terminal.

'Sounds lovely to me,' said Alice, by now almost running to keep up.

'I'm Ignacio by the way.'

'Nice to meet you Ignacio.'

'You too, Alice. May I call you Alice?'

'Of course.'

'Here we are.'

In front of them was a beautiful old yellow Rolls-Royce with a black soft-top roof and gleaming lights.

'This?' Alice felt a smile widen on her face.

'Yes,' he said opening the door.

'It's a yellow Rolls-Royce. Have you ever seen the film? It's one of my favourites. It's called *The Yellow Rolls-Royce* – the part of the plot with Alain Delon and Shirley Maclaine is the best ...' She trailed off, realising she was sounding like her mother.

'My airport collection car is at home. This is my wedding car. I was cleaning it up this afternoon when I got the call to come and collect you.'

'It's beautiful.' Alice put her hand out to stroke it.

Ignacio smiled. 'I do that too. It's my pride and joy. I've owned it for twenty years. Please, sit in. I will take your cases.'

As Alice climbed in her eyelids began to flicker. It had been a long, cold winter, and the underlying threat of redundancy had added to the gloom and torpor. Spring had been late, and was slowly coming to life, but she'd been so stressed and exhausted she'd barely noticed. Sinking into her seat as the weariness pulled her down, she slipped quickly into a light sleep, rocked gently by the low thrum of the engine, fuzzy images flickering across her tired mind of Adam pursuing her, waving a postcard, shouting 'give me my house back!' with her mother running after him brandishing a rolling pin and singing 'Follow the yellow brick road'.

'Madam ... madam ... Alice ...' Ignacio was smiling again as her eyes opened, the car paused at a set of traffic lights. 'Alice, we are almost on the Marginal. This will take us all the way to Cascais. Look how beautiful it is.'

They turned onto the sea road, and she sleepily glanced, as instructed, out of the window, to where the sea sparkled and moved, and the sun caught the waves as if a field of sapphires was being blown in the breeze. To the right were yellow, white and blue apartments, and bright pink houses wrapped in trails of red and purple flowers. In the distance was a long, golden beach. That morning, when she had left her house, the grey clouds were so low she felt she was actually walking through them. But now, suddenly, here was a place where the sky was so blue and clear it was as if someone had taken a brush and painted it onto the landscape. She sat up, curling her feet onto the seat and stared out of the window like an excited little girl.

Her mother used to sit at bedtime with her and her sister when they were tiny and living in the damp little bedsit they had fled to after their father had left them and their home was repossessed. She would read them *Alice's Adventures in Wonderland* and *The Lion, the Witch and the Wardrobe* by the light of the dim bulb in the mottled brown room, filling it with colour and fun and hope. Every night she had sung them 'Somewhere over the Rainbow', so when they finally went to sleep, they knew there was somewhere better. All they had to do was to find the right door or get blown by the right breeze and they would be in a place that was exciting and hopeful and full of life. They had only been there for a few months until her mother had swallowed her pride and they had moved in with her parents. But Alice had never forgotten that bedsit.

'It is beautiful. Paradise,' said Ignacio. 'You cannot be sad for long in Paradise.'

For the rest of the journey Alice stared out of the window, captivated by the colour she saw around her. Ignacio eventually turned off the sea road, and Alice felt her heart beat a little faster. It was only two weeks since she'd made the uncharacteristically spontaneous and ill-thought out decision to come here, and the rest of the time had been caught up in all the practical preparations to make it happen. And now she was here. As the Rolls glided into the hotel entrance, Alice saw Kathy, who was standing at the top of the steps. When she saw the car, she waved. Next to her was a white-haired woman in a stripy pink dress.

'Hello! Welcome!' cried Kathy, almost tackling Alice to the ground as she climbed out of the car. 'At last! I'm so sorry I couldn't get to the airport.'

'Lady Miseryguts, it was, wasn't it?' cut in the white-haired woman.

'The cow,' said Ignacio seriously.

'It's fine,' mumbled Alice, slightly overwhelmed. 'Ignacio explained. I'm here. Wherever here is?'

Kathy stepped back and smiled at her friend. 'Welcome to Cascais,' she said.

'Welcome to Paradise, love,' said the white-haired woman. 'I'm Mary. Do you like cats?'

'Hello, nice to meet you.' Alice smiled, a little confused by the question. 'And yes, I do.'

'Mary is one of my closest friends,' said Kathy. 'She used to help me at the salon. And she does have a cat, but I can't explain that question.'

'Ignore her,' said Mary. 'There is an explanation.'

'I'll leave you now,' interrupted Ignacio. 'Did you enjoy your journey along the sea road?'

'Oh yes,' she said. 'It was lovely, thank you. Beautiful. Much better than the motorway.' Alice smiled nervously. She'd noticed Mary was staring at her.

'Are you okay, Mary?' asked Kathy.

'I'm perfectly fine.' Mary smiled. Then she hugged Alice.

'I think she likes you,' said Kathy.

'She can hear you,' said Mary. She stepped back and scrutinised Alice again. 'I knew it,' she said. 'As soon as I found out you were coming over I knew it. It was meant to be.'

'Knew what?' asked Alice.

'That you were sent to look after our apartment. And Aphrodite. Our cat. We finalised our bookings for our trip on the exact day you called Kathy.'

'Your apartment?' Alice was confused. 'I'm sorry, I don't understand.'

'We're going off around the world and need someone to apartment sit and love our cat.'

'Oh,' said Alice. 'Um …'

'It's all free, obviously.'

Alice struggled to put her confusion into words. 'That's really kind of you, but I'm only here for a few weeks. Just for a holiday. I'll be going back home quite soon.'

'Good. That's settled.'

'I don't think it is, Mary,' said Kathy. 'She said she—'

'Now, now, Kathy, you know I have a gift.'

'Mystic Mary,' said Kathy. 'It's not a real thing.'

'You may mock, but I do,' said Mary firmly.

'But I don't know you,' said Alice, 'And you don't know me …'

'Alice, I feel I do. I've heard so much about you. Please say you will do it when we go, even if it's just for a couple of weeks. If you want to go home we have plenty of volunteers who will jump over you to take over. Believe me, it's lovely.'

'It's absolutely gorgeous to be honest,' agreed Kathy.

Alice stood and looked at them as if they were speaking another language that sounded like English but didn't mean the same things as any English words she knew. She decided her mind had been scrambled by the journey.

'It's perfect. We're going in two weeks. You are booked at the hotel for two weeks. Everything is in alignment,' said Mary.

Alice continued to look at them. 'I've only just arrived.' She was struggling to find the words to match her bewilderment.

'Well you are not saying no. So I'll take that as a yes.' Mary looked pleased with herself.

Alice glanced at Kathy pleadingly.

'Just think about it,' said Kathy.

Alice smiled weakly as Ignacio revved the engine of the Rolls. She'd say no politely and firmly later. She wasn't really sure whether she was awake or dreaming the whole thing. Or perhaps she was developing a film fixation like her mother and was in a new instalment of *Alice in Wonderland*.

'Right, why don't you get checked in, and we'll meet you at the bar in half an hour?' said Kathy.

'Yes, yes,' sighed Alice, passing her luggage to the doorman. 'That's a good idea.'

One cool, refreshing shower followed by a cup of coffee reassured Alice she was actually awake, but possibly in some bright cartoon alternative universe populated by yellow Rolls-Royces, glittering waves and women called Mary who asked people they didn't know to look after their apartments. She went down to the bar to meet her and Kathy. Once she'd taken a swig of the champagne they'd ordered she found the courage to bring the subject of the apartment up. 'It's a lovely offer, really, Mary. But I can't commit to it, it wouldn't be fair.'

'Honestly, Alice, just say yes. And don't worry if you want to leave in a few weeks.' Mary tipped three lumps of sugar into her coffee and smiled. 'It's very good timing, that's all. We've decided to travel very quickly and left all the organising for our apartment and Aphrodite till the last minute. The person who said they could do it has had to head back to Italy because of a family emergency. So you have dropped into our lives at just the right time. I knew you would. Ever since I'd heard about you from Kathy all those years ago, I knew you would.'

'But,' said Alice slowly. 'I may only be there for two weeks.'

'It's fine. And it's too late anyway. I've told Aphrodite.'

Alice fiddled with her bracelets. '*Alice is so rigid, never lets go.*' Adam was in her head again, throwing memories at her like stones. '*I love her, you know, and I'm all for being organised.*' He was on the phone to his friend in the kitchen and didn't know she was listening in. '*But it was so liberating, so freeing just to get up and go on the motorbike and see where I ended up. Bless her, she can't help it. Being so bloody grown up all the time.*'

22

'Alice, are you okay?' Kathy nudged her.

'Ah, well, I will have to leave soon. I have to look for work and I've got an issue, a thing, I have to deal with at home. At some point,' said Alice.

'*She can't help it. Being so bloody grown up all the time.*' There he was again.

'I'll stay in your apartment.' She almost shouted the words. 'Until it's time to go. Until I spontaneously decide to go home. Until ...' her voice petered out.

'Whatever you say.' Mary smiled.

'And who or what is this issue with?' asked Kathy.

Alice took another swig of champagne. 'Not in the mood to talk about it at the moment.'

'Well I think it's time to celebrate properly,' said Mary. 'Mine and Frank's great pensioner adventure by land, sea and air to Australia. We should be there just in time to see our new grandchild being born. And to celebrate Alice being exactly where she is supposed to be. As I always knew she would.'

'Not quite understanding that bit,' muttered Alice

'Do you remember, Kathy? When you told me about Alice and the nasty way that man of hers was treating her, I said she belongs here. One day she'll come.'

'Oh, well that's nice,' said Alice.

'And then when he left you I said it again. Didn't I, Kathy?'

'Yes she did, to be honest,' said Kathy, 'But I think it was just you being all Mystic Mary, Mary.'

'I have a gift. And you know it. Don't mock!' She held her champagne glass up. 'Come on girls, first toast of the evening – to me and Frank and our adventure!'

Alice took another big swig, and then realised Mary was continuing where she'd left off.

'And then when Kathy said she'd seen you a few weeks ago, I said is that your sad friend, the one who was abandoned and now doesn't go out much. The one who used to be fun but isn't now. Stays in all the time? And Kathy said yes.'

'I didn't. I said that you'd had a bad time, I didn't say any of that.'

Alice drained the champagne glass, then poured herself another. 'So, this gift?' she asked.

'Oh, yes, I've had it forever. I'm always trying to help Kathy with her love life but she doesn't listen. I knew that recent one, what was his name – Shergar?'

'Fergus.' Kathy sighed. 'I think you'll find Shergar was a horse.'

'My powers don't cover names, love, but nonetheless, I knew he would love you and leave you, just like that.'

'He lives in New Zealand. He was here for business. He's gone to Norway now. He was always going to leave.'

'But you need someone, love. You'll be forty in no time at all.'

'I've got a couple of years left until then and I'm quite happy,' said Kathy.

'There's something going on though, isn't there? Something, someone, I can't quite get it yet, but I will.'

'There is nothing and no one,' said Kathy firmly, shifting awkwardly in her chair.

As the sun set slowly over the ocean, they went on a toasting frenzy, clinking their glasses to life, the universe, Cascais, windswept barbecues on Guincho beach, beauty treatments, the shoe shine man in the square, Mary's cat Aphrodite, Fergus and his ilk, Serge their hairdresser, flip flops and toasts themselves. Their final toast was to Alice's little house, left alone and forlorn in London.

'I think Frank's trying to ring me,' said Mary finally, picking up her mobile phone and watching it ring. 'I love you Frank,' she said.

'He can't hear you, you haven't answered the phone, you're just shouting at it,' said Kathy.

Alice could feel her eyes flickering, desperate to close and sleep. 'I have to go to bed,' she said. 'Sorry. It's been lovely but I'll see you in the morning.'

Chapter Four

Alice woke up, feeling confused. This was a holiday, but not like one she'd ever had. Life had pushed her out of her routine, and she'd somehow jumped even further. It was as if everything had accidentally been put on pause. Her heart was racing as she went down to the hotel café to meet Kathy and Mary to talk about the apartment. Two palm trees swayed in the breeze, the sea roaring in the distance. As Alice breathed in slowly, a still calm oozed through her. Then it disappeared into a cacophony of doubt and fear in which the familiar words *What are you doing? What on earth are you doing?* rang around her head.

'Now,' said Mary, putting three large envelopes on the table in front of her.

'Please tell me you haven't got the tour guide stuff out.' Kathy laughed.

'I get nothing but compliments about these, excuse me Kathy,' said Mary. 'I get a lot of visitors, Alice,' she continued. 'But I'm a busy woman. I was forever ferrying people into Lisbon and the like. I mean, it's lovely, but it's down the road. I'm there all the time. So one day I decided to facilitate rather than participate. Cut the visitor numbers down considerably.' The envelopes were marked as 'Cascais in a Day', 'Discovering Lisbon' and 'A Morning in Sumptuous Sintra'. 'I used to work in a travel agency,' said Mary. 'Never lost the habit.'

'They are very good, actually,' said Kathy. 'I gave them to my brother and his wife the first time they visited and they raved about them.'

'Thank you very much,' said Alice.

Mary stood up. 'Right I have to go now – so much to do. There'll be more information in the apartment for you when you move in. Make sure you have a lovely pink dress for our leaving do the week after next.'

Nope, it's all real. Not a dream, thought Alice.

Hugging Alice, Mary whispered 'Just go with the flow love, and it will all fall into place.' And then she was gone.

Go with the flow, thought Alice. *How do I do that?*

'Another coffee?' asked Kathy.

'I am on holiday aren't I?' said Alice. 'I haven't moved here and forgotten to tell myself, have I?'

Kathy laughed. 'Mary is a whirlwind. Totally bonkers. Completely lovely.'

'But I feel bad moving into her apartment for a couple of weeks and then leaving.'

'She means everything she says. Just take the offer and don't worry about it. You'll enjoy it more here if you're not in a hotel for ages. Really. Trust me. And now you've committed to a month here – two weeks in the hotel and at least the same in the apartment.'

Alice took a deep breath. *Go with the flow*. There was nothing waiting for her at home except for the looming shadow of Adam trying to sell her house. Not to mention the mortgage repayments and the small matter of needing to find a new job. *So, nothing to go back for at all*, she thought. 'Okay. If you insist. Is it fabulous?'

'Views to die for dahhhlink.'

Alice sat back in her chair and closed her eyes, allowing the morning sun to warm her face.

'So?'

'So what?' said Alice, eyes still closed.

'What's he done?'

'Who?'

'Adam.'

She opened her eyes and took a sip of her coffee, the anger and panic surging up again at the mention of his name. She took a deep breath and said, 'He wants to sell the house.'

'Oh dear.'

'Quite.

'So?'

'So, I have temporarily left the country. He can go and bloody whistle for it.'

Kathy left her to go to work and Alice embarked on her first day of the first open-ended holiday she had ever had. She tried to relax. And she tried to relax the following day. Day four arrived, and she took an early morning swim, collapsing onto a sunbed and listlessly trying to dry herself in the sun. Alice found that the future always disappeared during her early morning swims but was generally waiting for her as soon as her feet touched the grass, like a big, throbbing, anxious question mark. *So, what are you going to do then? You can't go on like this for long. You'll have to look for a job. You have to live. This is all very well, but …* She had learned to deal with her own inner dialogue by putting her iPod on to muffle it and organising her time in order to avoid the question mark. It was exhausting. All she wanted to do was sit under a tree and read some books, but that was not her current default setting. She wrote lists even in thin air. That was her default setting. Already that morning she had grappled with whether to have eggs and bacon for breakfast or just some fruit as she was having lunch with Kathy later on. That had been followed with a long internal discussion about whether to have a sandwich for tea and a swim or not, or whether simply to walk along the prom to Estoril.

A family tumbled through the lobby as she headed towards the lift to her room, laden with towels, beach balls and buckets and spades. They were laughing and chatting and were visibly relaxed. The complete opposite of Alice in fact. 'But I *am* actually on holiday,' she sighed. 'I can just drift.' *That is all very well, but …* replied the voice in her head, as she walked to her room to get ready to meet Kathy.

'I can't switch off. It's wearing me out,' said Alice as she and Kathy left the café after lunch.

Kathy put her arm around her friend. 'It's only because you've been working non-stop for so many years,' she said.

'I suppose so.'

'Your brain isn't used to resting, is it?'

'I suppose not.'

'You will learn to relax.'

'Yes, sir!'

'You've got a nice redundancy package, haven't you?'

'Yes.'

'About to live rent free.'

'I know, but I still have a mortgage to pay.'

'It's not too big though is it?'

'No.'

'I'm going to give you a facial and body treatment on the house tomorrow.'

'Are you?'

'Yes. And look at this.' Alice followed Kathy to the sea wall. Below was a tiny, sandy beach framed by rocks. Children were jumping in the water, screaming happily. 'This is in the middle of town, this is,' said Kathy.

Alice smiled. 'Point taken.'

'There's a yoga class at the hotel every Wednesday. Why not give it a go? It will help.'

'Were you always this relaxed?' asked Alice, leaning against the wall. 'I can't remember.'

'No, I wasn't, as you know. But I love it here. What with all the lavender and jasmine and what have you I use in the salon I get so relaxed, I sometimes go and sit by a road just to get some fumes to break the calmness!'

Alice looked out to sea and kissed her friend on the cheek.

'I want you to be happy,' said Kathy.

'I want to be happy too.'

'You will be. You've just got to sort yourself out a bit. Give yourself some time. It will come. I promise you it will.'

'I also don't remember you being this wise.'

'I'm not! But I'm really good at sounding it. And stop checking your phone messages all the time.'

Alice had pulled her phone out of her bag and was scrutinising it.

'Sorry, just worried about the house and Adam.'

'I thought you'd decided to leave the country and do nothing for a while.'

'I have.'

'So, if your mum or sister texts you to say he's back in England, what will you do?'

'I've made a decision to do nothing.'

'So stop checking your phone all the time!'

'I know, I know, but I feel I should be doing something.'

'Do you want to do something?'

'No.'

'So, don't!' Kathy glanced at her watch. 'Better get off, my next appointment is in half an hour. I'm working tonight. Will you be okay on your own?'

'Yes. I will be practising going with the flow.'

'Very funny.' Kathy took a green scarf out of her bag and draped it around her neck. 'Right, ready for action!'

'I really like your hair short,' said Alice. 'It's very classy. Very business-like.'

'Thanks – that's the idea. And I like the way you're growing your hair a bit longer and curly. It's more like you.'

'Thanks. It's a complete accident and the result of neglect.'

'Don't forget you need to get a pink dress for Mary and Frank's party.'

'Oh yes. Does it have to be pink?'

'It's Mary's pink-themed party. The pinker the better.'

'Here,' said Alice, handing Kathy her phone. 'Can you drop it off at the hotel reception on your way back to the spa and I'll pick it up in a couple of hours.'

'Aha! Cold turkey.'

'Yes. But just for a couple of hours.'

'It's a start,' said Kathy hugging her, before hurrying off towards the cobbled main street.

Alice walked down the steps to enjoy the beach for a while, wiggling her toes in the sand, watching the ebb and flow of the tide. As she absent-mindedly put her hand in her bag to get her phone, she remembered she was going cold turkey and needed to force herself to forget what was going on anywhere apart from the centre of Cascais. So she took a deep breath and said out loud, but quietly, so as not to startle anyone, 'I *will* relax.' Alice rolled her shoulders and stretched her neck. 'Relax,' she muttered to herself through gritted teeth. She walked up to the street above and began to meander home and was distracted by a young man with a guitar who was following two older ladies. Pausing by a dress shop, the ladies began to discuss what was in the window, whilst the man stood next to them, strumming his guitar. As they moved off, he moved off too, still playing. Absent-mindedly crossing the road, she smiled at the thought of the women with their own personal busker and wondered if he did the same in the supermarket, or at the dentists.

Finding herself in a busy square, she paused. It was jammed with cafés, their coloured tables tangled higgledy-piggledy into one mass.

'Hey!' said a waiter, approaching her. 'Would you like to eat? Or a coffee?'

Alice wasn't thirsty. It hadn't crossed her mind. She had somewhere to go. Then she remembered that the whole point of this was that she didn't have anywhere to go. She was relaxing. But she still said, 'No thank you,' out of habit and began to walk on.

'Sitting in the square drinking coffee is an important part of the day,' he said.

Alice turned back to say no thank you again, but he was beaming at her cheekily, with the back of a chair in his hand, pointing at the seat with his other hand.

She laughed, admiring his bravado. 'Go on then,' she said, surprising herself at how easily she'd given in.

'Excellent.' He laughed too. 'These with the red tablecloths are my tables.' He smiled. 'They are the best to sit and watch the world go by. Look – you can see all three entrances to the square, plus that little hidden one there.' He pointed at some narrow steps between two small shops. 'To the old town.'

Alice sat down.

'So.' He smiled again, his dark brown eyes holding her gaze.

Alice smiled back.

'To drink,' he said. 'What would you like to drink?'

'Of course. Silly me. I hadn't thought about it. Um …'

'A *galao*?'

'A what?'

'Milky coffee in a glass. Like a latte, but Portuguese. And it's much better. You can have it darker or lighter.'

'Oh, darker then, I think.'

'Okay. One moment please.'

Alice watched him as he went inside still impressed at the ease with which he'd got her to sit down for a coffee when she really didn't want one at all. *The lion chose the slowest moving member of the antelope herd, monitored its prey and measured the exact time to pounce*, she thought, smiling. *You are that antelope.*

The waiter reappeared with her drink. 'On the house,' he said.

'Oh, that's very kind.'

'You're welcome,' he said. 'My name is Carlos.'

'Alice,' said Alice.

'You are here for a holiday?'

'Sort of. No … yes. No.'

'So, you have moved to live here?'

'No … well, no … but, well … I'm here for four weeks. Six weeks. Two months or more, or less …'

'A few weeks then. You are here with our husband? Your boyfriend?'

'No. Just me. Visiting a friend.' Alice smiled.

'Just you? Well, welcome to Cascais,' said Carlos, his smile now even wider.

'Thank you. I am here to ...' Alice trailed off then tried again. 'I am here to ... go with the flow ... and replenish my energy.' The words felt like a statement of what she should be doing instead of how she felt. *If I say it enough, though*, she thought, *maybe I'll believe it.*

A man with an Alsatian dog sat down at a nearby table.

'I have to go. Work calls,' said Carlos. 'Luis,' she heard him say. 'Don't see you here very often these days.'

'No,' said the man. 'I've been busy with a few house projects. Got a deadline for this one. Antonio's supposed to be helping me, but he's too busy pursuing his dreams. And gambling. Illegally.'

'Ha, the band,' laughed Carlos.

'He tried to get me to wear a white jacket ... a new image. Anyway, I've told him I'm leaving. Too busy for music these days.'

Alice realised she had forgotten how to sit and listen and watch. She had filled her life with work and the house, and when the house was finished, she had started re-decorating it. It meant she didn't have to think about Adam and money. She gritted her teeth again. There it was. The thing she was running from. The thoughts. The thing she was not supposed to be thinking about. Him. It. Forcing herself to eavesdrop to push it away, she leaned back in her chair, and took a sip of coffee.

'Where's this house? I lose count,' said Carlos.

'Over in Torre,' answered the man. 'I want to get it done so I can do the next one.'

'You've got another one already?'

'This one is different,' said the man.

A waiter, a property-developer and the busker who liked to sing for his mum whilst she's out shopping, thought Alice, wondering who else was nearby. A couple sat at a table next to her and quietly began to argue about whether to have beer or wine and a child began to chase some birds around the statue. Alice ordered another coffee and finally started to properly relax. After a while she looked at her watch. She'd been sitting watching people bustle by in the square for nearly an hour. *That was nice*, she thought to herself as she stood up, pushing her chair back. A loud, sudden whimper came from behind her, and she looked around, startled. The dog had stood up, whilst his owner, the man who Carlos had been talking to, tried to calm him down. All she could see was black, lustrous, wavy hair, with tiny flecks of grey at the temples.

'Oh, I'm so sorry,' she said, embarrassed. 'I didn't realise he was there. He or she? Is he alright?'

'He's fine,' said the dog's owner, brusquely. The dog continued to whimper. 'Elvis, calm down, it's just a chair,' he said. 'Well, a woman and a chair.'

'I'm so sorry,' said Alice again, a little flustered by the man's rudeness.

'It's fine,' said the man, barely looking up.

'Hope he's better soon.' She hurried out of the square, on edge again, and walked through the old town towards the sea, trying not to go over and over the incident – a habit developed in the last few years as she had tried to unpick the unravelling of her relationship with Adam. *For goodness sake, Alice*, she thought, frustrated with herself. *Stop over-analysing it. You'll never see him again. He will have forgotten it by now and the dog is fine*. Standing next to the sea wall she gazed at the expanse of blue ocean stretching out to the horizon and her mind slowed. Two small yachts were moored close to the town beach, bobbing up and down in the breeze, whilst a dog ran backwards and forwards into the shallows, barking excitedly at its owner. The sea did look very enticing, so Alice began to walk back down the hill. As she did a coach pulled up pouring its passengers out in a jostling crowd, every individual pushing to take photographs of the perfect view of the bay. Another coach arrived, spilling out even more holiday-makers, fighting for space on the narrow pavement. Suddenly surrounded by people she staggered out onto the road and took a deep breath.

'Miss Matthews ... Miss Matthews ...,' shouted a man from a sleek black car.

Alice heard it but ignored it. She hardly knew anyone here, so who would be calling her name?

'Miss Matthews ... Alice ... Alice ...' The man waved enthusiastically at her.

She peered at him, confused. He had hair like a hedgehog's prickles and a kind smile. 'Ah, Ignacio,' she said eventually. 'Sorry. You are driving a different car. And I didn't expect to see you, so I didn't see you, if you see what I mean.'

'I am in my workday car today. My yellow Rolls-Royce is tucked safely in its garage. I am going to the hotel to pick up a customer. Can I give you a lift? It is free. On the house!'

'Free? That's kind. Are you sure?'

'Of course. Please.' Ignacio jumped out of the car to open the door, whilst Alice discreetly checked her dress buttons to make sure they were all done up. She wasn't used to so much being 'on the house'.

'Everyone is so generous,' she said as she got in.

'How are you liking Cascais so far?' asked Ignacio as they pulled away from the crowd.

'It's lovely. I just sat on the beach for a while, then I had a coffee in the square. Then I was surrounded on the hill as you saw! The waiter in the square was very nice. He gave me a free *galao* ... *galao* ... is that right?' Alice could see Ignacio's eyes narrow in the mirror.

'What café was this waiter in?' he asked.

'Don't know the name. It had red tablecloths though.'

'His name. Was it Carlos?'

'Yes, that's right. Do you know him?'

'Madam. Alice … just to say that my brother, Carlos, the waiter in the square. He is very flirtatious. He is not always to be trusted with women. Always compliments. So, please be aware of this. A pinch of salt and some distance, as they say.'

'Okay.' Alice smiled. 'Thanks for letting me know.'

'You look lovely today if I may say so.'

'Oh. Thank you very much.'

'When you arrived in Portugal you looked tired and pale. And sad.'

'Right, um …'

'Very sad. But today. Only a few days of being here, and you have blossomed already.'

'Thank you. I think. The sunshine helps.'

'No one can be sad in Paradise,' he repeated what he had said when he had first met her.

'Is that why you get so many tourists trying to take photos of the bay?'

His piercing blue eyes lit up. 'Wait until July and August. All day the coaches come. The people jump out with their cameras, snap their snaps and then jump back in and leave.'

'Where do they go afterwards?'

'No one knows. They disappear.'

Alice smiled. 'Really?'

'No,' said Ignacio. 'I am lying. They take them to Estoril. Then Belem. Then Lisbon. And only then do they disappear.'

Alice laughed.

'We are here,' said Ignacio as they turned into the hotel.

'Well, thank you for the lift. That was kind. Are you sure you don't want me to pay?'

'No. On the house. *Ate logo*. Until later. Ciao.'

Alice involuntarily checked her dress buttons again as she got out. They were all done up. 'Bye then,' she said.

'Goodbye Alice,' said Ignacio. 'See you soon.'

Walking past reception, she remembered that Kathy had left her phone there. Her heart began to beat anxiously as the clerk handed it back. Checking it as she got in the lift, she sighed with relief. No missed calls. No messages. *Maybe I'll put it in the safe tomorrow when I go out*, she thought. Two hours without the phone seemed to have done her good. As the doors closed she smiled. 'It felt like Cascais kept interrupting my fretting,' she said to the wall. 'I liked it.'

Chapter Five

'Why can't you be friendlier,' he hissed into her ear.

'I am being friendly.'

'No you're not. You're hiding, as usual, in a corner and not speaking to anyone.'

'I sat down because I have worked five ten-hour days and I'm tired.'

'Where did you go? You used to be fun to be with. Now you are just so … oh, I give up.' He lost interest and scanned the room, his eyes finally fixing on a woman laughing with her friends by the bar. 'I've only just started freelancing for the company. I need to make an impression. You need to try harder. For us. Not just for me.'

'I am trying very hard, Adam. I am working very hard for us.'

'Yeah, right,' he muttered, looking at the woman again. 'And where did you get that dress? It's a bit bloody pink.'

'I bought it especially for tonight. My friends said I looked great. I thought …'

'Well, you are a bit too visible in that. I'm going out for some air,' he interrupted.

Alice watched him as he sauntered towards the door, hovering near the woman and catching her eye as he left.

There was a knock at the door. 'Madam, your laundry,' said the voice, as Alice struggled into consciousness, breathless. 'Madam?'

'Yes, please. Just a moment.' She climbed out of bed and took the bolt off the door. 'If you just put it over there, on the sofa,' she said to the maid. Then she ran into the shower and tried to wash the memory away. It was Mary's leaving party that night, and Alice wanted to enjoy the experience without Adam's shadow ruining it.

'You look fabulous,' said Kathy as they drove along the sea road to the hotel where the party was being held.

'Aw, thanks. So do you,' said Alice.

'I mean it. You look lovely and sun-kissed and relaxed. And that pink dress is fab-u-lous. Where did you get it?'

'Oh this? I've had it for about five years actually. Only worn it once.'

'Really? It's stunning.'

Alice looked out of the car window as the waves rolled onto the rocks. It was a great dress, despite what *he* said.

'So,' said Kathy eventually. 'Are you going to tell me?'

'Tell you what?'

'Don't you start with me, Alice. Why do you not want to sell the house so much that you have run away from home?'

'Well ...'

'Well? Maybe it's a good thing. A fresh start in a new place. I'm sure it's worth quite a lot of money by now.'

'Adam ... ' Alice closed her eyes and almost had to force the words out. 'Adam stopped paying for that house years ago. He was always working on his novel or in between freelance work.'

'Oh.'

'And it just drifted.' Then the words began to rush out, her heart beating fast. 'If I ever brought it up, he accused me of pushing him. He used to get defensive and say he would more than make up for it when things got more regular. But they never did. And you know I couldn't just stop paying. I owned the house too.'

'Ah. I see ...'

'So he left the first time for his fling after Paul died ...'

'Oh, yes, I forgot his brother died.'

'And I had to keep paying, and when he came back, all contrite and guilty, blaming his behaviour on that I took him back ... because I felt guilty ... and when he cleared off for the second time, he just went. And all I get is postcards, as you know.'

'Oh, Alice.'

'So it's not our house really. It's my house. And he can't have it.'

'Alice …'

'I don't want to talk about it any more at the moment.' She had learned not to talk about it as it made the hurt feel real again, so she shut down. Opening the window Alice breathed in the fresh air. 'Music please,' she said.

'Any kind of music in particular?' asked Kathy.

'Just music.'

'I have just the thing.'

'What is it?'

'I'm Gonna Wash That Man Right Out of My Hair.'

'And you have this because?'

'For emergencies. For when they annoy me, upset me or I just want them to go away.'

'Okay, let's sing.'

'And forget.'

'Forget about bastard Adam and houses and mortgages. And rain. And jobs. And being sad.'

'Take it away, Alice!'

Kathy dramatically almost skidded to halt in the car park of the Hotel Sessimbra as they continued to sing and laugh loudly and exuberantly. They almost shrieked the words as they got out, slamming the doors in time to the music that Kathy did not switch off, and they stood singing to each other next to the car. Out of the corner of her eye Alice noticed a man in a car apparently having a conversation with a large Alsatian dog at the same time as they tunelessly held the last word of the song as it ended.

The man looked out of the window, confused, as the dog's ears pricked up trying to identify the noise.

'Whoops, we've been spotted,' whispered Alice.

'Bit late in the day to be whispering,' whispered Kathy back.

Alice giggled.

'Right,' said Kathy. 'I will nonchalantly turn off the power and lock the door, and we will saunter towards the hotel entrance as if there was no singing.'

'Like there was no singing,' echoed Alice. 'Got it.'

The dog barked and whined briefly as they walked past. Alice glanced in the window and shuddered slightly. 'Oh dear. I think I stood on that dog,' she said in a loud whisper to Kathy.

'Oh dear,' giggled Kathy. 'That's not very nice.'

The man was looking at them quizzically. Alice put her head down and hurried on. 'Yes, it was the dog. The owner wasn't very happy about it. It was an accident to be fair.'

'Try not to do it again, Alice,' said Kathy pretending to be stern. 'Now look straight ahead and walk in the door as if you haven't noticed.'

They giggled again and went in.

Alice drifted onto the terrace whilst Kathy chatted to some of the other guests. Leaning against the balcony she gazed out to sea. The sky was slowly turning from pink to deep purple, the setting sun casting an orange glow over the horizon. 'Photo,' she muttered to herself, taking her phone out of her bag. 'Massive photo opportunity.' As she held it up, attempting to frame the shot, a man weaved slowly and drunkenly behind her, lurching suddenly into her back. The phone plummeted towards the concrete patio below.

'Ow. Jesus Christ!' shouted a startled voice.

Alice peered downwards, panicked. There was a man. A tall man. A tall, dark, very handsome man with flecks of grey in his lustrous, black wavy hair. He was looking up at her angrily. Next to him sat a large Alsatian dog, also looking up. It was the man in the car and the dog she'd trodden on in the square. 'Oh God, I'm so sorry,' she shouted.

'No need to shout, I'm not that far away.'

'Sorry. Sorry. Are you alright? It got knocked out of my

hand. Shall I come down? I'll come down.' Alice ran through the bar, ungainly in her pink kitten heels, pausing only to hiss at Kathy, 'I've dropped my phone on a man's head. I don't think he's hurt. I trod on his dog a few days ago too.' Rushing through the doorway, Alice nearly tripped over the Alsatian, as its owner was holding her phone in one hand and rubbing his head with the other.

'Here,' he said, giving her the phone. 'It's not cracked or anything. I meant my head. Not the phone.'

'What a relief. You must have a really soft head. Oh, that came out wrong. Do you need stitches or anything? Or should I call a doctor? Or just get a plaster?'

He stared at her, stony-faced. A man shouted over to him from the garden.

'Luis. Luis! Over here. We're late.'

Turning to leave, he muttered, 'Work. Got to go. Hopefully I'm not too concussed to play. First you stand on my dog, then you throw something at me. I've had more subtle pick-up attempts.'

'What?' said Alice as he walked away. 'What? But I didn't ...' She turned around to see Kathy almost doubled up with laughter at the bottom of the steps. 'What's so funny? The arrogant—'

'I know you've been off the circuit for a while, Alice, but you don't throw things at men to get their attention. Especially men who have their own guard dog. It's obviously happened to him before.'

'Oh, for goodness sake. I'm really embarrassed. And look, he's laughing at me now.' She tried to glare at him, but he was smirking at her instead of listening to what his friend was saying. 'Who is he anyway? Thinks a lot of himself, doesn't he?'

'Luis something or other. Australian. Or Portuguese Australian. He plays guitar in the band. Oh no ... oh no ...'

'What?'

'It's Stephano.' Kathy nodded her head towards another man who was walking towards Luis.

'Stephano?' I didn't know he was still around. I thought he'd gone to Brazil after you'd divorced.'

'He did. Then he came back.'

'Oh, well. I'll go and say hello later. That is allowed isn't it? I mean I was your bridesmaid. All those years ago.'

'Of course. Of course. But, um … oh, never mind.'

'Something I should know?'

'Girls!' shouted Mary from the balcony. 'Party time! Come on. I've Feng Shuied the venue you know. They've been moving furniture back and forth all afternoon.'

As they walked through the door of the annex they were enveloped by a sea of pink and white balloons: pink and white balloons on every table, pink and white balloons hanging next to almost every inch of the glass walls, and pink and white balloons in hammocks attached to the ceiling ready to be released and drown the partygoers in pink and white.

'It's like a Barbie ball pit,' muttered Alice.

'Mary is fond of pink and white,' whispered Kathy.

Once again Alice suddenly felt she wasn't really there. None of this was real. She was in her bed in her house in London having yet another weird and feverish dream in which she was sitting in a candyfloss room at a party for Mary and Frank. She was going to live in their apartment so she could look after their cat. Of course it wasn't real. But then Mary came over to give her a hug, and she could feel it. Then the man whose head she had dropped her phone on started to play the guitar, Kathy got them more champagne and a stray pink balloon floated onto her hair, so she knew it was real. It was strange. But it was real. Alice managed to suppress a sob which had come out of nowhere: all this strange, vibrant happiness threw into sharp relief the empty, frightened days, weeks, months and even years she had been living. Taking a couple of deep breaths she looked up and forced a smile at the waiter who placed the champagne on the table. 'Don't look back, Alice,' she said to herself. 'Just don't look back.'

Kathy nudged her and whispered. 'Your new friend is very good, isn't he?'

Alice looked over at him. 'Yes, he is. Arrogant, but good.'

Luis sat alone on the stage, playing a haunting Spanish folk song, apparently unaware that anyone was watching him, completely lost in the music. Kathy nudged her again. 'He's also rather gorgeous isn't he?'

'Yes he is. But in a rude and arrogant way,' said Alice, glancing at him again, because Kathy was right. He was gorgeous.

'Holiday romance?' asked Kathy with a wink.

'Um,' Alice swallowed her drink and began to cough. 'I think that's a bit of a leap of imagination. And I don't want a holiday romance. And very, very attractive though he is I really don't think that I fancy him.' Alice turned around to look outside and not at the stage, not wanting to acknowledge that the thought had fleetingly crossed her mind. 'And I don't want a holiday romance with anyone,' she said eventually. 'I cannot stress that enough.'

'Why not? It'd do you good.'

'I don't want to get involved. I've got too much on my plate.'

'A holiday romance isn't getting involved,' said Kathy, kicking Alice's ankles. 'You used to do it all the time before you met Adam.'

'We went on two holidays before I met him.'

'That's two holiday romances.'

Alice turned back round to the table and sipped her drink. 'Yes, well, that was a long time ago. And I was young. And carefree. And not like I am now.'

'I'm sure I could fix you up with someone.'

'Kathy!' said Alice, trying to be stern.

Kathy giggled and put her arm around her. 'Have some fun!' she said.

As the meal ended with pink and white meringues, the band leapt dramatically onto the stage, joining Luis and his guitar. 'Ola Cascais!' shouted the lead singer. 'It's great to be here for Mary and Frank's farewell. Are you having a good time?'

'Yes!' chorused the room.

'Are you ready to rock? Are you ready to dance?'

Kathy giggled. 'Now this one thinks he's Jon Bon Jovi. He always does this. But he never gets booked to play actual rock music any more.'

'Aw, bless,' said Alice, who was by now feeling quite pink and white herself.

'We are Blazing Heat!' he shouted over the top of the introduction to 'Hi Ho Silver Lining'.

'See what you mean,' laughed Alice. When she finally looked up she noticed Luis staring at her from the stage. Her stomach did an unexpected flutter, and she looked away to fiddle with her shoe. Then she glanced over again but he was looking at his guitar. The set covered most musical genres, including a few Broadway hits, a couple of Beyonce's songs and one song by The Clash as people crowded onto the dancefloor, happily dancing both in and out of time. The band wrapped up with 'I'll Get Along Without You Now'.

'I chose that,' shouted Mary. 'In fact, I chose it all.'

As the DJ took over, Alice drifted outside into the garden to cool down. The warm air was light with the scent of jasmine and wild sage. Taking off her shoes, she stood on the damp grass, stretching her arms above her head, and breathed in slowly, eyes closed.

'Are you meditating?'

Alice turned, startled. Luis was standing in a doorway, smiling. She hadn't realised how tall he was. Her stomach fluttered again and she tried to stop it by putting a hand on it.

'Oh, hello. I am so sorry about earlier. Someone knocked into me,' she said too quickly.

'And I was a bit surprised,' said Luis. 'I'm not normally that rude. I was feeling protective towards Elvis, too. And I was distracted. A lot on my plate.'

Alice smiled. 'Me too.'

'Shall we start again?' he asked.

He shook her hand, and Alice felt a tiny and very pleasant electric shock as he did so.

'Hello madam, my name is Luis.'

She smiled. 'Hello sir, I'm Alice.'

'Very nice to meet you. Would you care to dance?'

'That would be very nice, thanks.' His eyes held hers for a second. They were brown and warm and smiling.

'You'll need your shoes,' he said, eventually. 'Although if you like dancing without them …?'

'Oh yes,' she said, slipping them back on. 'I like the feel of the grass on my bare feet,' she said, wishing she hadn't said it as soon as it was out of her mouth.

'You do?'

'And I don't like walking in heels. I totter in heels,' she said, wishing she hadn't said that either. Alice felt a comfortable and nervous at the same time, something she hadn't experienced since before she'd met Adam.

'So your phone is okay?'

'Yes. Your head?'

'Yes.'

They began to walk back towards the party.

'Everything is so clean and fresh here, isn't it?' The words spilled out of her. 'I love London, but it doesn't smell as nice as here.'

'Well this is Paradise,' said Luis, leading her back into the party. 'And Paradise always smells nice.'

As they stepped onto the dance-floor 'Lady in Red,' segued seamlessly into a Disney song and they were suddenly surrounded by excited little girls swaying and waving their arms around. 'Shall we anyway?' asked Luis, pulling her close to him. And they both danced slowly to 'Let it Go' whilst trying not to laugh out loud.

'Luis! Luis!' Blazing Heat's lead singer was shouting at him from the door. 'Time to go. Next gig. Come.'

'Sorry,' sighed Luis into her ear. 'I thought I was finishing after this but he sprung another one on me.' He stood back and kissed her hand, gazing into her eyes again. Alice gazed back, then glanced away, nervously. 'How long are you here for?' he asked.

'I don't know …'

'You don't know?' He laughed. 'Interesting.'

'Luis! We will be late.'

'Sorry, I have to go. Antonio – my cousin – second, or third or fourth – anyway, he is family – likes to keep busy.'

Alice watched him walk towards his bandmates at the door as one of the waiters handed him Elvis on his lead. She had to stop herself from following him and asking him to come back. To dance again with her, and to talk, to be. *It's been a long time since I've been at a party*, she thought. *Calm down. It was just a dance.* As she walked back to her seat, happy and a little flustered, Stephano, Kathy's ex-husband approached her.

'Alice! What a surprise. It's great to see you after all this time.'

'You too,' she said, kissing him on the cheek. 'I didn't realise you still lived here.'

'I went to Brazil. Then I came back. I think it was nearly four years ago now.'

'Still doing the landscaping and gardening?'

'Yes. Business is doing well. I employ twenty people at the moment.'

'Good to hear.'

'So you finally decided to come and visit Kathy.'

'Finally.'

'How have you enjoyed the party?'

A laugh burst out of Alice, unexpectedly. 'It's been wonderful. A real tonic. Just lovely.' Her phone buzzed in her bag. 'Excuse me. I just better check this,' she said. It was from her sister, Tara. 'Phone me. It's about Adam.' The familiar sick anxiety returned. She stood up. 'Sorry, Stephano, I've got to ring someone,' she said, walking towards the exit.

The following morning Alice left the hotel for her temporary new home, waving goodbye to the staff at reception with a smile. But the conversation with Tara the previous night had punctured her happy mood with an unwelcome dose of Adam and the grey sky seemed to echo it.

'Why are you so sad, Alice? Today is a good day,' said Ignacio, ushering her into his car. 'Is it because it's raining? It has to rain sometimes, even here.' He gestured dramatically towards the sky. 'It is to make it green and bright and beautiful. So no need to be sad.'

'I'm not sad. Do I look sad?'

'You look sad. Like the day you arrived. Pale. Unhappy. Lost.'

'Oh, well. I'm none of those things, Ignacio. Look, I'm smiling.'

Ignacio glanced in the rear-view mirror and shook his head. 'That is not a smile.'

Alice looked into her handbag and began to rummage around it, so he couldn't see her face. 'How long will it take to get there?'

'Three minutes.'

'Three minutes. Is that all? I could have walked. I only have one suitcase.'

'Kathy thought you would get lost.'

She sighed. The car slowly turned into the long tree-lined driveway towards the apartments. Bushes of red and orange bougainvillea tangled around the bottom of the pink and brown block that was to be Alice's home for the next few weeks. As they drew closer, she tried to be excited. And grateful. And relieved. But the knot in her stomach was caused by anxiety, the tension in her neck by stress, the watery eyes hidden behind sunglasses by crying about the loss of something she didn't want anyway.

'I needed to let you know,' Tara had said quietly when she had called her after the party. 'He is coming back over. Next week. His sister-in-law told me. So I could tell you. She doesn't know about the house.'

'Oh well. I knew he was coming back. Better tell Mum and Joseph to brace themselves.'

'But there is something else. He's bringing his new girlfriend with him.'

'Oh.'

'Oh indeed. Are you okay? I thought you needed to know.'

'I do. Thanks for telling me. But it's okay. I'm not pining for him or anything.'

Alice swept out of the car, angry. She was angry because she wasn't feeling the way she thought she should be. And why should she not be happy on the first day of her new, if very temporary, life? Because of Adam. Because of bloody Adam. She did not want to think of Adam. But he was there, like a selfish shadow, throwing himself into her thoughts. 'Like the snake in Paradise,' she muttered. 'No, that's the Garden of Eden.' And then she got angry because she was struggling with metaphors about Adam when she should have been bounding out of Ignacio's car and looking up proudly at her penthouse home with – according to Mary – 'stunning panoramic views of both the sea and the mountains'.

Alice replayed the conversation in her head again and sighed. 'Have you ever been to Argentina, Ignacio?'

'No. Why?'

'Someone I know is coming back from Argentina to find

48

me. But not because he wants to see me. Because he wants to take something away from me.'

'So, I see now. That is why you are looking so sad.'

She glanced at the text her sister had sent her that morning. I checked his new girlfriend's name. It's Veronique. Are you okay? I thought you were going to spontaneously combust when I spoke to you. Tara xx

Leaning wanly against a tree whilst Ignacio struggled with her suitcase, she glanced at the swimming pool glistening like glass between the trees and wandered towards it. *I'm gonna wash that man right out of my hair*, said the voice in her head, as she studied the still, pale blue water. Humming the tune, she threw her sunglasses dramatically on the grass and ostentatiously kicked off her flip flops before jumping in and shouting, 'Bugger off Adam and leave me alone!'

Ignacio stood, staring down at her as she emerged, invigorated, from the depths of the pool, and said nothing as she squelched behind him towards the entrance. 'I feel better now,' she said.

'Madam,' he said without looking back. 'Don't pause too long in the foyer. Your shirt has become see through and that is not a good way to introduce yourself to the porter.'

Chapter Six

Alice was determined to fill her first day in the apartment with useful activities that would overwhelm any thoughts of Adam by their sheer volume. So she unpacked, went shopping, went for a swim – in her swimming costume this time – and walked into town and back. By six o'clock she had run out of things to do. Deciding to make a list of places she wanted to see, she sat down, pen and pad in hand and tried to think. But he pushed himself back into her head, with thoughts of his new girlfriend, who was called Veronique and was 'a little bit South American,' according to Tara. Alice hadn't questioned what a 'little bit South American' was but tried to ignore an image of long, swishy black hair. No face, but long black hair, swishing beguilingly. She stood up and drifted onto the balcony, putting her hands through her fringe to muss it up and pouting in an attempt to channel a young Debbie Harry to offset visions of the imaginary Veronique.

I don't want him, she thought. *I don't care. But ... but ... how has he found someone whilst I've been too busy to do anything because I've been working hard to pay the mortgage?* Her mobile rang and she walked back into the apartment, glad of the respite from herself.

'Hi. It's me,' said Kathy.

'Hi. I've had a lovely day. The apartment is gorgeous,'

'Good. At least Adam hasn't ruined your day as well as yesterday evening.'

'Nope. I woke up this morning and decided that I wouldn't allow it,' she lied.

'Excellent.'

Alice picked up a note of distraction in her friend's voice. 'It wasn't that easy, though. But I've done really well.'

'I'm on my way over with something for you,' said Kathy.

'Oh what? Wine? Cake?' A muffled noise of what sounded like another voice drowned her out. 'Sorry – is someone with you? I heard a voice?' said Alice.

'No. No,' replied Kathy. 'I didn't hear anything. I'm on my own.'

'My mistake! Are you going to tell me what the something is?' Another muffled noise interrupted her. 'What *is* that?' asked Alice, perplexed.

'I can't hear anything. Must be a glitch on the line.' A door banged in the background. 'I'll be with you in half an hour, with something from your past,' continued Kathy. 'I'm being mysterious,' she said mysteriously. 'I'm being mysterious because I'm trying to build up the excitement.'

'Oh, well it's working,' laughed Alice. 'See you later.' And as she laughed, she remembered the expression on Luis's face as they danced the previous night. For just a moment Adam had gone. She smiled and sat down, picking up a pink embossed notebook left by her landlords, full of instructions and helpful notes from Mary. There was also a basket of bath creams, pot pourri and some homemade herbal teas with 'drink me' written on the bags. She picked up the book and opened it at 'Welcome!'

Dear Alice love, welcome to our home. I'm sure you'll have a wonderful time in Cascais once you settle in.

I've put together some useful hints and tips for your stay. Read them as and when.

For food shopping, you'll already have seen the big supermarkets, but for day to day, there's a little shop five minutes away. Just turn left as you come out of the apartment block.

For sitting down and staring at people whilst drinking coffee, you know the square, and I know you've met Carlos – go there often – it'll do you good. And there's a little café opposite the lighthouse too. I know you like photography –

Kathy told me – you'll get some wonderful photos there. I think you should go there this week!

Aphrodite will make an appearance at some point. Just feed her twice a day and allow her to sit on your lap when she feels like it.

And there's my homemade herbal teas. They all have a different function – read the packets carefully and don't drink too much all at once as they are somewhat potent.

The doorbell rang and Alice jumped – it couldn't be Kathy already, she thought. Pressing the button she stared, confused at the image on the screen.

'*Bom Dia*, madam,' said the porter. 'I have your cat.' He held Aphrodite up to the camera as confirmation. Mary and Frank were so busy that there hadn't been any time for Alice to visit before she moved in, so this was her first sight of her. Aphrodite had been discussed with such reverence, Alice had pictured a prim and disdainful pedigree, but here was a tiny, raggedy, rather startled-looking black and white moggy.

'I'll put her in the lift,' he said. 'She brought in a mouse again, but don't worry – I won't put that in the lift!'

Alice saw Kathy rushing through the foyer. 'Me too, hold the lift. I'm here!' she shouted.

As the lift doors opened outside the apartment, Kathy almost threw herself at Alice whilst the cat stalked indifferently past her towards the food bowl in the kitchen. 'Adam's a bastard and I hate him,' whispered Kathy into her ear. 'Now remember, I'm gonna wash …'

'I've already done that,' said Alice, laughing and prising herself free.

'Good, good, excellent. That means you're okay?'

'Nope … but what's that noise?' A loud impatient wailing was coming from the kitchen.

'I think that's your cat.'

'Oh, yes. Aphrodite. She needs feeding I suppose.' Alice peered into the kitchen, 'She makes a big noise for such a tiny little thing.' The yowling continued until the food was in the bowl, replaced by contented purring and slurping. 'How lovely to find such happiness in a pink plastic dish full of smelly offcuts of who knows what,' said Alice putting the kettle on. 'Cup of tea?'

'Yes please,' replied Kathy walking into the living room. 'So, I've brought these things from the past.'

Finding a stash of what looked like homemade herbal tea bags in the cupboard, Alice picked a couple with the words, 'Really Very Relaxing' on them and put them in two vibrant coral pink mugs.

'Look.' Kathy smiled as Alice carried the tea into the living room.

'What?'

'Here, silly.'

Two necklaces lay on the glass-topped coffee table: one with entwined white porcelain beads and delicate blue ribbon, the other a cacophony of multi-coloured wires linked to a small silver and gold locket attached to a swatch of lilac silk.

Alice's eyes widened. 'Oh, you kept them. You've still got them after all this time,' she said, sitting on the floor and carefully picking them up.

'Open the locket. Go on.'

Inside was a minute photograph of two women, their hair covered in daisies, plastic glasses in their hands, laughing. Alice beamed. 'That's us at the little festival by the South Bank. I can't believe you still have them. You brought them all the way to Portugal.'

'I kept them because you made them just for me. Clever, talented Alice. I was so thrilled.'

'I did, didn't I?' Alice smiled again.

'And look.' Kathy held up a photograph on her phone. 'This is the painting you did for my parents of the view of the hills from their garden. I got them to take a picture of it hanging on the wall so you could see it.'

Alice examined the image and felt a little rush of pride. 'They still have it? Wow, that's lovely.'

'Of course they still have it,' said Kathy. 'You painted pictures, you took photographs and you made jewellery. And people bought all of it.'

'A long time ago.'

'Yes, but that Alice is still in there somewhere, lurking.'

Alice felt herself suddenly tense. That was another life, another Alice. 'No I think that part of me has gone,' she said firmly.

Kathy took a sip of the tea. 'Mmmmmm. This is nice. What's in it?'

Alice squinted at the writing on the label. 'It said it's really very relaxing. It's got chamomile, mint, catnip … catnip? And a secret ingredient.' Aphrodite jumped onto Kathy's lap and tried to stick her head in the mug.

'Well the catnip works then.'

Alice gently put the necklaces down and stared at them.

'I wanted to remind you of what you can do,' said Kathy, trying to push Aphrodite away.

'Could do.'

'Can do. Can I look at the bracelets you've got on? Can you take them off?

'Yes, why?' Alice was trying to forget what she used to do. It was something that had made her happy but she'd lost along the way, and it was easier not to remember.

Kathy stood up and went to the kitchen, reappearing with a pair of scissors. Alice sipped the tea and watched, confused for a moment, as Kathy picked up the first bracelet. The beads scattered onto the table as she cut it.

'What are you doing?' asked Alice, startled. 'That's mine. You can't just cut it up.'

'I'm doing what you used to do – cutting up something

mundane so you could make something special,' said Kathy, picking up the other three bracelets and doing the same.

'Why are you doing it?'

'You haven't got any bracelets now, so you'll have to make your own.'

'Kathy – they're my bracelets – that's a bit ... rude?'

Kathy laughed. 'Cruel to be kind.'

Alice sipped the tea again. Its relaxing properties were clearly taking hold as she was feeling only mildly surprised that she wasn't more angry with Kathy for destroying her jewellery. One minute earlier she'd been about to shout at her. 'This is very nice,' she said.

'It is, isn't it?' said Kathy.

'It's even more relaxing than all that chamomile tea I drank after I lost my job ... I am going to wash that man out of my hair completely,' muttered Alice quietly.

'And shall we send him on his bloody way?' asked Kathy.

'This tea is lovely,' said Alice, laying on the sofa. 'But I feel tired.'

'It is very relaxing isn't it?' agreed Kathy. 'I'm just going to lie down on the rug for a moment.'

The following morning Alice woke up face down on the sofa with the cat purring loudly into her left ear. Opening her eyes tentatively, she slowly realised that she had spent her first night in her new home and forgotten to go to bed. And it wasn't because she'd drunk too much wine. 'What the hell was in that tea, Aphrodite?' she muttered, sitting up and stretching. Cracks of light filtered through the shutters, dotting the floor like cats' eyes on a moonlit road. Following the dots to the terrace doors she opened them with a flourish and stood in a spotlight of white sun. 'Ta dah!' she said, nodding to an imaginary audience.

Stepping barefoot onto the warm tiles, she breathed in the fresh sea air and felt a surprising tingle of excitement. Walking to the kitchen to make breakfast she found a little note placed next to the necklaces Kathy had brought round.

Mad Mary strikes again. That tea was brilliant. I haven't slept so well in ages. I woke up on the floor … one of the team has phoned in sick, so I may have to do an extra few shifts over the next couple of days. I will be absent in body, but here if you get stuck. And don't forget: Fly Alice, fly! (or make yourself some new bracelets anyway) xxx

Alice giggled as she poured herself a glass of orange juice. 'Fly Alice, fly.' She smiled to herself. 'Maybe I will.'

Walking back to the living room, she picked up a handful of the beads that Kathy had virtually torn from her wrist. Then she moved onto the balcony and looked at the sea again. It was so blue she wanted to pick it up and put it in the room, so it could shine its light on the walls. She looked back at the beads, and then at the sea. Half an hour later she was walking out of the apartment with a camera in her hand. Turning right at the end of the drive she walked purposefully until she reached a crossroads. Following her instincts and where she thought the sea was she turned right again, and then left at another crossroads. Pausing under the shade of a tree to try to get her bearings, she heard a familiar man's voice from inside the house directly behind her.

The patio doors were open wide and her heart fluttered a little. It was Luis, waving a paint brush and apparently talking to his dog again. 'Ladies and Gentlemen,' he said loudly. 'Luis Simal has just decorated this room completely in under six hours. Solo, alone. With no help whatsoever.'

'It was a long night. I was working,' shouted another voice from inside the house.

'Working. Yes. At the casino,' said Luis. 'Hear that, Elvis, he's lying again.'

Alice stood, intrigued, and a little embarrassed. She

shouldn't be listening to this argument and so she began to move slowly around the tree, not wanting to be seen.

'Gambling. You were gambling,' continued Luis. 'He was, wasn't he, Elvis?' The dog barked apparently in agreement.

'I'm sorry,' said the other voice. 'But if I want to spend all night in the casino I will.'

As she walked, their raised voices seemed to follow her, dragging her in. 'I help you out,' she heard Luis say. 'Is it not too much to ask that when you say you will help me you do it?'

'I'm doing it for the band. And you owe me. Remember when we had the record deal? Nearly had the record deal? We could do it again. We're just as good.'

Record deal? thought Alice, intrigued again, and slowing a little so she could hear more.

'Yes I owe you. Thank you. But all that was a long time ago and I am leaving.'

'Just be patient,' came the other voice. 'Just for a few months, okay? Two months then? I am changing things. For old time's sake, Luis.' Alice sped up, guilty at her eavesdropping, and turned the corner towards the sea road. 'Alright, alright,' was the last thing she heard. 'For two months maximum. No more.'

She saw the sea glistening in the distance, and walked purposefully towards it, trying to shake off what she'd just heard, but noting that for the second time in a week she'd somehow listened in on details of Luis's life without meaning to. *I'm only here for a few weeks*, she thought. *I'm not interested. I'm not.* She crossed the road and paused on a stone bridge between a copse of trees in which stood a beautiful cream, red and green mansion with a triangle of blue-green sea to the front of it and a small café with a blue and white lighthouse opposite. The colours and light took her breath away, and she made her way to the shore. Clambering onto the rocks opposite the lighthouse, she stood close to the water, adjusting her camera to get the right light. The sea reflected the luscious green of the trees in the park overlooking a tiny beach under the bridge, oozing into a deep, bright blue as it stretched out beyond the headland.

And so she began, taking picture after picture, trying to capture the ever-changing palette of the water and sky, mesmerised and calmed by the soft ebb and flow of the tide as it washed against the rocks. Turning her attention to the mass of periwinkles clinging to the stones, she almost put her foot in the water.

'Hey!' shouted someone from the stone bridge. 'Hey! Be careful. The rocks are sharp under there, and you may drop your camera on a fish and concuss it.'

Alice looked up as if woken from a dream. There he was. Luis. Tall, dark, handsome. And laughing.

'Mmmmm. Yes,' she said, disorientated and frantically searching her brain for a witty response, or any response apart from 'yes'. But it didn't come.

'Do you have time for a coffee?' he shouted again, indicating the café.

'Mmmmm. Yes,' said Alice, nodding enthusiastically, wondering why she kept stepping on, eavesdropping on and bumping into him. She tottered inelegantly up to the café where Luis had already found them a table. Elvis yawned noisily, laying down in the shade and stretching.

'You looked lost in your own world there.' Luis smiled.

'Ahh. Yes … I was I suppose … taking photos of the sea and the rocks.' She trailed off, slightly embarrassed, not only at being discovered taking photos of shellfish, but at the fact that she'd heard him arguing with his friend only a little while earlier.

He leaned forward. 'The colours are magnificent aren't they? I've spent hours here myself. You should come when the sun is setting over the sea. It's the most beautiful sight.' Luis paused, waiting for a response.

'Mmmmmm, lovely,' was all Alice could say, trying not to stare at the attractive crinkles around his eyes.

He smiled. 'Are you taking photos for the sake of taking photos or for something else?'

She smiled back.

'So, are you …?'

'Ah, yes. I'm not actually sure,' she said, pushing her brain into gear. 'I used to … I studied art and I used to paint and make things. I sold quite a lot, actually, like a little cottage business, but I haven't for years.' The words tumbled out quickly. 'But I decided this morning that I wanted to do something again. But I don't know what.' She paused and looked at Luis. 'There's something about this place.'

'Yes, yes,' he said. His gaze was intense. 'I felt like that a few years ago when I first got here. It seemed to wake me up in a way. My paintings sell okay, but my photographs of this place do really well.'

'You're an artist? I thought you were a …'

'Guitarist?' he interrupted. 'Alice. It is Alice, isn't it? I am a renovator of houses, painter of walls, occasional guitarist, sometime photographer, and on rare moments a painter of paintings.' He rubbed Elvis's ear. 'I also own a dog as you can see.'

'That's a lot. You must be busy,' said Alice, intrigued.

'Can I see?' he asked, taking the camera and studying the photos. He smiled again. 'We should go out and take some photos sometime. Together?'

'Oh yes. That would be nice.' Alice tried to sound casually pleased rather than very pleasantly surprised.

He looked at his watch. 'Great. Give me your number and we'll sort something out. You're here for a few more weeks, aren't you? I've got to go. Got to see a man about a house.'

As he left, Alice glanced at her top to make sure the buttons were all done up. They were. She had felt invisible for a long time, but just over two weeks in Cascais seemed to be changing that. Ordering another coffee she sat for a while trying to calm herself down. Her comfort zone over the past few years had been hiding out of sight so no one could hurt her. Alice could feel herself smiling inside with excitement. Leaving some coins for the drink she picked up her camera and decided to walk into town. *Enjoy it, Alice*, she thought. *Whatever this is, try to enjoy it. Please. Because it's something and nothing. You're only here for few weeks. Be normal. Be bloody normal!*

As she headed along the sea road, she allowed herself to enjoy the fact that this hugely attractive man seemed to like her. Ten minutes later she received a text.

You can buy canvas, paints and brushes in a shop in Rua Dos Descobrementos. Luis.

Then she received another one.

Adam is definitely flying back to the UK tomorrow. It was from Tara. The sick feeling overwhelmed her again and her heart began to beat faster. A couple of hours without thinking about him, and there he was again, ruining it. *I don't want this. I don't want this. I don't want to know. It's easier not to know*, she thought, panicking again.

As Alice walked back to the apartment, the swimming pool shone in the distance, cool and welcoming, ready to wash Adam away. She ran past, fighting the impulse to jump in fully clothed again. By the time she had got back to the apartment, she knew she needed a rest from him and his news – she'd come here for a holiday, and to take stock, and as usual, Adam was doing everything his way, not hers. Gathering a tiny bit of resolve, she composed a text and sent it before she could change her mind.

Dear Mum, Joseph and Tara,
I love you loads. But I need a bit of a break from Adam, as every time I hear his name I want to jump fully clothed into any bit of water near me. I have actually done it once already. So, can you no longer use his

name if you text me– how about calling him by his initial, so he is now simply, A? And can you only let me know if he tries to contact you or break the door down in my house (not his house as it isn't his house)? This is an A lock down! Love Alice xxx

Then she hid the phone at the bottom of her underwear draw for a while, drained a cup of another of Mary's teas – this time 'Quite Relaxing' – and dragged a sunbed into the shade on the balcony. She drifted into a deep, dreamless sleep until the sun went down and the breeze woke her up. The distant lights of the fishing boats danced amongst the black waves in the bay to the screeched songs of the cicadas in the gardens below. Wide awake and restless, Alice threw on a cardigan and walked down the hill into the town, losing herself in the narrow, cobbled streets quietly buzzing with life. Pausing to inspect the tempting window display of the *pastelaria* in the main street, she caught sight of her reflection and smiled, pleasantly surprised at the healthy, tousled, happy-looking person staring back at her.

'Hello,' she said. 'It's lovely to see you again. You've been away a while.' Then she moved on towards the sea and sat for a while, staring peacefully at the dark ocean.

Chapter Seven

The shop that Luis had recommended was in a narrow, unwelcomingly dark street hidden in the old town, but as Alice pushed open the creaky door and stepped into the untidy room, a long-forgotten excitement bubbled up from somewhere deep within her. She wanted to laugh and clap her hands with joy. Full to bursting with brushes, paper, pencils, chalks and paints, the shop smelt of white spirit and oil and it felt like home. An hour passed as brushes were examined, colours assessed, paper measured and advice sought from the owner. Eventually falling out into the sunlight, Alice struggled to carry the two carrier bags of artists' materials and an A3 book of canvases she had bought. But she didn't care – she was happy.

'Hey, hey,' shouted Carlos as she walked through the square. 'Come back. Sit. Relax.' Alice glanced back as he pointed dramatically at a chair. 'Here,' he said.

She sat, obediently.

'Alice. It is Alice, isn't it?'

'Yes, it is.'

'You are in Portugal. It's important to take time to sit, drink coffee and watch the world. Even if you have other important things to do.'

'Okay. I haven't got other important things to do, though,' she said. *Apart from looking for a proper job at home*, she thought. Alice sighed wearily inside, annoyed with herself.

'What would you like?'

'Um *galao e* um *pastel de nata*.'

Carlos beamed. 'Ah, Portuguese. Very good, very good.'

'That's all I can say,' said Alice. 'Plus *Bom Dia, Boa Tarde, Boa Noite, adeius* and *ola*!'

'Excellent!'

'*Pudim flan*.'

'You would like a *pudim flan* too?'

'No. I can say *pudim flan*. I don't want one.'

'Just as well because we do not have any. But it will be useful to know if you want one from somewhere else.'

'Hopefully.'

'Okay, I will return with your order,' he said, turning to go. He paused. 'You should come here more often. Always welcome.'

Alice smiled, surprised. 'Oh, thank you,' she said.

Carlos beamed again.

Spreading out her new paints in a line on the table, she sat back and examined the tangled braids of bougainvillea clinging to the yellow wall opposite. Taking a photo, she picked out the paint colours she wanted to use and took a photo of them too. Scooping them back into the bag, she smiled, thinking about the painting to come when she got back to the apartment.

'Hello, Alice. *Bom Dia.*' Ignacio had sat down at the table next to her.

'Oh, hello,' she said, surprised. 'How are you? Sorry, I was caught up in what I was doing and didn't notice you were there.'

'I saw,' he said, nodding towards the bag of paints. 'What were you doing?'

'I was planning a painting with my new paints. That's what I was doing …' She trailed off. 'Do you have a day off?' she asked, changing the subject.

'Yes, I have taken my mother to her sister's and I'm now waiting to collect my car from the garage. It needed a little work done on it.'

Carlos returned with her order.

'Ola! Carlos! Did I tell you he is my brother?'

'Yes, you did. Small world,' said Alice, searching their faces for similarities. She couldn't find any.

'*Diga, diga,*' said Carlos.

'That means speak,' said Ignacio. '*Uma bica* … that means one—'

'—black coffee,' interrupted Alice, excitedly. 'Ta da!'

'Okay. I will bring it Ignacio,' said Carlos, gently touching Alice's shoulder as he left.

'You are friends?' asked Ignacio, eyebrows raised.

'No, no. I've just had coffee here a couple of times, that's all. He's very friendly.'

Ignacio leaned forward and spoke quietly. 'Alice, I believe I have mentioned this to you before, but be careful. He has a reputation. He is very fond of far too many women.'

'Oh, right,' said Alice, a little embarrassed. 'I just drink coffee here, that's all. Anyway, it's a lovely day, isn't it?'

'Paradise,' said Ignacio leaning back in his chair.

Carlos returned with his coffee and stood behind Alice. 'She is looking very well. Being here suits her I think.'

'Yes, yes, she does,' said Ignacio. He looked behind her. 'Does anyone know that dog? The one sitting next to you Alice? It looks familiar.'

She looked down. Elvis was staring attentively up at her.

'I didn't know he was there,' she said.

'He just arrived,' said Carlos.

'Well, I do know him. His owner, rather. A bit ...' She trailed off again.

'There you are, mate,' said Luis, seeming to appear out of nowhere. He pulled up a chair. 'You shouldn't run off like that. Although when you guide me to Alice it's allowed.'

Alice's heart fluttered and she involuntarily crossed her arms, as if that would stop it. 'I didn't see you,' she said.

'He just arrived,' said Carlos. '*Ola* Luis.'

'*Ola. Uma bica*,' said Luis. Carlos scratched his beard and nodded, unsmiling, before going to get the order.

'So,' said Luis, looking at Alice's carrier bags, 'I see you have been to my favourite shop.'

'Yes I have. It's wonderful. I was there for ages and I bought far too much.'

'Ah, Alice in Wonderland.' He smiled.

Ignacio tapped her on the shoulder. 'I will give you a lift

back to your apartment. I am collecting my car from the garage around the corner there.'

'Oh, thank you,' said Alice, a little surprised. 'That's very kind.'

'I'm going to take Alice to Sintra,' said Luis. 'Great photographic opportunities there.'

'Okay, that sounds good, great, I mean,' said Alice. An unbidden girlish giggle spilled out of her, which she tried to disguise as a cough.

'How is the band business by the way?' asked Ignacio.

'Busy, busy, busy. But it's Antonio's band. I'm leaving in a couple of months.'

'Getting a bit old for all that after all,' said Carlos, rejoining the conversation as he returned with Luis's coffee.

Alice picked up a strange tension in the air.

'Doing a lot of property renovations,' said Luis. 'Plus the painting and the photography. It's a lot at the moment.'

Alice took a bite out of her cake.

'I love *pasteis de natas*.' Luis was looking over at her. 'The best thing about living in Portugal.'

'They are delicious,' said Alice, mouth still full.

Luis's phone rang. He sighed. 'Here we go,' he said, as he answered it. 'Antonio. Why do you need me there earlier? To meet who? Why do I need to do that – can't I just come later for the sound check?'

Ignacio shook his head at Alice. 'Antonio,' he whispered loudly. 'He's no good.'

Luis rang off and smiled. 'He's right you know. He's not the best person to be around at the moment.' He took a sip of the coffee and stood up as Elvis darted to the other side of the square. 'Oh, no, he's got the hots for that Great Dane again,' he said. Swigging the rest of the coffee he threw some change on the table. 'Gotta go. He's not coming back. *Ciao, belo*.' He blew a kiss at Alice as he ran off.

'So you know him?' asked Carlos.

'Yes I do. A bit,' she said.

He bent down and whispered in her ear. 'Be careful. He has a reputation.'

Ignacio leaned forward. 'My brother is right. Be careful.'

Alice's phone beeped.

Got a day off music and painting tomorrow. Fancy Sintra? Will pick you up at the hotel at eleven, L. Alice glowed inside. Everyone seemed to have a reputation round here, she thought. And it didn't matter anyway because she'd be going home in a few weeks.

I don't know whether to go to Sintra with Luis or not. Alice's breathy excitement of the previous day had been replaced with her default anxious setting overnight.

Why on earth not? Kathy texted back.

I'm only here for a few weeks. I don't know if it's a good idea to get involved.

Alice! He's taking you out to take some photos! Why don't you just enjoy it? Going out for the afternoon is hardly getting involved. And anyway, what if you do? – you deserve to have some fun.

I don't know how to have fun anymore. I should be sorting stuff out, looking for work.

Alice! For goodness sake! Lighten up. Got to go, someone's come in. xx

Alice put the phone down and walked into the living room from the balcony. She was also dealing with a problem she had never had to deal with in London. 'I think geckos are cute, but I don't want to live with any,' she had muttered, nose wrinkled, picking up the tiny dead lizard left lovingly next to the kettle by Aphrodite that morning. Then she had spent half an hour hunting the live one that was scuttling around the apartment. She returned to her search as the cat sat elegantly on the sofa watching Alice crashing and banging around in pursuit of her prey.

'How the hell did you get them in?' she shouted whilst peering under the bed. 'Why did you only kill one of them? Why aren't you helping me?'

When she finally saw its tail disappear into a cupboard, she gave in and summoned the porter who arrived with a large glass bowl and a piece of card.

'She is a very clever cat.' He laughed. 'She hid them, I think.'

'You mean they've been here for a while?'

'Oh yes,' he said, walking into the bedroom and looking under the wardrobe.

'So they've been living with me and I didn't know?'

'Yes.'

'I feel a bit sick,' she said, sinking down next to Aphrodite on the sofa, wondering if there were any other small reptiles in residence. In London she'd had a few ants.

'I will close the door now,' the porter said, slamming it shut.

'I'm supposed to be getting ready to meet a very gorgeous man, not dealing with your dark secrets,' said Alice, jabbing her finger at the cat, who was now lying down and stretching, languorously. 'It's very irresponsible of you Aphrodite,' she said. 'I haven't been on a date for years. I mean I'm not even sure I should be going. But I'm going. Despite you, cat.'

A few minutes later the porter walked carefully into the living room, holding the covered bowl with a tiny gecko pressed inside.

'That was very quick,' said Alice. 'Thank you.'

'You're welcome. Please don't hesitate to call me next time,' he said.

'Next time,' she sighed to herself. 'Next time …'

Then she hurriedly changed into a sundress, put on some flip-flops, grabbed her camera and ran to the hotel, red faced and hair flying untidily in the breeze.

Luis was facing the sea when she arrived, taking photographs of the waves crashing against the rocks, oblivious to the clusters of people noisily bustling past him. Pausing for a moment she watched him intent on his task. Something in the way he leaned forward, lost in the moment, flicked a switch inside her, just the same as when he was playing the guitar at Mary's party, like he was in a world of his own. She felt still and calm. And it confused her. She walked towards him. 'Hello,' she said.

He looked up, smiling broadly. 'You look beautiful,' he said. 'Have you run here?'

'Oh dear, is it that obvious?' she asked. 'I was late. Gecko issues at home. I've never had to deal with gecko issues before. Is my face very red then?'

'Red? No, it's glowing.'

Alice laughed. 'Glowing? I like your style.'

Luis put his arm on her shoulder and guided her towards his car. 'Sintra, madam?

'Yes please.'

'Here,' he said, walking down a narrow track through a wall of bushes and trees. 'The gardens here are beautiful. And on a day like today with the sky this blue, the contrast of the flowers and trees is striking, don't you think? Hopefully we will get some good pictures. One of the guys who sells my photographs says people are talking about the place. So here we are.'

'It feels like a secret,' she said.

Luis turned towards her and held her gaze for a moment. 'I suppose it is.'

As he walked towards a clearing her stomach did the loop the loop again, and she patted it as if it was indigestion.

'Look at this!' said Luis gently, beckoning her over. A carpet of orange, pink, white and yellow wildflowers lit by the midday sun rolled into the distance, scattering colours into the gaps between the trees. 'Late spring, early summer, there are flowers everywhere,' he said. 'On all the road verges, between the rocks ...'

'It's beautiful,' said Alice softly.

'Take it all in,' said Luis. 'So that when it's dark and cold you can call it back into your mind.'

They stood for a few moments without speaking, as Alice

listened to the silence punctuated by lilting birdsong. 'I want to run barefoot through the flowers like when I was a little girl,' said Alice eventually.

'Elvis is obviously in agreement about this view,' said Luis. 'Look, he's just sitting and watching. Not like him at all.'

'He's obviously a dog who appreciates art and nature,' she said.

'Or maybe he's waiting for a bird or rabbit to arrive so he can chase them and frighten the life out of them.'

Alice laughed. 'Yes, probably, but I prefer my idea.'

'I prefer it too. That's a nice world you live in!'

'It's how you see it.' She smiled, enjoying his eyes glinting mischievously back at her.

'Shall we take some photographs, madam?' asked Luis, taking out his camera.

'Of course, that's what we're here for,' said Alice, torn between staring at Luis, and taking photos of the gardens.

They disappeared into their own worlds, and Alice moved through the grass, taking photographs of flowers and petals and the dappled patterns of sunlight through the trees, framing vistas and gaging colours and tones. Time stood still for a while. Only as the light changed with the slow movement of the sun did they begin to wake slowly up to the real world again.

'I fear Alice,' said Luis formally, touching her arm, 'that although it is only half past two, the inexorable rotation of the earth has beaten us and taken our light. And, of course, the trees make it very shady.'

'Shame,' said Alice, 'but I'm really, really hungry, actually, so thank goodness.'

'You're no artist, madam. Hunger would not beat a proper artist.'

'So, you're not hungry?'

'Starving.'

'Well then.'

'Well then.' He smiled. Placing his rucksack on the grass he slowly and ostentatiously unclipped it, producing a loaf of bread, a tub of olives, some slices of meat and some water. Fishing further into the bag he pulled out a large tartan blanket and placed it with a flourish on the ground. 'Alice, please sit.'

'That's Mary Poppins' handbag disguised as a common black rucksack isn't it?' Alice joked.

'Shhhhh nobody knows who I really am. Now spit spot, eat up ... and please keep it to yourself.'

'Alright Mary,' whispered Alice giggling. She felt herself giving into something, but she couldn't properly work out what it was. It was a kind of reminder of something past, something lost. Something she'd forgotten how to feel. They sat and ate, surrounded by hazy colours and vibrant butterflies, the air laced with pine scent and wild rosemary. As the sun wrapped them in a warm glow for the first time in a long time Alice did not think of the past or the future. All that was real to her was Luis and this beautiful garden.

'Time to go,' he said eventually. 'The world awaits.'

'No,' she wanted to say. '*I'm not ready, yet. Stay, let's stay here forever so I don't have to back to real life.*' But she just smiled at him. He stood and held his hand out to help her up, their eyes locking for a moment. *Deliciously soft brown eyes you have, Mr Simal*, she thought, as he began to pack up the picnic.

'I have another gig with the band later.' He sighed. 'Last minute. Antonio twisted my arm. Again.'

'It's a pity you don't enjoy it any more,' said Alice, rolling up the blanket. 'You're so good. When I saw you play at Mary's party, you seemed to be completely involved in it.'

He looked up again, surprised. 'I did? Well I do love it.' He put his rucksack on his back. 'I'll let you into a secret – sometimes I play guitar with a local band that play Latin music. Nothing serious – just occasionally on a Sunday we'll perform at a bar or a restaurant. It's just for fun. That's what I miss about Antonio's band – the fun went years ago.'

'What does Antonio think of it?' asked Alice, putting on her shoes.

'Oh, he doesn't know. He suspects of course. I think he feels I'm cheating on him.' He laughed and turned towards the path. 'Your chariot awaits, this way.'

The following day Alice awoke with a sense of purpose and excitement. The time she had spent with Luis had reminded her that men other than Adam did actually exist, and that inspiration was everywhere to feed her imagination. Also, she had an appointment with Kathy. She ran down the steps of the hotel towards the ballroom where the belly dancing class was being held – Kathy had told her it was either that or Limbo dancing, as whilst she was in Cascais she should try to assimilate. Alice had argued that she didn't see how either dance would help her assimilate as neither of them were Portuguese. Kathy had told her that she had to come anyway. As she rushed around the corner to find her friend, she bumped into Stephano hurrying the other way.

'Alice!' he said, looking surprised. 'You're looking well. Are you here for the belly dancing?'

'Yes I am,' said Alice breathlessly. 'And I'm late. Have you seen Kathy?'

'No. Why would I have seen Kathy?' He seemed distracted, looking over her head. 'I have to go, now. Lovely to see you.' He kissed her on both cheeks and hurried off.

'Oh, okay, bye,' said Alice, running towards the ballroom.

Kathy was standing at the back waving at her.

'I'm nearly late,' said Alice, trying to calm her breathing down.

'At least you're here. So?'

'So what? I just saw Stephano.'

'Oh, yes, he was just here for something.'

'He said he hadn't seen you.'

'Oh, okay.' Kathy bent over and did a stretch. 'So?'

'So what?'

Kathy raised an eyebrow. 'On the phone you told me Luis had dropped you home after Sintra …'

'Why did Stephano say he hadn't seen you then?'

'Because it's Stephano,' said Kathy standing straight and stretching her arms above her head. 'Come on, I want to hear about you and Luis.'

Alice stretched too. 'Well he dropped me off home.'

'And?'

'And nothing.' Alice looked at the floor and tried not to smile.

'Really?'

'Yes.'

'*Really?*'

'He kissed my hand.'

'Is that all?' Kathy laughed and bent down to touch her toes.

'I thought it was very gallant actually.'

'Rubbish. For goodness sake.'

Alice kicked her gently and laughed. 'I'm not used to this, Kathy, remember. No idea what's supposed to happen or when or if. And anyway, I'm just passing through, so it doesn't really matter.'

'Yes it does matter, Alice,' said Kathy, kicking her back. 'There is going to be a next time thought, isn't there? Do you plan to exchange letters or something?'

'Ha ha … he said next time he would take me to eat where there were actual chairs.'

'Oh?'

'He said it was somewhere at the edge of the world.'

'Oh. My. God!' said Kathy in mock disgust.

'It sounded funny when he said it.'

Kathy stretched again and tried to shimmy.

'I can't do belly dancing,' said Alice.

'Neither can I,' said Kathy, 'but the teacher is a client and finally managed to wear me down.'

'Well I suppose I am a blank canvas.' Alice started doing her own stretches.

'Yes I suppose you are.'

'A new page in a book.'

'Yes, another way of putting it.'

'A new novel. A new chapter.' Alice stood up straight.

'You can stop now,' said Kathy.

Alice hugged her. 'Thank you.'

'For what?'

'Just everything.'

'Alice loves Luis. Alice loves Luis,' sung Kathy.

'No I don't. No I don't. Shhh … teacher's here. She'll tell you off if you talk.'

'I suppose the cake will undo all the good work I've just done wiggling my belly,' said Alice, as they sat in the café after the class. She sliced a sticky, round bolo de chocolate in half.

'I saw you,' scoffed Kathy. 'You just shook your bits around for an hour.'

'That's what you were supposed to do!'

'Totally out of time with the music.'

'I don't care! I was expressing myself in a unique way,' said Alice, biting into the cake. 'What?' Kathy was looking at her with a smile on her face.

'It's so nice to see you back to being Alice Dorothy Matthews.'

Alice tried to smile back but her mouth was full of chocolate crumbs. 'Why thank you,' she spluttered.

'That doesn't mean that you're not disgusting.' Kathy laughed. 'Close your mouth when you're eating.'

Alice threw a lump of sugar at her. 'So then, Kathy.'

'What?'

'Stephano.'

Kathy took a slice of cake and began to eat it.

'You went a bit strange when he appeared at the party, didn't you?'

Kathy continued to eat and took her phone out of her bag. Alice leaned over and snatched the phone away.

'Excuse me, that's rude,' said Kathy.

Alice stared at her. 'And you were very evasive when he was here earlier.'

'We live in the same town. We're bound to cross paths occasionally.'

'I don't believe you,' Alice pulled the plate of cake away. 'I'm holding this hostage until you tell me the truth. I know you. I know you very well. And Stephano.'

Kathy bit her lip

'Is something going on between you and Stephano?'

'Nothing.'

'Are you sure?'

'What? With my ex-husband? What kind of idiot do you take me for?'

Alice smiled. 'Just the common or garden kind.'

Kathy sat back and sighed loudly. Alice grinned expectantly.

'Yes, okay, I'm an idiot. Sometimes things go on. And then I regret it immediately. And then I'm really horrible to him. And then after a period of months, something happens again.'

'Right.'

'Only this time ...'

'Ah, recently was it?'

'After Mary and Frank's birthday party, actually.'

'Yes?'

'Well he turned up at work the day after asking to take me out for a drink.'

Alice took a sip of her coffee. 'Well I'm no expert,' she said, 'but that sounds normal to me. Although, as you know, I have not had any experience of normal behaviour for some time.'

Kathy looked up at the sky in exasperation. 'We never do

that. It's always the same – hover round each other, sleep together, regret it, disappear …'

'Did you go for a drink with him?'

'Yes, reluctantly.'

'Did you enjoy it?'

'Yes, reluctantly.'

'You don't look very happy about it.'

'I don't trust him. Haven't for years. Since about two years into our very short marriage.

Alice took another bite of cake. 'Look at us still talking about boys,' she said.

Kathy took off her sunglasses and smiled. 'Shall we be grown up for a moment though? At some point you are going to have to deal with—'

'—oh no you don't,' interrupted Alice. 'For the moment real life consists of the following: sunshine, swimming, photography, painting, shopping for food and Aphrodite … and perhaps going for a meal at a restaurant with chairs with a very attractive man called Luis. Who apparently has a reputation. But has beautiful eyes. And I'm on holiday, so does it matter if he has a reputation? The biggest stress I should have to deal with is Aphrodite's pet geckos. Which is actually very stressful really and more than enough for me, thank you very much.'

'Finished?'

'Yes.'

'I thought you were going back in a couple of weeks.'

'I am. Just haven't decided exactly when yet. I can't stay indefinitely. It's not allowed is it? I can't remember exactly how long I can stay for a holiday, but it's not that long. I am regrouping my strength ready for the fight ahead. And looking for jobs … oh God. Spell broken. I'm feeling horrible again.'

'Sorry, have some cake,' said Kathy.

'Can we talk some more about boys?'

'Made any bracelets yet?' Kathy ignored her question.

'You sound like my mother,' Alice said with a sigh.

Chapter Eight

'Over there,' said Luis. 'Cities, roads, people, things, dogs, cats ... but over there—' he turned towards the sea stretching westwards to infinity '—nothing, nada. Well, until you get to America. Or the Azores.'

'So this is the restaurant at the end of the world?' asked Alice.

'Yes. Imagine. In the Middle Ages you would look out over exactly the same sea, thinking that not far beyond the horizon the world ended.'

'Frightening,' she said, looking at the black rolling waves roaring against the cliffs.

'There are fishing boats out there. See the tiny lights. They look like they are twinkling. It's nothing as romantic as that. They are just disappearing behind terrifyingly massive swells.'

Alice, smiled, glancing at the distant lights scattering down the hills, clustering into villages and towns, the glow of Lisbon in the far distance. 'This is beautiful,' she said. 'Another beautiful place. Do you only go to beautiful places?'

'They have to pass very stringent tests.' Luis nodded gravely. 'I refuse to live in a plain world.'

'So you not only visit beautiful places, you live in them too?'

'Australia is mostly beautiful,' he said. 'I'm from Melbourne. Well, I was born here and my family moved there when I was a baby. Then I moved back in my early twenties because Australia just wasn't quite beautiful enough.'

Alice sipped her wine. 'What really brought you here?'

Luis touched his chest. 'Broken heart.'

'Really? I'm sorry.'

Luis smiled. 'No, not really. Well, I always had what I wanted. Good at school, good at university, good at sport, good at being an architect for about five minutes. But just after I qualified and the world was my oyster, something happened. My girlfriend dumped me. And I loved her, and I had done for a long time. I couldn't cope at not being good at being a boyfriend. So I ran away.' He paused, and glanced down at his drink, embarrassed. 'And I wish I hadn't told you all of that. Please forget it.'

Alice wanted to touch his hand, but said instead, 'you were an architect? That's impressive.'

'Briefly,' said Luis, smiling again. 'Are you trying to picture me in a suit?'

'Why didn't you carry on doing it here?'

Luis looked at the table and took a sip of his drink. 'I think that's enough about me for the evening. That's as interesting as I get. What about you? What's your story Alice?'

'Boring really. I'm a runaway too.'

'I'm glad you ran away here. Am I being too cheesy?'

Alice's stomach looped the loop once again. 'Yes and no.'

He took a gulp of beer, then placed his drink firmly on the table. 'Alice.'

'Yes.'

'Do you like the chairs?'

'Do you mean the actual chairs?'

'Yes.'

Alice stroked the arms and looked down at the legs. Then she wriggled in her seat. 'As green plastic chairs go they are top notch.'

'Nothing but the best.' He sipped his beer again. 'Do you like the food?'

'Absolutely delicious as burgers go. Yes, thank you.'

He leaned forward. 'I have bought a new house. I'd like to show it to you. Next time. As long as you are still here?'

'For a few weeks yet. That would be lovely, thanks.' Alice realised that the extra 'two weeks only' was beginning to stretch a bit but also realised she didn't care. 'I like looking at houses,' she said.

'It's different, this one. Older. In need of some tender loving care. Been battered and bruised. A real project.'

'A challenge?'

Luis looked at Alice and smiled. 'A challenge and definitely something worth spending some extra time on. And on that note, shall we go? Tomorrow I am meeting the buyer for my completed house, and unfortunately, I am also playing in the band. It'll be a long and dull day.'

As they walked towards the car, Luis switched on his phone. 'I didn't want us to be interrupted,' he said, 'but the result is this.' It pinged over and over with messages received. 'No rest for the wicked.' He sighed, accidentally brushing his arm against Alice's then moving away quickly to listen to a voicemail. 'Alice,' he said as they got in the car. 'Do you mind if we stop by a bar on the way to your apartment? Antonio was supposed to drop some of my tools at the house, but he didn't, and I've got a couple of things I need to finish first thing. He's got them in his car. It'll be just after a gig. I'm so sorry. Five minutes?'

'No problem,' said Alice, 'It'll be nice to meet him.'

'Humph,' said Luis as they drove off.

'Right,' he said as he parked outside the bar.

'Right,' said Alice.

He turned to her, unsmiling. 'When we go in can you remember that I'm leaving this part of my life behind?'

'Of course,' said Alice, surprised. She hesitated for a moment. 'Is there anything I should know?'

'No, no,' he said, slightly agitated. 'It's just Antonio can be ... a little ... and some of his friends are ...' He sighed. 'Never mind, forget it. We'll be in and out in a few minutes.' He took her hand protectively as they walked towards the entrance, and as he pushed open the door, the calm peace of the night was punctured with chatter, laughter and loud, pumping music. They weaved around the groups of people towards the back of the room, where Antonio stood with three young women.

'Antonio,' said Luis. 'This is Alice.'

Antonio turned slowly around to look at her, and nodded, unsmiling.

'Nice to meet you,' said Alice, holding out her hand.

He nodded again, ignored her and turned to the women. Alice stepped closer to Luis, a little taken aback.

'Luis,' Antonio said. 'This is Marcella.' He put his arm around the shoulders of a tall, shapely young woman with glowing skin and dark brown lustrous hair. 'She's the one I've been telling you about. And her friends are Julia and Joanna.'

'Hi,' said Marcella, grabbing Luis and kissing him on both cheeks. 'I've been so looking forward to meeting you. I love the band. I've been telling Antonio I would love to get you more gigs. I'm in events management and my father owns some bars and restaurants. I know a lot of people. It would be great. We could get to know each other.'

Luis untangled himself and squeezed Alice's hand tightly again. 'This is Alice,' he said.

Marcella nodded. 'Hi,' she said, without smiling.

Alice smiled widely, trying to work out what was going on. 'Hello, lovely to meet you.' A long forgotten, half-hidden memory of the parties she went to with Adam shivered through her uncomfortably. She pushed it away but the shadow lingered.

'Right, mate,' said Luis, unsmiling. 'Where's my tools?'

'Your tools?' asked Antonio.

'You said you had my tools here. I need them.'

'Oh, that was a mistake. I managed to drop them off at the house after I left the message and it slipped my mind.'

'Great, what a waste of time.' He turned to go.

'Well, now you're here, why not stay?'

'I've got to take Alice home.'

Antonio glanced at her. 'Well come back after you've done that. Marcella has lots to talk to you about.'

Alice stepped back, wanting to get away, back to the car, back to the restaurant at the edge of the world. Luis put his arm around her.

'Yes, please come back.' Marcella pouted.

'No, thanks,' he said turning away. 'I'm taking Alice home and then I'm working first thing in the morning, as you know.' They walked towards the door without turning back, and as they headed to the car, he turned to her. 'I'm so sorry. They were very rude.'

'Surprisingly rude,' said Alice quietly

'Yes. Please remember. They are not my people. Antonio was not always like that.'

'Okay,' said Alice, trying to pretend that it didn't matter. Because she was only here for a few weeks, and this was all just fun.

He switched on some music and they drove to the apartment in silence.

'Thank you for a lovely evening,' said Alice after they pulled into the driveway.

'Well, I enjoyed it. Shall we forget about the last bit?'

'Yes, please.'

'And do you want to come and see this old house? My project.'

Alice began to relax again. 'Yes, I'd love to.'

'And perhaps we could go into Lisbon for a drink. You said you are here for a few weeks, didn't you? I keep asking you that. Sorry.'

'I am, and yes, that would be great.'

There was another pause.

'Okay,' she said, turning towards the door. 'Off I go.'

'Wait,' said Luis. Suddenly he pulled her towards him and kissed her gently.

As his lips touched hers, Alice felt herself change, as if she was shedding one of the layers she had grown to protect herself. And she couldn't stop it. She didn't want to stop it. *Don't go*, she thought as he stroked her hair.

'I have to go,' he said. 'I'd like to kiss you more. But I have to be up at half five tomorrow morning. You are now free to leave the vehicle.' He laughed. '*Ate logo*. See you very soon.'

Alice stepped out of the car and turned back so she could see his face again. He leaned over, touched her cheek and kissed her once more. 'Oh, Alice,' he said, 'I wish I didn't have to go but I do.' He closed the door gently.

She watched the car as it disappeared into the dark, and touched her mouth, smiling at the memory of his kiss. As the headlights finally turned out of sight, she almost skipped into the apartment and scooped up Aphrodite. 'Shall we dance?' she squeaked into the cat's ear.

She awoke the following morning, eager to meet the day. She thought of Luis, his eyes crinkling, the firm touch of his hand as he tried to make her feel secure when she met Antonio. Stepping out of bed she walked straight towards the living room, needing to see the sunlight and breathe the fresh, clear air. Flinging open the shutters Alice padded onto the balcony, embracing the morning sun. The sky was clear and cloudless, the leaves on the trees deep and green and the bougainvillea draping the bright white walls surrounding the garden was a velvety crimson. 'Heaven,' she said to Aphrodite, who was curled up on a chair in the sun. 'Mmmmm ... can you smell that? Is it pine trees? What do you think? Yes, pine I think, Aphrodite.' The memory of Luis's kiss fluttered through her like a butterfly. Two birds flew from the roof, swooping towards the swimming pool, and as they soared back up to the trees, Alice saw their bright blue chests shimmering in the sun. Then she walked into the apartment, gathered her easel, canvas and paints and staggered out of the door, almost giddy with excitement to spend the day painting the first thing she saw.

She had arranged to meet Kathy at the hotel so they could wander around the town in the evening, and as she sauntered towards the beauty salon, she heard raised voices from inside.

'You shouldn't be looking at my phone.' It was Kathy, her voice stern.

'Well you shouldn't be getting texts from strange men.'

Alice paused, not sure whether to go in or not. *I seem to be making a habit of listening into conversations I'd rather not hear*, she thought, putting her hand on the door, but not moving.

'You what? Stephano, we are not in a relationship. I can get texts from whoever I want.'

'Well I don't want you to.'

'All we do is have sex.' Kathy sounded exasperated.

Alice saw a customer walking down the corridor towards the salon and decided to interrupt before she did. She coughed loudly a few times, then shoved open the door. 'Hello!' she said brightly.

Kathy and Stephano looked up, surprised.

'Hello, Stephano. Lovely to see you. Do you have a customer due, Kathy?' She nodded pointedly towards the door.

Kathy looked confused as the footsteps from outside grew louder. 'Ah, yes. It's not me. I'm just finishing. It's with another of the girls.'

'I'd better go,' said Stephano. 'Nice to see you, Alice.'

As he turned to go Kathy said, 'you can't expect me to think it's anything more. You just pick me up occasionally, and I allow it.'

'I took you for a drink the other day.'

'Yes you did. You ambushed me outside work.'

Stephano sighed. 'Okay. Come on a date with me. I'm asking you out. Let's arrange something for next week. I'll text you with arrangements.'

Kathy looked bemused. 'Okay.'

'Okay, good,' he said, and left.

Kathy grabbed her bag and opened the door. 'Let's go then,' she said to Alice, as she turned towards the sea.

'Sorry I got in the middle of that,' said Alice.

Kathy untied her silk scarf from around her neck and shook her head. 'At last, uniform off,' she said. 'And thank you for warning me about the customer. Can't have the salon owner arguing with men in public!'

'That's okay,' said Alice, 'And now you're going on a date?'

'Yes, I don't know what's got into him. He didn't even take me out when we were married. Always wining and dining his customers then. But anyway, how was your date with Luis?'

Alice giggled. 'It was lovely.'

'Excellent!' Kathy looked pleased. 'When are you seeing him again?'

'Soon hopefully. But, um there was …' Alice stopped herself, not wanting to ruin the feeling she'd woken up with by raking over what had happened when she'd met Antonio.

'There was?' asked Kathy.

'Oh, nothing.'

'What have you been up to today anyway? I can guess as you have a blue spot on your arm.'

'I painted the swimming pool,' announced Alice.

'Don't they have handymen to do that?' joked Kathy, as they paused at a jewellery stall.

'Aren't you the funny one?' said Alice, picking up a beaded green bracelet and examining it.

'Yes, I am.' Kathy laughed and tried on a pair of purple sunglasses.

They meandered on into the town and Alice paused at the window of a very expensive looking clothes shop. 'That blue silky dress at the back,' she said. 'Maybe I'll treat myself to that for my birthday.'

'That's not for weeks yet,' said Kathy. 'Aha, that means you'll be hanging around for longer than a fortnight then!'

Alice was silent for a moment. 'I didn't say that. But I could buy it before my birthday and take it home.'

Kathy put her arms around her friend. 'You like it here, don't you?'

'Yes I do. The longer I stay the more I like it.'

'Well stay here then.'

'I can't.'

'Why not?'

'Because … what's that music? I know it, but I can't place it.' A slow, haunting melody drifted along the street.

'I know it too. But I've never heard it played on an accordion and electric keyboard before.' They paused and listened.

'It's coming from over there,' said Alice, pointing at two teenage boys standing next to a café.

'I know it, I know it …' said Kathy. 'It's … it's …'

'Some Day My Prince Will Come,' giggled Alice.

'Snow White!' chuckled Kathy. 'Remember, we used to watch it all the time on cold and damp Sundays?' She stood and listened. 'Maybe your Prince has finally arrived, Alice.'

'And maybe yours has too, again!'

'Yeah, right. I don't think so. Prince Charming, no. Prince Amorous more like. And anyway, what about you and Luis last night?'

'Well, it was rather lovely but …'

'But?'

Alice just needed to say it, because when she did, it would sound irrelevant and that would make her feel better. 'We had to go and get something from that Antonio, who's very rude by the way, and some girl was there who was also very rude. It was like a weird little soap opera.'

'What did Luis say?'

'He said before we went in that they weren't his people.'

'Well that's good.'

'And he did kiss me.'

Kathy punched the air. 'Yes, Alice Dorothy Matthews is back on the man-wagon!'

Alice laughed. 'Kathy!'

'Oh, look, there's Ignacio.' Kathy motioned her head in his direction.

'*Ola! Boa Tarde,*' said Ignacio walking towards them. 'My nephews are very talented, don't you think?'

'Your nephews?' As she spoke Alice noticed their spiky hair and piercing blue eyes. 'I see the resemblance.'

Ignacio smiled proudly. 'My sister's children,' he said. 'I will be taking them home soon. She will only let them do this for an hour a week and only if I am here to look after them.'

'Well they are excellent,' said Kathy.

'I'll tell them. And her. She doesn't really like them doing it, but they are teenagers. Wilful. Sometimes it's best to give them a little bit to keep them happy.'

Kathy and Alice took some coins out of their purses and placed them in the little plastic cup the boys were using to collect their earnings.

'Thank you,' said Ignacio, bowing. 'And where are you going to on such a lovely evening?'

'Nowhere really,' said Kathy. 'I'm training Alice to amble. They don't do it in London. She's picking it up very well.'

Ignacio beamed at Alice. 'It's working. The power of Paradise.'

'Do you know everyone?' asked Alice, smiling towards the boys. 'You seem to.'

'I have a very big family, so yes!' He laughed. 'Enjoy your evening. And Alice – you should stay for a while. You really look much better than when you arrived. You looked so exhausted, stressed, very pale.'

'Thank you,' said Alice. 'We'll see you soon.'

'*Ate logo,*' he said as they began to wander towards Fisherman's Beach.

'Maybe the song was about Ignacio,' whispered Kathy. 'I think he likes you.'

Alice slapped her on the arm. 'He's just being nice. Stop stirring!'

Chapter Nine

'There's none left!' shouted Alice from the kitchen, peering into the back of the cupboards to make sure that there wasn't a secret stash of Mary's herbal tea hidden away.

'I'm crestfallen. Do I look crestfallen?' asked Kathy, standing in the doorway.

'Well I'm crestfallen too. I can't drink ordinary tea now, or even shop-bought herbal teas. She didn't leave much, did she?'

'She didn't realise you were a herbal tea addict, I expect,' laughed Kathy, taking a biscuit from a pink tin.

'I wasn't until I bought all that chamomile tea after I got made redundant and Adam sent that postcard,' said Alice. She paused and poured herself a glass of water. 'You know I feel sick all of a sudden. I didn't, then I mentioned those two things and I feel physically sick.'

Kathy put her arm around her.

'I'm okay,' said Alice, trying to breathe the nausea away as she opened the cupboard door again. 'Old Mother Hubbard. Tea-wise anyway. We've drunk the Very Relaxing Ones, the Very Energising ones, the Very Cleansing Ones, and a couple of Oooh Watch Out Ones – I had to go for a walk, a swim, and then danced around the living room after those – my antidote was that one sample of the Sleep Like a Baby one. Never to be repeated. I didn't wake up for fourteen hours.'

Kathy opened the fridge door. 'Wine then,' she said, taking out a bottle of Vinho Verde.

'Ooooooooh, I'm so disappointed,' cried Alice. 'No more of Mary's herbal tea. What are we going to do?'

'Very funny,' said Kathy. 'Good whining.'

'I'm fairly relaxed mostly,' said Alice, 'apart from when real life pokes its nose in like just now.'

'That's because Luis is working his magic on you, my dear,' said Kathy, taking the glass of water from her and replacing it with a glass of wine.

'Well he really is much better than herbal tea. Really. Although I don't know when I'm seeing him again. He sent me a text saying he's very busy. But he wants to see me soon.' She took a sip of wine. 'Something about the property he's doing up, and then something about his friend Antonio's mum needing her car repaired and so he was doing an extra couple of gigs to help him get more cash. And, well, anyway ... you don't think he's trying to get rid of me do you, only nicely?'

'No I don't. He obviously likes you. And at least he told you. I find that level of communication in men admirable. I personally am not used to it.'

'I suppose you're right.'

'We could message Mary and ask for the secret recipe.'

Alice walked to the living room and sat down on the couch. 'You'd better do it. I can feel my fingers itching to get on social media and track Adam down. And that woman.'

'Well you can ...'

Alice took a bigger sip of wine. 'Nope. Not ready. I have spent two years trying to locate him with no success. He's either changed accounts or blocked me. And now I don't want to find him. Because if I do, it all becomes real again.'

Kathy put her phone down on the table. 'It's okay, I've just messaged Mary for the recipe. Hopefully she'll reply soon from wherever she is.'

Alice's phone pinged. She checked the message and felt her breath catch in her throat.

'What's the matter?' asked Kathy.

'It's a text from my mum.'

'What's wrong with that?'

Alice looked up. 'The first word starts with "A".'

Kathy took the phone gently from her. 'I'll check it, shall I?'

'Yes please.'

Kathy read the message. Then she hugged Alice before she read it out. 'It says, "Adam is definitely back in the country. He phoned us and left a message. I am completely ignoring the little shit. Rather enjoying winding him up. Will continue to do so but need to tell you he is here and on the loose. He's a bit upset that he can't get in the house. Was muttering something about changing the locks being illegal on the phone. Well done you! All my love, Mum."'

Alice breathed out slowly and stood up. 'There it is again,' she said. 'The nausea. Sorry.' She sat down again suddenly. 'In the last couple of weeks I've actually started to relax and enjoy myself. I mean, I know I have to go back soon and sort everything out. But just for a little while can't I have some peace? He's even ruining my break.' She managed to get to her feet and walk over to the balcony. 'I'm not ready to deal with all that. I don't want to. Not yet. Not at the moment.'

'You are in Paradise,' said Kathy softly, 'and you don't have to deal with anything you don't want to.'

Alice stared at the trees outside. 'No I don't'

'It's up to you to decide when you want to sort things out.'

'Yes it is.'

'And you'll have a lovely time with Luis in Lisbon.'

Alice turned and smiled at her. 'Hopefully,' she said. 'Funny, just thinking about him has calmed me down.'

'Calmed you down? Surely at this stage of your relationship he should be giving you hot flushes, and not of the menopausal kind.'

'Oh, yes, my stomach does a loop the loop when I see him. And when he texts. And when I think of him. But in a strangely calm way. I can't explain it.'

'Well are you okay now? You look less white.'

'Yes, thanks. I hadn't thought of that difficult stuff much for the past few days now. I've been so caught up in things here. It's been so lovely, Kathy. For the first time in years.'

'Did you really change the locks in your house?' asked Kathy.

'Of course I did. It's not his house. It's my house. Although strictly speaking I think if his name's on the paperwork I shouldn't have. But I did.'

Kathy laughed. 'Right, let's do something about this. Where's Mary's manual? We can see if she's left any ideas on what you can do to take your mind off things.'

'It's in the book case. The pink and white book with ribbons in the pink and white box with ribbons.'

Kathy retrieved it and opened it at a random page.

Alice closed her eyes. 'Okay, what does it say? Surprise me?'

'Paddle boarding.'

'Paddle boarding?'

'Paddle boarding. On this page anyway,' said Kathy. 'On the next page it's tile painting. But I opened it on paddle boarding, so that's what we do. It says, "Alice, sometimes when life gets you down it's a good idea to throw yourself into a physical challenge. I took up paddle boarding at the age of fifty-eight. There's a school at Guincho run by a very tall, blond and handsome Dutch chap called Hans. Tell him I sent you. You will love it. I know you will."' Kathy slammed the book down. 'Yes!' she said, punching the air. 'Time to get salty and sandy!'

'I don't want to.'

'Tough. Mary says you have to. I'm coming too. It'll take my mind off Stephano.'

'Can we not just wait for her to get back to us with her tea recipe?'

'I'm going to give them a call and book us in.'

'Water again,' said Alice, this time taking a big gulp of wine. 'Now the little swine has sent you jumping in it, too.'

'Yes, well, this will be controlled and wearing wetsuits, rather than leaping in randomly in sundresses. This is taking control. Day after tomorrow?'

'But …'

'No buts.' Kathy covered Alice's mouth with her hand. 'We are going to have some fun whether you like it or not.'

Alice smiled at her friend. Kathy was right. She needed to force herself to have as much fun as possible because when Adam finally managed to push himself into her life again, it would be in very short supply.

Alice had been hoping for a windy, wet day so the paddle boarding would be cancelled. But the sea was calm, the breeze was soft and the sun was shining brightly. 'I thought that the water had to be dead flat with no waves for us to do this?' she muttered to Kathy.

'It is,' she replied. 'And there's no turning back now. It took me twenty minutes to get into this wetsuit.'

'Looks a bit choppy to me,' said Alice.

'Hans says its fine.'

'Well, he would.'

'Ladies.' Hans walked towards them. 'Come a bit closer so you can hear better and I can introduce you to your boards.'

'Is the water cold?' asked Alice, anxiously

'Only moderately.' He laughed. 'That's why you have the wetsuits.'

They walked over to the small group of students comprising of three schoolboys, two long-limbed teenage girls and a man in his fifties who was telling everyone he was having a mid-life crisis.

'These are your boards,' said Hans. 'I need you to stand on them with one foot slightly in front of the other for balance.'

The group did as they were told. Hans handed out the paddles. 'Now,' he said, 'in less than an hour you will be experts in steering your boards whilst standing. Before that you will fall in a lot. And before that you have to learn to get on your board, and how to fall in the water properly. But first, I will show you how to stand up.'

Fifteen minutes later they were dragging the boards towards

the water. 'Remember,' said Hans, 'don't expect miracles the first time you go in the sea. Take it slowly. Have fun, and I will come out to see each of you individually.'

Alice looked at the sea warily. 'I won't be able to do this,' she said.

'Come on, just go for it. What have you got to lose?' urged Kathy.

'My dignity,' muttered Alice.

'Come! Come!' shouted Hans as the others trotted to the shoreline. He picked up Alice's board and carried it into the water. 'The rest is very easy,' he said.

'Thank you,' said Alice, looking up at his frame silhouetted against the sun. *I can't not do it with his gorgeousness watching*, she thought.

'Alice,' he said, 'everyone else is in the sea.'

'Oh, sorry, miles away,' she said. 'Off I go.'

The youngsters were already kneeling on their boards, trying to stand. Kathy was soaking wet and laughing hysterically. Alice paused, allowing the cold water to lap at her feet for a few moments, her heart beating anxiously. Suddenly she was back in her kitchen, loading the dishwasher, Adam sitting at the table, flicking aggressively through an exotic travel magazine. *'No sense of adventure,' he said quietly. 'Why can't you just forget about the bloody cost for once? Why do you have to be so bloody sensible all the time and lay on the guilt trip about the money?'*

The shrieks of the others brought her back to the present. She looked at the board attached to her wrist with the rope and down at the paddle stuck in the sand. She shook her head in an attempt to rid herself of the memory of Adam, took a deep breath, jumped and ran deeper into the sea. 'Yeeehaaaaa,' she screamed, 'Yeeehaaaaa!' Holding the board steady she climbed on and sat for a few moments with her legs in the water, watching a school of tiny silver fish swaying backwards and forwards with the tide.

'Right,' she muttered. 'It is time, Alice Dorothy Matthews.' Holding the paddle in one hand she slowly tried to move to a standing position, but the board slipped from under her and she tumbled into the sea. The cold, salty water sent a shock through her body, and she pushed herself to the surface, spluttering and coughing. 'Fabulous!' She laughed, climbing on again. 'Fabulous!'

Half an hour later after accidentally tipping herself into the sea at least a dozen times, Alice finally managed to stand, wobbling inelegantly but proudly across the bay. 'Look, look,' she shouted to Kathy. 'I can do it, I can do it!' Then she fell in. Clambering back onto the board she managed to stand again, this time with a little more aplomb and balance, and paddled towards the rest of the group.

Hans waved at her. 'Well done Alice,' he yelled.

'Ooooh, thank you,' she yelled back. And fell in again. Climbing back onto the board, she sat down and allowed herself to drift towards Kathy.

'It's wonderful,' said Kathy, sitting down too. 'But I'm exhausted.' Their boards knocked into each other and they laughed.

'I just can't drive this thing,' said Alice.

'Not ready to pass your test yet,' sighed Kathy. A small wave pushed the boards together again.

'Time to finish everyone,' shouted Hans. 'The wind's getting up now quite quickly, so best be careful.'

'Oh, pity,' said Alice, 'I was enjoying—'

A wave suddenly picked up her board and pushed her quickly towards the shore, and she screamed and giggled until she tumbled out in the shallows. She sat, shaking with laughter, sand in her nose and eyes. 'Kathy, that was brilliant!' she squealed, turning around to see her friend draped across her board laughing uncontrollably.

'I ... can't ... move ...,' snorted Kathy. 'That was ... so ... funny ... I just ... can't ...'

Alice rolled backwards, giggling, and lay in the water, gazing at the sky, still attached to her board, clutching the paddle with the other hand. Seagulls swept along the clouds and the sea swished gently in her ears. 'I did it,' she said to herself softly. 'I can paddle board.' A wave poured water over her face and she spluttered. *Time to get out*, she thought, and rolled over, dragging herself into a standing position. She began to stride out of the sea, the *Baywatch* theme playing in her head, when a large and friendly Alsatian dog ran towards her at speed, knocking her back into the water.

'Elvis! Oh, no, Elvis! For God's sake!' Luis was running towards Alice, horrified.

She resurfaced spluttering and wheezing whilst the dog gambolled playfully around her, barking excitedly.

'Are you okay?' shouted Luis.

'What are you doing here?' coughed Alice.

'I'm sorry. I'm so sorry. Let me help you.' He waded towards her as she tried to stand up. 'Here,' he said, holding out his hand.

Alice didn't think. The excitement she had felt in the sea overcame her and she couldn't help herself – she grabbed his hand and pulled him into the water. Then she laughed.

'That's not funny,' cried Luis. 'I'm on my way to a gig.'

'I'm sorry,' she said. 'I'm so sorry. I don't know what came over me.' Alice sat in the water, surprised at what she'd done. Then she laughed.

Luis looked at her curiously then his face broke into a grin. 'You look like you've been enjoying yourself.'

'I have. I didn't expect to. But I have.' She pulled the board back towards her. 'I thought you were doing up that house?' she said, finally managing to stand up.

'I am. But I promised Antonio, you know, to help pay for his mother's car repairs. I said I'd do a couple of gigs. I had to bring Elvis for a walk first. He must have seen you from the dunes. He can run very fast.' They looked at each other for a moment. Alice wanted to laugh again, because she was happy and invigorated, and Luis was sitting in the sea fully clothed.

'I have to go and do work on the house after that, too,' he said eventually.

'Oh dear, that's a pity,' said Alice, holding her hand out to help him up. Clasping it, he dragged her back into the water. 'Oh, dear ...' he said, as Alice screamed.

'Children!' shouted Kathy, as the rest of the group began to pack up. 'Hans says the lesson is over. Come back to school. We can have a drink with him in the beach bar with the others once we've changed.'

'I must say,' said Luis quietly, 'you look very good in that wetsuit.'

'Really?' Alice wasn't convinced. She pulled some seaweed out of her hair. 'I thought I looked a bit rough, to be honest.'

'You look very, very, very ...' he tailed off, smiling. Then he kissed her lightly on the lips and stood up, pulling her out of the water. 'I have to go. I will call. I promise. Bye gorgeous.' He turned towards the dunes, Elvis in pursuit.

Alice watched him walk away, her heart racing excitedly. *Gorgeous, me? In this?* she thought. *Well, if you say so.* Picking up the paddle board she carried on towards the changing rooms, smiling inside. 'I'll have a beer, please, Hans,' she shouted to the instructor as he walked towards the bar. After a quick, cold shower to wash away the sun and salt, Alice pulled her dress over her head and joined her friend. An hour later, she was feeling very relaxed.

'Did you see that sunset? It was just lovely.' Two more bottles of beer appeared in front of them. 'Ohhh, magic. Who put those there?'

'Hans did,' giggled Kathy.

The bar was now full of people eating, drinking, chatting and laughing, and a band had set up in the corner.

'Oh, live music,' squealed Alice.

'Ah yes.' Kathy waved towards them. 'They play Latin

music.' Then she put her head on Alice's shoulder. 'Alice, I've got a problem.'

Alice stroked her hair, comfortingly. 'Oh no, what is it?'

'Stephano.'

'Why is he a problem?'

'Well, despite the fact we split up years ago, we don't seem to have really. Not really. No clean break. And now I'm confused as he's getting all friendly again.'

'Don't you want him to be?'

'No. Yes. No. Yes … I don't know. I should never have slept with him that time. All those times.'

'I think you still love him,' said Alice softly.

Kathy looked at her, then shook her head. 'Nope. Hard as nails me.'

'If you say so.' Alice looked at the beer in front of her. 'Hans is being very generous, you know.'

'Ahhh,' said Kathy.

'What does that mean?'

'We've got a sort of bet.'

Alice sat back and looked at her, trying to be serious. 'A bet about what?'

Kathy looked at the floor. 'Whether you would dance on the bar or not,' she muttered.

Alice narrowed her eyes. 'So, you said I would or wouldn't?'

'Wouldn't,' muttered Kathy.

Alice looked at her and took a swig of beer. 'Why?'

'Because you've never done anything like that before!'

The band started playing 'Livin' La Vida Loca'. Alice looked at Kathy, wounded. So her best friend thought she couldn't be adventurous? Or silly? Or spontaneous? The music suddenly made her laugh, and she began to wiggle. 'I can be dangerous too, you know?' she said.

'Dangerous?' Kathy's eyes narrowed. 'What are you planning?'

'You are about to lose your bet, Kathy. For today I did

paddle boarding, and now I am going to dance on a bar ...'
Alice stood up and dragged her friend with her. 'Is it okay if
we dance on your bar please?' she said to the barman.

He looked confused. 'No you can't,' he said.

Hans, standing at the far end, beckoned him over and
whispered something to him. They laughed conspiratorially
as they glanced towards the women and the barman nodded.

'Alice!' shouted Kathy. 'You don't ask permission to dance
on a bar. You just get on it.'

Alice looked at her friend. 'But that's just rude, Kathy,'
she said, shaking her head. 'Have you ever danced on a bar
before? There's surely some etiquette.'

Kathy leaned in closer. 'No, actually I haven't. I think we
should do it.'

'You'll lose your bet.'

'Don't care. Let's go!'

They both tried to pull themselves up, but the bar was too
high, and they leaned on it, giggling.

'Why don't we get a chair and use that?' said Alice.

Kathy retrieved an empty bar stool and put it next to them.

Alice looked at it. 'Oh dear, think it's too high.'

'Nope.'

Kathy clambered up and stood on the bar triumphantly.

Alice hauled herself to a kneeling position, but the sundress
she was wearing made her pause for a moment. 'I'm going to
show everyone my knickers.'

'Are they nice?'

'Very.'

'Well, I'm sure everyone will approve then.'

Alice looked around. About half the people in the bar were
watching them, the other half hadn't noticed. Flashing even
half the bar was too much she thought, and she tried to tie the
back and front of the bottom of her dress together with one
hand, whilst clasping the bar with the other.

'Hurry up, the song's nearly finished,' said Kathy.

Suddenly, Alice was shoved up onto the bar by a pair of unknown hands. She manoeuvred around on all fours, shocked.

'Sorry,' said Hans. 'It was painful to watch. I couldn't stand it.'

Alice took a deep breath. The alcohol was beginning to make her feel a bit wobbly. 'I don't know if I can stand up,' she whispered.

Hans pulled himself next to her and slowly guided Alice to a standing position. A sea of faces looked at the three of them, surprised.

Alice laughed. 'I've done it!' she shouted.

And then the music stopped.

'Oh dear,' she said, and the room erupted in laughter and applause as the band began to play 'I Like it Like That', and Hans took Alice's hands.

'If Kathy is going to lose the bet, let's make her lose it good,' he laughed, and they began to sway together to the happy, vibrant rhythms.

Kathy took her other hand, 'We are dancing on a bar!' she shrieked, and they began to sing.

Then the barman passed them up a bottle of beer each and the whole room began to sway and sing along too.

Alice looked at the scene around her bathed in the mellow glow of the lights, and she realised she felt happy. She'd forgotten how to live in the moment, and a day of falling in the sea, and then singing randomly in a bar – the sheer physicality of it – had meant she hadn't thought about tomorrow or the day after that, and that hadn't happened for a long time. She held her beer aloft and toasted the room. 'To today,' she shouted. And then she saw him. Luis. Standing by the door, his arms folded, smiling at her. She waved at him. 'Come and join us!' she mouthed at him. He began moving towards her and their eyes locked as he walked. Alice's heart began to beat a little faster. She wanted to dive into his arms so he could carry her away.

'So,' he said, looking up at the three of them.

'Hello,' said Alice. 'I've had a lovely day.'

'I can tell.' He laughed.

'I think it may be time to get off the bar,' she said. 'I'm beginning to feel a bit limp.'

Kathy and Hans clambered down, but Alice remained rooted to the spot.

'I have to kneel down again,' she whispered.

'It's alright, I'm here,' said Luis.

Alice slowly sunk to her knees then tried to climb down, her legs hanging from the bar.

Luis swept her up and looked into her eyes.

'This is like a film,' breathed Alice. '*Officer and a Gentleman*. Or *Dirty Dancing*?'

Luis laughed. 'It's real life, Alice,' he whispered softly, his warm breath lightly brushing her neck.

Alice's feet touched the floor and their eyes locked once again as she leaned into him, smiling. Then her legs buckled. 'Oh, dear, I think that last beer was one beer too many. What with the sun as well. Mostly the sun, I think. Not the beer.'

'I think we'd better get you home.'

'Luis,' said Hans, 'I think you have some company.' He nodded towards the door where Antonio, Marcella and her two friends stood, staring at them unhappily.

'Are they glaring at me?' asked Alice in surprise.

Luis sighed. 'How did they know I was here?'

'We all know that Antonio thinks you are betraying him with the guys in the Latin band.' Hans laughed. 'He probably heard they were playing here and decided to head you off at the pass!'

Alice could feel Luis bridle and his shoulders tense. 'Well I came to see Alice,' he said.

'Did you?' Alice smiled broadly.

Luis kissed her lightly on the lips. 'It was the wet suit that did it. All I could think of when I was playing my set was you falling in the sea.'

Alice sank into him again, her eyes closed.

'Luis!' Marcella tapped him on the shoulder and almost pulled him back.

Luis turned slowly towards her. 'Marcella,' he said. 'What brings you here?'

'I thought you said you were going to work on your house after the gig?'

'I was but I decided to come and see Alice on the way,' he said levelly.

Marcella's eyes narrowed as she attempted a smile.

'Alice, of course,' she said. 'I saw you nearly fall off that bar. You must have had a lot to drink.'

Alice smiled, although the room was beginning to spin a little.

'Just as well I was here to catch her,' said Luis. 'And now it's time to take her home.' He took Alice's hand. 'Let's go.'

'Oh, what about Kathy?' she said.

'It's okay,' said Hans. 'My wife is picking me up in ten minutes, we'll give Kathy a lift.'

Kathy winked at Alice, as Luis gently guided her towards the door.

Antonio stepped in front of them.

'Antonio,' said Luis. 'What are you doing here? I thought you were off into Lisbon to meet some of Marcella's contacts?'

'She decided she wanted to come here,' said Antonio tightly. 'Anyway, I thought you might be here too, with those guys playing.' He almost spat the last few words.

'Ahh, so it was your idea,' sighed Luis. 'Antonio, just give me a break, won't you? I wanted to see Alice. My life does not revolve around your band.'

Antonio looked at her then turned to Luis. 'Another one,' he sneered. 'You didn't decide to pick up a guitar and join that band then.'

'No,' said Luis, 'I'm leaving before you say anything else. I'm not getting into an argument with you. And you should not refer to Alice as "another one".' He pushed the door open and led a bemused Alice out into the cool evening.

'I'm so sorry about that,' he said. 'Office politics. Again.' He sighed. 'It's complicated. Old loyalties – old friends – a shared history – knowing how much the band means to him.'

'No, it's fine,' said Alice, confused. 'He's still a bit rude though.'

The waves lapped softly against the sand as Luis kissed her softly.

'I think we need to get you home,' he said.

Alice's heart beat fast again, but the sudden shot of sea air made he woozy. 'I feel a bit …'

'I know.' Luis laughed. 'You need to get some sleep.'

Chapter Ten

'This is my apartment. Sort of my apartment,' said Alice as Luis guided her through the door. 'And this is my painting – my work in progress, if you will – of the swimming pool and surrounding area.' She picked up the canvas and held it above her head. 'Painting is not my best subject. But I am okay at it. I think.'

Luis studied it thoughtfully. 'You look like you're waiting for someone at the airport and have painted a picture on a sign instead of writing their name,' he said eventually.

'Yes. It's for Mr S Pool.'

Luis laughed. 'It's a good painting, you know.'

'Thank you.' Alice spun around the room with it and nearly bumped into the wall.

'Careful,' said Luis, catching her arm and guiding her to a chair.

'You are lovely,' said Alice, firmly, smiling up at him. 'Oh dear. Now I'm sitting down I feel a bit …' She put her head into her hands as the room began to tilt slightly.

'Oh dear, oh dear,' muttered Luis, kneeling down beside her. 'You really *do* need to go to bed.'

Alice looked up woozily. 'Oh, you know, Luis. That's a lovely idea, really. And thank you. It has been on my mind quite a lot. You know … with you … but I think I am about to be sick, so I think that we will have to do that another time. I didn't have much to drink today. I didn't. Must have overdone the sun. Although maybe I did have too much to drink … I don't know. Why are you laughing?'

Luis was looking down at the floor. Alice thought he may have been smiling, or even trying not to laugh, but the room was now spinning a bit, so she couldn't be sure. 'Alice …'

'It's okay. Crisis averted. I'm not going to be sick. Good news.'

'Nevertheless,' said Luis. 'I think when you are feeling better we could revisit that idea.'

'Alright,' said Alice meekly.

'Now I'll get you some water,' he said, walking into the kitchen. 'Is that your phone ringing?'

'Is it? It is.' Alice rummaged around in her bag. 'Hello? Tara? Tara? What's wrong? Why are you phoning so late? No, I'm not drunk thank you very much. I've had a bit too much sun today.'

Luis placed the glass on the table as Alice fell silent.

'Mum said he'd phoned her Tara, not that he'd been to their house. Is she okay? Who was with him? Oh ... oh ... what do you mean Mum said she had a moustache? Is she a man? No ... oh ... okay ... look, thanks for letting me know. I'll call tomorrow when I'm a bit more better. Bye then.' Alice stood up unsteadily.

'What's happened?' asked Luis, pulling her to him and putting his arms around her.

'My sister Tara said thingy ... he who must be named ... has been to my parents' house with his girlfriend who has a moustache.'

'I'm not sure I understand. But okay.'

'I wish it would all just *bugger off*!' shouted Alice into his shirt. 'Not you. I mean it all. Oh dear.' She sighed. 'This isn't going very well, is it?'

'Um,' whispered Luis into her hair. 'It could be better.'

'Bugger,' sighed Alice.

'Right, it's time for you to go to bed. Alone,' said Luis. 'Because I think you have had just a little bit too much to drink and I don't want to take advantage of you.'

'Too much sun,' corrected Alice.

'Of course,' said Luis. 'Now,' he said firmly. 'You need to go to sleep and I need to work on the house.' He picked up the glass of water and handed it to her. 'Drink this,' he said.

Alice sipped it obediently.

Then he took her hand and guided her to the bedroom. 'I'll let myself out. Goodnight.'

'Goodnight,' whispered Alice sleepily climbing into bed.

But he had already gone.

Alice slowly awoke to the sounds of children playing happily in the pool. Her eyelids felt like they were welded together, and her mouth was dry as sawdust. Rolling over onto her back she felt her head. 'No headache,' she muttered. 'Amazing. But so thirsty ...' She got out of bed tentatively and padded to the kitchen to put the kettle on. Aphrodite was sitting by her food bowl, waiting patiently. 'Don't make me feel so guilty by sitting there all quiet. I know you're hungry,' said Alice. 'Why didn't you yowl in my ear like you usually do? To make me feel bad, that's why.' She spooned the cat food into the bowl and took her tea to the living room. She took her first sip and then stopped. 'Oh no. Oh no. Oh. No.' Fuzzy images of dancing on a bar, falling into Luis's arms and the call from Tara about Adam flew into her mind. And suddenly with absolute clarity she remembered everything she had said to Luis when he brought her home. 'Oh, God, he'll never speak to me again. He'll think I'm desperate.'

She took another sip of tea, feeling ashamed and embarrassed. Aphrodite trotted into the living room and began to purr around her feet. 'I've got to do something to take my mind off this,' she said to the cat. 'All of it, Adam, the bar, Luis, me ... God I feel so stupid.' One of the children in the pool screamed with laughter. Alice couldn't think of anything else to do. 'Aphrodite, I'm going outside to paint. Don't look at me like that. Have you got a better idea?'

Alice showered then gathered her paints, brushes and easel, pulled her sunhat over her head firmly and hurried outside, settling herself under a tree. She began to paint and for a little while managed to forget everything except her task.

'You're up and about very early, all things considered,' said

Kathy, walking across the garden towards the pool, swigging from a large bottle of water.

'Didn't want to sit in the apartment thinking about things,' muttered Alice from under the very large sunhat, 'so I thought I'd finish the painting.'

Kathy settled herself on a sunbed next to where Alice was sitting and watched her move the brush across the canvas, scattering a trail of red buds behind it. 'How do you get the flowers to look like that? Like if you touched them they would feel real?'

'I don't know,' said Alice, not wanting to talk about what she knew Kathy was about to talk about. She assumed Tara had told her already.

Kathy sighed. 'Alice, do you think you should contact a solicitor now he's starting to cause problems for your family? Tara messaged me last night too.'

'Yes I should,' said Alice angrily, putting her paintbrush down.

'And?'

'When *I'm* ready. Not when he's ready.'

'Right.'

'He can stew in it. I've spoken to Mum. She agrees. Lockdown.'

Kathy took another gulp of water. 'Do you not think you ought to be more proactive?'

'I am being proactive. I'm deliberately not doing anything.'

Kathy peered closely at Alice's head. 'I think I can see steam coming out of your ears.'

Alice smiled weakly. 'He can't just click his fingers and get what he wants, Kathy.' She sighed. 'And I'm not even ready to give him a reaction let alone a house.' She looked up at her friend and decided to change the subject. 'So, what happened with you last night?'

'Hans and his wife dropped me off at home. I've known her for years. Although Stephano got wind of me getting in a car with a tall, handsome man and got the wrong idea. Honestly, even beach bars have ears. And what difference does it make to him all of a sudden? He sent me a very terse text. I have no idea what's going on in that man's head.' Then she leaned forward and held Alice's gaze. 'The real question is, however, what happened to you?'

Alice pulled her sunhat down over her eyes and put her head in her hands.

'Not that I'm an expert in body language,' said Kathy, 'but my instincts tell me that looks quite negative.'

'I sort of indicated to Luis that I was keen to go to bed with him,' said Alice quickly. 'And he said no because I was too drunk. I wish I couldn't remember, but I remember it all. I want to hide. I just want to crawl under the bed!'

'Oh dear.' Kathy giggled.

'That's not very helpful.'

'I think it's rather sweet. Have you heard from him this morning?'

'No.'

'Oh.'

'Exactly.' Alice pulled the sunhat back slightly and looked at Kathy. 'I'm so embarrassed. I don't know what to do.'

'He's probably busy. You said he was getting that house ready.'

'He seems obsessed with that house to me.'

Kathy laughed. 'Pot. Kettle. Black.'

'What?'

'You. Your house. You know.'

Alice sighed. 'Can't argue with that.'

'Look, in Portugal, the rules with buying houses are different to in the UK. You said he had another house on the go, didn't you?'

'Yes.'

'Well maybe something happened – there could be money issues, or a buyer has dropped out, or problems with a deposit. Or he may have to sell it quickly and so he's finishing it off. '

Alice sighed again. 'Common sense as usual. What would I do without you?'

'I really don't know,' said Kathy, taking another gulp of water. 'But on that note I have to go. My first appointment is at half eleven.'

'What should I do about Luis?'

'Nothing. All will be fine.'

'And Adam?'

'Ah, well,' she said, standing up. 'I have no idea about that one.'

Alice picked up her paintbrush. 'Please don't ask me to go paddle boarding again.' Then she remembered Luis pulling her to him as he helped her off the bar, and she smiled.

Alice dozed a little fretfully in the afternoon, and after a swim, which refreshed her slightly, she wandered restlessly into town, trying to push her concerns about Luis and Adam and the house to the back of her mind by taking photos as she went. Walking into the square she paused and examined the patterned cobbles at her feet.

'Hey!' shouted Carlos the waiter. 'Are you in disguise today?'

She looked up, confused.

'The hat,' he said, walking over to her. 'It's very wide.'

'Ah well, it's starting to get hot, isn't it?' Alice said. 'So I thought extra coverage would be a good idea.'

'It's nearly seven o'clock in the evening. I think the sun is not so hot.' He smiled. 'I can't see your eyes.' Carlos bent his knees and peered up under the brim.

Alice pulled it to the back of her head.

'Much better. Now I can see your lovely face.'

'I can see where I'm going too, which is much better as well.' She smiled back at him.

'Is there a problem with the floor?' he asked curiously, looking closely at the cobbles too.

'Oh, no. I was just looking for inspiration.' She held the camera up as if that would explain it.

'Right. I see.'

'I think I'll have a coffee then,' she said after a while.

'Of course,' said Carlos. 'Sit please.'

Alice pulled the hat back down to mask her eyes and waited for her drink.

'Are you in disguise?' Luis threw his phone down onto the table and sat next to her. Alice laughed and tried not to think about the previous night.

'Did I make you jump?'

'Yes,' said Alice. 'Actually you did.'

'That's because you can't see out from under your hat.' He looked tired and unshaven, and she wanted to touch his face and lace her fingers through his unkempt hair 'Are you okay?' he asked her.

'What? Sorry,' said Alice. 'The hat's so big it must be affecting my hearing too.'

'Have you recovered from yesterday?' he said, looking into her eyes and smiling.

Alice pulled the hat down even further. 'That's why I'm wearing the hat. I'm so embarrassed,' she said quietly. 'And I didn't want to get a headache earlier, so I wanted to keep the sun off just to make sure.' She glanced up again at Luis and smiled. 'Although as Carlos pointed out, it is beginning to get dark. But mainly I'm wearing it because I am hideously embarrassed.'

'Don't be.' Luis put his hand on hers. 'It was actually very endearing.' He smiled again. 'Who is "thingy"? You mentioned them last night. And who's the woman with the moustache?'

Alice sighed. 'One is from the past. And I think the other one is his girlfriend.' She took off her hat and put it on the table.

'Ah, the past,' said Luis.

'Yes, and I wish he would stay there.' Alice could feel a fission of anger shoot through her temples. She changed the subject. 'Anyway, have you finished the house?'

'Nearly finished. Worked through the night and most of today. Then I got interrupted and decided to give in and have a rest.'

Carlos bought the coffee over.

'Luis,' he said. '*Diga*.'

'He means speak,' said Luis

'*Sim, diga*!' said Carlos.

'*Um Imperial*. That's a beer. And here endeth the Portuguese lesson for today.'

Alice laughed. 'You've not had much sleep then?' she asked.

'I intended to have some. But you know – life!'

Alice sipped her coffee.

'I only live five minutes' walk from here,' he said.

Alice glanced up at him. Luis was staring at her, a playful smile on his lips.

'*Um Imperial*.' Carlos set the glass on the table dramatically. 'I hear Antonio is causing problems again at the casino,' he said.

'That was less than two hours ago,' said Luis irritably. 'How did you know about that?'

'Ignacio was outside waiting for a client. He told me Antonio was drunk and aggressive again. Drinking all day, I heard.'

Luis picked up the beer and drank half of it in one gulp. 'I had to get him out and drive him home before they called the police.'

'Again.'

'Again.'

Alice could sense the weariness in Luis' voice. 'Does he do this often?' she asked.

'Recently, yes,' sighed Luis.

'He gambles in the casino,' said Carlos as he walked

towards another table, 'loses his money. Doesn't like it. Drinks.'

Luis sat up and put his glass down on the table. 'But that's him,' he said. 'What about you Alice? It was your sister that called you last night?'

'Yes, Tara. Her middle name is Scarlett. My mum was really into escapism when Tara was born. She watched *Gone With the Wind* a lot at the time. Probably because she couldn't pay the mortgage on the house and had been at war with our father. Not that we had clothes made out of curtains or anything. We did get evicted though.' She looked down and took a sip of her coffee. *Said too much*, she thought.

'Sounds like you had a hard time,' said Luis. 'And I assume that your name was inspired by films too?'

'I'm the eldest and at the time I was born Mum was having a hard time too.' The words tumbled out of Alice and she was unable to stop them. 'Mainly because my dad kept disappearing and she had no money and so she watched a lot of films which made her feel that you could escape somewhere even if it was a little bit odd. So, I'm Alice off of *Alice in Wonderland* and my middle name is Dorothy – from *The Wizard of Oz*. I do have a pair of red shoes actually.'

Luis smiled at her. He leaned forward. 'So, you are really in Wonderland now? Or the land of Oz? Not Australia. That's where I come from. But the one with the wizard and the munchkins?'

Alice thought for a moment. 'I suppose it is very vibrant and colourful and home had become very grey and static.'

Luis took another gulp of his beer. 'Be careful of the Wicked Witch of the West,' he said. 'Or the north, or the south. I don't know. Just remember—' he was suddenly serious '—this is real life too. It may be beautiful and fun and exciting, but things aren't always as they appear on the surface.'

Alice felt a little uneasy. *What did he mean?* 'No, I know,' she said. 'But for me it's an escape.'

'I'm sorry,' he said. 'I've ruined the mood. That's what having no sleep does for you.'

Alice smiled. 'No, you haven't ruined the mood at all,' she said, still not sure how to take what he'd said.

He caught her gaze and for a moment she forgot what he had said and where they were. All she could see was him.

'Oh, sh—!' Luis grabbed his buzzing phone and put it in his pocket. 'That can wait,' he said. 'So you enjoyed the paddle boarding yesterday?'

'I did actually. It was difficult, but invigorating.'

'It suited you. You looked happy.'

His phone buzzed again and again. Taking it reluctantly out of his pocket, he read the messages, irritably. 'Now this is what I mean about real life,' he said, exasperated. 'Sorry Alice, I'm going to have to go. I don't want to but I have to sort out something I thought I had already sorted out. Bloody Antonio.' He leaned forward and kissed her gently, cupping her face gently in his hands. Then he kissed her again, more forcibly, pulling her closer.

Alice felt a warm glow encase her and her heart began to beat more quickly.

'I don't want to go,' he muttered. 'But his mother keeps ringing me. He's drunk and he's trying to drive his car back to the casino. I have to help. She's been good to me.' He stood up. 'Are you free tomorrow evening? I've got to visit the solicitors to sign the paperwork for the house then I'm celebrating.'

'Yes I'm free,' said Alice

'Great. I'll call you tomorrow,' he said, striding off towards the old town.

'Be careful of him,' said Carlos sharply, appearing out of nowhere to clear the table. 'He has a reputation.'

There it was again, thought Alice. That word. The niggle that was Marcella and Antonio raised its head. But she reminded herself that she was not in Cascais for long, so what did it matter? When she was with Luis, he made her smile.

She meandered up the hill back to the apartment, smiling at everyone and everything. Making herself a cup of ordinary tea when she got back she sighed and sat down. Aphrodite climbed onto her lap and stretched herself out on it. 'What exactly does having a "reputation" mean? I mean I know what it means but Luis doesn't seem like that to me.' Aphrodite dived off Alice's lap in pursuit of a fly. 'You're no help,' said Alice standing up and walking to the bathroom. She began to wash off her make-up, breathing on the mirror and staring at her reflection through the misty glass. 'Why do I care? Isn't this an interlude? Aren't I learning to just go with the flow and take things as they are? Real life can wait till I get home.'

'*And when will that be?*' said the reflection.

'Soon. Soon. But just leave me alone. For a little while. Please,' said Alice, turning and padding out onto the terrace, the tiles still warm underfoot. The moon hung over the sea, orange and heavy. She watched it for a long time, mesmerised, lost in thought. 'Adam didn't have a reputation, but he still turned out to be a complete bastard,' she said to Aphrodite, who had finally given up on the fly and sat purring at her feet. 'Oh bugger. I said his name. Bugger. Christ! He knows how to ruin a moment and he's not even here.'

Clumsily banging the shutters closed, Alice walked into the bedroom, wishing that Luis could somehow extricate himself from his real-life distractions, reputation or not. Then she picked up the camera, opened the shutters again and photographed the moon.

Chapter Eleven

Alice blearily awoke to see the clock on her dressing table pointing to 6.30 a.m.

'Oh early morning, how pleased I am to see you. Not. Thank you, cat.' Aphrodite nuzzled into her arm, purring loudly, bored with repeatedly jumping on and off the bed. Alice absent-mindedly checked her mobile phone. One message received at 12.30 a.m.

Are you still awake? It was Luis

Alice sat up, surprised. 'Aphrodite, why did you decide to do this now and not at 12.30? That would have been much more helpful.' The cat purred on, oblivious, as Alice replied to Luis. I wasn't. But I am now. I suppose you are asleep? She lay down and closed her eyes, not expecting a response. The phone buzzed.

Wide awake, said the message.

Her heart fluttered. The cat woke me up, she replied.

Are you dressed?

Alice's heart flipped a bit. Where was this going? No …

I've got to meet my architect at my new house. – the project. Want to come? I'm meeting him at 7.30. That's morning, not evening! I can pick you up at the hotel at 7.15.

'Strange feeling,' she muttered to Aphrodite. 'Being disappointed and not disappointed at the same time.' Okay. See you there. Pressing send she leapt out of bed and headed to the shower. Twenty-five minutes later, she ran out of the apartment, excited for her early morning date, and intrigued to see the house. Luis was waiting for her in the car with Elvis in the back and turned the engine on as soon as he saw her turn the corner. She jumped in, smiling, and he kissed her lightly on the lips. 'Sorry to be in such a rush,' he said, 'but my friend has to go to work after this and I want to get as much advice from him as I can.' Elvis barked as they drove off and nuzzled in her ear.

She laughed. 'Ah, Elvis. It's lovely to see you too!'

Luis squeezed her hand. 'And sorry I texted so late last night,' he said as he drove them up into the hills behind the coast road. 'Yesterday was quite tiring what with work and Antonio's games. When I got home I wanted to hear a friendly voice.'

'Is Antonio okay now?' asked Alice gently.

'Who knows? I know he was lying when he said his mother needed work done on her car. She didn't know anything about it.'

'Why would he do that?'

'Antonio being Antonio. Well, he's not always been like that. Just in the past couple of years.' He turned the car up a narrow track. 'Look,' he said, his voice becoming more animated. 'Just up there – my new project. My baby!'

Alice saw a tiny dilapidated old house hidden behind some olive trees, surrounded by overgrown bushes shot through with multi-coloured flowers. It looked like it needed some love, she thought.

'I used to drive past this all the time and never noticed it,' he said. 'But a guy I know was selling it – it was his grandparents' house – and he showed me the photos. And I wanted it as soon as I saw it.'

'It looks lovely, full of character,' said Alice.

'I don't know why it affected me so much. All my other projects are hard-headed business opportunities. Buy, refurbish, sell. No emotion. But this one … I wanted to save it.'

'Love at first sight,' said Alice.

Luis stopped the car and smiled at her. 'Must have been,' he said, and opened the door. 'Joel,' he said to the tall, elegant man walking towards them. 'Thanks for coming so early. This is Alice.'

'Hello Alice,' said Joel. 'Pleased to meet you. Be careful,

Luis will have you knocking down walls and painting ceilings before you know it.'

Alice laughed. 'Just my cup of tea,' she said.

'I know you've got to be quick,' said Luis. 'Shall we start?'

The heavy footsteps of Luis and Joel moved slowly around the bedrooms of the farmhouse, as Alice quietly explored the worn-out kitchen, brushing her fingers along the abandoned worktops, trying to imagine how the men were going to bring it back to life. There was something about it, she thought, a sense of warmth that probably came from all the happy families that had lived there over the years. Pushing the back door open, she stepped through the early morning light into the overgrown garden: a riot of red geraniums, white bougainvillea and yellow pansies, dark green moss dotted with tiny blue wildflowers and tall sprigs of lavender. The remnants of a vegetable patch, covered in weeds hugged a dirty white out-building at the far end of the land, and beyond it the hills tumbled down towards the sea.

Walking to the end of the garden she turned to survey the house. Luis, hair unkempt and face unshaven, was talking animatedly to Joel, both of them framed in a brown, dusty window. Alice smiled, her stomach doing the familiar loop the loop. An image of herself walking barefoot on the grass and clipping a bunch of crimson roses to take inside to a sunlit kitchen suddenly popped into her head. As it did, her phone buzzed. Another message from her sister, Tara. Adam has been to Mum and Dad's house. You have to do something. He's trying to wheedle his way in again. You need to contact him. You can't run away forever.

Alice felt a tiny knot of anger in her stomach.

The men walked into the garden, smiling. 'So,' said Joel, climbing into his car. 'Big plans. Glad you have a project to finally get your teeth into, Luis. I will send you the drawings in the next two weeks. Good to meet you Alice. Now I have to go to my work. *Ate logo.*'

'He's a busy man,' said Alice. 'Does he always do consultations this early?'

'Joel is doing me a favour. We go back a long way. He was once in the band.'

'Was he really?'

'Yes, and then he grew up and left and got a proper job,' laughed Luis, guiding Alice into the living room. 'What would you do with this space?' he asked.

'Me?' Alice looked around at the neglect and felt a stab of sadness. It was such a lovely place, with so much history, and even more potential.

'Yes, you. You mentioned you had decorated your house didn't you? You made it beautiful? I do up old houses, paint the walls white then leave.'

'But you are a painter and a photographer and—'

'Alice, I am a mere man. I need a woman's vision.'

'Oh, that's quite a compliment.'

'Yes, it is.'

'Well then,' said Alice, eager to help. 'I would – and this is at first glance – rub this wooden floor down and re-varnish it – don't put tiles in here – and I would paint the shutters blue, not green, and I would make those windows into glass doors from floor to ceiling, the entire wall, opening up onto decking, with a wooden roof or something, make an outside room and I would have voiles – with blue flecks – and big voluptuous tassels hooking them to the wall … and a couple of rugs here.' She glanced at Luis to gauge his reaction.

'Go on.' He smiled. 'What about the kitchen?'

'I would have a lovely modern kitchen, with an island in the middle, dark grey or black tiles. Or would the terracotta ones be better? It's a big space, so you could have a table at the end there – make it an open plan kitchen diner. It has such a lovely feel to it, you'd want to be true to its past. Do you know what I mean? I watch a lot of property programmes.'

'Property programmes?' asked Luis.

'Programmes where people look for their dream houses, then decide they are going to change them completely anyway ... knock down walls, build an extension, that kind of thing.'

'It'll look great when I clean it up,' said Luis, pacing around the room, scanning the walls and the floor. 'I feel so excited about it. Can't wait to get started.'

'Are you going to do that soon?'

'As soon as Joel gets the plans back to me. In the meantime I've got to get some more prints of my paintings and choose which photos to supply to the tourist shops. It all helps the finances. And a couple of gigs, unfortunately. Those I could do without.'

'Busy, busy, busy.'

'Not today. I was supposed to be finalising the paperwork with the guy who's buying the other place but he's had to fly to Madrid for urgent business. Hopefully nothing to worry about. What have you got planned?'

'A swim, a walk, and a bit of painting, so nothing really. I took a photo of the moon last night and I wondered what it would look like in watercolour.'

'Can I see?'

'I haven't got my camera with me. It's in the apartment.'

'Well,' said Luis. 'Have you had breakfast?'

'No.'

'I will take you for breakfast. Then I need to walk Elvis. He's fast asleep in the car, lazy dog! We could drive by your place and collect the camera after that?'

Alice thought of Tara's text. *Push Adam away*, she thought, *push him away*. 'Just a sec,' she said. 'Just got to respond to a text.' She looked at the phone, pictured Adam's face and deleted the message. Then she looked up at Luis. 'Sounds like a plan.' She smiled, trying to sound nonchalant. *You wouldn't know nonchalant if it knocked on your door and said hello, I'm nonchalant*, whispered the voice in her head.

But during a convivial breakfast where they discussed what colours to paint the walls, the texture of the tiles and whether stand-alone baths were a good idea, it crossed Alice's mind that she'd started to say yes to things instead of standing still and hiding. She liked it.

Luis drove them to the apartment afterwards. 'I'll turn the car around while you fetch your camera.'

'Oh, you can come up if you like,' said Alice. 'Mary won't mind. I mean she's not there, so she wouldn't know. But I live there, so people can come up and ... It's to see the photos. On the camera ...'

'I can't leave Elvis in the car. It's too hot already. Bit unusual this time of year. No wind. I mean the weather not Elvis. His wind never subsides ...' Luis trailed off. 'So, I can't come up.'

'I didn't think. Sorry,' said Alice clambering out of the car as if her life depended on getting away from Luis. Which at that moment it felt like it did. 'I'll be a couple of minutes,' she squeaked, almost sprinting to the foyer. If someone asked her to write a definition of 'acute embarrassment' for a new dictionary, she thought, this experience would definitely be used to illustrate it. 'I have no idea what I'm doing, Aphrodite,' she said to the cat, picking up the camera. 'It's been so long since any man has come near me. Really. And that's only if I count Adam as a man. Which he isn't. In my opinion. Bugger, I've said his name again.' She raced to the lift and out to the car trying to look calm. Opening the door and sitting down, she smiled very brightly. She waved the camera at Luis. 'Here it is ... I took loads of photos. Got a bit carried away actually. Do you want to see?'

He took the camera, put it on the dashboard and kissed Alice, long and lingering, his hands gently framing her face, stroking her hair then lightly touching her neck. 'So,' he whispered.

'So ...' she echoed, knowing that everything was about to change.

'These photos of the moon ...'

'Yes,'

'I have some, too ... they are in my house. Shall we go there?'

'Yes.'

Luis kissed her again. 'I really do have photos of the moon in my house,' he said turning on the ignition.

'I'm sure you do.' Alice smiled.

'I do. Really.' They drove down towards the road, Elvis stirring noisily in the back.

'So you really *do* have photos of the moon,' said Alice, looking through a box of pictures as Luis opened all the shutters, flooding light into the darkened room.

'Yep,' he said. 'They sell very well, especially the black and white ones for some reason.'

'Well, I'm going to paint mine, so that will be a bit different.'

'Yes it will, but ... follow me ...' Luis took her hand and led her upstairs. On the landing was a large painting of a big orange moon hanging over a dark sky, the lighthouse to one side, the café to another, a triangle of light on the glistening black sea.

'Wow!' exclaimed Alice. 'Genuinely, wow! I took all those photos of the orange moon last night. When did you paint this?'

'A couple of years ago. Just for me. I don't paint much now,' he said, standing behind her. 'Just walls ... white ... as you can see. No time.'

Alice felt his arms around her waist, his breath on her neck and her heart began to beat faster. She turned to him. 'I haven't ... there's been no one since ... I'm out of practice.' She sighed, exasperated with herself. 'Did I just ruin the moment?'

'No,' murmured Luis, his lips brushing her mouth. 'I have paintings in my bedroom too. Do you want to see?'

'Yes,' whispered Alice, as Luis guided her towards the bed.

'I will show you later,' he breathed into her ear, as he moved his hand gently down her neck, following the outline of her breasts to her waist.

'Alice, Alice?' whispered Luis.

'Mmmmm?' she muttered sleepily.

'It's 8 o'clock.'

Alice rolled over to him, opening her eyes slowly.

'8 o'clock …? What time did we get here?'

'About half past ten …'

'All day … really?'

'Really.'

'Well, it's been most enjoyable.'

Luis kissed her. 'Yes, *most* enjoyable.' He stood up and put on his shirt.

'Do you have to?'

'No I don't' he said, taking it off again. 'But I have wine in the fridge, plus some bread and ham, and so I must put on my trousers. Don't look at me like that, we need to eat. I need to regain some strength!'

Alice stretched lazily and climbed out of bed as he walked down the stairs. Pulling her sundress over her head she opened the doors to the terrace and stood breathing in the warm, calm evening air. In the distance was an ocean liner making its way out of Lisbon towards the Atlantic. Luis came back and stood beside her, setting the wine glasses down on a table.

'There's no breeze,' he said softly. 'Look how calm the sea is. No swell, no waves.' The ship seemed to float slowly through the sky, sailing through the stars, the sea and sky the same jet-black, the moon obscured by clouds. They stood for a while, entwined, caught up in the stillness of the night as the lights of the boat became more and more distant, finally disappearing around the headland.

'You don't have anywhere to go tonight?' asked Luis.

'Nowhere. I can message the porter and ask him to feed Aphrodite.'

'Good. Stay. Tomorrow I will take you home. We won't check our phones or e-mails until then. For now, it is just us.'

Luis handed her a glass and she sipped the wine thoughtfully. 'So, Luis, why are you so in love with that house?'

'I'm thinking of living there.'

'What and selling this?'

'Yes, eventually.'

'Oh, so you don't only buy and sell for profit?'

'Normally I do, but it's different with this one. I fell in love with it at first sight. I've never done that before. And so …'

'And so …?'

Luis kissed her again. 'Bring your wine back to bed,' he whispered.

As he took her hand again, she knew she was giving into life, for once. She didn't care about anything at that moment, about the house, about Adam, about Antonio or Marcella. Real life could wait.

'Where have you been? Why haven't you been answering my calls? I was worried sick about you.' Alice was back in her apartment, and real life, also known as Kathy, was crashing in.

'I'm fine,' said Alice, answering the buzzing of the intercom. 'No need to keep buzzing the door like that.'

'Well, I've been here for ages,' shouted Kathy, exasperated.

'Sorry, I had my headphones on. I was concentrating. I just stopped to have a drink of water.'

'Are you actually going to let me in?'

'Sorry, I forgot I had to press the button.'

'Yes, and when I come up in the lift, I have to press another buzzer, and what you have to do is this: you have to walk to the door and open it and what happens then is this: I can come in.'

'Very funny.'

'I know. Press the button. Please.'

Alice pressed the button, then opened the door and headed for the kitchen

'Very funny,' said Kathy two minutes later from the hallway.

'I know,' shouted Alice. 'You already said. Tea?'

'Mary's special recipe?'

'No. Common or garden English Breakfast.'

Kathy followed her into the kitchen. 'Must email her again to chase her up about that ... Alice ...'

'What?'

'You've got paint all over your face.'

Alice wiped her face with the back of her hand and glanced at it absently. 'Oh, yes ... orange ... I've been painting on the balcony. God, I hope I haven't got it on the furniture.'

'Looks like just the face to me, and now the hands.'

'Oh.'

'Alice,' said Kathy sharply. 'What is going on with you?'

'What?'

'I've been trying to call you for two days. And your Mum has. And your sister.'

'I've had my phone turned off.' Alice suddenly tensed. *Here it was, real life*, she thought, *it's back*. 'God what's happened? Are they alright?'

'They are okay, but Adam ... sorry He Who Shall Not Be Named ... has been back to your mum's house. Had an argument with your stepdad. And says if you don't contact him in the next two days he's getting a solicitor involved.'

'Let him,' said Alice, handing a mug of tea to Kathy. 'Let him spend his money. I don't care.'

'You've got to speak to him, Alice,' said Kathy.

'I will. When I'm ready. And obviously I'm not. I'm busy painting. I'm going to wash my hands.' Alice felt a twinge of defiance. *When I'm ready*, she thought. *Not when he's ready. Not this time.*

'Why did you turn your phone off?' asked Kathy following her to the bathroom.

'I didn't. I just forgot to turn it on again. We were just enjoying being away from all the stuff … you know …'

Kathy stood in the doorway, arms folded, grinning. '*We?*'

'Yes we. Stop smiling like that. I can see you in the mirror!'

'You're doing it too. I know you are.'

Alice turned to her friend and giggled. 'Come on,' she said, 'Let's take tea on the terrace.'

'Where did all these dust sheets come from?' asked Kathy, perching awkwardly on a chair.

'Luis brought them round when he brought me home last night. He uses them when he's painting houses. I've been doing some painting too. Luis was encouraging me.'

'He's your mentor now, is he?'

'Amongst other things, yes, and he's fulfilling the role very well, thank you very much!'

'I can see that!'

Alice sighed. 'I'd better ring my mum. Was she upset?'

'No. She loves a good fight. And your stepdad too, by the sounds of it. But Alice—'

'I know, but Kathy, I've just started to relax. I've found something … someone … for a while at least, and I'm fed up of bloody Adam upsetting me with what he wants all the damn time. It was always like that. What *he* wanted—' Alice's voice rose with a sudden anger that seemed to come from nowhere '—he wanted to buy the house, then he wanted to go freelance, and he wanted to wait a bit longer until we had children. I wasted all those years thinking he meant it, and I went along with it because I am too loyal. I'm not doing it any more.'

'Oh, Alice,' murmured Kathy. 'I hadn't thought … I didn't think.'

'And now something lovely has happened.' Alice could feel tears pricking her eyes. 'And I don't know what it is. But it's for me. At last. And he's trying to ruin it.'

'But he can make real trouble for you.'

'He already has. Ever since I've known him.' Alice studied her half-finished painting. 'I want to enjoy this, Kathy. I know I have to sort it out. But not now. It's taken me a long time to get here.'

Kathy stood up and hugged her. 'I know. And you look wonderful, you really do.'

'He doesn't know where I am does he?' asked Alice suddenly.

'No he doesn't. Let's forget about him. When are you seeing Luis again?'

'Tomorrow. He wants to take me to one of his gigs. Will you come?'

'Can't. I'm having an actual date with Stephano. It's only taken six years since we split up.'

'And I thought I was slow.'

Alice clasped Luis's hand tightly as they snaked through thick crowds of people towards the stage. 'Are they all here to see you?' she shouted above the noise.

'No,' shouted Luis. 'It's a charity gig and we're one of the supporting acts.'

'Still,' she said. 'Impressive turnout. Will Elvis be okay with the guy on the door?'

'Sure – his son will be along soon – I pay him a few euros to keep an eye on him while I'm on stage sometimes.' He turned to face her, his expression serious. 'There was a time when I loved this and everything to do with it. But not now. This isn't me any more. It was once. But it isn't now,' he whispered into her ear.

Their eyes locked together for a moment and Alice smiled. 'Okay,' she said.

'Right,' said Luis, holding her hand even more tightly. 'Let's do it.' They moved forward then halted suddenly.

'Hi Luis,' said a small attractive woman blocking their way. 'It's Susannah. Remember?'

'Hello, Susannah', he replied. 'It's good to see you again. I'm sorry, every time we meet I just seem to be passing through.'

'I know. Same at the gig I came to a couple of weeks ago. Still, nice to see you too.' There was a pause as she spotted Alice.

'This is Alice,' said Luis, still holding her hand.

Susannah nodded politely then turned back to him. 'You're looking so well, Luis. I've been thinking about you. All the old times.'

'Ah, the old times.' He smiled, glancing at the stage. 'Sorry, I really do have to go. Enjoy the gig. There are a lot of good bands on tonight.' Turning towards the stage, he squeezed Alice's hand, and continued to push forwards, up the steps and into the wings. Luis put his arm protectively around her as Antonio hurried towards them, his right eye swollen and black.

'I'm afraid I have to take Luis away from you now. He has work to do.'

'She'll watch from the wings,' said Luis firmly.

'There's not enough space,' replied Antonio.

'She's my guest.'

'I'm so sorry, Alice, is it? Luis is always bringing one woman or another backstage and I'm always having to shoo them away. You understand?'

Alice took a deep breath. It was as if he was using words instead of fists, she thought.

Luis stared hard at Antonio. 'Don't speak to her like that. If we weren't in public I'd tell you what I really think of you when you do that. And where did you get that black eye?'

Antonio touched his face and rubbed his eye. 'Damn. The make-up hasn't worked. Don't look at me like that.' He said to Luis. 'Someone wanted some money from me and I didn't have it.'

'You are a mess,' said Luis. 'And not just physically.' Luis guided Alice away from Antonio with his arm around her waist. 'What time are we on?' he shouted back, without looking at him.

Alice's stomach churned uncomfortably. She longed for the still, quiet days the two of them had just spent together.

'Half an hour. Five songs.'

'Good. Then we'll be away.'

Antonio grabbed Luis by the shoulder and tried to pull him round. 'But you have to see Marcella.'

'Why?'

'Marcella wants to see you. She organised the event. Invited us onto the bill.'

'Why does she want to see me?'

'You know why.'

'No, I don't. Now, I'm just going to see a few people and introduce them to Alice. Then I'll be here five minutes before we go on.' Pulling Alice into the darkness further backstage, he wrapped his arms around her. 'I'm so sorry. I thought this would be fun for you. He was very rude.'

'He was. Again,' she said, trying to disguise the shakiness in her voice. 'I should be able to say something rude back, but he stuns me so much, I can't find the words.'

'We'll disappear straight afterwards, I promise. Then it will be just us. If it wasn't a charity gig I'd walk out now.' He kissed her and held her hand. 'Come on. There are some very nice people here who will be more than pleased to meet you.'

They pushed back through the crowd and found Joel the architect with his wife. 'A-ha, Alice,' he said. 'Lydia – this is the woman who Luis is going to sneakily get to help him with that old house I told you about!'

Alice laughed. 'Oh, I love bringing houses back to life. Although I think he only asked my advice.'

'Just watch him,' said Lydia, smiling. 'He's very persuasive.'

'It's a beautiful old place though, isn't it?' said Joel. 'I'm glad you bought it. I was worried someone would buy the land and turn it into an apartment block.'

'It would be a shame to do that,' said Luis, taking out his phone. 'Look.' He began to show Lydia photographs of the house, his face intense and enthusiastic.

Alice watched him, enjoying the passion with which he was describing the project but as the singer who was performing came to the end of her set, his face began to tense. He glanced at the stage, unsmiling. 'Time to go,' he sighed. 'Lovely to see you two.' He grabbed Alice's hand again. 'Come on, we're up next!' They walked around to the back of the stage where the band were waiting to go on.

'You were nearly late,' spat Antonio.

Luis didn't say anything. He kissed Alice and followed them onto the stage. When the band began to play the man she'd seen performing at Mary's leaving party was entirely different. Then, he was lost in the music, relaxed and in the moment, but now, she could feel the tension between him and Antonio, and the animosity that seemed to have grown in only a few weeks. Luis flew off the stage barely before the applause had died down.

'Did you like it?' he whispered to Alice. 'How was it? Was it okay?'

'It was great. *You* were great.'

Pulling her to him, he kissed her lightly. Then he kissed her again, hungrily. 'Time to go,' he said.

'Are you like this every time you come off stage?' giggled Alice.

'Yes,' he said, kissing her again, as they walked towards the door.

'Luis! Where are you going?' Antonio had placed himself between them and the exit.

'Home.'

'You can't.'

'I'm going home, Antonio.'

'You were really good,' said Alice, trying to change the subject.

Antonio looked at her. 'Right,' he said dismissively. 'Marcella wants to speak to us, Luis. She has more work for us. It's important.'

'You don't need me for that,' said Luis impatiently.

'It's good manners. She has helped us.'

'Hello, Luis. You were all so good. As always.' Marcella walked confidently towards them flanked by her two giggling young friends.

'He's trying to rush away. I cannot keep him still,' said Antonio.

'Oh, what a pity,' said Marcella. 'I was hoping you could stay on for the after party.' She leaned close to Luis, her glossy hair brushing Alice's face. 'It would be fun,' she whispered. 'And my father may be coming later. He would be a good person for you to meet.'

'Marcella thinks her father may book us for some of his restaurants and bars,' interjected Antonio.

'But I'm leaving the band,' said Luis. 'I'm just helping Antonio out until he finds a new guitarist. So, you don't need me.'

'Oh!' said Marcella stepping back, surprised.

'He's said that before,' said Antonio. 'Haven't you, Luis? He never actually leaves.'

Marcella glanced at Alice as if she had only just noticed she was there, then she smiled. 'Oh, I see,' she said. 'Just a temporary phase, then. I have to go. Why did I think organising a big event like this would be easy!' She hugged Luis and flounced off, accompanied by her friends. As they got to the other side of the stage, they all glanced back and laughed.

I am in the middle of a particularly bad teenage film, said the voice in Alice's head. But she didn't find it funny.

'Once you're bored with this—' said Antonio '—you'll want the band again … she likes you, man.'

'All the more reason not to stay,' said Luis firmly. Grabbing

Alice's hand, he moved Antonio out of the way and pushed the door open, slamming it behind him. 'I am so sorry Alice. So sorry.' They stood silently for a few moments.

Say something clever or witty or acerbic, screamed the voice in Alice's head.

'That really wasn't very nice,' she said eventually, a niggling feeling creeping up on her that being involved with Luis wasn't the escape from real life she'd thought it was. But then he smiled, and kissed her, and she didn't care about any of it.

'Shall we go to the beach bar just down there?' he asked.

'Whatever you say,' said Alice, as they began to walk.

The lights in the beach bar were turned down to a dusky yellow, the quiet chatter ebbing and flowing with the sound of the waves softly rolling onto the sand.

'That's better,' said Luis, stretching his arms and moving his head around slowly. 'I come here sometimes just to be able to clear my head.' Elvis suddenly appeared and barked, padding around restlessly. 'And to walk the dog, obviously.'

'You know what just happened,' said Alice slowly. 'I didn't know how to react.'

'Neither did I,' muttered Luis.

She looked at him expectantly. 'Is Antonio always like that?' she asked eventually.

'Unpleasant and rude, you mean? Not as bad as that. There's something going on with him. I don't know what it is … I saw his ex-girlfriend in the audience at the gig. She was with some guy. Antonio developed very expensive tastes when he was with her. There's something else, but I don't know what it is.'

'There's always something. And it's always other people. And it's the same for me,' sighed Alice.

'Well, now there isn't. There's just us.' Luis leaned forward and winked.

'Alice!' Kathy and Stephano were standing in the doorway, waving.

'Now there isn't just us,' he said.

'What are you doing here?' asked Kathy as she came over and Stephano pulled up some chairs. 'I thought you were at that charity gig thing?'

'We were going to go there after our meal but the night is so beautiful, and I've seen your band too many times already, ' Stephano said and laughed.

'Did it finish early?' asked Kathy.

'No. We just decided to leave and have some time to ourselves,' said Luis.

Stephano peered dramatically into Luis's eyes. 'What have you done to him? Hypnotised him? He could never be dragged away from these things in the past.'

'That was a long time ago,' said Luis to Alice.

'Just joking, just joking,' laughed Stephano. 'I can see why he would want to spend time with you away from all of that.' He turned to Alice. 'How is your extended holiday going?'

'I'm beginning to slowly relax. But keeping myself busy.'

'Alice is a very talented artist,' said Kathy.

'Yes, I remember. I thought you'd given all that up?' said Stephano.

'I'm not really. I've just started to dabble, you know.'

'Yes, she did. And she is now again an artist... did that make sense?'

'I have been plying Kathy with expensive champagne,' said Stephano. 'I am trying to impress her.'

'Trying to!' Kathryn giggled. 'He turned up wearing a tie so tight it almost made his eyes bulge. I persuaded him to take it off.'

Stephano pulled the rolled-up tie from his pocket. 'Best place for it,' he laughed.

Elvis barked again, jumping up at Luis. 'I can't put him off any longer,' said Luis. 'He needs a walk.' Standing up, he checked his phone and sighed wearily.

'A message from Antonio,' he said to Alice. 'I'm not going

to read it. It can wait until morning. Shall we take Elvis home after his walk? And without being too forward, can we go to your apartment afterwards?'

'Alice this is ridiculous and childish. For God's sake why are you being so bloody stubborn? I know where you are and if you don't call me back I will just get on a plane. I'm running out of patience. Fast.'

Alice threw the phone onto the table. She hadn't heard Adam's voice for two years. And there it was. In that little piece of plastic. Like a malevolent genie stuck inside the voicemail. She stood up and paced around the room. His little messages had always made her feel like a trapped animal trying to get out of a cage made of his words. They would arrive without any chance of redress from her. No shouting, no questioning, no telling it to him straight. She used to picture him sitting in some bar creating the 'I'm having such a good time and you're not' postcards, as she'd used to call them. Alice knew he didn't want to know how she was, he just wanted her to know that he was doing very well, thanks. So, the only way she could deal with them was to tear up the postcards or set them alight or jump in some water. She remembered the evening she and Kathy had scattered the remnants of the last few over Tower Bridge and almost shivered with pleasure. She thought about the sea and the image of the phone flying gracefully through the air and landing with a splash in the stewing waves near the Boca do Inferno made her smile; Adam and his threats disappearing into the deep at The Mouth of Hell.

But she needed the phone. It wasn't as disposable as cardboard. It was her lifeline to her family and Kathy. And Luis. Alice smiled to herself as she thought about him. He had left hurriedly that morning, kissing her forehead when she was half asleep, muttering something about Antonio and his mother and real trouble this time. 'Why when I am trying to escape does real life come a knocking?' she said to the phone. Then she stood up and shouted at it. 'And how does Adam know my new number anyway?' It was obviously her sister who had given it to him, so she phoned her. 'I told you not to give my number to Adam. For God's sake, Tara.' Alice paced around the living room.

'He was upsetting Mum and Dad. They wouldn't tell you. They didn't want to worry you. You can't just clear off to another country and expect everyone to deal with your rubbish.'

'My rubbish? You know what he's done to me. Have I ever asked you to do anything like this before? Have I? No.'

'If he gets a solicitor involved it'll get Mum and Dad more stressed. For God's sake Alice, why can't you just speak to him?'

'You don't understand. Nobody understands me.' The tears began to fall, staining her face.

'For Christ's sake, stop wailing. You sound like you did when you were fourteen.'

'He wants to take my house away from me.'

'If you spoke to him you could come to some arrangement. You can't hide forever.'

Alice paused by the window and looked out onto the terrace at her drying paintings. She took a deep breath and the tears began to subside. 'But I want to hide for just a bit longer,' she said quietly. 'I'm frightened. You know what he's like. He's always managed to walk all over me. I'm scared I'll let it happen again.'

Tara sighed. 'Oh Alice. You won't. Not this time. You've only been away for a few weeks and you sound different already. More like you than you've been for years.'

'Does he know where I am?'

'He knows you're in Portugal. Near Lisbon. That's it.'

'He said he'd get on a plane and come to see me.'

Tara laughed humourlessly. 'Well he must have become psychic. Maybe that potter girlfriend of his is mystical or something.'

'His girlfriend is a potter?'

'Yes. Apparently. They're setting up some venture together in Cheam. Arty thing ...'

It felt like a blow to the head. Alice sat down, a sick feeling in her stomach, a sudden pressure on her temples. 'He wants to sell my house to help her, doesn't he?'

'God, I hadn't thought of that.'

'He always laughed at me ...'

'Alice ...'

'I've got to go.'

She put the phone down and somehow managed to clamber into bed, suddenly exhausted.

Alice woke up, sweating, to a half-dreamt image of herself pushing the real world of problems and rain and Adam away with her two outstretched arms and standing in a beam of light with Luis and Aphrodite and her painting of the moon. She could hear a strange metallic buzzing interspersed by a weird yowling noise in the distance. For a moment she couldn't remember where she was. The room was all wrong. It was white and silver with smatterings of pink. Her bedroom was dusky green and cream and gold and the window was opposite the bed, not to the right. And there was no door to a terrace. Because she didn't have a terrace. The buzzing stopped, but the cat-like noise continued. Alice rolled out of bed, reality slowly seeping into the daylight.

'I'm in Portugal,' she said. 'And that noise is coming from Aphrodite, my cat.' Standing up she padded to the kitchen. Aphrodite was on her hind legs peering into the toaster. At this point Alice achieved full consciousness. 'Please, please, please, please, please don't let there be a gecko in there,' she screeched, slightly panicked, realising she would have to look inside to check. *How did you get a gecko out of a toaster?* The buzzer went again. And again. Alice leaned against the wall and pressed the intercom.

'It's me. Tara phoned. I'm coming up. I've got a remedy.' Kathy's voice was sharp and frantic, and as she let her in Alice imagined her careering into the lift and bouncing off the wall.

'Where's the gecko?' Alice took the steaming hot tea from Kathy and sat down, finally feeling almost human after a very hot shower and some slow, deep breathing.

'No idea. Aphrodite is still guarding the toaster,' said Kathy. 'I need to sort it.'

'Forget about that. Neither the cat or the gecko – if there is one in there – are going anywhere for a while, and we can get the porter to sort it. He likes a challenge. You need to sort you first.'

Alice sipped the tea. 'This is lovely,' she said. 'Tastes a bit different to the last lot, though.'

'It does, doesn't it? Maybe because it's fresh? Got the magic potion directions from Mary herself.' They sat in silence for a few moments. 'She sends her love, by the way. Currently in Thailand. I told her all was well. I was lying obviously.'

Alice sighed. 'So Tara told you everything?'

'Yes, she did. She's right. You can't hide forever, Alice. Did you respond to the message?'

'No. I deleted the voicemail and the number.'

'Well, he'll be in touch again.'

'This girlfriend … why is he helping her when all he did was take from me?'

'Don't think about that,' said Kathy. She picked up her phone and began tapping away angrily. 'Time to get some information so you can start to fight back. Drink some more tea.'

Alice watched her friend and tried to get as angry as she was, but it wasn't there – just a sense of weariness and defeat, somehow accumulated over time without her even noticing. Until now.

'Aha!' Kathy waved the phone at her triumphantly. 'Here they are, look.'

Alice took it and read the Facebook page she had found.

'VeroniqueCeramics: The Flavour of South America. Argentinian ceramic artist and potter, Veronique Longbottom and partner, travel-writer Adam Kennedy launch new online art supermarket with a studio and shop to be open soon.' Alice read it out loud, glancing up at Kathy to see her reaction.

'Bastard,' spat Kathy, drinking more tea.

'There are photos of some of her bowls and stuff,' said Alice.

'Not interested,' said Kathy. 'Where's your camera? Can I look at all these photos you've been taking?'

Alice looked at her.

'Time to take a stand,' said Kathy. They both peered at the canvas on the terrace. 'That's beautiful, but too big for today.'

'I've downloaded my photos onto the computer,' said Alice, picking up on the sudden excitement in Kathy's voice.

'Are they ready to print?'

'Not all of them.'

'Can you pick out six of the best?'

'Yes, but why?'

Kathy picked up her phone. 'Just a sec, I've got a friend that runs a print shop, I'll see if he can help us out urgently.

'I'll put the kettle on,' said Alice. 'We need more tea.'

Chapter Twelve

'Come on, I'll introduce you,' said Kathy, walking into the shop. 'I know the owner. It's fine. It'll be easy.'

Alice wavered, pausing outside, clutching her freshly bought portfolio holder, containing a selection of her photographic prints which Kathy's friend had produced free and on the spot.

'Alice.' Kathy walked back out towards her. 'She's lovely, but I can't sell these for you. You have to be confident.'

'Sorry,' said Alice. 'But three hours ago we were having a cup of tea, now suddenly I'm here to sell photographs. I forgot what you were like. Although, that tea has relaxed me a bit, I think.' Then she found herself giggling.

'I think you forgot what you were like,' said Kathy, putting her arm around her friend and guiding her into the shop, 'And hurrah for the relaxing tea – goodness knows what you'd be like if you hadn't had a few brews. And stop giggling,' she said, giggling too. 'Now, into action!'

Alice scanned the room to get her bearings. On the walls were a mixture of modern paintings and large photographic prints of cities around the world. Her heart began to beat a little too fast as she tried to visualise one of her works on the wall next to a spectacular view of Funchal and a cityscape of Barcelona. *Not good enough, I'm not good enough*, she thought, and began to back out of the door.

'Kathy,' said the woman behind the counter. 'How lovely to see you.'

'It's been ages, hasn't it, Farrah? Time goes so quickly and you suddenly realise it's been months since you've seen anyone. I'd like to introduce you to my friend Alice … wait, where are you going Alice?'

Alice paused, realising reluctantly that there was no escape.

Kathy was on a mission again, and she was bringing Alice with her. 'Thought I heard something, sorry. Nice to meet you.'

'Nice to meet you too,' said Farrah.

'Alice is a very talented artist and photographer from London. She's staying here for a while and has been taking some wonderful photos. I suggested she show them to you, as you have a great eye.'

'I'm always looking for new artists,' said Farrah. 'Can I look?'

This is it, thought Alice. *Judgement*. 'Of course,' she said, her heart beating even faster. She unzipped the case and lay the prints slowly out on the counter. Farrah picked them up one by one, her face serious and intense. Alice shuffled nervously as Kathy checked her phone.

'The area is so beautiful,' said Alice eventually, 'I just felt I needed to capture as much as I could. I've just been doing it for me to be honest, but Kathy said I should show them to you.'

'She's right,' said Farrah looking at Alice and smiling widely. 'They really are very, very striking. I love the way you have digitised some of them to keep scatterings of colour. Particularly the ones of the gardens and the lighthouse.'

'Oh, thank you,' said Alice, beaming back, eyes wide, supressing a sudden sob of happiness. 'You like them?'

'Yes, I do,' said Farrah.

'I told you so,' said Kathy.

'Can you get me two of each of these?' Farrah asked. 'We'll see how they go. Sale or return. Let's discuss terms, shall we? Cash in hand, of course. For the first few anyway.'

Alice stared at her in silence for a moment. 'Really?'

Farrah laughed. 'Of course. I have no doubt they will sell.'

Then Alice began to cry. And laugh. She wanted to jump up and down for joy, but Kathy had hugged her in a vice-like grip and she couldn't move.

Following the success in the first shop, Kathy had dragged Alice to two more in the centre of town, both of which had taken the photos and asked for them to be delivered to them at the end of the week.

'That's how you do it,' said Kathy. 'You are now officially an artist again. And by the way, Alice Dorothy Matthews, they took them because they were good, not because they knew me. I know what you're like – you'll start deconstructing it and deciding they did it as a favour to me. They didn't. They have businesses to run. And they don't stock rubbish. And here endeth my speech.'

They sat down at a café and celebrated Alice's new status with one glass of wine each.

'Thank you, thank you, thank you,' said Alice, 'but I'm not sure I could have done it without the calming effects of those cups of tea.'

'You did try to bolt at one point,' said Kathy.

'Imagine what I'd have been like without it. I probably would have run and jumped in the marina when Farrah said she liked the prints.'

'Or you would have grabbed hold of the door frame and not let go!'

The giggling started again and carried on for the next half an hour.

'Are you alright?' Kathy asked after they paid the bill. 'My stomach's a bit iffy all of a sudden.'

'I'm alright,' said Alice.

'God. I think I'd better go.' Kathy stood up unsteadily. 'Good day, though. Wasn't it? Are you fine to get home?'

'Yes. Yes. Yes.' Alice smiled and felt as if she was floating calmly an inch above the pavement.

'Right. I'm going that way.' Kathy hugged her and walked swiftly towards the taxi rank.

'Which way shall I go?' muttered Alice. 'Left towards Estoril, or right towards the square, or behind me to the supermarket, or straight ahead to the sea. After all, the world is my oyster.' She chuckled to herself for no particular reason and leaned against the wall. The sea looked particularly blue today. And the sky was shinier. 'And the boats in the bay are much bouncier,' she said to herself, 'or floatier.'

A couple walking past glanced at her and smiled.

'Oh dear, said that out loud,' she said out loud, then sat down, realising that she was feeling a bit light-headed. And a little bit happy. That wine must have been strong, she thought. Or it could have been the tea. What had Kathy put in it? Coffee, she suddenly thought. That's what she needed. And then she would walk home and begin her new life as an artist. *Olive oil*, said the voice in her head, which also seemed to be affected by the tea. *You need olive oil. You've run out of olive oil. For cooking.* So she glided into a tiny supermarket off Rua Frederico Arouco and picked up a bottle of olive oil. And some wine. Why not? And those oranges looked nice. She tried to pick up two of those. But as she did so, the bottle of oil slid slowly out of her hands and smashed onto the floor. Alice stared at the liquid seeping slowly from the shattered bottle along the aisle.

Oh dear.

'What have you done? Why did you not use a basket?' the owner hurried towards her, brush in hand. 'Move, move,' he shouted.

'I'm so sorry,' said Alice. 'I don't know what I was thinking.'

'Nothing. You were thinking nothing,' said the owner sharply, trying to clear up the mess.

A woman, possibly the owner's wife, came over and took the wine and oranges from Alice. 'Come,' she said kindly. 'Pay for these and we will clean up your feet. There is oil all over them. You can't walk like that. You will slip.'

'I'm so sorry,' muttered Alice again.

'He has seen worse,' said the wife. 'Do not worry about him. Come.'

Alice found herself outside watching the woman squeeze washing up liquid onto her feet and spray them with the hose used to clean out used bottles of beer. 'You are so kind,' said Alice. 'I feel so silly.'

'It could happen to anyone.'

I don't think so, thought Alice. Carefully walking to the square, she was aware of tiny bubbles puffing from her flip-flops every time she took a step. And then there was the oil that had not quite been washed away; it was more like sliding than walking. She sat down, slumping her head onto the table, laughing uncontrollably. A cup of coffee was soon placed gently on the table.

'Perhaps drinking at lunchtime doesn't suit you?' said Carlos.

She looked up, startled. 'I think it was the tea, Carlos,' she said.

'Of course it was,' he replied.

'No, really.' She giggled. 'And look at this.' She stamped her feet on the floor to make more bubbles escape.

Carlos smiled.

'Olive oil,' she said solemnly. 'And washing up liquid.' Then she giggled again.

'What have you done?' Ignacio had materialised beside her. 'I saw you crossing the road. You looked a bit ill, like you couldn't walk properly.'

'I dropped olive oil. On my feet.' She stamped them again to show Ignacio the bubbles.

'I will take you home,' he said brusquely. 'Perhaps you should not drink so much at lunchtime.'

'I have had one glass of wine only,' she shouted. 'Sorry, I didn't mean to shout.'

'Well, something else then,' said Ignacio.

'No, I haven't, actually. Don't you think the bubbles are funny?'

Ignacio looked like he was trying not to smile. 'No.'

Alice sighed. 'Okay, you're right. A lift home would be most welcome. I don't know if I could walk uphill on extra virgin olive oil coated flip-flops.' Standing up inelegantly, her bag swept her empty cup onto the floor.

'Don't worry, don't worry,' said Carlos. 'Just get home safely.'

Following Ignacio mutely towards the road she noted three young women glaring at her from another table. 'Do I know them?' she asked him loudly.

'I do not know, Alice,' he said, putting a protective hand on her shoulder.

She didn't realise it was Marcella and her friends until she fell into the back of the car.

'Are you sure you have time to do this?' asked Luis as they drove up to the farmhouse the following day. 'If you have to get the photos ready to be printed professionally for the shops, shouldn't you be doing that?'

'It's okay,' said Alice. 'I went into town first thing this morning to put the orders in. Amazingly I had an excellent night's sleep last night and woke up as fresh as a daisy at six a.m.!'

'Ahh, Mary's tea.' Luis laughed

'Never again. Never, ever again,' groaned Alice. 'I dread to think what I must have looked like with those bubbles pouring out of my flip-flops.'

'I wish I'd seen it,' said Luis.

'I'm glad you didn't,' laughed Alice. They drove in silence for a while, Alice's mind darting between the excitement of selling her prints and the pain caused by Adam's behaviour. No matter how hard she tried to push it to the back of her mind, she felt betrayed.

'You may not be happy about this,' said Luis eventually. 'But Antonio is going to be at the house. He's helping out today with the heavy work.'

'Good news,' sighed Alice. 'I'll just keep out of his way.'

'It's the money. He's been gambling. His mother's worried sick. I'm paying him to help – I'm doing it for her,' he said.

Alice squeezed his hand. 'Well that's what friends are for,' she said.

'And here he is. Mr Happy,' said Luis, as they drove up towards the house.

Antonio was pacing back and forth, smoking a cigarette and rubbing his temples. As the car parked up he turned towards them and stood, staring at Alice. 'What's she doing here?' he hissed, as they got out of the car.

'Alice is going to help with the house. She has a lot of experience. And a good eye for detail,' said Luis.

'She's a woman. What could she know about construction?' scoffed Antonio.

'Do you want to earn a day's wages, or do you want to walk to the road and catch a bus home?' said Luis angrily. 'I'm helping you out of loyalty to your mother, for no other reason.'

Antonio walked into the house in silence and Alice and Luis followed.

'I'll start on the bathroom,' said Alice, hurrying to get away from the anger she could feel from Antonio. As she did, he picked up a hammer and smashed it into one of the kitchen cupboards, then smashed it again. And again. Alice could feel the walls vibrate.

'That's a much better way to deal with your anger issues,' said Luis. 'Now, I need you to get everything in here off the walls and into the skip.'

'Yes sir,' muttered Antonio, swinging the hammer at a worktop and bringing it down with a crash.

Alice began to work, prising the tiles from the wall, focusing her energy on that rather than the muddle in her mind.

Luis appeared at the door. 'Are you okay?' he asked. 'I'm sorry about him. He's even worse than usual. If I'd have known, I wouldn't have asked you to help.'

'I'm okay,' she said quietly.

'No you're not.' Luis began to work on the other wall.

'Well Antonio is the least of my problems at the moment, but his attitude is very unpleasant,' Alice said, dropping a broken tile onto the floor. She dropped another tile and watched it bounce. 'That was supposed to shatter into hundreds of little shards,' she said.

'I thought you'd be happy about selling your photographs.' He wrapped his arms around her and kissed her. 'I'm very impressed.'

'So am I. Thank you.'

'So what is it then?'

Alice sighed. 'The past. Adam left a message on my voicemail. And now I know why he wants to sell the house.'

'Why?'

'To help him and his new girlfriend set up a ceramics business.'

'Oh.'

'Oh. Indeed.'

'Did you speak to him?'

'Of course not. I'm so angry. All the love I put into that house. And the money. When I was doing my sensible job to pay the mortgage, bringing it back to life and making it beautiful, it saved my sanity. And when he went, it was ... it was ... I hid in it. It made me feel safe ... and now he wants to take it and use it to help someone else. Someone else ... when ... it's not hers to have. Or his.' Tears began to prick her eyes.

Luis held her tighter. 'Oh, Alice. Bricks and mortar. They can't protect you from everything, can they? They can protect you from the wind and the rain and the cold, but they can't protect you from your emotions.'

'That was very profound.' Alice sniffed into his shoulder.

'Thank you. I thought so.'

'I'm not finished though.'

'Okay, carry on.'

'And now I'm here, and I feel good and safe and it's making

me better, and now he's leaving me messages. I don't even want to hear his voice here, let alone have him here. It feels like he's invading. Even talking to him feels like giving in.'

'Look. I'm here. I'll support you. You are not on your own.'

'Well he can stew in it a bit more as far as I'm concerned.'

'Whenever you are ready to talk to him, do it. I'm here.' Luis kissed her again.

'Hey,' said Antonio from the doorway. 'Some of those worktops are difficult to move, I could do with some help.'

'Okay, okay.' Luis gave Alice one more kiss on the top of her head and followed Antonio down to the kitchen.

As Alice began to pull the tiles off she heard their voices drifting into the room.

'Cosy, you and her,' said Antonio.

'Yep,' grunted Luis. 'This sink is heavier than I expected. Let's get it through the doorway into the garden and put it over there.'

'How long is she staying here for?'

'I don't know. Let's put it here.' There was a pause. 'I'll take it to the hardware shop later. It's in good shape, should get some money for it.'

'So she's a tourist?'

'Antonio, I think you should listen to yourself.'

'I know things.'

Luis walked back into the house.

'She was in the square yesterday afternoon. Drunk or drugged. Knocking things over. Shouting. Marcella was there, she sent me a message.' Alice could hear the sneer in Antonio's voice.

'Instead of telling tales about someone you hardly know, shouldn't you be thinking about paying off your gambling debts and getting your life sorted out?' replied Luis. 'You sound like a twelve-year-old girl.'

Alice stood up, shocked that anyone could be that interested in what she was doing. And angry that they'd decided to gossip about it.

'I heard all that,' said Alice as Luis climbed the stairs.

'Don't worry about it,' he said rubbing her back.

'What on earth are those silly little girls doing spying on me and spreading rumours?'

'You've got it. They are silly girls.'

Alice glanced out of the window at Antonio. 'And what's a grown man doing behaving like that for goodness sake?'

'He has a lot of stress,' sighed Luis. 'But that's no excuse. If it's any help, he's like this to a lot of people at the moment, not just you.'

'Well, I'm going to say something,' she said, walking towards the door. 'I'm hardly a drunk or a drug addict, but he and those nitwits have been around on the two occasions I have actually relaxed and let my hair down just a bit. And they won't even let me have that.' Fury and frustration took hold of her and she had to fight away tears again.

Luis grabbed her gently. 'Don't. You don't need to get involved with this. For me. Please.'

Alice looked out the window at Antonio. 'Well, for you. Just for you.'

Luis smiled, obviously relieved. 'Well,' he said. 'Big day for you tomorrow. Picking up your pictures to deliver for sale.'

Alice prised another tile off the wall and forced a grin. 'Yes, that's me. An artist.'

'Luis! Help me with this!' shouted Antonio from downstairs again.

Luis sighed, then blew Alice a kiss. 'Here I go again,' he said, backing out of the room and smiling until he turned and walked down the stairs.

She looked at the wall and her mind drifted back to the last time she was chipping at an old tile stuck fast to the bathroom wall of her house. A pang of guilt guided her hand to her bag to look for her phone. She sat on the floor and clicked onto the photographs she had taken the day she left. The living room looked warm and inviting and safe. In her mind's eye she saw Adam standing on a ladder just after they had moved in – he was painting the ceiling in broad, clumsy strokes with a roller which was dripping onto the wooden floor instead of the dust covers. She had giggled. *'Careful you're putting more paint under the ceiling rather than on it!'* He had looked at her menacingly and pretended to tip the paint bucket over. *'I'll paint you in a minute,'* he'd said. And then he'd laughed. Alice leaned against the wall and felt empty. It felt like another life that had happened to someone else. Because the man she had been with for so many years couldn't really be trying to take the thing she loved the most to give it to someone else, could he?

Well, sadly yes. Yes, he could.

'Concentrate on the good stuff. Concentrate …' Alice stood on the balcony and stretched her arms wide. Closing her eyes she breathed in the warm, fresh air and smiled.

'Is that the sweet gentle aroma of jasmine?' she said to herself. 'And can I hear the gentle rustle of the trees swaying in the breeze? Yes, I believe I can.'

Aphrodite brushed around her feet, purring. *This is nice*, Alice thought, picking her up and stroking her ears. 'I am an actual artist,' she said. Aphrodite nuzzled her head into Alice's arm. 'I thought you'd be impressed.' Closing the shutters, Alice put on her sandals, picked up her bag and opened the door. *Although*, said the voice in her head. *Don't forget Adam and his girlfriend with the moustache.*

'Focus, focus,' muttered Alice out loud. 'What do I have to do today? Pick up the prints. Bring them back here. Sort them out, and then deliver them.'

He could find out where you are, you know? It's not that difficult, said the voice.

'Think I'll get a cab back with them. I'll text Ignacio.'

You can't hide forever.

'I think I'll get him to take me back into town afterwards, too, to deliver them. Precious cargo after all.'

And now you've got Antonio and those girls talking about you for some reason.

'Wonder if Kathy is feeling better. Maybe she can meet me on the last delivery and we can celebrate.'

You've got to do something. It's not going to just go away.

'Bugger off!' shouted Alice. And she slammed the door behind her.

How do I get rid of all that negative energy in the apartment? she thought, pressing the button for the lift. *Or is it negative energy in my head?* She took out her phone and called Kathy. 'Hi. It's the big day today. Do you want to come and help? We can celebrate afterwards ... well, you do sound terrible ... is it a sickness thing? ... have you been to the doctor? ... no, you really should go ... I felt a bit wobbly but I put it down to a mixture of tea and wine! I was okay within twenty-four hours. Are you sure you're up to it? Okay, I'll see you there.' She put the phone back into her bag. 'Don't you even dare,' she said to the voice in her head as she walked through the foyer towards the doors. 'I'm going to the printers to collect my photographs, so just leave me alone.'

As Alice walked down to the harbour and through the town, she could feel herself smiling. She had taken a small step towards something new, and it felt exciting. Turning the corner to the shop, she saw Luis standing in the doorway.

'Surprise!' he said, gathering Alice up in his arms. 'I thought as it's such a big day, we – that is myself and my dog – should be here outside the printers to mark it.' Elvis barked and jumped up at Alice excitedly.

'What a lovely idea.' Alice smiled. 'That's so sweet.'

'And ...' Luis presented a large pair of scissors to her.

'Oh, that's useful ... thanks!'

'Go on,' he said, winking. 'Go in.'

Set down in front of the counter were two boxes full of her prints. In front of it were two wooden chairs one foot apart linked by a bright pink ribbon tied in a bow. The manager stood behind the counter smiling widely and turned on some music.

'Is that Wagner he's playing?' asked Alice quietly.

'It's to give a sense of occasion. Now go on.' Luis laughed.

'I now pronounce that I Alice Dorothy Matthews am officially an actual artist.' Cutting the ribbon to enthusiastic applause from Luis and the manager, Alice paused, suddenly overwhelmed with emotions that felt as if they had been bottled up for years: happiness, sadness, joy, fear, pain, love. *Love?* Tears arrived out of nowhere and poured down her face.

'What's the matter?' asked Luis. 'I thought you'd be happy.'

'I am,' said Alice 'I am so happy, this is the kindest thing … really this is.' She buried her head into his shirt and sobbed. 'I never thought,' she gulped. 'I'd given up hope that this could—'

'It's okay,' said Luis softly, stroking her hair.

'I'm so happy,' she muttered into his chest. 'But I've got your shirt wet.'

'Madam,' the manager was next to her, holding a handkerchief. 'Please, do not cry.'

She turned her head towards him, eyes bloodshot, nose red. 'Thank you so much for doing this.'

'Alice. What's wrong?' Kathy was standing in the doorway, leaning limply on Stephano.

'Luis and the manager tied a ribbon to the chairs and I cut it with scissors like I was the Queen,' she said, quietly.

'Oh, what a lovely thing to do,' said Kathy.

Alice pulled herself away from Luis and looked properly at her friend. 'Oh my God, you look terrible.'

'Thank you. Believe me, I looked a lot worse half an hour ago,' sighed Kathy.

'What the hell was in Mary's tea?' muttered Stephano.

'Stephano will drive us back to yours with your prints,' said Kathy faintly. 'Sorry, I didn't know you'd be here, Luis.'

'It's okay. I have to go to see my solicitor – in ten minutes. Kathy, they're right, you look terrible.'

'You need to see a doctor,' said Alice firmly.

'I will, I will. If it's no better tomorrow.'

'I have to go,' said Luis. 'Good luck today. Do you want to come to the house tomorrow? I'll be pulling up the floor.'

'You old romantic,' said Kathy.

'I will if it's just you and me,' said Alice.

'It's just us tomorrow. And Elvis, of course.'

'How could I say no? *Ate amanha* ... that's tomorrow isn't it?'

'And almost fluent in Portuguese, too.' Luis laughed, kissing her. 'I'll text when I'm on my way. *Adieus*.'

Sitting on the floor of the apartment, legs crossed, Alice began to sort through the boxes of prints.

'Look at you,' said Kathy, munching through breadsticks that Stephano was handing to her one after the other from a large box. 'Totally engrossed in what you're doing.'

'Well, it's my job. It's my actual job. You look a lot better.'

'I feel better thanks. Think the worst is over.'

'Ordinary tea from now on, I feel.'

'Yes, probably best to put Mary's on the back burner until she returns.'

'Pity.'

'They look great,' said Stephano. 'Excellent. And that one ... may I?'

'Which one?'

'The one with the flowers in the wood.'

'Ah, the one at Sintra.' Alice handed it to him.

'The colours are beautiful,' he said.

'Thank you. That was the first time Luis took me out to photograph things. We had a picnic. I'm going to do a painted version, too. I love the colours so much. And look ...' Alice stood up and walked into the spare bedroom. 'My painting of the pool,' she said, 'I've displayed it on the dressing table.'

'Wow! That's fantastic. I'm so proud of you.'

Stephano picked up his car keys from the table. 'Sorry

ladies, but I have to go. Meeting with a client. Well done, Alice.' He kissed her on the cheek.

'Thank you,' she said, glowing inside.

'Okay, well I've got to go too,' said Kathy. 'I'm feeling a bit better, so I can do my late shift at work. How are you going to get the photos to the craft shops?'

'I'll get a cab. I'll call Ignacio, see if he can do it.'

'Great. Well, see you in a couple of days. And don't forget. We must sort out your birthday celebrations. Only just over three weeks to go.'

'Oh God. Do we have to?'

'You are not hiding. It's your birthday. It's going to be good. And you may need to buy another packet of breadsticks. I seem to have finished the box.'

As Alice saw Kathy out, she heard her phone ring then stop. Walking to the table, she took it out of her bag and looked at the number. She didn't recognise it. Thinking it was a wrong number she put it down, but then it buzzed again, with a voicemail. Puzzled, she started to listen.

'I knew you'd block my number, so I thought I'd try again with another one.'

Alice felt sick again. It was Adam. His voice was calm and measured, but the words were like knives.

'Alice, we can sort this out amicably. I know you're attached to that house like it was a person, but my dear, I don't know how you're managing now you've been made redundant. I mean, the pennies must be reducing every day you're not working. What are you using to pay the mortgage and the bills? It's in both our interests to sell. Now come on, you don't want to lose everything in a fight with me, do you? I remember how you used to talk about how you were evicted when you were a girl. Don't want to go back there, do you? Unblock my number and give me a call.'

She threw the phone on the sofa and stared at it, her heart pumping. This time she wasn't floored, she was angry. He knew exactly what to say, and he knew what she would do next. She hated herself almost as much as she hated him as she picked up a pen and pad, grabbed her phone and logged onto her bank account.

There it was, the proof that she hadn't been paid for six weeks. She knew it, and she'd planned it, but seeing the gap on the fifteenth where her salary should have been still made her panic. She scrolled down to the beginning of the previous month and carefully made a note of her outgoings and added them up. Then she double-checked how much money she had put in for the next couple of months from her redundancy package. Her breathing began to steady as she also checked the email confirming how much her redundancy was. *Plenty*, she thought, *plenty more for at least ten months*. But not much more. Not forever. Her heart rate picked up again. She knew at that moment she had to do something to make her feel she wasn't just floating. She had to feel some forward momentum. So, she found the contact details of an ex-colleague who had set up a consultancy, took a deep breath, and sent her an e-mail asking if she had any work going.

Alice felt sick, because at the moment the e-mail was sent, she knew with absolute clarity that she didn't want that life any more. But she also understood that financial security was what had kept her sane for the past few years. And the cocoon of the house.

She stood up and closed the shutters to the balcony. Alice despised Adam more than ever at that moment, because he knew how to push those weak, sad buttons. Then Aphrodite knocked one of her photos onto the floor, and as Alice picked it up, she gritted her teeth, and almost physically pushed away those past ten panicked minutes. He wasn't going to ruin this, and she wouldn't let him bully her. Slowly packing the prints she needed to deliver, she finally strode out of the apartment to Ignacio's waiting cab, feeling determined.

* * *

Ignacio stopped his car outside the shop in the marina.

Alice didn't move. This was it, a step forward, away from Adam. But what if no-one wanted to buy anything? she wondered. How would she feel?

'Do you want me to help you with the box of prints?'

But how would she feel if someone *did* buy one of her prints?

'Alice?'

She glanced out of the window and saw a couple walk through the door; her eyes followed them as they stood pointing and talking about one of the pictures on the wall.

Ignacio sighed and got out of the car. He opened the boot and took one of the boxes.

Opening her door he held the box in front of her. 'Alice,' he said. 'This is a very good thing, isn't it?'

She smiled and relaxed. 'This is what I've wanted all my life, Ignacio,' she said.

'Well, it's time to have your dream come true,' he said.

'At least I will have tried,' she said, stepping out and taking the box.

'And you will succeed,' said Ignacio. 'Now I think you should go in.'

Alice took a deep breath, smiled and strode towards Farrah.

'Alice! How are you?' she said. 'Thank you for these.'

Alice handed over the prints. 'I'm fine. Very excited to be honest'

'I'm glad. That shows passion and commitment.'

The couple waved at Farrah to get her attention.

'I have to go,' said Farrah. 'I'll be in touch.'

'Lovely,' said Alice and walked out to Ignacio who was standing by the car.

'First one done!' she said.

'Congratulations!' He laughed. 'And now to the next one?'

In her mind's eye, Alice saw herself sticking two fingers up at Adam, and she smiled.

Chapter Thirteen

'I forgot to show you the plans for the house. I got sent them last week.' Luis sat on the terrace step and spread out the paper whilst Elvis lay down in the shade. 'I want it to be light and airy. Not all dark wood and shade like it is now. That's how they built them years ago. I know it's like that to keep you cool from the sun and the heat, but we can just pull the shutters closed and that would do the trick.'

'So you are building a terrace on the first floor?' asked Alice.

'Yes, just at the front. It will be beautiful. We are going to have to do some structural changes on the ground floor and build pillars, creating a terrace on the ground floor too.'

'Ah, if you're in that bedroom, you can waft out and gaze at the sea. Or the mountains.'

Luis smiled at her. 'Wafting … that was top of my list.'

'I do like to waft out onto the balcony at home, I mean at Mary and Frank's home … you know what I mean.'

'Yes. And I know you do …'

'This is very exciting. I did a lot to my house in London. But it was more organic, really. One room at a time, then deciding how to decorate it. Although my step-father is a builder, and he has done a few renovations. I used to like helping him out when I was younger. I couldn't do much, but I loved seeing how everything changed.'

'So you are an expert,' said Luis, rubbing her back gently.

'Well, I can paint, and stencil, and bring a wooden floor back to life.'

'You don't mind helping, do you? I know you need to build up the photography and the painting.'

'I like helping,' she said softly. 'I was always changing something or other in my house. It was a bit of an addiction. And anyway, we get to spend time together.'

'We certainly do. Although you are quite distracting. In a very nice way.'

'Am I now …?' Alice laughed, and stood up. 'We'd better work in different rooms then!'

Luis's phone buzzed. 'No rest for the wicked,' he sighed. 'I've got to take this, sorry.'

'I'll carry on pulling the tiles off the wall in the lounge, shall I?'

'Great, thanks.'

'Yes, sir. Will do, sir.' Alice walked slowly into the house, wiggling her bottom.

Luis laughed and answered the phone.

Alice walked inside and began to prise a tile off the wall. It fell to the floor with a satisfying crack. She imagined it was Adam's head. Staring at it for a moment, an idea began to form, and she began to get drawn into it, her problems dissipating as she began to lose herself in bringing it to life.

'Well, good news and bad news,' said Luis from the door as Alice examined the patterns on the tile.

'Oh, you surprised me.' She laughed. 'I was miles away.'

'Yesterday my solicitor told me that he thought the buyer for my last house was going to pull out and I should look for another option.'

'Oh, no … is that going to be a big problem?'

'No, no. I'm sure it's not. It's not confirmed yet. I'm still hopeful. But any extra cash to help get over the glitch will help.'

'Absolutely,' said Alice.

'So the call was from the shop I supply in Sintra – the owner has asked for more photographs. But different. So that's good.'

'Yes, that's excellent.'

'And I've negotiated that he'll pay half up front rather than just a percentage on sales. So that's good.'

'That is good news. What's the bad news?'

'I've got to spend a day taking photos, then developing and mounting them. So that's a couple of days away from here.'

'Needs must,' she said.

'Although …' Luis walked outside and stood thoughtfully for a moment. 'I've got it!' he said. 'Here. It's beautiful. The view's beautiful, the garden's beautiful, the house is old and decrepit and beautiful. I'll take photographs here.'

'That's an excellent idea', said Alice. 'Um … I've got an idea, too, and a favour to ask.'

'Go ahead.'

'You see these tiles I've pulled off the wall … can I use them for a project I have in mind?'

'Of course, you can.'

'And can I do that here? I just don't want to do any harm to the apartment, and I think it might get messy …'

'Now?'

'Yes please.'

'Good, we can keep each other company. Now, back to work Miss Matthews please. Elvis, follow me.'

Alice picked up some of the tiles and carried them outside in a bag, excited at the prospect of trying something new. She emptied it onto the ground and checked what tools she had with her. 'Do you have any cement?' she said as she sorted through the pile of broken tiles on the grass.

'I'm not really at the stage of making things yet. I'm still at the pulling everything out and destroying it stage,' said Luis. 'What do you want it for?'

'I'm going to make some mosaic pictures. I'll try the adhesive I've got in my bag.'

'Adhesive in your bag?'

'It's my special "I am an artist and am prepared to 'art' at any time" bag,' said Alice. 'Stop laughing. I am being very serious.'

'I'm sure you are,' laughed Luis. He held his camera above his head. 'And this is my special, "I am a photographer and am prepared to photograph at any time camera".'

'Ha, ha. Very funny,' said Alice. 'I'm going to make some bracelets, too, with other bits of tiles. The muse is upon me. Must be this place.'

'Right,' he said, suddenly business-like. 'The light is great so I'd better get working. Don't mind me, I'll be roaming around photographing things.' He stood and stared at the horizon to the west. 'I can see some clouds coming in. So I'm going to have to work quickly. See you in a bit.'

Alice looked up to say something, but he was already striding off into the distance with Elvis close on his heels.

She sat in the morning light, cooled by a soft mountain breeze, working to a soundtrack of birdsong and the occasional buzz of a small plane flying above the beaches. For a while nothing else existed apart from the patterned shards of porcelain tiles and the shapes they made on the wood. A distant bark finally broke the spell and Alice looked up. The midday sun was high in the sky, and the breeze had dropped to nothing. A bead of sweat trickled down her back. Standing up unsteadily, she stretched and scanned the garden for Luis. The bank of rainclouds hovered close over Guincho beach.

'Think we got the best of the day,' shouted Luis.

Alice spun round to see him leaning out of an upstairs window, camera in hand. 'How long have you been up there?' she said.

'Not long. Got some great photos. How have you done?'

'I've made the first one,' she said. 'I'm going to stop now. My back is beginning to hurt.'

'Is that a tile picture of this house? It's good. I'd put it on my wall.'

'Do you think so? That's a relief. I've seen a few others in the past, so it's not exactly original, but it is original because it's mine. My interpretation.'

'I took some photos of you. I hope you don't mind.'

'Me? I'm not—'

'You are beautiful. It was as if you were part of the landscape. I couldn't help it.'

'Oh, I …'

'And now you're lost for words.'

Alice giggled. 'Mmmm,' she mumbled.

'Come. I've bought some bread and cheese for lunch. Picnic at the old table round the back. See you there!'

'So how do you feel now that you're a professional artist then?' asked Kathy as she and Alice walked slowly towards the square.

'One part of me is very excited,' said Alice. 'Another part of me knows that I can't make a living out of it and I need to start looking for work at home again. And I sort of have.' She felt strangely guilty saying it.

Kathy stopped walking and stood in front of Alice, her face serious. 'I know I keep saying you should face up to Adam, but actually I wish you could just enjoy yourself and stop worrying just for a little while, too.'

'I have been enjoying myself' sighed Alice. 'More than I've done for years. But that nagging voice always comes back. Usually after something wonderful has happened. I got some post forwarded from home today. My electricity is going up next month. That reminded me that there's no money coming in.' She decided not to mention Adam.

'Apart from your big chunk of redundancy.'

'That's true,' said Alice, starting to walk again.

'And what about Luis?' said Kathy. 'It's not just a fling is it?'

Alice looked at her. 'But that's what's it's supposed to be. It's all happening very quickly, and I can't seem to stop it. I don't want to. But I can't stay here for much longer. Life was much less confusing when it was just me hiding in my house.'

'But much less fun.'

'True. And I don't really want to go back yet. I want to live this bit for a little while longer.'

'I don't want you to go back,' said Kathy. 'It's lovely having you here.'

Alice glanced into a shop. 'There's that gorgeous dress,' she said.

'Stop pressing your face against the window. If you want to buy the dress we have to go into the shop'

'I was only admiring it. I didn't say I was going to buy it.'

Kathy held the door open and pulled Alice in.

'It's a lot of money,' she whispered. 'I'm living on my redundancy money, remember?'

'I need to remind you that you are living rent free in a wonderful apartment in Cascais,' said Kathy quietly.

'God, you know, sometimes I forget,' sighed Alice.

'Alice Dorothy Matthews. It is your thirty-eighth birthday very soon. Live a little. You'll stay until after that, won't you?'

'Of course, I will,' said Alice. 'The dress is beautiful though, isn't it?'

'You need to celebrate your life as a successful artist and buy it,' said Kathy.

Alice lightly brushed the blue silk dress and took it off the rail. Holding it up against her she danced coquettishly in front of the mirror.

'Would madam like to try it on?' The sales assistant appeared by her side.

'Yes, she would,' said Kathy. 'And shoes. Do you have any shoes that would go? And a wrap or a light jacket or something?'

'Of course,' said the assistant guiding Alice to the changing room. 'Give me a few minutes and I will come back with a selection.'

'Now. Are you feeling better, Kathy?' Alice pulled the dress over her head and wiggled it onto her body.

'Today, yes. Yesterday, no. If it comes back tomorrow I will definitely go to the doctors. I must have picked up a bug or something. It can't just be Mary's tea.'

'No. I was fine after a day—goodness me. I love this colour.'

'Come on then,' said Kathy impatiently. 'Give us a twirl.'

Alice pulled back the curtain dramatically and jumped out. 'Ta da!'

'Wow!' said Kathy. 'That so suits you. You look gorgeous.'

'I do like it. Love it actually.' Alice twirled around again.

'Ahh madam. That is stunning.' The sales assistant had reappeared with four pairs of shoes and two wraps.

'They're all lovely,' said Alice picking up each shoe in turn. 'But these are too high for me and these are too low. I love the blue silk ones and love, love, *love* these.'

She put on a pair of light blue leather sandals with tiny blue flowers on the sides.

'Perfect,' sighed Kathy.

'Excellent choice,' said the assistant.

Then Alice picked out the bright blue silk wrap with shots of silver and gold thread weaved in and put it on.

'It is from Morocco, madam,' said the assistant.

'It is spectacular,' said Kathy. 'Awww, Alice is all grown up. I'm so proud.'

Alice walked past the mirror a few times, smiling at her reflection.

'Stand still for a minute. I'm going to take a photo.' Kathy took her phone out of her pocket and pointed it at Alice.

'I'll take them. All,' said Alice. 'All of them. Happy early birthday to me.' She felt slightly giddy with the excitement of buying it all despite worrying horribly about money only half an hour before. Then she remembered last year's birthday – a slightly low-key visit to the pictures, followed by a drink with her parents. She deserved this, she definitely did.

'Just a sec,' said Kathy. 'I want to show you something. Here.' She held out the phone and showed Alice an old photo.

'That's me a few months ago isn't it?' she said. 'Gosh, I look tired and pale.'

'Well, look at this.' Kathy held up another photo. 'That's the one I just took.'

Alice's eyes widened. 'Are they both me?'

'Yes, they are. Before and after. Remember that. Remember how far you've come and how much you've changed.'

'Gosh, I thought I looked shocking today, my hair's all tangly and I forgot to put on my make-up … and dear God I *still* look better now!'

'Being here. All of this. It suits you.'

'I must have looked awful for years.'

'No you didn't, you've always looked lovely. You just look a lot better now.'

'I used to think I looked alright. No supermodel but alright. But I didn't realise I looked *that* bad!'

'Well that's a trick I won't be using again,' sighed Kathy putting the phone back in her purse.

'I'm definitely buying this outfit then,' said Alice. 'It's worth every penny.'

That evening Alice watched the sky slowly turn from blue to pink to pitch black. She had sat on the balcony immersing herself in the colours, photographing every change, Aphrodite purring at her feet. Everything she saw had become something she could create another piece of art with. She couldn't remember when it had started, but she knew it made her happy. Taking something beautiful and making it into something else that was another kind of beautiful.

'I feel like I've been dipped in colour, Aphrodite,' she said eventually. 'I have said it before and I will say it again. It's like I left my monochrome life in London and flew into a palette of paint.'

Aphrodite stood up and stretched.

'Time for food, then?'

The mosaics she had made the day before were leaning against the living room wall. Luis had suggested she approach the owner of a craft stall near the station with them. She paused for a moment, inspecting her handiwork, excited and nervous about the prospect. Luis had told her what to say and how to negotiate. Her stomach fluttered when she thought of him, and she smiled, but she remembered the problems he had with the sale of the house and wondered how he was. How he *really* was, not just what he chose to tell her.

Aphrodite mewed irritably.

'Okay, okay, food coming.'

As the cat gobbled her food hungrily, Alice stood at the door of the study, pondering the computer. Should she? Shouldn't she? She did. As it flickered into life, Alice took a deep breath and typed in Adam's name on Facebook. The name she had typed in so many times in the past couple of years with no results, was suddenly visible again. Rows of his girlfriend's pots were assembled decoratively in professional-looking photographs. And this time Alice did not feel sick. Not at all. Switching off the computer, she poured herself a glass of water and got ready for bed.

I am now an artist, Adam. Despite you, she thought, *and tomorrow I am going to sell my work without the aid of a safety net. I mean without Kathy or Luis being around to hold my hand.* But as she climbed into bed the image of Adam dropping one of her bracelets into a drawer and slamming it shut, his face full of contempt shot into her mind.

'*I know you said you'd been making these things since you were seven*,' he'd said. '*It's for little girls really, isn't it?*' Through the open bedroom door, Alice contemplated the bag of tiles on the table for a few minutes.

Then she stood up, opened her wardrobe, took out an old blue work dress she had brought to Portugal by accident, grabbed a pair of scissors from the kitchen and set to work. Four hours later, Alice had five bracelets made with smoothed out shards of tile, white and blue beads, and little scraps of her dress. Then she went back to bed, sticking another two fingers up at Adam as she did.

Ignacio opened the door of his car for her and bowed. 'Madam, please.'

Picking up her samples, Alice began to struggle into the seat.

He tutted, taking them off her and putting them in the boot.

'Are you well?' he said finally as they drove off.

'Yes I am, thank you. In fact, I'm quite excited.'

'You have recovered from whatever it was that affected you the other day?'

'What? Oh, Mary's tea ... yes, I'm fine thank you. Won't be drinking that again.'

'Tea?'

'Tea. And one glass of wine. They don't mix apparently.'

Ignacio pulled out onto the sea road and sighed.

'Is everything okay, Ignacio?' asked Alice.

'Yes, well. If you have to know. I think you should be careful about your behaviour.'

Alice felt a sudden dull ache in her stomach. 'I haven't done anything.'

'Word spreads easily here, and not everybody is friendly. Those girls ...'

'What girls .... oh *them* ... what about them?' She slumped into the seat, her heart beginning to beat faster again. *Please not today*, she thought. Not when she was fighting back and feeling hopeful. Not today. She didn't want to hear it. Not today.

'Carlos heard them talking. They are silly young women. But one of them ... her father has a lot of money and she thinks she can always get what she wants.'

'What has that got to do with me?'

'She wants your boyfriend.'

'What? He's nearly forty for goodness sake.'

'I'm just passing it on. They were not nice about you.'

'Oh.' Alice felt uneasy. 'I feel like I'm back in school.'

'I don't want to upset you. But just be careful. Luis, he—'

'—has a reputation, I know.'

They sat in silence for a while, Alice's mind turning over and over, wondering why no-one would just let her be.

'I think all that is behind him,' said Ignacio eventually. 'But sometimes people don't let go of those ideas. I think those girls haven't. She sees him as a trophy.'

Alice stared out of the window, wondering why she just couldn't have some fun without someone commenting on it.

'So, what are all these paintings and jewellery?' he asked, trying to change the mood.

Alice sat up, defiant. 'I'm going to try to get a craft stall to stock them. Luis suggested it. I've got some of my photographs in some shops at the moment.'

'That is good news, Alice.'

'I never thought in a million years I'd be doing this. I mean this time last year I was just looking ahead to years and years of the same job in the same place.'

'Well, it is Paradise,' smiled Ignacio. 'And when in Paradise …'

'Beware the Wicked Witch of the West. Or the north,' muttered Alice.

'Sorry?'

'Nothing.' She took a deep breath and smiled. 'Thanks for the warning. But today is going to be a good day!'

The car pulled up next to the beach, and Alice got out determinedly. But as she walked towards the craft stalls, her confidence began to dissolve. Hovering next to the stall that Luis had suggested she approach, she pushed herself forward, holding on to her portfolio bag containing her mosaic houses and bracelets as if it was welded to her hand.

'What could go wrong?' she asked herself. *You could get turned down. Brutally,* replied the voice in her head. 'And I could get my stuff accepted. I've got my photos on sale.' *Somewhere else*, reminded the voice in her head.

'Yes, but …' Alice looked at the floor and frowned. I used to sell my bracelets when I was at school, she thought. They are a part of me, my bracelets. Everyone used to love them. It was just Adam who seemed not to like them. But then I think by then he didn't like anything about me and I was beginning not to like anything about him. She looked at the stall again. 'I like my bracelets,' she said quietly. She stepped towards the woman who was tidying up baskets of hair grips on the other side of the stall. 'Hello,' she said.

'Hello,' said the woman. 'Are you looking for anything in particular?

Alice took out two of her ceramic mosaic houses and handed them to the woman. 'Would you be interested in stocking these? I have made them out of old tiles from a house near Guincho. You can hang them on the wall.'

The woman examined them, then turned them over to check the back. 'Good, you have put the hangers on. Not everyone does.' She ran her hand over them and held them up against the awning. 'They are very nice. I like them. I could take four to start. As I don't know you or how they will go it will be sale or return. No money up front.'

'Excellent,' said Alice, her whole body feeling like it was lighting up with pleasure. 'When would you like them by? I have several already made at home.'

'By Friday. That would be best. The woman smiled expectantly. 'You look as if you have something else for me?'

'Yes, yes, I do,' said Alice, pulling her bracelets out of the case, and placing them on the table.

'My goodness,' said the woman. 'These are beautiful, and unusual. And are these pieces of tiles?'

'Yes,' said Alice, beaming.

'How did you get them to be that smooth?'

'Secret technique,' said Alice.

Turning them over in her hand, the woman pulled on them. 'Just making sure they won't fall apart,' she said.

'They won't.' Alice smiled. 'I always make sure that the binding is strong.'

'Okay. I will have ten by Friday. Can you do that? Sale or return again?'

'Fabulous,' said Alice. 'I'm glad you like them.'

'I love them,' said the woman. 'Now, let's talk prices.'

Paddling off Fisherman's Beach again, thought Alice. But this time she was eating an ice cream. It was a strange way to celebrate, but after successfully selling her wares to the stall-holder, with a possible order for more if they went well, that's where her feet took her. They almost skipped there in fact. 'Breathe in slowly,' she said to herself. 'And breathe out.' Things had kept shifting inside her ever since she arrived. It was as if she was shedding skins. Like a snake, she thought. But she didn't like snakes so she imagined it was more like a butterfly emerging from a cocoon. *I am a butterfly*, she thought. *Maybe not quite. But almost*. Padding back onto the sand she tried once again to call Kathy and Luis. Kathy was proving very difficult to get hold of, but Luis eventually answered.

'That's great news Alice. I knew you could do it. Look, I'm going to have to go. I've got to deliver these photos to Sintra. And then I've got this gig with Antonio.'

'Oh, I thought you were giving that up.'

'I don't want to do it, believe me. But he needs help. Old loyalties ...'

'Okay, well.'

'I'll be playing the guitar whilst gritting my teeth. I'd rather be with you than be there ... I've got to go. I'll call you tomorrow.'

Alice watched her ice cream slowly melt onto her hands.

An image of Marcella flickered into her head. She tried to ignore it. Then the phone rang, and as it did, she knew instinctively it was Adam calling from yet another number. She waited until he left a voicemail, and clicked the phone to listen to it, but this time, it was with a cold, hard defiance.

'Hey Alice. Just checking in. Have you checked your bank balance yet? Come on, why not just sell the damn thing and put the money to good use? It's half of quite a lot. Call me. Soon. Or I'll start to chase you. You know I will.'

Half of quite a lot, she thought. *Half. He doesn't own half. For the amount he's put in he only owns the downstairs toilet. The rest is mine.* She sighed and began to walk up the hill, wondering how Adam and Marcella had been allowed to ruin her day. As she stepped back to avoid a group of people, a pair of patterned trousers hanging high on a clothes stall brushed her face with green, yellow, pink and orange, as if they were waving at her. She smiled. *I'm not the person you think I am*, Adam, she thought. *And you aren't going to undermine me, Marcella. I'm not going to hide.*

Picking the trousers up, she held them against her legs and laughed. She loved them, and she knew Adam would hate them. So she took some euros out of her purse and bought the most noisy clothes she had ever owned in her life.

Chapter Fourteen

As Alice walked along the path through the gardens towards her apartment, she noticed a figure sitting in the shade of a tree, leaning back against its trunk. As she got closer, she realised it was an exhausted-looking Kathy, her silk scarf lying next to her and her bag discarded about a metre away. She began to walk faster. 'Kathy, are you okay?'

Kathy looked up, her face pale and drawn. 'I think so. I thought I'd pop in to see you as I had a bit of time between appointments. Felt like some fresh air, to be honest. But I felt faint and couldn't go any further. No idea what's the matter with me. I haven't felt right for a while really.'

'Do you want me to help you up?'

'Can we just sit here?' sighed Kathy. 'I'm quite comfortable to be honest. And I've got to get back in about half an hour.'

Alice sat down next to her. 'Do you want me to get you anything?'

Kathy held up a bottle of water. 'No, thanks. All fine.'

'You do look a bit pale.'

'I know. It'll pass though. I'll be okay. What have you been up to?'

Alice reached into her bag, pulled out a bracelet and eased it onto Kathy's wrist. Her friend examined it and smiled weakly.

'You made this? A bracelet? Just like the old times.'

Alice whispered into her ear. 'I did more than that.'

'What?'

'I took my mosaic pictures down to that stall-holder by Fisherman's Beach. And she's going to stock them.'

'Fabulous! What about the bracelet?'

'She loved it. I've got to take more down as she's stocking them too! Alice "the bracelet queen" Matthews is back in town.'

Kathy hugged her. 'Ah, so my brutal "break your bracelet so you had to make a new one" tack worked!'

Alice laughed. 'I suppose it did. And just wanting to stick a couple of fingers up at Adam, I suppose. Great motivation.'

Kathy sipped some water and leaned back against the tree.

'Kathy …' said Alice.

'Yes, I know. I've made an appointment to see the doctor tomorrow. Stephano's been on at me too. He's in a state – thinks I'm pregnant. I'm just going to prove him wrong.'

'Well,' said Alice quietly. 'To the untutored eye you are showing all the signs.'

'The untutored eye that's watched too many films you mean,' said Kathy, picking up her scarf and tying it around her neck. 'I'm on the pill. It's all fine'

'Well at least you're going to the doctor.'

'Indeed. Fancy walking with me to the hotel? You can catch me if I faint dramatically, then.'

They walked slowly up the steps towards the beauty salon, and Alice breathed in deeply and dramatically. 'Ahhh, lavender. Gorgeous. I feel relaxed all of a sudden.'

Kathy grimaced. 'This bug I've got or food poisoning or whatever – its making me feel sick at the merest whiff of lavender. And patchouli. I have to keep leaving the room when I'm doing facials.'

'Bit difficult for a beautician,' said Alice.

Kathy kissed her on the cheek. 'Time to go. Deep breath. And congratulations my clever, talented friend.'

'Thank you for helping me.' Alice smiled. 'Or pushing me. I really wouldn't have had the nerve to do it if you hadn't.'

'Ciao for now,' said Kathy as she walked through the salon door.

Alice watched her go, a slight niggle of anxiety prickling at her neck. She'd never seen Kathy ill before. Not even slightly. The door shut gently as her friend slowly disappeared from view. Alice decided to get a glass of wine on the terrace and walked around the corner of the building. Luis was sitting at a table, dressed in a red shirt and black trousers, drinking a beer and talking to a man Alice hadn't seen before. Even though he looked very uncomfortable in his band outfit, and she could sense irritability around him, her heart did the usual loop the loop and she shivered happily. 'Luis,' she said, waving at him.

He turned to her, surprised, and stood up with his arms open. 'Alice! I was just thinking about you and here you are.' He brushed her lips with his and squeezed her tight. Alice tingled. He pulled out a chair for her. 'This is Nuno,' he said, nodding towards his friend.

'Ah, Alice,' said Nuno. 'I have heard a lot about you. Enchanted,' he said, taking her hand and kissing it.

'Lovely to meet you,' said Alice. 'I was just chatting with Kathy, but she's gone back to work, so I decided to treat myself to a lovely glass of wine here instead of going home.'

'I'm glad you did,' said Luis. 'I've said yes to doing more gigs with the band and here I am again.' He squeezed her shoulder. 'Don't look at me like that, it's out of necessity.'

'Look at you like what?' said Alice.

'Your face hides nothing,' he said. 'And I understand why you're not happy.'

'What do you mean, out of necessity?' asked Alice. 'Is it that other house?'

Luis sighed. 'Yes.'

'The buyer pulled out,' said Nuno. 'I warned him about him.'

'Nuno is my solicitor,' said Luis. 'And he used to be in the band, so he looks after me.'

'You were in the band too?' asked Alice incredulously.

'Yes. But I had to get a real job in the end.'

'Another one,' said Luis, shrugging his shoulders. 'Nuno is a solicitor, Joao is an architect. They all leave and grow up.'

Nuno got the waiter's attention. 'What would you like Alice?' he asked.

'A large glass of vinho verde, please,' said Alice.

Luis took a sip of his beer. 'So, now I have the house I live in, the house I have finished, and the farmhouse.'

'I told you not to buy the farmhouse until you'd sold the last one,' said Nuno.

'I know, I know. But it was love at first sight.'

'What are you going to do?' asked Alice.

'I don't know. Find a buyer quick. Or a renter. Before the bank start getting difficult.'

'Well, I know you don't like it, but thank God for the band,' said Nuno.

'Yes,' Luis. 'I hate to say it.'

Alice squeezed his hand. 'It'll work out, I'm sure,' she said.

'What have you done today?' he asked.

'Sold those mosaics I made at the farmhouse,' she said. 'And some bracelets.'

'I told you they were good!' Luis stood and pulled her out of her chair. He held her close and kissed her again. 'You're wonderful,' he whispered into her ear. The waiter placed the glass of wine on the table, and Luis passed it to her. 'A toast,' he said, picking up his beer. Nuno stood up and held his beer aloft, too. 'To Alice,' they both said.

Alice laughed. *Everything will be alright*, she thought. *Everything will be alright.*

The side door slammed open and Antonio walked out, followed by Marcella and her two friends.

'Luis,' said Marcella. 'I am so glad you could be part of this. I keep saying to everyone, the band will not be the same without Luis.'

Nuno looked at Luis. 'I see some things never change,' he said quietly.

Marcella noticed Alice and nodded. Antonio just glared at her. 'We've got to change the set list,' he said.

'Whatever you want,' said Luis.

'No – we need to talk about it inside.'

'No, it's fine,' said Luis, smiling calmly. 'I've been doing it long enough. Any order you want.'

Marcella moved closer to Luis. 'I'd love to play music,' she said. 'Do you do lessons?'

'Not enough time and no patience,' he said.

Antonio walked towards the door. 'We're on in ten minutes,' he said. 'Don't be late.'

Nuno looked at Luis. 'And some other things don't change either.' Then he smiled at Alice. 'It's been lovely to meet you,' he said. 'Hopefully I will see you again soon.' He kissed her on both cheeks as Marcella swept swiftly round, flicking her hair, and stalked after Antonio. Nuno raised his eyebrows. 'I will be in touch,' he said to Luis. 'I'll put the word out that you're looking for a buyer, but you need to talk to the estate agents first thing tomorrow.'

'I will,' said Luis, shaking his hand as Nuno moved to go. He turned to Alice. 'I'm so sorry about those people,' he said to her. 'This isn't out of choice. You believe me, don't you?'

Alice grabbed him round the waist and looked up into his dark brown eyes. 'I know, I know. It's fine.' He held her tight for a few moments. 'You can come over after the gig,' she said.

She could feel him sigh. 'I have to be up early tomorrow – I have a guy to talk to about work on a building site in Lisbon, so I need to drive in early. Then there's the estate agents.' He paused. 'Do you want to come over tomorrow afternoon? You wouldn't need to help. You could work on your art.'

Alice squeezed his waist again. 'That would be great. Around two?'

Antonio shouted from the door. 'Five minutes,' he said.

Alice could feel Luis's body tense up.

'At two tomorrow,' he said kissing her hair.

As he turned to go, his shoulders slumped, a little defeated.

Alice stared at his back until he was out of sight and decided she didn't want her wine any more. She walked slowly down the hotel steps and onto the sea road, and as she did so, her phone began to ring.

'Everything's going to be alright? What was I thinking!' Alice nearly shouted to the empty garden. She plunged into the pool, the cool, clear water breaking through the panicked fug that had descended one minute into her conversation with her sister. And it had engulfed her completely when she finally got off the phone to her mother. Tara had phoned minutes after she'd left the hotel. 'Literally minutes,' said Alice to herself. 'Literally minutes of, "everything's going to be alright".' It was 9 p.m. and it was dark, but she didn't know what else to do except throw down the phone, pull on her swimming costume and run down to the gardens.

Floating on her back, she looked up at the stars. As her eyes began to focus they sharpened into recognisable shapes. 'Adam knows you are in Cascais. He is on his way,' she read.

It's written in the stars, said the voice in her head.

'Not funny,' said Alice.

I told you, you can't hide forever.

'Not fair.'

No, it isn't.

She began to swim again, as if the force of her strokes would make her head clearer. Or just make all thoughts and talk of Adam go away or at least go somewhere else. 'Preferably back to South America,' said Alice at the sky. But it just made her angry. *Stand your ground*, said the voice in her head. *Don't give in.*

'I wish he'd stuck to the bloody postcards,' said Alice climbing out of the pool and collapsing onto a lounger.

Lying on a sunbed in the dark she wrapped herself in a towel as exhaustion replaced the fury. *Time to fight, Alice*, whispered the voice in her head. She closed her eyes for a moment, trying to rouse the energy to walk back to the apartment, the conversation with Tara going around and around in her head.

'How did he find out I was in Cascais?' she had asked.

'One of your university friends mentioned that Kathy lived there, and he said he put two and two together.'

'Does he know where she works?'

'No – she's not very good at keeping touch with anyone apart from you, is she?'

'Thank goodness for that!'

'But Adam is desperate enough to sell the house to fly into Lisbon and try to track you down. So maybe you could use that to your advantage – get the upper hand,' said Tara.

'He likes to get his own way. It could be that,' said Alice. 'Although I could make myself really difficult to find.' Then she became Alice again. 'But this is real life, all he has to do is call loads of beauty salons and he'll find Kathy.' After she'd finished talking to Tara, she tried to call Kathy, but her phone went straight to voicemail.

'Mind you even I can't find her at the moment,' she'd muttered.

The familiar Aphrodite-purr alarm roused Alice slowly from her dreamless slumber, but this morning it was accompanied by tiny droplets of water on her back. And the cooing of the doves was a lot louder. But there was something different about the way the cat nuzzled into her ear. Slowly Alice lifted her arm and moved her hand along the animal's soft coat. It didn't feel like Aphrodite. She rolled over and opened her eyes. The ginger tom from downstairs stared back at her.

'Oh God.' She sighed. 'Still on the sunbed.' The lawn spray splattered her with water again as it rotated and she rolled down onto the grass.

'*Bom dia*, madam,' said the gardener pushing a wheelbarrow full of weeds towards a bin.

'*Bom dia*,' replied Alice, sitting up.

'*A dia e lindo*, lovely day.' He smiled.

'Sure is.' Standing up unsteadily, Alice remembered why she had fallen asleep by the pool. 'Right, one more time before I take on the world,' she said to the cat, and jumped in.

Just what taking on the world meant, Alice couldn't decide. All she knew was that when she went into town to deliver more bracelets and buy more art materials she was on high alert. The spectre of Adam potentially lurked around every corner, even though her mother had assured her that he had no real idea of exactly where she was. She was angry, she was determined, but she was scared. Because when he finally did find her, Alice knew she'd have to deal with him, and that meant fighting for her home. And even though she was wearing her new defiantly vibrant trousers, she wasn't sure they would help with that.

After dropping off her bracelets, she grabbed a taxi to Luis's farmhouse, her stomach churning with stress. And there, too, in the back of her mind were Marcella and Antonio and Luis's supposed reputation. But as soon as Alice caught sight of him sitting on the step talking to Elvis who had dropped a stick at his feet, everything disappeared, except for him.

'Alice!' he waved at her, smiling. 'It's so good to see you.' He swept her up and kissed her, stroking her hair, whilst Elvis sat barking happily. He stood back. 'Great trousers,' he said. 'They suit you. Make you look like an artist.'

Alice stroked them and laughed. 'New uniform then. I was thinking of getting some hairbands and stuff, just to go the full hippy.'

He took her hand. 'I've already made a start. I've got to do as much as I can today because …' He trailed off.

'Because?'

He looked at her and paused. Then said, 'Just because.'

They began to wash down the surfaces in the main bedroom, both of them facing different walls, quiet and lost in thought.

Tell him, said the voice in Alice's head. But something strangled the words in her throat, as if letting them out would put Adam between them.

'So,' he said, eventually. 'Once I clear everything here, I will have to leave it until the other things are resolved.'

'Oh, that's a pity.'

'Once I have sold the other place I can buy what I need for here.'

'Any progress on that?'

'Not so far.'

They worked on for a while, silent again. The sunlight shone through the window, illuminating Luis's back. It looked a little hunched, a little despondent, Alice thought. She walked up behind him and put her arms around his waist. 'It'll be all right,' she said.

'Its business,' said Luis. 'I have to take the rough with the smooth.'

'I know.'

'Tomorrow evening I have another gig.'

Alice stood back. 'Oh,' she said.

'It's only work, Alice,' said Luis.

'I know, but I thought you were—'

'This is real life,' he said, suddenly sharp. 'It's okay for you. This is your escape. You are in a little cocoon. For me this is real.'

'I …' Alice felt like she'd been slapped.

Luis turned around. 'I'm sorry, I'm so sorry.' He grabbed her and held her to him. 'I'm under pressure. You didn't deserve that.'

Tell him, said the voice in her head. But she didn't.

Chapter Fifteen

Alice walked through the doors to the beauty salon determined to speak to Kathy. She hadn't replied to three voicemails so Alice knew something was wrong. And she needed to warn her about Adam. And get some reassurance for herself. Immediately calmed by the soft aroma of lavender, Alice walked over to talk to the receptionist who had her gaze fixed on her computer. 'Hi. Is Kathy free?'

Juanita, the receptionist looked up, a tight smile fixed on her face. 'Well, sort of,' she said.

'Sort of?'

'She's, um ... you're Alice her best friend, aren't you? I've seen you here before and she talks about you a lot.'

'Is she okay?'

'She's behaving a little bit oddly today. I've managed to squeeze her appointments in with the other girls.'

Alice felt the anxiety return. 'Is she sick? Hang on ... can I hear "Greased Lightning" coming from somewhere?'

'She is just lying on the treatment bed in room one with the soundtrack from *Grease* playing over and over and over again.'

'I think I'd better go in.' Alice remembered two broken love affairs for Kathy at university. *Grease* was her 'being sad' album.

'Please. Can you? I mean she owns the place. It doesn't give a very good impression. You can hear it through the walls.'

Pushing the door slowly open, Alice walked into the darkened room as the song changed to "Beauty School Dropout". Kathy was lying on the bed, her eyes covered with a mask.

'Go away,' said Kathy weakly.

'Nope,' said Alice.

Kathy sighed and slowly pulled the mask off her face. 'Sorry,' she said. 'I thought it was Stephano.'

Alice forced herself to smile brightly. 'So, you're playing the soundtrack from *Grease* then. Why?'

'Mmmmmmm.' Kathy rolled off the bed onto her feet as Alice's heart began to beat faster. There was a tense, anxious look on her friend's face she hadn't seen before. 'It wasn't the tea, after all,' said Kathy, 'Apparently, I *am* pregnant.'

Alice looked at her, stunned. 'You're what?'

Kathy sighed again and said evenly. 'I'm pregnant.'

'That's great news,' said Alice too quickly, wanting to help, but unsure exactly what to say. She moved towards Kathy to try to hug her but she stood back holding her hands up to keep her away.

'Sorry. I don't mean to, but I only found out about four hours ago, I'm in shock.'

'Have you told Stephano?'

'I left him a message. He hasn't phoned. I don't want to see him.' Kathy began walking around and around the treatment bed. 'Where is he? Why hasn't he been to see me? I hate him for doing this to me. I don't want him to come.'

Alice poured her a glass of cold water from a jug on the table and held it up to her. 'Drink this,' she said.

Kathy looked at her. 'I want a cup of tea,' she said quietly.

Alice stepped out of the room. 'Can you order us a pot of tea and two cups from upstairs,' she said to Juanita.

'Is she okay now?' asked Juanita quietly.

'Almost,' Alice whispered. 'Tea coming,' she said, turning back to Kathy and trying to sound bright, but her stomach was in turmoil, as she tried to understand how to help her friend. Positivity, she decided, was the best approach. 'This is exciting news. Isn't it?'

'Not quite the words I'd use. Screwed. That's a word I would use. In its literal and figurative sense.'

'Have you decided what you are going to do?'

'Nope. Well, I know what I'll do. But I still have to agonise for a while yet before I finally get my head around it.'

Alice sat on the treatment bed and patted the space next to her. 'I think you need to sit down.'

Kathy nudged in next to her. 'Careful, I am an invalid.'

'You're pregnant my dear. That's not an illness.'

'Well vomiting constantly makes me feel ill. So it is.'

There was a knock on the door and the receptionist brought in some tea. 'Thank you, Juanita,' said Kathy. 'I apologise for my behaviour. Is all okay out there?'

'All okay,' replied Juanita, 'Don't worry. But could you turn the music off?' She closed the door behind her.

Alice switched it off and stirred the tea in the pot.

'So, your birthday,' said Kathy eventually.

'I should remember how many sugars you take, but I can't,' said Alice.

'It used to be a half. It's now three. Because I'm pregnant and that's what I want.'

'Fine. Okay. What about my birthday?'

'End of next week, my dear. What are your plans?'

'I hadn't thought. I have that dress and—'

'Useless!' Kathy took the tea. 'All I do is go off and get accidentally pregnant and you go completely to pot.'

Alice looked at her, wondering whether to tell her about Adam or not. 'Shouldn't we be talking about your pregnancy rather than my birthday?' she said eventually.

Kathy took a sip of her drink. 'You're looking shifty,' she said. 'You weren't here just to check on my welfare, were you?'

'Um. Well. There is something I was going to tell you that is affecting my potential plans.'

'What? Is it Luis? Is everything alright?'

'It's not Luis … Adam is here. Apparently. Somewhere.'

Kathy's eyes widened in surprise. 'You're kidding!'

'That's the liveliest I've seen you for days.'

'Ha! Adam always did wind me up.'

Alice picked her cup up and breathed in the hot steam thoughtfully. 'It is a bit odd, though isn't it? Flying in to try to intimidate me. Because he may not find me.'

'Could be a colossal waste of time and money.' Kathy giggled softly.

'Although. He's actually looking for you.'

'Me?'

'He found out you were here from someone from uni and he knows you're a beautician. And he used his considerable intellectual talent to work out that I was somewhere near you.'

'We'll have to go out in disguise.'

'Very funny.'

'You know what he's like. He's going to try to bully you again. He must really need the money from your house.'

'I've said it before and I'll say it again ...'

'He can't have *my* house,' they said in unison, 'he only owns the downstairs toilet!' And then they laughed.

'None of this is funny at all, though,' said Alice staring into her tea. 'None of it.'

'You should see him, though. I'm being serious now.'

Alice shook her head slowly.

'The usual Alice tactic of dealing with something by pretending it's not happening.'

'I'm not ...'

'You are.' Kathy put her arms around her friend. 'You are either going to have to buy him out of the house or you are going to have to sell it. I suppose you could rent it out to pay the mortgage but if he wants to sell it you can't, can you? The brutal truth. I am either going to have to have the baby or ...' Kathy stood up again and put her cup down. 'Neither of us can run fast enough to get away from any of this.'

'I'm fighting it,' said Alice quietly. 'In my own way. But I'm fighting it. He only paid for about an eighth of it. And that downstairs toilet? I decorated it!'

'Do you really want to go back to it, Alice?'

'It's my home.'

'Is it? Oh … oh dear.' Kathy clambered up and bolted out of the room towards the bathroom.

'This baby doesn't like your tea.'

As Alice ate a biscuit there was a soft knock on the door. 'Kathy?' It was Stephano.

'Come in,' said Alice. 'She's in the loo.'

He eased himself slowly into the room and stood with his back against a wall in between a trolley full of bottles and cotton wool and an alarming looking white machine that had a red flashing light on it.

'She told you?' he said.

'Yes,' said Alice. 'Congratulations?'

'Hmm,' he said, looking at the floor, as Kathy pushed the door open.

'You!' she said.

'Kathy …' he said stepping towards her, as she backed away,

'Don't "Kathy" me!' she shouted.

Alice began to shuffle around the table, hoping to make her escape.

'I'm so excited,' he said.

'Are you?' said Kathy, beginning to cry.

Alice closed the door behind her and began to walk back to her apartment, so she could give her friends some space to talk.

When Alice got home she attempted to block her anxiety by concentrating on work and began gathering some more prints. But it kept coming back. *Her* house, *her* money, *her* everything. He wanted to take it away from her. Now Kathy had her own issues to deal with she had no-one to help calm her down. And she couldn't tell Luis. She just couldn't.

'It's *my* home.'

Is it? said the voice in her head which sounded very much like Kathy.

'It's my home. I made it.'

The House that Alice built, said the voice in her head.

'The House that Alice built,' she said sadly.

She put the prints to one side and picked up Aphrodite. 'Fancy a walk?' she said, padding into the kitchen. 'My kitchen in London has cream cabinets and a black marble worktop. The tiles are white and terracotta and the floor is the same.' Aphrodite purred and dug her claws into Alice's shoulder.

'I remember helping the builders pull the old one out. Dust and debris everywhere. Just a shell. And then it slowly took shape – it sort of grew out of the murk and dirt. I got the fabric for the curtains from Camden Market and I made them myself. Magnolia with delicate splashes of bronze and green and yellow, with thin dark gold tie-backs.'

I used to make myself a nice cup of tea and look out at our tiny garden, watching the birds swoop onto our feeding table, and glimpsing the occasional London sunset. All framed by my hand-made curtains. Then we ... I ... ran out of money and we ... I ... had to wait for a year before I decorated the living room. I used to spend hours on the internet late at night researching colours and fabrics and furniture ...'

Aphrodite started to wriggle impatiently, jumping onto the floor with a squeak.

'You're right,' said Alice. 'Back to work. Today I shall be living in the present for once. Because he's even taking that away from me. I won't let him. Got to choose some more photos to print.'

The entry phone buzzed. Alice glanced at the clock. It was just past midnight. She picked it up.

'It's me,' said Luis. 'I wanted to see you.'

Alice's heart fluttered. He was here, just when she needed him. 'I thought you were at that gig?'

'I was. It finished. I left. As early as I could.'

She let him in and ran to the bathroom to tidy up her hair.

'I wasn't sure you would be awake,' he said, holding out a bottle of wine and kissing her lightly.

'I was sorting through the photos I took the other night. Got completely involved and didn't look up until you arrived.'

He sighed wearily and sat on the sofa.

'Oh dear, like that is it?' she asked. 'I presume you'd like a large glass?'

'As long as you have one too.'

'If you insist.' She sat down next to him and they snuggled in together. 'Was it a good crowd tonight?'

'Pretty good, I suppose. Couldn't wait to leave.'

'Well you have a lot on your mind.'

'I can't believe I didn't get out of this years ago, you know? It was just easier to stay. I'm lazy, I suppose.'

'You can get out of it.'

He sipped his wine. 'Unfortunately, recent events have meant that I have to stay in it a little longer. I can't help feeling that Antonio is enjoying having some power over me. It's a mess.'

'Oh well.'

'Three houses. I have three houses. One to live in. One to sell. And one to renovate.'

'You are property rich.'

'But cash poor. I'll sort it. It's this bit in between. I'm going to have to be a bit scarce over the next few days. Sorting this mess out. Playing in the band, and I've managed to get a few days working on some apartment renovations in Lisbon.'

'Needs must,' said Alice. 'As long as it's all okay in the end.'

'In the end,' he said. 'I haven't forgotten your birthday. Don't worry. I'll be there.'

'Wherever there is. I haven't really organised it yet.'

'Well, wherever it is.'

She forced a smile.

'Are you okay?' he asked. 'You seem different. Distracted.'

'No. No. I'm fine,' she lied. 'Probably tired from staring at photos.'

'Don't be too tired,' he said, kissing her. 'I was hoping you would make the most of me tonight. As I'm going to be scarce!'

The aroma of freshly ground coffee roused Alice from her deep sleep. Relieved to discover she had woken up this morning in her bed rather than by the pool she stretched, pinpricks of sunlight trickling through the shutters dotting her arms. 'Luis,' she said. 'Come back to bed. It's too early.'

'I wish I could,' he shouted from the kitchen. 'But I have to be in Lisbon by eight. And I have an Alsatian dog to walk before I go.'

'I know, I know …'

'But,' he said standing in the door holding a tray. 'Being a perfect man, I have made you breakfast in bed.'

Alice sat up, smiling. 'Yes, you are the perfect man. Thank you! But what about you? There's only enough there for one person.'

'Oh, no you don't,' said Luis, placing the tray on the bedside table. 'I already ate. If I got back into bed with you and the breakfast I'd never get out again.' He kissed her lightly. Then again deep and intense. Then again. 'Oh Alice, Alice, Alice,' he murmured, pulling himself away. 'I have to go. I will call. Promise.'

And then he was gone.

Chapter Sixteen

Alice worked for two hours wrapped in the warm, happy glow that spending time alone with Luis gave her. But then the phone rang. 'Hi, Mum,' she said.

'Alice. Oh Alice.' Her mother's urgent tone sent a surge of panic through her whole body.

'What's up?' she said, her heart racing.

'Adam's on his way to Portugal. He may already be there.'

She felt sick. Here it was. 'I already know he's coming, Mum,' she said, pretending to be calm so her mother wouldn't get more upset. 'There are plenty of people here. He's hardly likely to bump into me, is he? Don't worry.'

'But if you do see him, what will you say?'

'He may not find me.' Her voice was still calm, her heart beating fast.

'His mother called me. The little bastard is really on the warpath.'

'I'll deal with it if it happens. Please don't worry.'

'I can't help being worried.' There was a pause. 'You need to speak to your solicitor. I know Tara has tried to persuade you.'

'I will when I'm ready.'

'You are so stubborn, Alice.'

'Yes, I suppose I am,' she said, knowing it wasn't stubbornness. It was fear.

'I know. You could fly home. Confuse him by not being there.'

Alice saw herself sitting at her computer in her living room looking for jobs she didn't really want, exhausted and fragile. She couldn't go back to that. Not yet anyway. 'Interesting idea, Mum, but I think here is better for the time being. Besides, I've got some more orders for bracelets, photos and a couple more of my mosaic houses. I actually have work to do. I mean it's for tiny amounts of money, but I'm really enjoying it.' She could sense her mother relax.

'Well done, darling. Really, well done. Don't let him spoil it.'

'I won't. And don't worry, please. It will be resolved. When I'm ready. Bye, Mum.' She put the phone down and walked onto the balcony. The sky was a perfect blue, the air still and warm. 'I won't let him spoil it,' she said. And something inside her shifted again.

The following day Alice worked on her projects, swam twice and walked along the sea road towards Guincho to clear her head. The spectre of Adam seemed to put an invisible force field between her and the centre of town. Why tempt fate? she thought as she turned and strode west rather than east. But the day after, she sat up bolt upright in bed.

'Right,' she said to Aphrodite who was sitting on a pillow, staring at her. 'I'm allowing him to bully me into hiding, and I don't even know if he's here. For. Goodness. Sake.'

Aphrodite jumped onto the floor and began to walk towards the door. 'Why tempt fate?' Alice muttered. The cat stood and turned her head. 'But then, why hide from him, Aphrodite?' She climbed out of bed and walked towards the kitchen 'I suppose I do need to get more bits for the necklaces – and paints. And I suppose I should check how my photos are selling. If at all. It's my job, after all. The one I've always wanted.'

She fed the cat, showered, dressed, put on her bright trousers and enormous straw hat, and headed into town.

It was the middle of June and the streets were full people, busy locals zipping around clusters of ambling holidaymakers. Alice was always impressed with the ability of the tourists to slow down to a snail's pace seemingly almost minutes after they'd arrived by the sea. It had taken her a few weeks to master the art of the amble. But now she was an expert. But not today. Today Alice was darting from shop front to display board to shadowy corner like a very bad cartoon spy wearing very visible clothing, trying to avoid eye contact with everyone, ears alert for the sound of Adam's gruff laugh, searching for the top of his head above the crowds.

Pausing outside one of the shops stocking her photographs to let a family out, she saw a couple pick up one of her Sintra prints and admire it.

'Look at the colours,' said the woman. 'They are so vivid. Where was this taken?'

'The gardens at Sintra,' said the owner. 'In spring the woods are full of wild flowers.'

'It's beautiful,' said the woman, placing it on the counter, and stepping back to get a better look.

'It would look good in the study,' mused her husband. 'Get it framed in silver, or blue.'

Alice beamed, pretending to look at postcards.

'We'll buy it,' said the woman.

Yes! thought Alice. *Yes, yes, yes! Someone likes my stuff!* She tried to imagine it hanging up in their home. Something that she saw and captured only a few weeks ago was about to become part of their lives. She hadn't thought of it like that before. She walked into the shop and smiled at them as they carried her work of art out into the big wide world.

'I just sold one of your prints,' said the owner.

'Yes, I heard! That's really good news,' said Alice. 'How are they going?'

'I sold two yesterday, two today. Last week five.'

'Is that good?'

'It's very good for a new artist.'

'Do I need to supply any more?'

'In two or three weeks maybe. I will let you know.'

Alice floated along the street. *A new artist ... a new artist ... that's me!* The craft stall that sold her bracelets was surrounded by people examining its goods, so she hovered by the window of the *pastelaria* next door, pondering the rows of meringues, pastries and tarts displayed tantalisingly inside, unable to decide which to buy. A baby began to cry, snapping her out of her reverie and she glanced up. Behind her reflection, she caught a fleeting glimpse of a familiar-

185

looking tall man with wavy fair hair striding purposefully by. Heart pumping, Alice pulled her hat further down over her head and furtively examined his back as he waited to cross the road. *It's not him. It's not him. It's not him.* The words spun around her head as she hurried into the shop and joined the queue, glad of a place to hide.

Ten minutes later, four *pasteis de natas* were packed into a gleaming white box. Alice held it in front of her as if it was a shield and re-joined the throng.

The calm shade of the art shop provided a pleasant respite from the anxious journey around town. Alice lingered, picking up pencils and brushes, examining them closely, then placing them back on the shelves. A pale blue watercolour paint held her attention for a while, and she held the palette up to the light to compare it to a slightly darker version. By the time she had decided which glue to buy, after ten minutes of carefully reading labels, Alice felt strong enough to re-enter the world outside.

'How are the bracelets going?' Alice scanned the craft stall for her creations.

'*Muito bem*,' beamed the woman who ran it. 'Very good. I have one left.'

'One?' Alice beamed back. 'One left?'

'Have you any more?'

'Yes, back at the apartment. How many do you want?'

'Forty. Same price as before.'

'Okay. I can get them here the day after tomorrow.'

'Tomorrow would be better.'

'How about after three o'clock tomorrow then?'

'Okay, fine. That would be good. It's coming up to peak season, so I like to keep good sellers in stock.'

Alice wondered if any of the passers-by could see the golden happy glow that surrounded her body, then realised she would have to hurry home. She only had ten. Thirty more bracelets had to be made by the following afternoon. Weaving around the crowds purposefully, mind buzzing with beads and tiles and ribbon, she automatically cut through the square. A brightly patterned scarf caught her eye and she dipped into the shop to look at it. Everything was inspiring ideas for more projects, and she felt invigorated. Smiling to herself, she noted how the colours intertwined and merged. She checked her purse and found only three euros. *I'll buy it tomorrow*, she thought, *and drape it over a chair so I can see it whilst I'm working*. About to step once again into the bright sun, a familiar deep laugh stopped her in her tracks, and almost physically pushed her back inside. For a few minutes Alice had completely forgotten him. But now her heart was racing again, and her mouth began to feel dry. Turning her attention to a rack of postcards, she tried to decide what to do next. *It may not be him*, she thought. *But what if it is?*

'Alice!' Carlos shouted at her from his café. 'You dropped some paint from your bag … and you are wearing your big hat again. Those trousers are very bright. That's not like you. Are you going to take more photographs of the cobbles?'

She stepped back behind a row of sunglasses.

'Are you in disguise again?' he laughed.

'Is Alice in there?' It was Ignacio. 'Oh yes. Alice. I see the brim of your hat! Will you have coffee with us?'

Pulling the hat further down, she waved limply and picked up a German newspaper, holding it in front of her face, clutching at her cakes and bag of materials.

'Carlos,' said Ignacio loudly, 'Alice is in the shop. I've asked if she would like to join us. It's such a beautiful day.'

'Oh God, why don't you just put a giant arrow pointing at me,' she muttered, literally backing herself into a corner.

'Alice?' Ignacio was now in the shop. 'Alice? My nephews are about to perform again across the square. Do you remember them last month? They have been practising … listen …' A slow and tentative jumble of accordion and electric keyboard drifted into the shop. '… I think it's …' He closed his eyes and concentrated. 'Ahh … "I Still Haven't Found

What I'm Looking for" … U2? They are very ambitious boys. Don't like to make it too easy.'

She put the newspaper down and stepped forward. 'Could you drive me home?' she said. 'I don't feel all that well.'

Ignacio looked at her for a moment, confused, then nodded. 'Of course.'

'Can you not stay?' asked Carlos as she scuttled behind Ignacio.

'Sorry, no. Not well,' she said, head down. 'See you soon.'

She glanced across the tangle of tables stretching across the cobbles. A man with wavy fair hair sat next to the statue of Luis de Camoes, watching the commotion. His female companion leaned towards him and whispered in his ear. It was Adam. He was here.

Clambering out of the taxi, Alice almost ran to the lift, to the safety of the apartment. As the doors opened, her phone rang. Another unfamiliar number. Her heart beat fast. It was Adam. He'd seen her. There was no hiding now. She jumped into the lift, and reluctantly clicked on the voicemail, her heart pumping. It wasn't him. It was the ex-colleague she'd emailed about work. 'Hi,' she said. 'Great to hear from you, Alice. I haven't got anything at the mo, but I've got a friend who's looking for training consultants. I've sent him your details and he'll be in touch soon.' As the doors closed, her heart lurched with relief that it wasn't Adam. But she wasn't as happy as she had expected to be about the possibility of a job at home, even though that was what she wanted. Wasn't it?

Rushing through the apartment door, Alice threw herself onto the sofa and phoned Kathy, deciding not to say anything about the job. 'He's here. I saw him.'

'Oh. Well, he'll never find you. He may not have seen you.' Kathy's voice sounded weary.

'I've got to go back into town tomorrow to that craft stall.'

'It's so busy. Don't worry. He'll never spot you.'

'I don't want this to happen. Everything is going so well.'

Kathy sighed. 'Alice. You were always going to have to do something eventually.'

'He should have waited for me to go back to London.'

'You may never go back.'

'Of course I will,' snapped Alice. 'I've got a mortgage to pay, a job to get.'

'Mmmmm … well…' There was a pause.

'You sound terrible,' said Alice eventually. 'Do you want me to come round later?'

'No. I'm okay. Just tired. Getting through the working day then falling asleep as soon as I walk into the apartment.'

'Do you want me to get you anything?'

'Oh, for some of Mary's special tea.'

'No. Never ever again,' said Alice.

'You could calm Stephano down for me,' said Kathy.

'Is he pleased?'

'Yes. And nervous. And over-protective. And driving me mad.'

'He always did drive you mad.'

Kathy sighed. 'Yes, yes, I suppose. It's all a bit overwhelming. Unexpected. He's smothering me a bit.'

'You both need to get used to the idea. It'll be fine.'

'I suppose,' said Kathy. 'Are you okay? How are you going to deal with Adam?'

'Don't know.'

'Thought so. Look I've got to go back inside. My next appointment's arrived. I'll call tomorrow and we can do something. Even if it's just me coming to your place and falling asleep.'

Alice put the phone down and stared out of the window. Funny how you can just stand still but things change around you, she thought, remembering her much-loved house where she had stood still and safe for so many years. She suppressed a sob caught in her throat. Everything jumbled together in her head – Adam, the job, Luis, Cascais, her house. Her home. He was going to try to take it away. Not this time. She took a deep breath and began to gather the beads for the bracelets.

Chapter Seventeen

Aphrodite jumped into the middle of the pile of broken tiles, kicking several off the plastic sheeting onto the marble floor.

'Stop it!' shouted Alice, as the cat skittered around the room, pushing and chasing the tiny shard which had caught her eye. 'I think you're hungry,' she said, taking the opportunity for a rest. Aphrodite abandoned her prey and trotted to stand at her feet as she opened a tin of cat food. Alice stretched and glanced at the clock. 'Eleven already. Twelve bracelets made ... eighteen more to do.' She glanced at her phone to check there were no notifications. There weren't, and she sighed with relief, longing to go back only two weeks ago when Adam was just a shadow outside her little bubble, something she knew she had to deal with, but hadn't crashed through yet. Suddenly her mind was in London again. Adam was walking through the door dragging a suitcase. *I'm back,* he'd said. *I made a mistake. Please please forgive me ... I wasn't in my right mind.*

And she had. Or she'd thought she had. It was grief that had made him behave that way. His brother. Killed in a car crash. So young. How could she not understand? How could she not try to forgive his betrayal? Then she was standing at the table in the hall six months later reading a note.

I'm sorry. I can't do it any more. I'm going travelling. I'll be in touch. A.

And that was that. Everything left hanging in the air. A drip, drip of jaunty postcards from trendy destinations across the world. Never a return address. So even if she had wanted to sort out the legal side of the house, she couldn't. The sick, sad, frightened, lonely feeling that enveloped her back then began to seep into her again. 'No no no no no,' she said, almost physically pushing the dull, sad ache away. 'I am never ever going to allow you to make me feel like that again, Adam. Ever.' Pouring herself a glass of water she walked back into the living room, fighting the urge to go and lie under the bedcovers and give in to the feeling.

'I'll make three more bracelets tonight then get up at seven to finish the rest,' she said loudly as if he could hear. 'I have work to do.' She restlessly picked up some beads and sighed, suddenly wanting to speak to Luis, hear his warm, deep voice comforting and reassuring her. She picked up the phone and called him. He answered immediately.

'Alice,' he said. 'I haven't long – I'm on in ten minutes. I'm so glad you called.' His voice sounded tense.

'I'm so glad you answered,' she said.

'Is everything okay?'

'Yes,' she lied again. 'I just wanted to hear your voice, that's all, as you're going to be a bit scarce.'

'I know, I wanted to hear your voice too. It's starting to get a little difficult with the bank. They've started to drop hints that their patience may run out very soon.'

'Oh dear. I'm sure you'll find a buyer.'

He sighed. 'Yes. I'm sure. But it's a little bit stressful.' Someone shouted his name in the background. His voice dropped. 'God, the band. I don't want to do it, but I need it.'

'It'll be fine.' She wanted to reach her arms through the phone and put them around him.

'Luis … busy again …' Alice could hear Marcella's voice close by. 'I was hoping I could talk to you about a little proposition. I want you to teach me to play the guitar. I mentioned it to you before, remember?'

'I'm sorry Marcella, I'm on the phone …'

'Luis …' said Alice, feeling uncomfortable.

'It's okay, Alice,' he said. 'People get like this when a gig's about to start.'

'How much do you charge an hour?' It was Marcella again.

Luis's voice was quietly irritable. 'I don't give lessons Marcella, I'm sorry. And I'm on the phone. Excuse me.'

Her voice began to get shrill. 'You seemed perfectly happy to speak to my aunt earlier on.'

Alice almost stopped breathing. Something wasn't right, she knew it. 'Her aunt?' she said.

'Yes. An old friend from when we first started. It appears her and Marcella are related.'

'I'd bet you would give her guitar lessons,' said Marcella.

'Does Marcella know you are talking to me?' asked Alice impatiently.

'I'm going into another room,' he sighed. She could hear a door close. 'That's better.'

'Luis?'

'We bump into people all the time who used to follow the band,' he said. 'Older, wiser, married, children, but still want to know what we're doing.' He paused. 'Are you sure you're okay?

'Yes. Just wish I could be there with you.'

He laughed a hollow laugh. 'Even I don't want to be here with me! I've got to go. I'll call tomorrow. *Bejinhos*. Kisses.'

'Kisses,' whispered Alice and put the phone down. She forced herself to make the three bracelets and went to bed.

Alice breathed in the hot spicy steam from the tea. She knew it was a bad idea, but it was all she could think of to distract her from her visit into town to make her delivery. Luis hadn't responded to a text she'd sent just before she went to bed and Kathy was struggling through her working day. With no motivational talks from them she was on her own with the potential 'Avoid Adam' assault course awaiting her as she left the building.

So it was just her and the stash of tea she'd found shoved to the back of the cupboard; the remainder of the potent batch Kathy had made. The first sip made her shiver with guilt. Then she sat on the balcony and savoured it slowly, knowing that there was none left. This was it. She'd infused all of it into the hot water – probably about four cups worth. As she drank she tried to visualise a calm and successful journey into town and back with no interruptions from intimidating ex-partners. In fact, she visualised Adam on a plane home at that very moment.

'Oh, the shame of it,' she said to herself. 'Only able to deal with him with the assistance of some dodgy herbal tea … I never could argue with him … he can hypnotise me into agreeing to anything. He always could.' She took another sip. 'For God's sake! Bugger off bloody negative thoughts,' she said, standing up and putting the cup down forcefully. With her big hat on, her bag of goods over her shoulder, Alice Dorothy Matthews stepped over a dozing Aphrodite and closed the door behind her. As she stepped out of the lift, she pulled herself up to her full height and strode out of the apartment gates towards the town.

'Here we are,' said Alice when she got to the stall, pouring her bracelets onto the table.

'Thank you,' said the stallholder, gathering them up quickly and putting them into a box. 'Don't want them to fall on the floor and break, do we?'

'Whoops, didn't think,' said Alice. 'I had a long night and didn't get much sleep.'

'I know how it is. I'll call you when I need more. I'm sure these will go quickly.'

'Okay. See you soon.'

Alice decided to do a bit of window shopping at some of the more expensive clothes shops around the corner, so meandered slowly off, glad of the protective properties of Mary's tea. A long flowing green silk top caught her eye, drawing her inside one of the larger boutiques. As she absent-mindedly went through the rails looking for matching trousers, she heard a noisy clutch of young women chattering behind her as they left the shop.

'My aunt. Really. She should know better. You should have seen her last night. They were all over each other. It was disgusting. I don't know what Luis thinks he was playing at. What is it with him and old women!'

Alice stood frozen, staring hard at the top, trying to pretend that this person that sounded a lot like Marcella wasn't standing behind her talking about Luis. She watched them walk past the window and felt a terrible feeling of dread. Luis hadn't returned her text last night or this morning. Stepping out into the street, Alice physically tried to shake off what had just happened. Marcella was barely out of school, she reasoned with herself. She was just young and naive. And nasty.

But he has a reputation. There it was. The voice running around in her head again.

She found herself back near the craft stall. 'These are very cute.' A woman was talking about Alice's bracelets. She examined one closely, stroking one of the tiny, smooth ceramics. 'This is beautifully done. Do you know where you can buy these beads?'

'I don't think you can. My supplier uses old tiles and cuts them into these circles. I don't know how she does it.'

'These are a very good idea. Don't you think so, darling? I'm sure I could run some similar ones up and sell them when we open the shop.'

Alice stood, watching, slightly hidden. Luis's recent behaviour had been running through her head, each action dissected for clues as she wandered aimlessly along the cobbled streets, and she'd somehow found herself near the stall again. That's when she saw them. Adam. And Veronique. His girlfriend. The artist. She was stealing her idea.

'Alice!'

She was rooted to the spot, feeling woozy and vague. Was she dreaming this?

'Alice!' his voice again. Then a touch on her hand.

'Alice,' he said softly.

His pale blue eyes stared into hers.

'I'm not Alice,' she said.

'Yes, you are.'

'No, I'm not.'

'Yes, Alice, you are. Are you alright?'

His face came into focus. Time hadn't made much difference. The laughter lines around his eyes were a little more visible, and his chin had the beginnings of a pale beard. But it was as if they were standing in their kitchen on the day he'd come back.

'I'm not Alice. You are mistaken. Easily done.' She turned and walked hurriedly up the hill.

'What on earth are you doing?' He was following her now. 'Alice! Alice!'

Turn around and tell him what you think of him, screamed the voice in her head.

But she knew she couldn't. Because if she did he would look into her eyes and speak his soft words and he would make it all right. Somehow. Just for a while. Until he'd got what he wanted.

'Alice, for God's sake!' He was shouting, and people were turning to watch.

Why had she drunk that bloody tea? Her head was feeling so light and disconnected. 'Leave me alone,' she said. 'Please just leave me alone. I have no idea who you are.'

'We need to talk.'

'No. I don't want to. And I'm not Alice.'

'Stop being so strange. Are you alright?' he asked again.

'Like I said, I'm not Alice.'

'Stop being so childish. I've come all this way to talk to you. I could have gone through a solicitor you know. I could have started to send you formal legal letters.'

The street narrowed; people filled it; she couldn't push through the crowds to get away from him. There was no way out. Anger began to replace the panic and she stood still for a moment. 'Why didn't you go through a solicitor?' she said finally, turning towards him.

He smiled almost triumphantly. 'I thought we could settle this amicably. You know. Old friends.'

'Friends?'

'We've known each other a long time, Alice.'

'Well you don't know me any more.'

He held his hand out to her. 'Why are you making this so difficult?'

She took a deep breath. 'If you went through a solicitor you wouldn't get the house, would you? But like this you think—'

'It's my house.'

'It's my house actually.'

'We bought it together.'

'Is that what you told her?'

Veronique had caught up with them and had put her hand on Adam's shoulder. Alice's phone buzzed. A text from Luis.

Sorry I didn't get back to you. Long nights and longer days. See you in a couple of days hopefully. Another gig tomorrow.

She looked at them both. 'It's not your house. You own the downstairs toilet. And tell her that those bracelets she thought were so clever – I made them! And I'm not telling you how I made them. You can't have my house, and you can't have that. But—' she pointed at Veronique ' —you are more than welcome to him.' Then she turned again and pushed through the crowds. Her phone rang.

'Kathy. You wouldn't believe what's—'

'It's Ignacio. I'm using her phone. She collapsed at work, Alice. She's in the hospital.'

Kathy lay listlessly on the bed. 'I hate feeling like this. I hate it,' she moaned.

'It won't last. Tara was really ill when she was first pregnant with her first. Then after three months she was blooming.'

'That's just something everybody says to make you think it will get better. I don't believe it. I want to feel blooming now!'

Ignacio hovered by the door. 'I should go back to work,' he said. 'Now you're here, Alice.'

'Thank you so much, Ignacio,' said Kathy. 'You've been a real star. I don't know what I would have done without you.'

'It's fine,' he said, kindly. 'Someone has to look after you two. *Adieus*. I'm going.'

As soon as he left, Kathy began to cry.

'Oh, poor you,' said Alice, softly kneeling on the bed and putting her arms around her friend.

'I had a panic attack,' she sobbed. 'I wasn't just feeling sick. I don't know what to do. I really don't.'

'I've never seen you like this,' said Alice.

'That's what Stephano said.'

'But you will be fine. It's all a bit overwhelming isn't it.'

'Stephano is missing,' said Kathy quietly. 'I knew he'd let me down. Chasing me again and pretending he wanted something more than before. And now ... why did he do that? I don't understand. I didn't get pregnant deliberately. I don't know what happened. I'm so careful. We're so careful.'

'What do you mean, missing?'

'I haven't heard from him for two days.'

'Is that technically missing?'

'His phone just goes to voicemail and he hasn't returned my messages.' Kathy's voice began to rise. 'And I'm in hospital and he's not here, and I'm having his baby. And he's not here.'

'I'm going to find him,' announced Alice, standing up unsteadily.

'What's the matter with you? You know you're swaying a bit?'

'Yes ... well ... nothing.'

Kathy managed to stop crying and stared at her friend. 'I don't believe you.'

Alice leaned against the wall and sank slowly to the floor. 'I drank the last lot of that batch of tea ... the last few lots ...'

'Why?'

'In case I saw Adam obviously.'

Kathy wiped her eyes with a handkerchief and sat up. 'Did you see him?'

'Yes.'

'Really? What did you do?'

'I told him I wasn't Alice.'

'You ... what?' Kathy began to giggle.

'I told him I wasn't me.'

'You twit!'

Alice began to laugh. 'I know. I think he guessed it was me, though ... well, obviously. Oh dear, what was I thinking?'

'Not a lot. Well, you've made me laugh. Which is better than panic.'

'Then we argued about the house and I ran away.'

Kathy's shoulders shook she was laughing so much.

'Thank you for your sympathy. Thank you!'

'And for the next instalment?'

'No idea. I don't care at the moment, though. I'm going to find Stephano for you.'

'I think in your current state you would fare worse than me.'

'So are they letting you go home or keeping you in?'

'Letting me home later.'

'Stay with me and Aphrodite, then.'

'Okay. Do you have breadsticks?'

'Boxes and boxes of them,' said Alice. She hugged Kathy and walked towards the door. 'Message me when you're ready to go and I'll come and get you.'

When they finally got back to the apartment, Alice and Kathy sat, exhausted, on Mary's balcony.

'Thank God there's no more of that tea,' sighed Alice.

'You sound more wistful than grateful,' said Kathy.

'Probably a mixture, I think.'

'It's a bit of a turnaround this.'

'How do you mean?'

'Well, you were supposed to come over to Portugal and I'd take you under my wing and help you and look after you, and suddenly, you're looking after me.'

'I hadn't thought of it like that.'

They both gazed silently at the trees for a while.

'Shall we watch a film?' asked Alice eventually.

'Okay. But it shouldn't need too much concentration.'

'Mary's got a small and fairly eclectic mix of movies. Do you fancy *Pulp Fiction*?'

'No.'

'*Aladdin*?'

'No.'

'*Notting Hill*?'

'No. Seen it too many times.'

'*The Railway Children*?'

'Doesn't daddy disappear and reappear at the end?'

'Yes.'

'Then no. Too much daddy disappearing for me.'

'*The Yellow Rolls-Royce*?'

'Don't know that one.'

'It's about a yellow Rolls-Royce.'

'Yes, got that ... no.'

'*Breakfast at Tiffany's*?'

'That's the one.'

'We can both sing along to "Moon River", and then we can cry ...'

'Oh no, is that my phone ringing? I'm going to have to walk to the table.' Kathy got up and answered it, wearily. 'What? Do you know who this man is? You didn't tell him ...? Okay, thanks for letting me know.' Kathy slumped onto the sofa. 'That was one of the girls from the salon. A man came in earlier and asked if I worked there. Then asked where I lived. He was English, tall—'

'They didn't tell him, did they?'

'No, of course not. How did he find out where I worked?'

'He's a journalist. He probably just picked up the phone and rang around loads to find you.' Alice slumped next to her. 'I can't have this, can I? Can't get you involved in fending him off. I'll have to see him and talk sensibly to him.'

'Don't worry about that. I'll quite enjoy playing with his mind.'

'You have enough to worry about at the moment.'

'No, I'll definitely enjoy playing with his mind. Now – your birthday,' said Kathy, suddenly changing the subject. 'We'll do something, promise. Has Luis told you what he has planned?'

'No. Haven't spoken to him properly for a couple of days.'

'Anything you need to tell me?'

'No. Nothing.'

Kathy touched Alice's arm. 'Alice,' she said softly.

Alice sighed. 'I know, I know. I've got to do something about Adam.'

'He's here. There's no more hiding.'

Alice picked up a cushion and hugged it to her like a comfort blanket.

'You'll just have to let him find you.'

'What? Go into town and allow myself to be caught? And say what exactly? Here's the number of a reliable plumber? Take the downstairs toilet and go!' They giggled.

'Well this is another fine mess we've got ourselves into,' said Kathy.

'How are you feeling now?'

'Better. Still panicky. But less panicky. Angry with Stephano. Sad. Sort of excited. But not much.'

'I'll put the film on.'

Chapter Eighteen

Alice knew that now Adam had found Kathy he would start pushing so he could track her down. And she couldn't let that happen. Not any more. She looked at the text. Okay. I will meet you by the statue at 12.30 tomorrow. A.

So she was here, despite every bone in her body urging her to get on a plane and disappear. The cafés in the square were almost full; a mixture of locals and tourists chatting, reading, drinking and listening to the mariachi band which had been passing through town a few days ago and apparently had decided to linger for a while.

Their joyful music was completely at odds with the feeling of impending doom Alice was currently experiencing. And the blazing summer sunshine just made it worse. Kathy had persuaded her that going into town and waiting to be found would not be effective or useful. Alice knew that, but the part of her that did not want to deal with Adam had been in control when she'd decided that was the best plan of action.

The rational part had slowly been drawn to the fore, partly because she did not want Kathy to get involved. Tara had sent her Adam's mobile number and Alice had gritted her teeth, composed a message in five seconds and pressed send immediately, before she could change her mind.

'Why are you sitting here and not at one of my tables?' Carlos was weaving through the chairs towards her.

'Because you're full!'

He glanced back and nodded. 'Ahhh. Of course. So … you are not wearing your too big hat?'

'No. No longer in disguise.'

'And you are okay? I heard you had problems yesterday. A man upsetting you?'

'I'm okay. Thank you for checking though.' Alice smiled.

'I have to get back to work. *Ciao*.'

'*Ciao*.' Alice watched as he disappeared into his restaurant and sighed. *I know about five people here*, she thought. *But everyone seems to be fully aware of all my movements.*

'Hello.' She looked up. A shaft of sunlight framed his face. It looked like a halo. She felt sick. He pulled out a chair. 'Veronique will be along in a moment.'

'Veronique?'

'My partner. You met yesterday.'

'I mean, why is she going to be here when we are talking about the house?'

'Come on Alice, be nice. It involves her.'

'No it doesn't.'

He leaned forward and smiled. 'I'm sorry if it's a bit of a shock. Veronique and everything. But you know. I've moved on.'

Alice leaned forward and smiled back, anger raging in her stomach. 'Adam. I really don't care what goes on in your private life. Not at all. But this business is between us. Not her.'

He sat back and looked around. 'Ah, there she is.' He waved. 'Veronique … over here.'

'Well, I'm not talking about the house now.'

'Alice. It's over between us,' he said loudly as Veronique sat down. 'There's no point fighting it or arguing about it.'

'I'm glad it's over Adam. It's been over for years.'

'This is Alice, my ex,' announced Adam.

'Hello. We meet at last.' Veronique smiled.

'Hello,' said Alice sweetly.

'I know you are having problems with this, Alice,' said Adam evenly, 'but by clinging onto the house, you are clinging onto me and the past.'

Fury shot sharply through Alice's body like a sabre. 'I'm just fighting for what's mine – the house. I'm not clinging onto anything.'

Veronique smiled again and rummaged in her bag, pulling out two of Alice's bracelets and placing them on the table. 'Oh, do not take any notice of me,' she said. 'They really are lovely. You are clever. Adam never mentioned what you did at all.' She picked up one of the bracelets and examined it. 'Just trying to work out how you made the tile shards look like that. I've always got a few misfired pots hanging around. I could do my own version. Couldn't I, Adam?'

Alice stood up. 'No. Not doing this,' she said.

'Alice … come on. Let's sort this out amicably. The house is our joint property. That means half belongs to me, obviously. Solicitors cost money and cause aggravation. Let's just put it on the market and split it. Then we can both move on. I don't know how long you've been here, but you can't be earning anything. How are you paying the mortgage?'

Alice took a deep breath to calm herself down. 'On paper it's joint property, Adam. But I paid for most of it and did most of the renovations. And that means that it is not half yours.'

Adam rose to his feet and they faced each other across the table. 'Do you know how much that house is worth now? We bought it years ago and it was a wreck. For God's sake.'

'I'll sell it when I want to. And when I do, ninety per cent of what it's worth is mine.'

'I can force you to sell it.'

'Why? Do you need the money now, Adam? Do you? What for?'

'For our business.' Veronique smiled, without looking up. 'Our ceramics business. I have been very successful in Argentina, and we want to bring it to the UK.'

Alice turned to walk away. 'Not with my money,' she said. 'Now excuse me, I have work to do.'

Adam leaned across the table and pulled her arm. 'Oh no you don't. You can't keep running away.'

'I haven't been running anywhere Adam,' she said quietly.

'You're the one that's been running. And now you want everything to go your way. In your time. And I say NO!'

Adam's arm dropped limply to his side as Alice strode away.

'What's going on? Who is that? Are you okay?' Carlos appeared by her side.

Alice was almost hyperventilating. 'Don't let him see me cry,' she whispered.

'Come inside and I will make you a coffee,' he said. 'On the house.'

She played with her phone as she sipped the hot milky *galao*, wanting to call Luis; longing for him to suddenly appear with Elvis in tow, laughing and flirting and teasing her; wanting not to have heard Marcella's gossip. Wanting to turn the clock back to the magical day they had spent at his house on the hill – him taking his photos, her creating the mosaic pictures, when the whole world was just Luis and Alice.

If she called him, would he tell her something she didn't want to hear? Something she didn't have the strength to deal with now? Adam's words crowded her head. He made everything seem grey. He had done for years, she realised. What had happened to him? She remembered falling in love with someone completely different all those years ago. How had he changed so much? Or was it her?

'How are you now?' Carlos sat down next to her.

'I'm okay. Thank you.'

'That man. Who is he?'

'My ex. With his new partner. They want to sell our house. But I don't want to.'

'It is cruel that he has brought her.'

'Yes, I suppose it is.'

'Shall I call Ignacio and ask him to get Kathy to collect you?'

'No. No. It's fine. Kathy's not very well.' Alice took a sip of her coffee again. She had to do something. But she wasn't ready to face Adam again. 'Actually, are you in contact with Stephano? You know, that landscape gardener?'

'No. I'm not. But Luis is his friend. Try him.' He stood up and smiled at her. 'I have to go back to work. You know I can spread the word about that man. He won't be able to get a glass of water in the square, let alone a meal.'

'Could you?' Alice felt her eyes light up.

'Yes!'

'No. That's cruel, although ...'

Carlos clapped his hands together. 'Leave it to me.'

She sat back. Adam was bringing out the worst in her. Then she sent a text to Luis asking whether he had Stephano's number.

The reply came immediately. Yes. Here it is. At the estate agents. Trying to sort things out. See you soon. Xx

Alice smiled inside, a warm glow suddenly spreading through her, but it soon began to cool as a picture of Marcella crept into her mind. *'What is it with him and old women?'* Alice gulped as Marcella's words extinguished her smile and made her heart beat faster again.

Belem glistened in the afternoon sun; the grey bricks of the Torre and the Monument to the Discoveries reflecting the milky blue of the river. Alice took a photo. The colours would be useful for something.

What are you doing here? asked the voice in her head.

'No idea.'

Well you didn't accidentally beam in from outer space did you?

Alice had fled the square, her head a cacophony of Adam and Veronique, of Marcella, of Luis, of houses and solicitors, Stephano and Kathy, of duty and responsibility and not knowing what she wanted. She forced herself to walk, as if her body would move faster than her thoughts and she could leave them behind somewhere on a bench or a wall so they could argue with themselves. Her feet took her to the station, onto a train, and off it at Belem. And somehow for a while she managed to lose herself in the old buildings and narrow streets. But it was always there, somewhere in the background.

She sat in the park next to the fountain and closed her eyes for a moment. *I have to do something*, she thought. *I can't let him walk all over me any more.* Taking a deep breath she turned on her phone. Five missed calls from Adam and three texts. She deleted them without bothering to read them and blocked his number again.

She looked up at the Monument to the Discoveries and stood up, taking her small guide book out of her bag.

Built on the north bank of the Tagus River in 1960 to commemorate the 500th anniversary of the death of Prince Henry the Navigator, the Monument to the Discoveries portrays a three-sailed ship ready to depart.

Alice leaned on the wall, watching the River Tagus ebb out to sea to the west, imagining what it was like for those men sailing off into the unknown. She read the next paragraph of the book.

The sides are decorated with sculptures of important historical figures such as Vasco da Gama, Magellan, Cabral and other Portuguese explorers, crusaders, monks and cartographers. Prince Henry the Navigator is at the prow holding a small vessel.

Putting the book in her bag, she sighed. It was time to do something. Hiding from the truth was not an option any longer. Tapping the details of Cooksley and Sons solicitors into her phone, she got an email address and wrote a message asking them to get three valuations on her house as soon as possible.

Heart beating fast and hands shaking she leaned into the breeze and tried to breathe slowly. For the second time that day Alice wanted to cry. But this time the tears did not come, just something hard and strong and determined. And angry. Her breathing slowly calmed down as her head began to unjumble.

So the Good Ship Alice Dorothy Matthews is about to set sail into a new world? questioned the voice in her head.

'Not necessarily,' said Alice.

Oh I think so, it replied. *This is all very symbolic, isn't it?*

She glanced at the river again and allowed herself a limp smile. 'I suppose it is.'

Her phone buzzed. It was a text from Luis. Hi. How's your day? X

'Tell him, tell him,' she said out loud. But she didn't. I'm okay, thanks. What about you? Still busy? X.

Yes, but I haven't forgotten your birthday. Day after tomorrow. I will wine and dine you. X

Looking forward to it.

But she didn't believe her own text this time. Because finding out the truth about Luis was something she needed to do but couldn't face. What if Marcella was right? What if even this was about to crumble away too? Then she'd have nothing.

Chapter Nineteen

Despite leaving two voicemails and several texts the previous evening, Stephano was obviously still in no mood to be found. And a listless and fretful night had led to an unwanted and heavy sleep until almost midday. A long and energetic swim had not rid Alice of her irritability or anxiousness, so she had decided to track him down in person.

Deciding to ask Ignacio if he knew where Stephano was, she walked to the hotel. The foyer was a cool and welcoming respite from the dry heat of the mid-afternoon sun. An airport coach had just dropped off several groups of excited holidaymakers, so Alice paced around, fanning herself with her hat, waiting for Ignacio to arrive.

I should be dealing with my own problems, she thought. But she was in no mood to talk with Adam until the house valuations had been done. And the nagging doubts about Luis were dragging her down. So she continued to wait.

'Alice. How are you on this lovely day?' Ignacio appeared from the middle of the crowd of tourists, smiling.

'I'm okay, thank you. How are you?'

Ignacio looked at her curiously for a minute. 'I am very well, Alice. But I think you are not.'

'No, I'm fine.'

'I think you are not.'

'I am!' She tried smiling.

'Ahhh, good, that is better.'

'Do you know where Stephano is?'

'No. No, I don't. But I think I can find out. Have you asked Kathy?'

'I don't want to bother her. She's a bit busy today.'

'I can give you his number.'

'I have it, thank you. He's not answering his phone.'

'Perhaps he is busy too?'

'Maybe. But it is urgent, so …?'

Ignacio turned towards one of the receptionists, who was still surrounded by a sea of people. 'Okay. For you,' he said eventually. 'Can you tell me why?'

'Um, no.'

'It is okay, Alice. You are like family. You do not have to say.'

'Oh, that's kind. Thank you,' she said, slightly taken aback, and suppressing the sudden urge to throw her arms around him.

He pushed through the throng to the reception desk and returned with a piece of paper.

'He is here,' he said. 'Costa Caparica, the other side of the river. He has rearranged his days looking after the grounds here so he can remodel the gardens of a guesthouse owned by his friends.'

'Thank you. Is there a train or a bus? How do I get there?'

Ignacio looked at his watch. 'I can take you. I have had a cancellation already today. I was working very late last night. A trip to Caparica would be a nice break.'

'I will pay you.'

He held his hand up. 'No, no, not today. As I said it will be a break. I have not been south of the river for months. It will be good to go.'

'Are you sure?'

'Alice, I would not do it if I was not sure. Come.'

As the car turned onto the bridge over the Tagus, pulling away from the sprawl of Lisbon over to the south of the river, Alice felt her mind quieten with the steady thrum of the engine. Her eyes began to flutter closed and she fell into a calm sleep. She woke as the car stopped, to the sound of Ignacio's voice shouting into his phone, but it was so fast she could not decipher the Portuguese. Although, from his tone it was obvious he was not very happy.

Stepping slowly onto the road, her hair was caught by a gentle breeze, heavy with sand and sea. To the left was a beautiful old guest house, enclosed by a tangle of bushes and trees and ahead a wall of sand dunes tumbling to a vast expanse of gold beach stretching into the far distance.

Kicking off her shoes she followed a wooden walkway to the beach and sat staring, mesmerised, at the sea. Her brain seemed to have emptied of the chaos of the last few days, soothed by the gentle, rhythmic breaking of the waves.

'Excuse me, Alice. I am sorry about that.' Ignacio sat down next to her. 'I was asked to collect someone from one of the golf courses, but I said no. They were not happy. Is a man not allowed a few hours rest!'

'This is beautiful,' she said. 'So different to the other side of the river. Less rugged, I think. Softer, in a way.'

Ignacio took his jacket off. 'I am on holiday.' He smiled. 'I will cut loose and be just in my shirtsleeves.'

'Is that the guest house that Stephano is working at?'

'Yes. But he will probably be at lunch. It is not quite three o'clock yet. That means you can stare at the sea for a little while longer.'

'It's like a meditation aid.' Alice shook her hair and stretched her arms above her head. 'I've been a bit tense.'

'I have heard that your ex-husband has been here bothering you,' said Ignacio.

'Word does get around doesn't it? He's not my ex-husband though. We never married.'

'More fool him.'

'No. I think I'm the fool here.'

'We can tell he is upsetting you. I know it's about your house. What will happen?'

'Well.' Alice closed her eyes and took a deep breath. 'I cannot ignore him any more. Either we sell the house or I buy him out. He wants more of it than I think he's entitled to. If I want the proportion that is rightfully mine, then I think I will have to fight him in court. That's what my solicitor says. I e-mailed her yesterday. And if I win he could go to appeal … and it will cost money. It's so unfair. All of it.' She put her head in her hands and fought back the tears.

'Yes, yes, it is unfair,' said Ignacio quietly.

They both sat in silence for a few moments.

'Where do you live, Alice?' asked Ignacio eventually.

'Where? I live in London.'

'So, you don't live here?'

'I sort of do.'

'Do you want to live in London?'

'It's where my house is.'

'You didn't answer my question.'

She smiled. 'No, I didn't.'

'Because you want to live here.'

'I was just here for a rest.'

'And now?'

'I can't just give everything up and move here. It's a bit of a risk. It's not like moving to Bristol or something. I think I need paperwork and stuff. I need to work and I think I need to get permission to stay? Oh, I don't know.'

'What will you be giving up?'

'I have to get a job. And that's where my kind of jobs are.'

Ignacio looked at her and shook his head. 'Alice, have you ever thought there are other ways to live your life other than the way you have so far?'

She pulled up some ragged scrub grass and began to tear it up slowly. 'In my mind I was supposed to be married, have two or three children, be a successful artist and have my dream house by now. That's what I wanted when I was a little girl. I wanted the kind of man my stepfather is. Not an irresponsible, selfish, cruel waster like my father. But I chose Adam. Who despite outward appearances has turned out to be exactly like him. My mistake! I got my house though. That's all I've got.'

'I have seen your pictures. You are an artist.'

'I can't make a living out of them.'

Ignacio leaned back and shielded his eyes from the sun. 'My family loved it here. My grandparents owned a farm close by.'

'It's a beautiful spot.'

'Yes, it is. My parents used to drive us down to stay with them as often as they could. We children used to sit in the back of my father's truck with all our suitcases and extra food. I don't know why we needed extra food – we were going to a farm after all ... still, that is how my mother is! Even now. We were so happy – all I can remember is long, sunny summer's days with my family – my cousins and aunts and uncles would all come too. There would be noisy meals on a long table amongst the lemon trees, arguments, laughing, and when my grandfather had drunk too much, singing.'

'It sounds lovely.'

'It was. A lot of them are gone now – either died or moved away, or too busy to keep in touch. But I remember those days and it makes me love this place. And I have let new people into my life as I have grown older, and so I love other places, other things too.'

'Are you trying to tell me something?'

'Just that you must do what makes you happy. Because it can be gone in an instant and if you always look to the past you may never have what makes you happy there and then. Now.'

'That's very wise. You sound as if you've had some big sadness in your life?'

Ignacio laughed. 'No, not at all. My sister reads a lot of self-help books and I read them when I am at her house so I can't hear my nieces and nephews arguing.'

Alice wanted to throw her arms around him for the second time that day. 'Oh Ignacio.' She laughed. 'You do make me smile.'

He stood up and began to put his jacket back on. 'Come,'

he said. 'I think Stephano will be back from his lunch now. Do you want me to come with you?'

'No. No, thank you. I need to speak to him in private.' Alice shook the sand from her feet and put her shoes back on, and as she walked towards the building she turned. Ignacio was pacing along the beach dialling a number on his phone.

Stephano was standing under a small copse of trees taking photographs of the hotel gardens as Alice walked through the gates. 'Stephano?'

He looked up, startled. '*Ola*,' he said as Alice walked towards him. 'What are you doing here?'

'I came to see you,' she said.

'To see me?'

'Yes. I tried phoning you but couldn't get through. Is the signal bad here?'

'Yes, it is. And I haven't been checking my phone. I don't have long to finish the project.'

'Anyway,' she sighed, sitting on a bench in the shade. 'Have you got time to talk to me for a few minutes as I've come all this way?'

'Of course,' he said, sitting at the opposite end of the seat.

'Kathy's not very well. She was rushed to hospital a couple of days ago.'

He stood up in shock. 'Is she all right? Is she okay?' he asked, anxiously.

'Not really. She's out of hospital though.'

Stephano sat down, bowing his head and rubbing his temples.

'Why have you not been in contact with her, Stephano?'

'I needed some space. To think,' he said quietly.

'Now that's a bit of a luxury, isn't it?'

'You don't understand.'

'Understand what?'

'This wasn't supposed to happen. Not yet, anyway.'

213

'Not supposed to happen?' Alice could hear her voice rising with anger.

'I'm not ready for—'

'I don't think Kathy was ready for a family. But she's having to deal with it, isn't she?'

'But it's such a commitment.'

Alice stood up. 'Hang on a second. A few days ago you were really excited. Then suddenly you stopped contacting her.'

Stephano looked at the floor. 'We don't contact each other every day, you know?'

'Well I think things have changed,' she said, sharply, surprising herself.

He looked at her, shame creeping across his face

'I think you need to be in regular contact with her now you are having a baby together.' She moved closer. 'I think you made her think you wanted more than you had before,' she said, calmer now.

'I did. I do. But a baby ...'

Alice looked at him, confused. 'You know her so well, Stephano. I mean you were married to each other for a few years. You must know you can't play around with her emotions. This is serious. There is now another human being involved. It hasn't been born yet, but it's there.'

They sat silently for a while. 'Does she hate me?' he asked eventually.

'Yes and no. Look, I don't know what you two are going to do. But you need to speak to her. She's floundering. And I've never seen her like that.'

'I know, I know ... I hadn't either.'

'Well Stephano, do something about it.'

'I will call her now.'

'I thought the reception here was bad?'

He smiled thinly. 'If I walk up those steps it will probably be fine.'

'Go on then.'

'Okay, okay. I'm walking, look.'

'If I discover you haven't called, I know where you are, don't I?' said Alice to his back. She watched as he made the call, then stood up to go.

'Straight to voicemail,' he said. 'I left a message.'

'Go and see her,' sighed Alice. 'Please. For her.'

Stephano hung his head again. 'What must she think of me?' he said.

'Only one way to find out,' said Alice. 'I have to go. Good luck with it.'

As she walked out towards Ignacio and his waiting car she said to the sky, 'I know. Who was that? Was that me? Laidback Alice. Right, now to sort myself out.' She paused. 'Oh yeah, right,' she muttered, 'because it's so easy to sort *me* out. Not.'

The table was covered with baubles, beads, ribbons and tiles as Alice carefully threaded them onto the bracelet wire. Twenty lay in a wicker basket destined for her stockpile.

Talking to Ignacio had somehow triggered a restlessness inside her; she needed to do something positive and proactive that would occupy her completely for a while, so life wasn't all about the house and Adam and fear of what her life would be like in a month, or a year, or ten years from now. And somewhere from the back of her brain came the word – internet. Sell them on the internet.

Then she said the words out loud. 'Sell them on the internet.'

'Sorry? What did you say?' Ignacio had asked as they drove back to the apartment along the Marginal.

'Nothing. Don't worry. I just have an idea, that's all.'

The excitement came with the words. 'Sell them on the internet.' Of course, she thought. It was so obvious. 'Got to make them first,' she muttered as she almost ran into the apartment. 'Going to make a mountain of them. Then I will do the internet bit.'

And there she had sat for three hours, thinking of nothing but the colours and shapes and textures of the materials she had in front of her; how they should fit together; would some have to be exactly the same or did they all need to be unique? Should she make necklaces, too, and rings?

Everything else had gone. But there was something she knew deep down. She was dealing with Adam but couldn't quite put her finger on how.

Kathy took a two-hour lunch break before working late and rested at Alice's apartment. She glanced in the mirror and grimaced. 'At what point am I supposed to start glowing with imminent motherhood?' she said. 'I look like I've been living in a cave all my life surviving on a diet of pasties and washing my hair with lard.'

'Well I think you look gorgeous,' shouted Alice from the living room.

'Are you talking to your bracelets or to me? You haven't really looked up since I arrived.'

'Sorry, I'm on a roll. My ambition is to build a mountain of shiny beady pretty things and then take over the world.'

Kathy moved a pile of fabric to the side of the sofa and sat down. 'What's the material for?'

'Don't know. I nipped out earlier to the market and bought some just in case I needed it.'

Kathy laughed. 'I haven't seen you this manic since university.'

'Oh, no, really?' said Alice whilst curling some wire with a pair of pliers.

'It's lovely to see actually.'

'There! Done it.' Alice put the finished bracelet onto the mound of beads next to her and looked up. 'Oh, poor you. Do you want a cup of tea?'

'There! I knew I looked like crap,' sighed Kathy.

Alice stood up and gave her a hug. 'Sorry. But you will glow soon. I'm afraid I only have common or garden tea, not Mary's special brew.'

'Pity. I could do with some. Stephano's been ringing me virtually every half hour.'

'Oh, good. I'm so glad he's stepping up.'

'You think so? I've been ignoring him.'

'Why?'

'Because he cleared off when I needed him and now I'm not so sure I want him.'

Alice took Mary's book of ideas from the table and rifled through it.

'What are you doing?'

'Seeing if Mary's left a recipe for "Tea that gives you common sense"!'

'Good. Then you can have some of that yourself!'

'What do you mean?'

'You're making bracelets when you should be dealing with the practicalities of your house and Adam.'

'I am dealing with the practicalities!'

'No you're not. How is making bracelets sorting your life out?'

'Just two minutes ago you said it was lovely to see.'

'It is, but you are still sticking your head in the sand.'

'So are you!'

'No I'm not. I'm suffering from raging hormones. You, on the other hand should be out there fighting.'

'I am. By making bracelets.'

'Oh God. Just give me the tea. I don't understand.'

Alice walked to the kitchen. 'I've asked my solicitor to get three valuations for the house quickly. I should hear in the next few days.'

'And then?'

'Don't know to be honest.'

'Please stay. I need you. I don't know how to change nappies.'

'Neither do I!'

'But you're so happy here.'

'I know. But I only came for a break. And I don't know how I'd feel. It's a bit like stepping into a void. And I love my house. And things are so uncertain. How do I stay? Do I have to fill in forms? And my life is in London. Isn't it?' She walked back with a cup of tea for Kathy and a glass of wine for herself.

Kathy winced. 'Oh dear. My life is over!'

'Only for a few months.' Alice sat down and gulped down some wine.

'You haven't mentioned Luis,' said Kathy.

'He's been very busy.'

'Really?'

'Yes.'

'Yes?'

'Yes … look, I heard something when I was in town about him and some other woman.'

'From who?'

'That girl Marcella, with her friends.'

'Oh, for goodness sake. She's a spoilt brat. Stirs things up. Have you asked him about it?'

'No … I've had all this rubbish with Adam … but this whole playing with the band thing … I'm not very comfortable with it actually.'

'Only because she's hanging around. Look, he adores you. It's obvious. And frankly, he was playing in the band when you met him. What's he doing for your birthday?'

'Not sure. Something …'

'Well, I'll meet you straight after work, and then he can catch up with us!'

'Done.'

'Done.'

Alice's phone buzzed. 'Ah. Luis wants to meet for a quick coffee in between working on the building site, visiting estate agents and doing a gig tonight.'

'Told you. When?'

'Around six.'

'Right – I'm going to have a nap. Can you wake me in an hour and point me towards work?'

'I'll wake you up and escort you there so you don't fall asleep on the way.' Alice smiled. 'Meanwhile I'll be making a mountain of bracelets.'

'Here,' said Kathy guiding Alice into her treatment room, 'I've got this great pillow spray stuff that's been sent to me as a sample. You spray it on your pillow and apparently it makes you sleep really well.' She opened another door at the back of the room into a storage space and office. 'My secret room,' said Kathy, laughing. None of the other treatment rooms have it. It means I can hide away and do paperwork.'

'It smells lovely in here,' said Alice.

'It's torture at the moment,' said Kathy, cracking a window open. 'It's still making me feel sick.'

There was a soft knocking at the treatment room door. 'Kathy. There's a man here to see you. He says he's an old friend.'

'Is that what he's calling himself now? Really?'

The receptionist walked in looking confused.

'You mean it's not Stephano?'

'No.'

'Oh.' Kathy opened the door slightly and peered through. 'Great, that's all I need,' she muttered.

'Is everything all right?' asked Alice uneasily.

Adam pushed through to the room, and Kathy shoved Alice into the store cupboard, slamming the door shut.

'Kathy, it's been a while,' he said.

Alice put her ear to the door, heart beating, anxious, angry and longing for the solitude of her little house in London, where she could hide from everything and everyone.

'Adam,' said Kathy.

'Surely it's a hug for an old friend like me?'

'A hand shake is fine,' said Kathy. 'Well this is a surprise.'

'It would have been rude of me to be in the area and not try to see you.'

'It would have been fine,' she said. 'I would have understood if you couldn't.'

'Who'd have thought you would have ended up as a beauty therapist?' he said eventually, 'what with your business degree and everything.'

'Well, here I am. Beauty therapist. Running my own business. All this is mine.'

'Been here long?'

'About ten years actually. Remember? I got married to a Portuguese man. You came to my wedding. Then I moved out here.'

'Of course … look, I suppose … well, you know why I'm here don't you?'

'No.'

'Alice must have told you.'

'Alice hasn't mentioned you at all.'

Alice somehow managed to smile under the tangle of emotions she was feeling. Flight or fight were two of them.

He laughed in disbelief. 'Now I know that's not true.'

'Why?'

'Please don't play games, Kathy. We need to sort out this house. I want the capital to invest in my future.'

'Oh, what is your future?'

'Me and Veronique – my partner – we are opening a gallery and ceramic shop. She already has one in Argentina. We're bringing the model to the UK.'

'Oh.'

'And Alice is refusing to discuss it. Can you talk to her?

Reason with her? She's not returning my calls again. I don't want to get solicitors involved but I will have to if she doesn't grow up.'

A surge of anger made Alice try to open the door to shout at him, but it was stuck.

'What's the matter with that door?' he said. 'It seems to be shaking.'

'Nothing,' said Kathy. 'Looks fine to me. And grow up? Mr Flakey telling Alice to grow up?'

'No need to get personal.' His voice began to rise in frustration.

'From here, Adam,' she said slowly, 'it appears you are trying to push her into something she is not ready to do.'

'It's my future.'

'And hers.'

'This is ridiculous. You're as bad as she is. Tell her I want this resolved urgently. The house is as much mine as it is hers.'

Alice leaned against the door, breathing hard. *The lies!* He was no better than a thief.

'You know that's not true!' said Kathy, raising her voice.

'On paper it is. It doesn't really matter who paid for what. Both our names are on the mortgage and the deeds. She's not going to win this. We all know that.'

'Leave now!' said Kathy angrily. 'Now! Or should I call a security guard?'

'I'm going. I'm going,' he said. Alice heard his footsteps getting more distant. 'Just tell her to talk to me, all right? Because I'm beginning to get irritated.'

Alice tried the door again. She wanted to run after him and confront him. To show him she wasn't scared. But the door wouldn't move.

Kathy tried opening it from the other side. 'Oh, for goodness sake,' she said. 'I'm too weak to push. I'll get someone …' then she started giggling. 'Bit like one of those stage farces isn't it …'

Alice leaned against the door and sank to the floor as she began to laugh herself. 'Life used to be so much less complicated. Boring, sad and empty. But less complicated.'

There was another knock at the treatment room door.

'You've got another visitor,' said the receptionist.

'God, I thought he'd gone,' sighed Kathy.

'No, this is a different person,' said her colleague, lowering her voice.

'Is she in there?' It was Stephano. His voice grew louder as he pushed into the room. 'Are you okay? I heard you'd been in the hospital.'

'Oh, it's you.'

'Don't be like that, please.'

'Oh no you don't.'

'We need to talk.'

'No we don't.'

'I'm not going anywhere until you talk to me.'

'All right, but not out here. I've got five minutes before my next client.

Alice stood up and moved into the office, further away. She didn't want to listen to their private conversation, but their voices were raised, and she could hear everything.

'You must think I'm a terrible man.'

'Yes.'

'I panicked.'

'And?'

'I've pulled myself together.'

'Oh lucky me.'

'I'm here now. I'm not going anywhere.'

'And what makes you think I want you?'

'Alice said—'

'What's Alice got to do with this?' cut in Kathy.

'She came to find me and—'

'You mean you only came to see me because my friend told you to?'

'It wasn't like that.'

Alice began to wonder if she needed to get away from Kathy too and looked at the window longingly.

'Well, you just said it was.'

'You're being unreasonable.'

'I'm being what? What?!' she shouted.

'It's your hormones. The baby … our baby.'

'No – it's because you ran away. And I needed you.'

'I'm sorry.'

'And now I don't need you!'

'Yes you do.'

Alice tried to ease the window open, but it was only designed to open a few inches.

'Let's get married!' said Stephano quickly.

'What? Again?'

'Marry me. I love you!'

'No you don't. You ran away.'

'But I'm back.'

'You're unreliable.'

Alice pulled a book about herbal remedies from a shelf and opened it, trying to focus on something else.

'Not any more'

'For goodness sake. I don't trust you.'

'Learn.'

'Learn? You have to earn trust.'

'I will.'

'You stopped contacting me for nearly three days. And I was in hospital.'

'I'm sorry. We don't always speak to each other every day.'

'Well now we're having a baby so it's different.'

'Yes, that's what Alice said.'

'Alice again!'

The book she was pretending to read fell open on a page dedicated to the soothing powers of chamomile. Alice wondered if there was any in the storage room.

'Look. It's always been there, hasn't it? Us. Even when we got divorced. I never stopped loving you. Never…'

There was a pause. 'Me neither,' Kathy said.

Alice felt so happy for them she wanted to cry. The room fell silent for a few minutes, then Alice heard the outer door slam open.

'She's still not answering her phone and I absolutely demand you tell her I want to see her now!' It was Adam.

'Who said you could come in here?' cried Kathy angrily.

'Adam? What the hell do you think you're doing!' said Stephano.

'That girl tried to stop me from coming in, but I'm sick and tired of all this. Veronique is getting stressed from it and I need to sort it out. She's crying and wailing and shouting.'

Alice stood up and rushed towards the door again – she couldn't allow him to do this to her friends – but she tripped over a loose carpet tile and stumbled.

'You should be ashamed of yourself. We all know what you're trying to do. Get out now,' shouted Stephano.

'I want to speak to Alice!'

'Why don't you just leave her alone?' said Kathy.

'I want what's mine,' said Adam. 'She'll have to speak to me soon. I'm not giving up.'

'Get out!' shouted Kathy.

There was the sound of a scuffle, and a door slamming.

'I feel sick again,' said Kathy. 'I need to get some air. And I want another biscuit. Get me another biscuit. Please.'

Alice stood up and tried the door again.

'Kathy, Kathy! Has he gone?'

'Yes, for now. Big bully,' sighed Kathy.

'Can I hear Alice?' said Stephano.

'I'm stuck in the storeroom,' Alice said. 'Help' she called limply.

Stephano tried the door, then pushed it hard. Alice almost

fell out into the room. 'I'm so sorry that he got you involved,' she said.

'God he's aged,' said Kathy.

'We're looking after you,' said Stephano.

'Don't let him ruin your birthday,' said Kathy, putting her arms around her. 'And don't forget you're meeting Luis later.'

Stephano kissed Alice on the cheek. 'And thank you,' he said. 'Oh, you smell nice.'

'Fifteen minutes trapped in the store cupboard of a beauty salon,' said Alice. 'I'll go now. I think you have a lot to talk about.'

'Thank you for speaking to Stephano,' said Kathy. 'I really don't know what I'd do without you.'

Luis was sitting in the café by the lighthouse, his head bent over the table, flyers and paperwork piled in front of him, Elvis at his feet. As Alice walked towards him, she began to relax, relief washing over her with every step. Of course everything was fine. She'd allowed herself to be poisoned by other people and Adam's presence was making her anxious about everything.

Elvis trotted to her, his tail wagging, and Luis stood, smiling warmly, his arms open, inviting her in. 'Oh, Alice,' he said, wrapping them around her. 'I'm so glad to see you. So sorry I can't stay long, but you make me calm and happy and I needed to see you.'

'I needed to see you too,' she whispered. She sat down opposite him and waved to the waiter for a coffee. 'How are you feeling?' she asked.

'Better now you're here. But tired. And stressed. All will be fine in the end, but I need to sell that house quickly.' He rubbed his temples and showed her some of the paperwork. 'I printed out some of the e-mails I've had from the estate agents – it's easier for me to compare what they offer. They all suggest I drop the price significantly for a quick sale.'

'Ah,' said Alice. 'Is that something you can do?'

He sighed. 'I may have to. It's not good though. My mind is so muddled at the moment I can't think straight.'

Alice put her hand on his. 'You're very tired, aren't you?'

'Yes. But tomorrow evening I'm all yours. A night off from all of this for your birthday. Where would you like to go?'

Alice smiled. 'Do you know I think I want to sit in the square and relax with you and Kathy and just be. Is that okay?'

He kissed her hand. 'If that is what you want, that's what we'll do.' He looked into her eyes. 'Is everything all right? You seem a bit subdued.'

Alice hesitated. She didn't want to tell him – the time she had with Luis felt precious and talking to him about Adam would only contaminate it. He squeezed her hand. She took a breath. Should she speak to him about it? He'd know what to do. 'Well, there—'

'There you are!' She was interrupted by Antonio shouting from the road as he got out of a car.

Luis looked at the sky. 'Just a moment's rest from him. Please.' He looked at Alice. 'I'm sorry about this.'

Antonio was followed by a sulky-looking Marcella and another woman.

Luis put his head in his hands. 'I don't need this.'

Alice squeezed his hand. 'Should I go?' Antonio was glaring at her already and she was in no mood for confrontation. She knew that if he pushed her just a little she would react – slow-to-anger Alice had been replaced over the past couple of days by the one who wouldn't take it any more. And being trapped in a cupboard listening to Adam ranting hadn't helped.

'No, please. I'll get rid of him.'

'Who's this?' said the woman as they arrived at the table.

'This is Alice, my girlfriend,' said Luis. 'Alice, this is Susannah, a very old friend and surprisingly, Marcella's aunt.'

'Hello,' said Alice, standing up and holding out her hand.

Susannah shook it half-heartedly. Alice remembered Luis talking to her briefly at a gig a few weeks before.

Marcella tossed her hair sulkily. 'I don't know what you're doing here, Auntie. It's my idea.'

'Because you don't have the business to do it, Marcella,' snapped Susannah.

Alice sat down and looked at Luis, realising that for the second time in a couple of hours she was trapped in something she couldn't run away from.

'Can I ask what you're all doing here?' Luis said impatiently.

'I told Marcella and Susannah about your predicament about the houses, and Susannah can help you.'

Luis stood up. 'What were you doing telling them about my business? You had no right.'

'I was trying to help,' said Antonio. 'You've been bad-tempered, tired and over busy. It's beginning to affect the band.'

'How many times have I told you?' said Luis irritably. 'I'm leaving the band. I'm doing this short term.'

'You've said that before,' said Antonio.

'This time I mean it,' said Luis. 'I'm sorry Marcella, Susannah, I'm sure you mean well but he shouldn't have told you.'

'But I can help,' said Susannah sitting down. 'I have a property development business. I know you bought the old farmhouse on the hill and I'm interested in buying it.'

'I'm not selling that one,' said Luis.

'But the land is perfect for a new development.'

'Does that mean you want to knock the farmhouse down?' asked Alice.

Susannah ignored her. 'Luis, it is a perfect opportunity.'

'It's not for sale,' he said. 'Thank you for the offer though.'

She took a card out of her purse and gave it to him. 'If you change your mind,' she said. 'I could meet you there tomorrow.'

'Tomorrow I'm working and celebrating Alice's birthday. And as I said it's not for sale. But thank you for the offer. It's very kind.'

Susannah stood up. 'Okay.' She smiled. 'We had better go. Marcella is determined we dress up for the gig tonight. We'll meet you in the car Antonio.'

As they walked away, Antonio sat down next to Alice. 'You should watch her, Luis,' he said, looking right past her. 'Marcella says she saw her arguing with a man in public, and she's seen her drunk or drugged or worse.'

There it was again, the anger. She could feel it welling up inside her. 'You should be careful about spreading unfounded rumours, Antonio. I could take you to court.' She picked up a bottle of water from the table and threw the contents at him then stood up, shocked at what she'd done. And surprised at how much she'd enjoyed it.

Antonio faced her, angrily. 'See, she's unhinged,' he said. 'See you later. And tonight, make sure you smile.'

Alice began to shake again. 'I'm sorry, Luis. Sorry, it's just—'

Luis grabbed hold of her and pulled her to him. 'It's okay, I knew something was wrong. And I've been wanting to do worse to him than throw water at him. Well done. Now sit down next to me and tell me what's been going on. I've been so wrapped up in my problems I haven't thought about yours.'

'Adam is here,' she blurted out. 'Him and his new girlfriend. He's trying to intimidate me. But he's just made me angry. He's ruining everything. He's trying to take my house and he's barged in here. And he went to see Kathy at the salon, and I was trapped in a room and couldn't tell him what I thought …' She tailed off, tears trickling down her cheeks.

Luis picked up a napkin and dabbed her eyes. 'Oh, Alice. It will be okay. I'm here and I won't let him hurt you. I promise.'

She looked up at him. 'And I've been hearing things about

you – Marcella gossiping with her friends about you and her aunt. And I've been worried and …'

Luis looked at her, surprised. 'Susannah? I have no interest. She's married and as spoilt as her niece. They are playing mind-games with each other. Could you see? She's from the past. Completely the past. And nothing happened then with her either anyway. It's Antonio trying to control things again. His gambling debts are catching up with him and he needs their support to get more gigs. It's his mess, not mine.' He pulled her to him. 'How could you ever think that?'

'It's all happened so quickly. I don't know where I am or what to do, and when Adam turned up with his girlfriend it made me insecure.'

He kissed her face softly. 'I only want you,' he whispered. 'Only you.'

The panic in Alice subsided again, the familiar happy loop in her stomach making her smile. 'I only want you too,' she whispered back, holding him tight.

His phone buzzed suddenly. He sighed. 'It's my alarm – I have to get ready for this gig.'

Alice touched his face, and he grabbed her hand again, kissing it softly.

'And I will see you in the square tomorrow at 7 p.m. for your birthday. Now, come, I'll give you a lift back to the apartment.'

Chapter Twenty

The dots of sunlight on the bedroom floor promised a sunny day and Alice smiled, stretching along the bed and rolling onto her feet, the words Luis had whispered last night wrapping her in a warm, happy glow. *'I want you. Only you.'* She stretched again and picked up her phone, clicking onto a voicemail from Kathy singing 'Happy Birthday' very loudly.

Walking towards the balcony, she began to sing quietly, 'Happy Birthday to me, Happy Birthday to me, Happy Birthday to me … heeee … Happy Birthday to me.' Pulling open the voile curtains, she moved back the shutters and opened the glass doors.

'Tah dah,' she said, arms outstretched, stepping into the morning sun as if she were taking a curtain call. Aphrodite mewed noisily at her feet, so Alice picked her up.

'It's a beautiful day today,' she announced, nuzzling into the cat's soft fur. 'And it will continue to be so. Nothing … hear that, *nothing*! … will stop it being a beautiful day. Real life may continue tomorrow. But today, Aphrodite, today is *mine*!'

Leaning on the balcony she surveyed the garden below remembering a birthday not so many years before when she got caught in a severe summer thunder storm on her way to the pictures with a couple of friends. 'I spent my birthday evening smelling distinctly musty watching an action film about a man who thinks he's a spider because there was nothing else on, Aphrodite. Anyway, this birthday will be the one I remember because I have stepped outside to a cloudless blue sky. And I reek of jasmine, not city rain, because jasmine wafts everywhere around here, not traffic fumes.'

But somewhere at the back of her mind an unwanted word began to repeat itself. *Adam.*

'... does not exist today,' she said out loud. 'Is that the doorbell?'

Opening the door, Alice found a green basket full of beautiful flowers. Surprised, she picked them up, eagerly opening the card to see if they were from Luis.

Happy Birthday lovely Alice. Stand Firm. Fight.
And enjoy your day, love Mary and Frank xxxx

So kind, she thought, wondering how Mary knew it was her birthday, and only mildly disappointed they weren't from Luis. *Kathy's probably been e-mailing them with all the news*, she thought, carrying the basket into the apartment and enjoying the flowers' light scent. Her phone rang and she answered it mid-sneeze, balancing the flowers in her other hand.

'Bless you!' said an irritable-sounding Kathy.

Alice put the flowers down. 'Sorry. I was smelling a bunch of flowers and got a bit carried away.'

'Happy Birthday. How are you today?'

Alice wandered back onto the balcony. 'In a good mood actually. Thank you for your voicemail. How are you?'

'Didn't sleep a wink. Could do with staying away from work but I have to go in. I should be refreshed and ready for birthday drinks later though. Shall we say seven in the square?'

'Sounds good. Take care. Try to rest.'

'I'll nap on the treatment bed in between clients. I'm only half joking you know!'

'I know! See you later.' As soon Kathy hung up, the phone rang again.

'Happy Birthday.' Alice's insides did a loop the loop at the sound of Luis's voice.

'Thank you!'

'Can't wait to see you later. I'm so sorry I haven't been around much recently. But I will make it up to you. I promise. It was so good to see you last night. What are you doing today?'

'I think I may take a trip into Lisbon this morning. Take in the view from Castelo Sao George. Have a coffee. Come home and get all dressed up for this evening.'

'I'll come and get you.'

'Okay. But I'm meeting Kathy in the square at seven for a drink. Can you get here before that?'

He sighed wearily. 'I can't no. And would you believe it, I'm not playing in the band. Never again. I'll tell you all about it tonight. But there was another blow-up last night …' He hesitated. 'That can wait until I see you. I'll meet you there at half seven. Is that okay? It's going to be a beautiful day and a beautiful evening.'

Alice felt a little twinge of relief. No band to pull him away, no Antonio playing his games. 'Well I'm glad you're not in the band any more, but doesn't it make things difficult for you, you know, financially?'

There was a pause. 'I've been missing you Alice,' he said. Then he rang off.

Alice's stomach did a loop the loop again. 'Marcella was being vile,' she said to Aphrodite. 'I was worrying for nothing.'

Rifling through the wardrobe for a sundress, she knocked over the pile of bracelets she'd packed into a case the night before. As they spilled out onto the floor she giggled, watching them tumble like a multi-coloured lava flow of beads and ribbons. Deciding she liked the sight of the rainbow mountain they created, she left them where they stood, mentally patting herself on the back for creating so many in such a short space of time.

She got dressed and sat sipping tea on the balcony. The green of the trees, the blue of the pool and the pink of the bougainvillea below shone bright and deep, the smell of freshly cut grass was clean and crisp and even the growl of nearby cars sounded melodic. 'Happy Birthday to me,' said Alice again, raising her cup to the sky. 'Happy Birthday to me.' Then she took her camera and headed to the station for the half hour journey to Lisbon.

Alice gazed over the rooftops of Lisbon across the Tagus to the statue of Christo Rei. She wanted to stretch her arms out and sing but decided to take out the camera and make it a working day. Because she knew that as soon as she gave her mind a rest and stared, Adam, Luis, the house and money would all crowd in and spoil the view. The rooftops were already framed in her mind's eye before she even pulled the camera to focus, the photography taking over, driving her around the castle and down the narrow streets of Alfama to the shade of the Miradouro de Santa Luzia. The Tagus shimmered below as the red roofs jostled for space towards the water.

'Excuse me, madam. May I?'

Alice looked up, mildly startled. For a moment she had forgotten where she was. The young man smiled at her.

'I'm sorry. Did I surprise you?'

She smiled. 'A little bit, yes, to be honest.' She looked at him, wondering what he meant by 'may I?'

He bowed his head. 'I do apologise. I just wondered if you wanted your photograph taken with the view from Miradouro Santa Luiza in the background. You seem to be taking photographs of everything but you won't be in any of them!'

Alice smiled again, a little bit surprised that he'd noticed. 'Oh, that's very kind, but …'

He held his hands up. 'This must look terrible,' he said. 'I'm just waiting for some friends and I saw you looking so wrapped up in taking pictures I had to find out why.'

'Oh.' Alice looked into his kind brown eyes and relaxed. 'I sort of sell some of my photos as prints, so I'm exploring what I can do with all the beautiful things and views in Lisbon.'

'Ahh, an artist … but you can still be in a picture, can't you?'

Alice hesitated. He looked nice and normal, but you couldn't always tell. A waiter from the café walked over to him and said something to him in Portuguese.

He nodded. 'My table is ready. I've reserved it for my friends, but they won't be here for half an hour.' He smiled reassuringly. 'You can trust me.'

Alice laughed. 'It would be lovely to have my photo taken, to be honest.' She handed him the camera and posed for the photograph.

'If you move over there by the bougainvillea, that can frame it,' he said.

She moved obediently and waited for him to take the photo.

'There you are,' said the man, handing her back the camera.

'Thank you. You didn't tell me your name?'

'Sebastian,' he said, bowing.

'I'm Alice. You've been very kind.' She turned to walk away.

'Wait,' he said. 'My table is ready and my friends aren't here. Would you like to join me for a coffee? I've never spoken to a real artist before.'

'Well, I'm not ...' said Alice instinctively. But then she looked at his smiling face, and thought, *but I am, aren't I? And it's my birthday*. She nodded. 'Thank you. That's very kind.'

They sat down and ordered coffee.

'Is this your first visit to Lisbon?'

'I've been in a couple of times. I'm staying in Cascais.'

'Cascais is perfect.'

'Yes, it is lovely.'

He sipped his coffee and checked his phone then he turned his attention to Alice again. 'Have you been here long?'

'About six weeks or so.'

'Six weeks? I apologise. I assumed you were a tourist just passing through.'

Alice thought for a moment. 'I sort of am and I'm not I suppose.'

'So what do you think of Portugal?'

'I've only seen a very small part of it, but I think it's gorgeous. I'm rather taken with it actually.'

'Where are you from?'

'I live in London.'

'London … I was at university in London. St Mary's. It was a good time for me. Now I am back home in Portugal.'

'Do you ever go back to London?'

'Yes, I stay with friends whenever I can.' He leaned forward and touched the camera. 'May I?' he asked.

'Yes of course. Don't know if they're any good. I've just been snapping away.'

He began to click through the images. 'This first one is very good of you,' he said, seriously. 'The photographer is very talented.'

Alice laughed.

'So, can I see any of your prints here?'

'Well, I have just sold some of my mounted photos to a couple of shops in Cascais.'

'These are excellent. I can see why.'

Alice watched him as he concentrated, his dark curly hair pushed back behind his ears, sunglasses perched on top of his head. He looked up and their eyes met briefly.

'Are you here alone?' he asked, smiling.

'It's my birthday. I am treating myself to a morning in Lisbon.'

'Your birthday? I hope you have a lovely day.'

He gave the camera back to Alice and leaned back in his chair.

'So, Sebastian, what did you study at University?'

'Chemistry.'

'And is that what you do now?'

'Oh, no, of course not. I came home and work in the family business. We own some bookshops and I help manage them. I wanted to strike out and do ground-breaking chemical research, but I took the easy route.'

'There's nothing wrong with that,' Alice said.

'So, why did you come to Portugal?'

'I lost my job and I needed a break.'

'When are you going back?'

'Now that's a good question. I don't know!'

'And that is a good answer.' He leaned forward and smiled at her. 'And where is Mr Alice?'

'My boyfriend is at work in Estoril. I think.'

Sebastian closed his eyes and put his hand to his chest dramatically. 'I am stricken,' he said. 'There is a man in your life already.'

Alice giggled like a schoolgirl. 'Don't tell me there is no woman in your life.'

'Sometimes yes, sometimes no. I am fickle.'

Alice sipped her coffee, glancing at the tourists looking for the best spot to take the perfect photograph of Lisbon.

'It's a beautiful place,' Sebastian said. 'And you suit it perfectly.'

Alice smiled, then glanced at her watch. 'Ah, I've got to go – I'm due in Cascais in a couple of hours.'

Sebastian stood and kissed her on both cheeks. 'Goodbye, Alice and thank you for your company.'

'Bye, Sebastian. And thank you for yours.'

She hurried along the pavement, navigating the narrow streets towards Cais do Sodre to catch the train back to Cascais. It felt like she was floating above the cold hard cobbles with tiny wings on her back carrying her softly home. She smiled at everybody, and everybody smiled back. *This is where I'm meant to be*, she thought as a warm glow enveloped her body from somewhere inside. 'I belong here.'

Then her phone buzzed with a text. Going to be a bit late. House stuff. Could be positive! Will be there by 7.45. Luis xx

Alice walked down the hill to the square, as the sky over the bay rippled with delicate pink clouds and the boats glowing in the last light of the day. The stalls along the seafront were full of people browsing and chatting, the multi-coloured trousers, dresses and skirts billowing in the breeze. One man was trying on a straw hat, laughing with the stall-holder, his wife fussing around, picking up different kinds for him and a child was pulling her mother towards a stall selling beach toys, focused on an inflatable unicorn. Alice moved through them all, enjoying being part of the early evening ritual, looking back over the day and anticipating with pleasure the evening to come, with Luis, Kathy and Stephano and her new friends in the town. She had managed to push the worries about the house, her job and Adam right to the back of her mind. Turning into the square, she smiled – three dogs lay at the foot of the statue, a man was juggling on a tricycle outside a shop, and the tables of the restaurants and cafes were brimming with people eating, chatting and laughing. She sighed with pleasure, found a table next to the wall of Carlos's restaurant and sat down.

'Alice, you look beautiful today!' Carlos took her hand slowly and kissed it.

'Thank you. I thought I'd dress up for my birthday.'

'Your birthday! *Feliz anniversario*! Happy Birthday!'

'Thank you.'

'The blue of the dress suits you perfectly. So – a drink on the house from me.'

'Lovely. Glass of wine please.'

'You are not spending your birthday alone, are you?'

'No. I'm waiting for Kathy and Stephano. And Luis. But he's going to be a bit late. Actually, can I have some bread and olives to keep me going?'

'Of course.'

'Kathy should be here any minute.'

'Just sit back and relax.'

'I will.' Alice checked her phone. No new messages. Looking through her purse she realised she'd forgotten to get any cash. 'Actually, Carlos. I've got to nip around the corner for a minute. Could you keep the table for me?

He placed a reserved mark on it. 'It's yours for the night, Alice.'

She smiled at him and stood up. 'Thanks. I won't take long.'

Weaving through the tables towards the road Alice rushed to the cashpoint and impatiently waited for the money. Putting her card back into her purse she felt someone standing too close behind her, a strong smell of aftershave hanging in the air around them. She tensed and stared intently at the screen.

'Ahh, Alice. I was hoping I'd bump into you. Veronique is having a one-to-one yoga session so I thought I'd have a bit of a wander before dinner. That's a lovely dress – it looks like its cost you quite a bit of money.' Adam leaned in closer. 'Are you checking your bank account? Your money must be getting less and less every day. I mean, how are you supporting yourself?'

She looked up at him and forced a smile. 'None of your business really, is it?' She tried to sound calm, but her heart was beating angrily.

He put his hands gently on her shoulders. 'You know I'll get what I want in the end.'

Alice removed his hands and began to walk away. *Go away, Adam. Just go away*, she thought as he followed closely behind.

Sitting down at her table, she picked up the wine Carlos had brought and took a gulp as Adam pulled up a chair. Alice said nothing.

'I know it may surprise you, but I come in peace. It's your birthday and I wanted to say hello and wish you well,' he said.

Carlos appeared behind Alice. 'Is everything okay here?' he asked.

'Yes. It is. Thank you,' said Alice.

'Can I have a beer?' asked Adam.

Carlos glanced at Alice. She nodded reluctantly. There was no point in causing a scene. Especially not on her birthday.

'Coming right up.'

'Amazing. The service here has been incredibly bad. Veronique and I have been three times to various cafes in this square and have sat waiting for ages to be served. We gave up. She was getting quite upset actually. She's very emotional. It's her creative side, you know.'

'I find the service excellent,' said Alice, remembering the conversation she'd had with Carlos a few days earlier.

'So where is everybody? Surely this isn't your birthday celebration?'

'I'm waiting for Kathy. And Luis.'

'Luis? A gentleman friend?' he said, almost sneering.

'That's right,' said Alice, smiling hard and taking another gulp of wine.

Adam pretended not to hear. 'I'd check on Kathy if I were you. I saw her yesterday and she looked distinctly queasy. No doubt that aggressive hairy chap Stephano bundled her home. I thought they were divorced years ago.'

Alice picked up an olive and shoved it in her mouth to stop herself from saying anything. She was not going to rise to anything he said. *Not today. Let me have today*, she thought. *Let me have today.*

Carlos banged the beer onto the table and glared at Adam.

'Why haven't you been replying to my messages or calls?' he asked casually, taking a gulp.

'Because I blocked your number. I block and unblock it when I feel like it.'

Adam looked up at her, surprised. 'That's not like you. You were always so ... so ... doing the right thing.'

'Yes, I know. Things change.'

He glanced at his watch. 'Quarter to eight. You've been sitting here a long time on your lonesome? Are you sure they're coming?'

Alice popped another olive into her mouth and smiled.

'Look.' He leaned forward. 'Let's be civil. Once upon a time

239

we loved each other a lot. We can remember that and not get nasty.'

'I'm not getting nasty, Adam.'

'You've changed. I can't quite put my finger on how.'

'You haven't seen me for over two years. Of course, I've changed.'

They sat in silence for a while. Adam tapped his foot irritably whilst Alice scanned the square for nothing in particular.

'The house,' he said eventually.

'The house?'

'It's half mine.'

Alice sighed visibly and smiled at him again. 'You're like a broken record.'

'Legally. It's mine.'

'If not morally.'

'One has to do one's best to secure one's future.'

'Does one?'

'Alice!' Ignacio weaved through the tables towards them, followed by his nephews and his sister. 'You look beautiful today,' he said. 'Is everything all right here?' he continued, glancing at Adam.

'It's okay, thank you.'

'Good,' he said, pulling out a chair at the table in front of them and sitting down, along with his family. 'These are my nephews,' he said, 'you have met them already, and this is my sister Cristiane.' They all waved at Alice and smiled. Then the nephews ran to the other side of the square to see some friends.

'Thanks for coming,' she said. 'What would you all like to drink?'

'This is totally out of character for you,' said Adam leaning back, his voice beginning to sound aggressive.

Ignacio glanced at Carlos and beckoned him over.

'What is?' said Alice.

'Coming here. Being adventurous. Taking a leap of faith ...'

Carlos stood next to the table and began to clear some space. 'The usual for you all?' he said to Ignacio.

'Not sure what you mean—' Alice smiled at Adam again.

'—not being obsessed with decorating that bloody house,' he interrupted.

'I wasn't obsessed with it. I was redeveloping it.'

'But you didn't do anything else.'

'I did actually. But someone had to be the grown up. Once you stopped paying towards it I had to pay the bills and stay in my proper, sensible, well-paid job.'

'Don't blame me for that. You chose to do it.'

'Because you chose to fart about freelancing and never stuck to anything.'

'You got boring.'

Alice turned to him and smiled widely. 'So did you.'

'Me?' Adam looked astonished.

'You're not as interesting as you think.'

'I'm enjoying this,' said Ignacio to his sister. 'We are all very fond of Alice.'

'If you had let the bloody house go before this we could have travelled together,' hissed Adam. 'I wanted us to. You know I did. So we may have lost a bit of money, but we would have had experiences. Why do you think I left?'

Alice stared into her drink. 'You just lose interest in things. Pick them up, put them down,' she said eventually.

'You're so stubborn, Alice.'

Carlos reappeared with a tray of drinks and began to place them on the table, glaring at Adam.

'You don't know what it's like to be thrown out of your own home with nowhere to go,' she said slowly. She took another drink, trying not to throw it over him.

'No I don't. But you were so obsessed with it you didn't give me any time. Didn't nurture me. Didn't understand. Is it any wonder I looked for excitement in other people?' He

241

stood up. 'I'm going to get half of the house Alice. You might as well give in. It will save a lot of time and money.' He threw some money on the table for his drink. 'I have to get back to Veronique. We are going to source some suppliers in Portugal for the shop in Cheam so have to plan. It's our big leap into the unknown.' He stood up. 'Happy Birthday, Alice.'

As he walked away Alice saw some of the diners at nearby tables staring at them, whilst others were concentrating very hard on eating. She wanted to run after him and tell him he was a liar and a bully. She knew he'd deliberately tried to upset her on her birthday. She bit her lip. Where was Luis? Where was Kathy?

Ignacio moved his chair towards her. 'He has very feminine hands. I do not like him.'

Alice smiled thinly. 'Nope. Neither do I,' she said quietly. *Leave me alone Adam, leave me alone, please leave me alone*, cried the voice in her head. Just one day without worrying about the future. That's all she'd wanted, but it was closing in on her no matter how much she tried to ignore it. Another text arrived. Delayed. Be there as soon as I can. Luis x. Alice sighed with relief. He was on his way – he would put his arms around her and it would all go away, just for a while.

The flowers and the busker arrived out of nowhere, like someone had rubbed a lamp secretly and wished them up for Alice, and there they were in a kind of puff of smoke. The someone turned out to be Carlos and the smoke was the fuddle in Alice's brain left behind by Adam's verbal assault. She'd looked down again for a second to check her phone for messages. There were none.

When she looked up a young man with a guitar stood next to her smiling, a dozen red roses scattered decoratively on the table. Carlos, Ignacio, his nephews and sister stood around her, smiling. The busker began to sing 'Happy Birthday' and Ignacio turned and waved at the hubbub of people in the square. The musician played another chord, and Ignacio conducted the throng to sing 'Happy Birthday' to Alice as Kathy and Stephano walked around the corner.

Alice beamed happily as a cheer erupted from a multitude of people she didn't know in a place that suddenly felt like home. Standing up, she hugged her two knights in shining armour and the busker. 'Thank you,' she said.

'I'm Felipe. What would you like me to sing?' he asked. 'I am all yours for the evening. I am your birthday present.'

'My own busker?' Alice laughed. 'Thank you! How about "Daydream Believer"?' she asked. 'Yes. "Daydream Believer" please. And I'll leave the rest to you.'

'Sit,' Carlos instructed. 'Stay here for the evening. Why would you want to be anywhere else?'

'I really wouldn't want to be anywhere else.' She smiled as Kathy and Stephano arrived next to her. 'Come on. Party time!'

'I'm so sorry we're late,' gasped Kathy sinking down into a chair. 'You did get my text, didn't you? It's just you normally reply and you didn't.'

Alice checked her phone again. 'Nope, nada, ninguem, nothing.'

Stephano popped a bottle of champagne in an ice bucket. 'None for you my darling,' he said, kissing Kathy. 'It's all for us!'

'I had a bit of a turn.' Kathy sighed. 'And I just sort of fainted. Again.'

Carlos set down the glasses. 'Today is a good day. Look around you. And then look up'.

The sky was shot through with spirals of red and pink clouds, as the sun began to set.

'It's getting dark already?' sighed Alice. 'Where did the time go?'

'Where is Luis?' Kathy scanned the tables.

'Not here. Late. I got a text a while ago.'

'Well, I'm sure he'll be here soon. And if you didn't get my text either perhaps there's something wrong with your signal. Speaking of which.' Kathy pulled an iPad out of her bag and switched it on.

'What …?' Alice was pulled up from her seat and twirled away by Ignacio's cousin who had decided to dance to a reggae version of 'In The Summertime.' Suddenly the square was a spontaneous mass of dancers and diners, with smiling waiters dodging uncertainly around the tables. Alice laughed. It erupted unbidden and cascaded out unstoppably, as if someone had pressed a button in her back that pushed it out of her body. She had no control over it as it bubbled joyfully into the crowd, mingling with the shouts and shrieks and tuneless singing surrounding her. As she danced, she almost forced herself to be happy. Adam could wait. The house could wait. *Live in the moment*, she thought. She was like two people – the dancing, happy birthday girl, and the one who was hurt and terrified of what was going to happen tomorrow and the day after and the day after that.

'Alice … Alice!' Kathy shouted as the song finished. 'Look here!'

Bursting out of the mass she almost fell onto the table.

'Happy Birthday, darling,' said her mum.

'Mum? Where are you? I can't see you?'

'Focus dear. I'm on Skype. Look at the screen.'

'Mum!' Alice shouted at the iPad.

'We're all here, look!' Alice's stepfather, sister, brother-in-law and her nephew and niece all crowded into the frame. 'Happy Birthday!' they all shouted.

'Can you sit down Alice? I can only see your stomach at the moment not your face,' said her mum.

'Is this better?' Alice asked, pulling a chair close, wanting to reach into the screen and hug her.

'You look lovely,' said her mum. 'You look so well. Portugal suits you.'

'Does it?'

'Yes. Well, I haven't seen you for weeks. And what with your internet lockdown caused by He Who Shall Not Be Named we haven't even done this, have we?'

'He was here earlier.'

'My God!' shouted her mum. 'You're not trying to be friends again, are you?'

'Calm down, Myra,' whispered her stepfather in the background.

'No, Mum. He's just being a pain. But can we not talk about him?'

'Lovely bracelets,' said Tara, pushing her face into view.

'Oh these …' Alice shook them at the screen. 'I made them. I sell them through some stalls. I've got this idea now, too. I'm going to sell them on the web. Set up a site.'

'Fab idea!' said Tara.

The screen began to fuzz over. 'I've got something to—' But the connection went dead.

'Oh,' said Alice. 'They've gone.'

'Nice idea though,' said Kathy. 'It was mine.'

Alice hugged her. 'I love you,' she said. 'Did you mention to Mary what was going on in any e-mails at all?'

'No. I've not contacted her for a while to be honest. Why?'

'Just got a bunch of flowers and a cryptic message for my birthday.'

'Mystic Mary strikes again.' Kathy laughed as Carlos handed Alice another full glass of champagne.

'Drink up, birthday girl,' he said.

She took a sip just before Ignacio pulled her towards the edge of the tables for a dance.

'My song!' he shouted into her ear. 'What a Wonderful World.'

Alice laughed again, but as she looked up, she felt a chill down her back. Marcella and her friends were standing near the statue, disdain oozing from their every pore.

Alice hugged Ignacio. 'Thank you,' she whispered, 'for being such a good friend.'

For the next hour, despite Adam's attempts to upset her, and Marcella's brief appearance, Alice relaxed and enjoyed being with people who cared about her. She drank and ate and laughed, wanting the evening to go on forever so she wouldn't have to deal with the real life waiting for her in the morning.

Kathy glanced at her watch. 'I know it's quite early o clock for me, but I am so tired, Alice. Is it okay if I go now? I've got to work tomorrow and every day is quite a struggle at the moment.'

Alice put her glass down and grabbed her friend. 'Don't be silly, silly. Thank you for coming. It's been wonderful.'

'Where is Luis? I'd feel much better about going if he was here.'

'God, he is late isn't he? I'll call him now. Don't worry. I'm fine here with Ignacio and Carlos, and my friend Felipe, the busker.'

Stephano picked up his coat. 'Thank you for giving me a kick up the backside, Alice,' he said. As they left, Alice scanned the square once again for Luis. Then she called him but it went to voicemail.

'Hi it's me. Are you okay? It's just you were supposed to be here over two hours ago. I'm still here, but I'm just going to have a quick walk around to stretch my legs. My table's the one with the man with the guitar next to it. See you soon. Hopefully...' She turned to Ignacio. 'I'm getting some fresh air.'

'But you are outside already!'

'I know but I'm going to a different outside.'

She walked towards the beach and paused, enjoying the silver slithers of moonlight on the water. The ice cream booth was still open, so she bought herself a chocolate cone and sat on a bench.

'If I sit totally still and look into the distance,' she said to herself, 'I will look like I'm in a painting entitled "Lady sitting near a beach with ice cream cone with two scoops" or

"Enigmatic woman stares at the sea" or "It is dark but the stars make it light" or "Woman at a crossroads not literally but figuratively" or "The woman in blue" or "Woman wondering where her boyfriend is".' Melted ice cream began to seep onto her fingers as she gazed at the horizon absently. *Strange evening*, she thought. *Started well, went a bit badly – thank you Adam – improved immensely again – thank you all – now a bit stale – thank you Luis*. She stood up and stretched. 'Time to go back to my table,' she said, checking her phone again. Still no messages.

'Has he not got here yet?'

Alice turned around. Marcella was walking towards her flanked by two po-faced friends.

'I thought he'd be here by now,' she said. 'I need to speak to him. Is he still with my aunt?'

'Your aunt?' said Alice, confused.

'He must still be with her? Didn't they arrange to meet at that ruined old house he is doing up?'

Alice shivered again, uneasily. 'He's late. He's already contacted me to tell me.' Alice wished she could just turn on her heels and exit the scene coolly and serenely, but her feet remained rooted to the spot and the words had continued to come out of her mouth. 'He'll be here soon.'

'She's been interfering in my life. Talking to my father. Making things difficult for me.'

'I'm sorry. I'm not sure what this had got to do with me. I'm going back to my friends. Goodbye,' said Alice, flustered, standing up and walking away.

Disappearing into the crowds Alice detoured up a narrow side street, trying to calm down before she returned to the square, angry with herself for allowing some young woman she hardly knew to knock her off balance. Walking down an alley between two apartment blocks she found herself on the sea road, and as she turned into the square she found herself face to face with a very angry looking Antonio.

247

'Where is he?' he snarled.

Alice stepped back, surprised. 'If you mean Luis, he's on his way,' she said slowly.

Antonio glared at her. 'This is your doing isn't it? Him trying to leave the band again. Letting me down.'

Alice tried to walk past him. 'It's nothing to do with me,' she said.

He grabbed her arm. 'He'll be back. He always is.'

She prised his arm away and hurried away. 'He's probably still with Susannah,' he shouted after her. 'Because that's what he's like.'

Alice wanted to scream. *Stop, stop, stop. Leave me alone. Just leave me alone.* But as she began to rush on her phone pinged. Then again. Then again. The first message was from Luis.

Will be as quick as I can. So sorry. L xxx

And the second, which had been sent half an hour later.

I'm sorry. Things have changed. I can't see you anymore. It's done. L.

She stared at the words. Then she read it again and again trying to make sense of it. But she couldn't. Marcella and Antonio – they were right, they must have been telling the truth. The wine at lunchtime and the champagne at dinner were fuzzing her thoughts. She began to run up the hill. *This couldn't be happening. How could this be happening?* First Adam, then Luis. Both of them. Betraying her. In one day. On her birthday. She wanted to cry, but she couldn't. Not here.

The phone pinged but she couldn't bear to read the message in case it was Luis telling her again that they were finished. *If I get back to the apartment it will disappear*, she thought. *I've got to get back to the apartment.* As she got to the stone bridge opposite the lighthouse, the phone buzzed again. Images of Luis with a woman with horns and vampire teeth at the house Alice had been helping him to restore spun round her head, joined by Adam and Veronique laughing manically, wrestling the keys of her beloved home in London from her cold, tight hands.

She remembered how free she'd felt as the torn-up remnants of Adam's postcards fluttered down from Tower Bridge into the Thames all those months ago. She glanced at the moon. It made a triangle of glistening light on the tranquil ocean. So she took the phone and aimed for the middle then ran again, not waiting to hear the satisfying splash.

Two men that had been following her to make sure she was okay waited until she was out of sight, then scrambled onto the rocks. 'It is just as well she is a very bad shot,' Felipe said to Ignacio. 'She missed the sea. The phone is just here.'

'Typical woman,' said Ignacio. 'Can't throw.'

Chapter Twenty-One

The unfamiliar pitter-patter of rain roused Alice from her slumber. For one peaceful moment she thought she was at home in London, but then Aphrodite nuzzled into her face and previous evening's events came crashing into her mind. A raging thirst drove her out of bed rather than a desire to get up, and she lumbered to the kitchen, feeling heavy and sad.

Taking a glass of water through to the living room, she opened the shutters and watched the rain splash onto the glass as the clouds rolled by. *How could he end it like that?* she wondered. *So callous, so cold.* That's the kind of man she attracted into her life, obviously. One's that could change how they felt in the blink of an eye. The sky was every shade of grey, not a patch of blue or even white in sight. 'I don't want to be here any more Aphrodite, I'm sorry. I want to go home. This is too hard.'

Aphrodite sat, gazing up at her with big green cat eyes. 'Stop looking at me like that,' sighed Alice. 'Do you want to come to London at all? I'd be lonely without you.'

Scooping her up and nuzzling into her fur, Alice searched for the phone in her bag for a few moments until she remembered what she'd done the previous night. Sinking onto the sofa helplessly, she lay motionless for a while, immobilised by thought until she drifted off into a listless sleep full of rapid dreams of hammers and walls and paint and bells and being sucked into a children's ball pond full of tiny shiny beads. Down, down, down she went, sucked down to the bottom of the pool onto a cold, hard floor.

Her eyes flickered open. For the second time in an hour Alice awoke unsure where she was. This time it was the floor in the lounge. She had slipped off the sofa. 'Ow!' she said. 'Aphrodite. Ow!'

The cat meandered disinterestedly towards her and jumped on the table to get a better view. 'I wanted some sympathy, actually,' muttered Alice clambering to her feet.

Smatterings of blue and white dotted the sky outside, the grey clouds dispersing, blustered away by a fierce west wind which shook the trees in the garden, scattering leaves on the grass. 'Yep. I feel like that now. Am I controlling the weather?' She sat down, exhausted again.

'Cup of tea, I think. Sugar,' she said, pulling herself up. The laptop in the spare room caught her attention. Staring at it for a minute, she darted in, turned it on, and ran towards the kitchen. 'Real life is out there,' she shouted to Aphrodite who was still sitting on the table in the living room. 'And I suppose I have to deal with it … don't want to though.'

Valuations of 32 Creek Street, Muswell Hill. Alice reluctantly opened the email, heart racing, wanting to read it, but not wanting to read it. She read it.

Further to your request, we have instructed three local estate agents to value your property …

'Oh … really … *really*?' Her eyes widened. 'Good Lord! No wonder Adam wants half of it, right. So we bought it for … so we've made … and all the reports say that substantial value had been added by the renovations … plus the housing market in London … so …'

This is a tentative enquiry, she typed. *The property is in joint names, but the mortgage has been paid by myself for most of the time we have owned it, as well as the majority of the renovation work. I have mentioned this to you via the phone, but can you put in writing how would I go about dividing the assets fairly should we decide to sell? Also, how would I go about buying the other party out should I decide to go down that route?*

Her finger hovered over the send button. *Are you sure?* said the voice in her head. *They will reply. You will have to read it. And you will know the truth. Whether you like it or not. Are you sure?* She sighed, pressed send, then turned off the computer and closed the door. 'Nobody is going to take my hard work and love and commitment and throw it in my face ever again,' she said to the room.

Who are you talking about? said the voice in her head. *Adam or Luis?*

As she closed the shutters, Alice spotted the birds with the bright blue bellies that swooped and fluttered to the pool every morning. But today as they soared up from the water there was no luminous plumage – just ordinary grey mottled feathers. And she realised her mistake. When the sun shone they reflected the blue of the swimming pool. Today there was none.

'Idiot,' she said, walking out of the apartment, glancing at the piles of bracelets on the table. 'Idiot. About everything.'

Her feet guided her because her head did not know where it was going – it was so full of regrets and questions, anger, frustration and an overwhelming, crushing disappointment. *What was I thinking anyway – getting involved with a man like Luis? With a reputation. And I only came here to recharge my batteries. It was never in my head to stay. At all. I have to pay a mortgage for goodness sake, I have to live. I could only do this for a few months more. Although I may not have to pay a mortgage soon.*

She stopped as a dog walked languidly across the cobbled lane, collapsing in the shade of a shabby yellow cottage with a 'for sale' sign hanging from its balcony.

She realised she was in the old town. She continued to walk, not knowing and not caring where she was going. *I don't know what to do about my house,* she thought, *I just don't. I can't afford to buy Adam out – I know that at least. So, I have to sell. My house ... and I don't even know if I'll get what's mine. I don't even know if I can fight for it ... and once it's sold what do I do? Where do I go?*

A car squeezed up the hill towards her, driving through

a tunnel of tiny pink, white and yellow houses, draped in yellow bougainvillea and purple wisteria. *Nice colour combination for a bracelet*, she thought and almost smiled. Even in the middle of all this anguish she was thinking of bloody bracelets. She moved on. *Well at least I can sell my jewellery on the internet from anywhere.*

Putting her head down and looking at the floor, the thoughts tumbled out of her mind. *I may as well admit it to myself. I did, on silly days, think I could stay here. And my house would be over there for me, waiting just in case, open arms. But that was when Luis was around. I should never have fallen in love with him in the first place.* She stopped suddenly, surprised. *Did I just think that? Oh no ... idiot – IDIOT! Better book my flight home. Must let Mary know so she can get someone else to look after Aphrodite ...* Aphrodite. A tear hung on her cheek. *Stop crying about a cat!*

Alice walked on, head still down, inspecting the cobbles. 'Idiot.' she whispered.

The tables clustered under the almond tree, and the sun cast a dappled shade over the chairs as Alice sat, nursing her drink. She had stumbled upon the tiny square as she had wondered aimlessly through the narrow streets, the sun slowly breaking through the darkness of the morning. A family was moving furniture into a tall, narrow town house, their children running around noisily whilst an older man barked orders at everyone. Alice tried to imagine what the rooms looked like, where they would put the solid old wooden table being manoeuvred through the door, where the family photographs would hang, where their dog would sleep.

She thought of her own empty house, so lovingly brought to life, now to be abandoned. To whom? she wondered. Would they love it as much as she did – those four walls that had protected her and kept her safe? It would have to be a family that bought it. A family like the one she was watching.

Big and noisy and warm. That's what her house deserved. A happy family. She stood up and walked back up the hill towards the apartment. A new phone could wait until later. Time to Skype her mother. Time to act.

She rushed through the apartment building's foyer and pressed the lift button quickly, in no mood to make small talk with the porter. As she stepped inside and the doors began to close she glimpsed him darting out of his office towards her. 'Madam. Madam. I have ...' The doors closed and she sighed, closing her eyes. *No more news, no more anything*, she thought. Just hide.

As she walked through the door another wave of sadness overwhelmed her. She was leaving. This place had been her home as well, and now she was being pulled away from it. She turned on the computer and Skyped her mum, hoping she was there and could hear the call.

'Alice! How lovely to hear from you again.' Her mum's nose was visible on the screen. 'Why are you Skyping me? Where's your phone?'

'I lost it mum,' she lied. 'Can you sit a bit further back so I can see your face properly?'

Her mother scraped the chair away from the screen and Alice smiled as she came into full view.

'I'm glad you phoned. We tried to tell you last night. A letter has arrived for you. It's from a solicitor. It must be from Adam. Anyone else would have sent it to your house. Do you want me to open it?'

The anger returned in a rush. 'I think you should open it,' said Alice 'I can't believe he's already got his solicitor to send a letter. He told me he hadn't got a solicitor involved yet. He said he was going to. But he hadn't.'

'Alice Dorothy, sit down. Stop pacing around.'

'Sorry mum.' Alice perched reluctantly on the sofa as her mother began to open the letter. 'When did it arrive?'

'Yesterday.'

Alice sprang to her feet again. 'I can't believe it. Actually I *can* believe it. I bet he deliberately timed it to arrive on my birthday. What did I see in him, Mum? Why didn't you warn me?'

'I did, darling.' She sighed, unfolding the paper and placing it on the table in front of her. 'Now please sit down. You keep disappearing from view on the screen.'

'Okay, okay.' Alice sat down again. 'What does it say?'

'As expected. He wants to sell the house and get the money. In a nutshell.'

'Right. Right …' Alice bobbed up again.

'Alice, please …' Her mother sounded frustrated.

'I know I've got to sell it.'

'Yes.'

'But I don't want him to have half of it.'

'No.'

'But if I fight, he may fight back and all the appeals will cost a lot of money.'

'Yes, they will.'

'And I may not win, and he will get half and I would have lost that money.'

'That's right.'

'But I want to fight. I don't want him to have the money for this business.'

'Of course.'

'But I haven't … No, no! I will find the money when he appeals it. I will. I will find a way.'

'Alice Dorothy Matthews. Sit *down*!' shouted her mother.

Alice quickly sat down again.

'Look, Alice. I have spoken to your stepfather because we anticipated this. And we will help you financially with the legal fees until the house is sold. Then you can repay us with the proceeds. We would love to help you buy him out, but I think the house is now probably worth a lot of money and we can't afford it. But the legal fees we can help you with.'

Alice wanted to cry with gratitude. 'Will you? Are you sure?'

'Of course, we are. I'm not letting that arsehole take your money without a fight.'

'Mother. Language please! But thank you, thank you.' Alice stood up and kissed the screen. All of a sudden everything was clear. She knew what she had to do. A little flicker of excitement lifted her mood for an instant, and then it was gone.

'No more hiding, Mum. I'll speak to you tomorrow once I've got a new phone. Now I'm off to hang around some hotel lobbies.'

The screen flickered closed to the sound of her mother saying, 'What? What do you mean? Alice?'

Alice rushed out and strode through the apartment foyer towards the path. As she did, the porter came out of his office again trying to get her attention. 'Madam, Madam … I have …'

But she didn't even realise he was there. She had something she needed to say and that's all she could think of.

She walked through the main square hoping to find Carlos. 'What hotels do you think would provide private yoga instructors? There's one with yoga classes and they do belly dancing – do they do private sessions there or is there anywhere else?' she asked him as he was clearing a table.

He looked up, surprised. 'Alice,' he said. 'How are you? I heard there was some confusion last night? That you were upset?'

Alice couldn't look him in the face. She knew if she did the tears would come again, and she had to stay angry.

'I'm okay.' Then she asked her question again.

Carlos narrowed his eyes thoughtfully. 'Not the one you were thinking of on the seafront close to the station.' He paused for a moment. 'A Barrio,' he said eventually. 'That would be the one. Always holding that new age chanting stuff there.'

'Is that the one above the beach just across from the little shopping centre?'

'That's the one.

'Right. Wish me luck.'

'Did you speak to Luis?'

'Luis? No.'

'Well he is looking for you. He has your phone.'

'But I … how has he got my phone?'

'You had better ask him. Or Ignacio. Or Felipe.'

Alice looked at him blankly. 'I don't understand …'

Carlos shrugged. 'He turned up here after you had left. He had a black eye – something about a fight with Antonio. And he tried to call you, but of course you had thrown your phone away.'

Alice began to feel mixture of nausea and hope.

'They went to your apartment building but couldn't get an answer from you. Luis left some messages with the porter.'

'But he sent me a message,' she said, mind searching for explanations. *How could he be looking for her when he had ended their relationship?* She remembered the conversation with Marcella on the beach. Perhaps he hadn't sent the message. Had she made a mistake? But she couldn't deal with it, not now. Not when she had to confront everything. 'Well as Luis has my phone, so I can't call Ignacio. Can you tell him I'll need him sometime next week to take me to the airport?' she blurted out.

'Okay.'

Alice walked across the square.

'Are you going on a holiday?' shouted Carlos at her back.

'No. I'm going home,' shouted Alice, hurrying towards A Barrio Hotel.

The hotel lobby exuded lavender scented tranquillity as Alice sank into a plush cream and scarlet sofa in a gold and red alcove. Indian music drifted from the reception desk.

I am annoyed. I am annoyed. I am very *annoyed*, she repeated in her head. *Don't let your guard down. Be alert. Be alert.* Alice sat and watched, stroking the raised flower pattern on the arm of the sofa. Glancing briefly down, the way the leaves were drawn caught her attention, so she surreptitiously grabbed her camera from her bag and snapped a photo. Eventually a door opened and about fifty people in white robes padded out of a darkened function room, bringing an overwhelming blast of patchouli oil with them. Alice stood up, searching for Adam, the anger and indignation rising through her again, heart pounding, ready to fight. Finally. Pushing her way into the middle of the group to find him, she stood, listening for his deep, gruff voice.

'I must say, since I started Tai chi I've been a better person.' There he was, somewhere to her left. 'It was Veronique that got me into it.'

Alice moved towards the noise, easing her way between chatting groups.

But his voice moved. 'It's just so helpful,' he said.

Alice spun round and waited for him to speak again. It wouldn't take long, she thought. Adam couldn't keep quiet for longer than a minute. She wondered why everyone was so tall. Maybe there was a height requirement for this particular class, Tai chi for the longer body?

'Ssssh,' she said to herself out loud. 'Be quiet. I'm listening.'

A couple turned around, embarrassed. 'Oh dear, very sorry,' said the woman. 'I didn't realise we were speaking so loudly. We'll keep it down.'

'Oh, no, I didn't mean you,' said Alice, reddening. 'Please take no notice.' She squeezed around a cluster of people nearly getting walloped by a heavy-set man demonstrating a very slow move.

'… our new business … just getting it going, yes …' There he was, in the corner with his arm around Veronique.

Alice walked purposefully towards him. For the first time she was ready to deal with him properly. 'Adam,' she said. But he didn't respond. 'Adam!' She hit him on the back to get his attention. 'Adam!'

'Alice,' he sighed, turning around looking down at her. 'What are you doing here? I should have known by the jingle of those bloody bracelets that you were in the vicinity.'

'What is she doing here?' echoed Veronique.

'I have something to say.' Alice straightened her body.

The crowd began to disperse, sensing drama.

'Oh dear. Here we go again,' said Adam wearily.

'Oh dear,' sighed Veronique.

Alice took a deep breath. 'I am prepared to sell the house.' There. She had said the unsayable, the unthinkable, the unimaginable. She stood, waiting for the panic to return, the sense of loss, the fear. But it didn't. She felt light and free. Her house had given her a gift. The gift of pushing Adam out of her life. The house she had built was letting her go.

'At last!' said Adam, triumphantly.

'I am also prepared to let you have a proportion of the proceeds.'

'Right, well, it is my house too, so I don't know why you are saying it like you are giving me some kind of present,' he said irritably.

'Your name is on the deeds and the mortgage agreement but it isn't your house, is it?'

'Yes it is.'

'No it isn't,' said Alice firmly. 'I have checked through my bank statements online and I also have all the paper ones going back to when we first moved in. I can track back to the date when I started to pay for the mortgage payments on my own from my account. And it was a long time ago, Adam.'

'Yes, but my name is still on the mortgage and the deeds so it is technically half mine.'

'Technically. But I'm going to take it to court if you won't

259

settle via our solicitors. And I have kept every single receipt for all the work I had done and all the materials I bought.'

'Alice, why are you doing this?'

'You always used to laugh at me for keeping all those records, but you know, I think they will help me prove my case.'

The people in the lobby were stood, silent, pretending not to listen. Some were looking at Adam and Veronique curiously.

'But you are just delaying the inevitable,' said Adam slowly and condescendingly. 'It is just a bloody house. This will cost us time and money.'

'Not necessarily. I will instruct my solicitor to offer you a percentage of the profit from the sale.'

'How much?'

'Not saying. I haven't decided yet. Wait for the letter. When's your birthday again? I'll make sure it arrives then. Just like you arranged for your solicitor's letter to arrive on mine.'

'This is ridiculous. I'm going to use the money for something useful. The business. Not just sitting in some old bricks and mortar.'

'And I need it for my business.'

'You don't have a business,' scoffed Adam. 'Selling bracelets to market stalls in one town in Portugal is not a business, Alice.'

'I have just started an online business selling jewellery and photographs, actually.'

'Do something,' muttered Veronique. 'The money is part of the plan.'

'Sorry. No can do,' said Alice firmly. 'At least eighty per cent of the house is mine in my opinion. Probably more to be honest, and I'm going to fight for it.'

'But it will cost you a lot of money. You haven't got it.'

'I will find it. I will, Adam.'

He looked at her confused, unsure what to say.

Alice stood, her feet planted firmly on the ground, knowing exactly what she had to do. The man she had laughed with and dreamt with and made plans with, who had captivated her and won her, and who she had loved more than she thought she could ever love anyone was standing in front of her. But it had gone. She could finally remember why she had loved him. And she didn't want that any more. She stepped forward and touched his arm. 'You were all I ever wanted once. You overwhelmed me. Do you remember? But when you started to go, bit by bit, I filled the space you left with the house. I gave it all the love that was meant for you but you didn't seem to want any more. And now, and now,' her voice began to shake. 'You want to give all of what I put into that house to someone else. How dare you do that to me!'

'Alice I … I …' he faltered.

'I don't love you any more. And I don't like you. And I'm beginning to despise you. Don't you think that's sad? I don't want anything to do with you. I'm selling the house, and I'm fighting for what's mine.'

'Don't listen to her,' said Veronique sharply. 'You should fight for what's yours – ours.'

'Why don't you earn your own money,' said Alice, 'instead of trying to steal it from me?'

There was an audible intake of breath from the people around them in the lobby.

'Do not speak to me like that,' shouted Veronique.

'Don't try to steal my house, then.'

An elderly lady at the far end of the room began to clap. 'Bravo my dear! You tell them!'

'He told me it was half his,' Veronique said quietly, her voice trailing away.

Alice turned to see Luis walking towards her in the lobby. He was unshaven and one of his eyes looked like it had been hit.

'Luis!' For a moment her heart loop the looped with relief and happiness. 'Your eye. What….? 'Then she remembered the text he had sent the night before.

'Who is this now?' Adam's face hardened again.

'I'm Luis. I'm with Alice,' he said.

'No you're not,' said Alice. She couldn't calm down. Her anger at Adam and Veronique was now being directed at him even though she now knew something about the message she'd received wasn't right.

'What do you mean?' asked Luis, confused.

'You texted me. You told me you had met someone else. It was on my birthday. You had kept me waiting all evening. How could you?'

'Bastard!' shouted the elderly lady.

'I didn't do that,' he said.

'But I got the text. I'd show you, but you have my phone apparently.'

'You threw it away,' said Luis. 'You tried to throw it in the sea but it landed on the rocks. Ignacio and Felipe were following you to make sure you were okay and rescued it.'

Alice looked at him, trying not to crumple, finally realising how much her friends had been trying to help her.

Luis handed Alice her phone. 'Now show me this text.'

'How did you know I was here?' asked Alice.

'Carlos worked it out. Then he called me to tell me you were leaving. And I just heard every word you said to that man. Oh Alice …' he held his arms out to her, but she backed away.

'I knew it,' said Adam angrily. 'I knew there was another man, otherwise you'd still be wasting away in London.'

Alice spun round towards him. 'What do you mean?'

'I knew there was another man. I knew it.'

'Is that what this is about, Adam? You left me a long time ago. What is it to you? Is that why you came out here really? You could have done this all by letter'

'No, I'm with Veronique and I'm very happy.'

'So you just don't want to lose your grip on me then? You don't want me to move on? Well I have. The only thing keeping us locked into this is my house. And I'm prepared to let it go.'

'Yes, but on your terms.'

'Yes on my terms.'

She looked at Luis.

'Show me the text,' he said.

She scrolled down and opened it, unable to read it again.

'I did not write this text. I promise you I did not write it. Look at the text after it. I said I was on my way.'

'Who wrote the text then?' Alice bit her lip. Luis looked confused as he looked at her, then ashamed.

'I know who it was,' he sighed.

'Who was it?' asked Alice. But she already knew.

'I need to explain but not here,' he said.

'What was her name?'

'I was showing Susannah the farmhouse. She said she was interested in buying it. The bank manager had phoned me that day. It was bad news. I was very worried. I panicked. And so I agreed to meet there. But she wanted to buy the land and knock it down. And I don't want to sell it.' Beads of sweat began to form on his forehead as he looked at her.

'Go on,' she said quietly.

'She made a wrong assumption about me too and when I corrected her I think she was angry.'

'What was she doing with your phone?'

'I accidentally left it behind, and when I went back she handed it to me.'

'Why wasn't it locked?'

'I forgot to lock it … and then I texted you to tell you I was on my way.'

'But you never came. Where did you go?'

'I did come, but you were already gone.'

'I was there for hours, Luis.'

Luis looked around. 'Please can we do this somewhere else?' he pleaded.

'Where did you go?' repeated Alice.

'She drove home and I drove behind her because I was worried. And then I had a fight with Antonio. He was waiting for me at the café and blamed me for the fact that Marcella is no longer supporting the band.'

Alice looked at his black eye, fighting every instinct to go over and touch his face and throw herself into his arms. But she felt too betrayed. 'I was sitting in the square all evening waiting for you. It was my birthday. Why did she get the wrong idea about what you wanted? Tell me, please.'

Luis sighed. 'It was the past. She thought I was someone I never was.'

'The man with the reputation,' said Alice, sharply.

'It was a long time ago, Alice.'

'Did she know about me?'

'... yes.'

'Did she know it was my birthday?'

'Yes.'

'Did she know you were supposed to be meeting me?'

Luis looked at the floor. 'Yes.'

Alice turned and walked away. 'You idiot,' she said, pushing into the revolving door. 'You *idiot*.' And this time she knew she wasn't just talking about Luis, she was talking about herself.

Enveloped by the crowds of people outside, Alice allowed herself to be carried along with their footsteps, once again, not knowing or caring where she was going, grateful to be able to lose herself in their midst. *Luis didn't turn up for my birthday. Luis followed that woman home to make sure she was all right. Luis put her before me.* The words rang around her head. *Adam is trying to take my house to please his girlfriend. He doesn't care what it's doing to me.*

And as the word repeated over and over, Luis and Adam merged into one man until she couldn't remember who had done what or why. Ignoring her ringing phone, she drifted, until she found herself standing in the square, looking at the tables, not really seeing anything. Then she felt an arm guiding her towards a chair.

'Sit,' said Carlos, waving his arm at a colleague. '*Um galao*.' The glass of milky coffee was placed on the table. 'Drink,' he said.

Alice sipped it silently.

'Did he find you?'

'Yes.'

'Then why are you sitting here on your own?'

She looked at the wall. 'It's complicated,' she said. *You have to look after yourself and not rely on anyone else, Alice Dorothy Matthews*, she thought. *Thank God I have the house*. She took her phone out her bag. 'No signal. Again.' She sighed. 'Is there an internet café near here?' she asked Carlos.

'Yes, about fifteen minutes' walk. Straight up that street until the end then turn left.'

'Thank you,' she said, pulling out her purse to pay for the coffee.

'On the house,' he said.

Hiding herself in a corner of the tiny café, Alice clicked the computer onto her London address, then switched on the satellite map, moving the icon onto her street and in front of her house. Captured on a perfect spring day, candy pink blossom burst from the cherry trees along the avenue framed by a crisp blue sky. Two doors down Mrs Thomas was tidying up her front garden under the watchful eye of her ginger cat, Marvin.

Alice remembered the family she had watched move into the town house in Cascais earlier that day, hopeful and happy, planning their new life. Then she conjured up another family in her mind's eye – a mother and a father, a baby in a pram and a little girl with curly blond hair, walking up the narrow path of red roses and lavender to the front door and into her house. Inside were toys and mess and laugher and warmth, a teapot on the kitchen table, a dog barking in the garden.

The baby's room was blue with a stencil of yellow and green birds on the walls, a mobile of clouds hanging above the cot. Next door, his sister's room was strewn with dolls and dresses around a bed with a bright pink duvet covered with rainbows. The walls of the study were covered in books and nick-nacks and the main bedroom, pale and tranquil, lavender and cream.

'Enjoy the house I built,' she said to her imaginary family. 'It's for you to make your own now.' Then she clicked the computer off and left. She looked at her phone. Four missed calls from Luis and a voicemail.

'Alice, Alice, please,' he said. 'I know why you're angry, but I couldn't tell you how bad things were. I thought I was going to lose everything. But when she told me she wanted to knock the house down it all came into focus. I spent today sorting things out. It's all okay now.'

Another voicemail pinged into the phone. 'I wanted to sit in the foyer of your apartment building. I would have done all day, but I had to sort out the houses. It's for us. For *us*. I left messages with the porter for you. Oh Alice, where are you? I'm at the apartment block and you're not here.'

Then a text arrived. I have to go to see my solicitor and the estate agent. I need to sign some paperwork urgently. I'll be back. Luis xxx

All the emotions Alice had ever felt seemed to be coursing around her body. She knew she should call him, but she didn't have the words. She was being forced to sell her home and being thrown into an uncertain future and she was scared. No amount of sending in happy imaginary families on google could stop her feeling that. As she wandered aimlessly around the backstreets she noticed something. Someone had sprayed green graffiti over the dilapidated 'for sale' sign hanging wanly in front of a little yellow house. Alice paused in front of it and felt a pang of sadness. *That house needs someone to love it*, she thought.

'Yes, well, I'm leaving aren't I?' she said brusquely out loud, beginning to hurry up the hill and onto the sea road. 'So not me. I've got to get back and book a flight home. And let Mary know. She's got to find someone else to look after Aphrodite.'

Red, white and green fishing boats bobbed on the crystal blue sea, a school of tiny yachts skidding over the white crested waves in the bay. Alice tried to ignore it. 'Stop being so beautiful,' she muttered. 'Stop making it so difficult to leave. Just. Stop. It.' Cutting through the shade of the park to escape from the seductive ocean views, the scent of rosemary and lavender gently calmed her. So she began to breathe through her nose to block it out, running, trying to ignore the calls of the peacocks amongst the trees and the happy laughter of children skipping along the grass.

Alice threw the mobile phone into the bathroom because she didn't want to see any more messages or hear any more excuses. Her heart was breaking and she had to go. She closed the door as Aphrodite trotted towards her.

'Hello you,' she sighed. She switched on the computer and as she was waiting for it to connect, took the bowl she'd bought from her house in London out of her backpack and put it on the table. 'I think it's just you and me kid,' she said to it sadly.

The intercom buzzed.

'No,' she said, trying to ignore it.

'Alice,' said Luis, buzzing again. 'I know you're there. The doorman told me.'

Aphrodite jumped onto her lap, purring.

'Alice, I know you're angry. But nothing happened. Nothing. I was stupid. Please.'

Logging onto her e-mail, she tried to work out how to tell Mary and Frank that she couldn't stay any more. Should she ask to take Aphrodite back with her to England?

I have to leave because I have to sell my house because of my ex, she typed. Then she deleted it and started again. *I have to leave because I have to sell my house because of my ex. I have to earn money to pay the solicitors because I know he will try to get more of it than he is entitled to ... I have to leave because I have been stupid over a man ... I have to leave because although I love it here, I can't stay ...*

She opened a new e-mail. It was from the work contact her friend had told her about. *I've heard great things about you*, it said. *We're expanding in the new year and could have some consulting work for you. Could you let me know when you're available to meet up in the next month or so?*

There it was – a message that only three months ago would have made her jump up and down with excitement and relief. But now ... she sighed ... but now she needed to earn some money, even if she was going to sell her bracelets. The redundancy would run out soon enough.

The buzzer went again. 'I'm not going anywhere,' said Luis. 'I will keep buzzing until you let me in.'

A new e-mail flashed up. 'From Mary,' said Alice, clicking it open. 'A bit of a coincidence.'

In Australia at last! it said. *Our granddaughter is beautiful. We are both in love. Staying here for a couple of months then we are off to New Zealand. You are obviously loving it there. My friend sent me this. We used to drive past the farmhouse and imagine ourselves owning it. It's such a beautiful spot. She found this photo print in a shop in Sintra and scanned it in to send to us. You look so content.*

Alice opened the attachment.

The intercom buzzed again. 'Don't go, Alice, please. Talk to me. Don't run away. Please.'

She stared at the screen for a moment, then stood up and

walked backwards towards the door, not taking her eyes off the computer. Everything was suddenly clear, and relief washed through her. She began to cry.

The photo was taken of Luis's farmhouse from an outbuilding. The overgrown bushes and plants in the garden sloped down to rolling hills dipping towards the sea beyond. On a step next to a tangle of bougainvillea and clematis sat a woman examining some broken shards of tiles, a paint palette and mounting board next to them. Her reddish blonde hair glowed in the sun, her golden-brown bare arms were dotted with paint. She was part of the landscape.

She pressed the button to let Luis in and opened the door moving back towards the photograph, mesmerised. It was her. She was the woman in the photograph, happy and relaxed, like she belonged there.

Luis almost ran through the door.

'Alice, Alice, I am so sorry.'

'That's me,' she said, eyes still fixed on the photograph.

He stood next to her and took her hand. 'Yes, it is. Do you mind?'

She looked up at him. 'I look happy,' she said.

'You were happy.'

'You're not going to sell the house, are you?'

'No, never.'

'Things have been going on, Luis. I have to sell my house. I have to fight Adam for what's mine. I have to go back to do it.'

'Don't go,' he said.

'That woman you were with. I needed you. He was there. In the square. On my birthday. And you were with her.'

'I am a very stupid man,' he said. 'Alice, all the time I was there I wanted to be with you. I wanted to get away. But in my mind was the fear I was going to lose everything. This past month I got myself into a real mess. I couldn't think straight.'

She stared at the screen.

'You can fight him from here. Just go back when you need to,' he said. 'Don't go Alice, please. Stay. Stay with me.'

'With you?'

'Yes. I love you.'

'Do you?' Alice turned towards him.

'Yes of course I do.'

Alice began to smile even as the tears continued to fall. 'I love you too.'

Luis cupped her face in his hands and kissed her gently, then gathered her in his arms and held her.

'I felt so alone,' said Alice. 'Like I had to do it all myself.'

'I'm here now. We will do it together.'

'I still have to pay the mortgage until it's sold.'

'We will work it out. We will. Don't worry.'

'But …'

Something hit the balcony shutters with a clatter.

'What's that noise?' said Alice.

The intercom buzzed. 'It's Kathy. Go onto the balcony now. NOW!'

Alice and Luis looked at each other, puzzled. There was another clatter. 'Better do as she says,' said Luis, unlocking the doors and stepping out.

'What are you laughing at?' said Alice.

'You better come here.'

She walked onto the balcony and looked down into the garden.

Kathy, Stephano, Ignacio and Carlos stood under a tree, along with Alice's birthday busker and Ignacio's nephews. 'So you two have finally sorted it out then?' shouted Kathy. 'Thank goodness for that.'

'I told them you were going,' shouted Carlos.

'But we don't think you should go. It's Paradise!' shouted Ignacio.

He nodded to Felipe and his nephews, who began to play.

'What's that?' whispered Luis.

'"Daydream Believer",' laughed Alice. 'He played it last night in the square.'

As her friends began to join in the singing, two children climbed out of the swimming pool to watch and the people lounging on the sunbeds stood up, smiling.

'Don't go,' said Luis, kissing her ear. 'You belong here.'

'Don't go,' shouted Kathy above the noise. 'I need you, Alice. You have to help me run the spa when baby here comes. I'll do whatever paperwork is necessary. I need you Alice.'

'But what about real life?' said Alice quietly to Luis. 'The house and earning money? I can't just stay …'

'Real life? You are standing on a balcony in the blazing sun, with the sea glistening in the distance, the birds chirping in the trees, standing next to a man who loves you, and your friends and what looks like a newly formed boy band and some random strangers singing to you. And apparently that's what happened last night too. What's not real life about that?'

Two silver birds swooped down to the water, their chests catching the blue of the pool as they rose and rested on the trees beyond. Alice kissed Luis, to cheers from the small crowd below. Then she shouted 'are you coming up then?'

'Of course we are. Stephano's got a few bottles of chilled champagne in the car.'

Stephano turned to Kathy. 'But not for you darling. I also have lemonade.'

After a while everyone began to drift off back to their lives, smiling and happy, leaving Alice and Luis alone again.

Luis stood up. 'We have something to do Alice,' he said. 'Come.' He held out his hand.

'You look serious, all of a sudden,' she said. 'Is there anything else I should know?'

He looked into her eyes. 'Will you trust me?'

They held each other's gaze for a few moments, still and

calm, and just as he was about to turn away, Alice noticed a sudden fire in Luis's eyes.

'I trust you.' she said.

'It's around the corner, not far,' he said, leading her down towards the gates.

They walked in silence, Luis's face stern and tense.

'Are you going to tell me what's going on?' asked Alice.

'What you said to Adam yesterday was brave. You were stronger than I've ever been. And because of you I'm going to put the past to rest.'

They continued, Alice in a muddle of thoughts, hoping there wasn't going to be yet another argument, but understanding she had to allow Luis to do what he needed to.

He turned and kissed her gently. 'Here we are,' he said squeezing her hand at the doors to a dingy bar. 'Antonio uses this as a kind of office sometimes.'

They walked in hand in hand and saw Antonio and Marcella deep in conversation at a small table in the corner. They didn't notice Alice and Luis until they were standing next to them.

Antonio looked up, surprised. 'What do you want?' he spat. 'We had all this out the other day. You've left the band. I get it. Have you come for another fight?' He stood up aggressively. 'We can go outside and carry it on if you want.'

Marcella stood up. 'I don't want to be here with him or her. They've made enough of a fool of me, and as for my aunt ...'

Alice saw something shine and shake on her wrist. 'That's a nice bracelet,' she said.

Marcella looked down. 'Oh, this little trinket. My father bought it for me from one of the stalls.'

'I thought you were angry he wouldn't let you work with the band any more?' said Alice calmly.

'He says things like that, but then he forgets. I'll walk around wearing it for a few days to keep him happy.' Marcella almost smiled, defiant.

Alice squeezed Luis's hand. 'It's nice to see one of my bracelets actually being worn.' She beamed at Marcella, who looked down, shocked.

'This is yours?' She paused. 'I'm only wearing it because I have to. I'll throw it away in a few days.'

'I've got something to say to you Antonio,' said Luis.

Antonio looked down and started to write on a pad, ignoring him.

'We were more than cousins once, Antonio, we were great friends. I'm grateful for all the help you gave me when I moved here from Australia.' Luis walked over to him.

Antonio stopped writing but didn't look up.

'The band was great for a while, but it stopped being fun. I stayed for you. We all did. But you drove us all away. You've chewed over the lost record contract for so many years. Move on or find another dream or someone else to help you. Now you drink, you gamble, you lie, you bully and you're a mess, and you've used our friendship as a way of making me stay for too long.'

Antonio sat in silence for a moment then looked up. 'You always thought you were better than me. But you weren't. You *weren't*.' He turned to go and Marcella began to follow him.

'Don't get caught up in these games, Marcella,' said Luis. 'He's been using you. And you've been bullying Alice too. Both of you owe her an apology.'

She stopped. 'An apology? I haven't bullied anyone,' she said. But as soon as the words were out of her mouth, the bar door flew open.

'Marcella!' A middle-aged man in a smart suit and sunglasses stood at the door, the light behind him casting his body into shadowy darkness.

'Daddy, I...'

'I told you not to get involved with this. I told you. And yet you are still here, making a fool of yourself.'

He stepped forward into the light.

They all stood in silence for a moment.

The man took his sunglasses off. 'You won't remember me, Antonio, but I remember you.'

Luis examined his face. 'You look familiar,' he said.

'I auditioned for the band years ago. I didn't get in. You said I was a good bass player. Antonio was very rude about my abilities as I remember.'

Alice looked at them all. 'Every man in Cascais seems to have been in the band, or wanted to be in the band,' she said without thinking. 'Bit like *Spartacus* … you know – I am Spartacus … I am Spartacus …' she trailed off realising the room was silent and she was sounding like her film-obsessed mother again.

The man laughed. 'You'd think it was the only band in town!'

Marcella looked at her father. 'You mean you wanted to get in, and you couldn't?'

'Yes. I was cool once you know. Obviously not *that* cool – like I said I didn't make it in.'

'You mean I've been helping a band you wanted to be in when you were …?'

'Young?' he cut in. 'Yes.'

Marcella's face curled into disgust. 'That's embarrassing,' she muttered. 'I can't believe I…' She stared at Antonio and then at Luis. 'You are so much older than I thought. She glanced at her father. 'Did Aunt Susannah know?'

'Oh, your aunt?' he laughed. 'Your mother says her little sister is having a mid-life crisis – revisiting her youth by hanging around these two again. She's old enough to know better. You're young enough to learn. Now, get in the car and we'll talk about this later. If you still want your allowance that is.'

Marcella stomped towards the exit. She turned around as if she was about to say something, but simply spluttered 'I can't believe it.' Then pushed the door open and left.

'Well, I'd best go. Don't let me see you anywhere near my daughter again, Antonio.'

'It wasn't like that,' stuttered Antonio. 'She was helping the band. She wanted to help.'

He smiled at Luis. 'My name is Duarte – Duarte de Silva, by the way. I've heard that Latin band you play with sometimes is pretty good.' He took a card out of his wallet and handed it to him. 'I book some bands for my restaurants and bars. And the hotel I've got some shares in. Get one of the guys to give me a call.' He shook Alice's hand. 'Nice to meet you. I hope we'll meet again.'

'Nice to meet you too, Duarte,' she said. 'I'm glad you like my bracelets. You bought one for Marcella.'

'You made them? I like them a lot. I bought ten. My wife has so many aunts, sisters and nieces I like to keep stocks of little presents for them just in case!' He took another card out of his wallet and passed it to her. 'Send me your contact details. If I need any more I'll come to you direct.'

As he walked towards the exit he paused and said, without looking back. 'I thank my lucky stars I didn't get in the band you know. It would have distracted me. My father owned two bars and I took that and built his business up to what I've got now. I've just bought a small record label too.'

Then he pushed the door open and left through a flash of sunlight.

Alice, Luis and Antonio stood in silence for a few moments.

'Well, that was a bit of a surprise,' said Alice eventually.

Luis smiled. A door slammed behind them. 'I think Antonio has left the building,' he said.

Chapter Twenty-Two

'I saw this house,' said Luis as they walked through the old town the following day towards the square. 'But I had to stop myself from thinking about it. I want to concentrate on the farmhouse. I need to. But there was something about it … look it's down here.'

They stood outside the grubby little yellow cottage with the dilapidated 'for sale' sign on the door. Alice smiled. 'I noticed it too. Someone needs to love it. I had to give myself a good talking to. I haven't sold my house in London yet. And I was going to be leaving.'

'I had a call from the agent earlier,' said Luis. 'I have rented out the refurbished house. Looks like I am going to be a landlord. And someone is keen to buy the house I am living in. They just haven't seen it yet! So all being well, I'll be moving into the farmhouse soon.'

'That's wonderful news,' said Alice. She stroked the wall. 'I wonder if it'll still be for sale when I finally sort myself out.'

'We could do it together. I could buy it, and you could give me your half when you have sold your house.'

Alice threw her arms around him. 'That's such a lovely thought,' she said. 'But you haven't signed on the dotted line for your other two yet, and I think the next house I make will have to be mine and mine alone. Just the next one though. Just because I have to.'

Luis kissed her. 'You are very wise, Alice. So when you finally move into my beautifully and lovingly refurbished farmhouse, should I charge you rent?'

'Yes. Or I'll buy half of it … or ….'

'You know it will all be all right, don't you? I can't see Adam fighting for long. I only saw him for five minutes but I could tell he had no commitment to anything.'

'Well, we'll see,' said Alice. 'When it's finally done, which could take a while, will you come to London to help me move out? My house means so much to me. I'll need you to hold my hand.'

'Like I said, I will be with you every step of the way. Now say goodbye to the little yellow house,' said Luis.

'Goodbye little yellow house,' said Alice. 'For now, anyway.'

'Later, do you want to see some friends of mine play? For the Latin music band I sometimes play in. It's relaxed you know?' said Luis. 'Just fun.' He took her hand and they continued down the hill.

Alice turned to glance at the little yellow house. It looked like it was glowing.

Thank You

Dear Reader,

Thank you for reading about Alice and her new adventure in Portugal.

If you have enjoyed reading this story it would mean a lot to me if you had a few minutes to share a review on the platform you purchased the book or on Goodreads, as this is a great way for people to find out about my books.

If you have any thoughts, comments or questions you can contact me via the contact details at the end of my author bio on the next page.

Hopefully I'll see you again soon with a new story.

Chris x

About the Author

Chris Penhall is a freelance writer and radio producer. Born in South Wales, she has also lived near London and in Portugal, which is where *The House That Alice Built* is set. It was whilst living in Cascais near Lisbon that she began to dabble in writing fiction, but it was many years later that she was confident enough to start writing her first novel, and many years after that she finally finished it! She is enjoying her new career as a novelist.

A lover of books, music and cats, she is also an enthusiastic salsa dancer, a keen cook and loves to travel. She is never happier than when she is gazing at the sea.

Chris has two grown-up daughters and lives in the Essex countryside.

Chris is a member of the Romantic Novelists Association.

Follow Chris:
www.chrispenhall.co.uk
Twitter: https://twitter.com/ChrisPenhall
Facebook: https://www.facebook.com/ChrisPenhall
BroadcasterWriter/

More Ruby Fiction

From Chris Penhall

New Beginnings at the Little House in the Sun

Book 2 – Portuguese Paradise series

Follow your yellow brick road …

Alice Dorothy Matthews is on the road to paradise! She's sold her house in London, got rid of her nasty ex and arranged her move to Portugal where friendship and romance awaits. All that's left to do is find a place to call home.

But Alice's dreams are called into question when complications with friends, work and new relationships make her Portuguese paradise feel far too much like reality.

Will Alice's dream of a new home in the sun come true?

Visit www.rubyfiction.com for details.

Finding Summer Happiness

You won't find happiness without breaking a few eggs …

Miriam Ryan was the MD of a successful events and catering company, but these days even the thought of chopping an onion sends her stress levels sky rocketing. A retreat to the Welsh village of her childhood holidays seems to offer the escape she's craving – just peace, quiet, no people, a generous supply of ready meals … did she mention no people?

Enter a cheery pub landlord, a lovesick letting agent, a grumpy astronomer with a fridge raiding habit – not to mention a surprise supper club that requires the chopping of many onions – and Miriam realises her escape has turned into exactly what she was trying to get away from, but could that be just the thing she needs to allow a little bit of summer happiness into her life?

Visit www.rubyfiction.com for details.

Introducing Ruby Fiction

Ruby Fiction is an imprint of Choc Lit Publishing.
We're an award-winning independent publisher,
creating a delicious selection of fiction.

See our selection here:
www.rubyfiction.com

Ruby Fiction brings you stories that inspire emotions.

We'd love to hear how you enjoyed
The House That Alice Built. Please visit
www.rubyfiction.com and give your feedback or
leave a review where you purchased this novel.

Ruby novels are selected by genuine readers like yourself.
We only publish stories our Tasting Panel want to see in
print. Our reviews and awards speak for themselves.

Could you be a Star Selector and join our Tasting Panel?
Would you like to play a role in choosing which novels
we decide to publish? Do you enjoy reading women's
fiction? Then you could be perfect for our Tasting Panel.

Visit here for more details …
www.choc-lit.com/join-the-choc-lit-tasting-panel

Keep in touch:
Sign up for our monthly newsletter Spread for all the latest
news and offers: www.spread.choc-lit.com. Follow us on
Twitter: @RubyFiction and Facebook: RubyFiction.

Stories that inspire emotions!